EMILY HILDA YOUNG

(1880–1946) was born in Northumbe... She was educated at Gateshead Hig... wyn Bay, Wales. In 1902, after her ma... she went to live in Bristol, which was... novels. Her first, *A Corn of Wheat*, was p... (1912), and *Moor Fires* (1916).

During the First World War Emi... ...munitions factory, and as a groom in a local stables. However, after her husband's death at Ypres in 1917 she left Bristol for London, going to live with a married man, Ralph Henderson, Head Master of Alleyn's School in Dulwich. She continued to write. *The Misses Mallett*, published originally as *The Bridge Dividing*, appeared in 1922, preceding her most successful novel, *William* (1925). Then came *The Vicar's Daughter* (1928), *Miss Mole* (1930) – winning the James Tait Black Memorial Prize, *Jenny Wren* (1932), *The Curate's Wife* (1934) and *Celia* (1937). She lived with the Henderson's in South London until Ralph Henderson's retirement at the time of the Second World War when he and E. H. Young went, alone, to live in Bradford-on-Avon, Wiltshire. Here Emily Young wrote two children's books, *Caravan Island* (1940) and *River Holiday* (1942), and one further novel, *Chatterton Square*, published in 1947, two years before her death from lung cancer at the age of sixty-nine.

Virago publishes *The Misses Mallet, Miss Mole, Jenny Wren, The Curate's Wife, Chatterton Square, William* and *Celia*.

VIRAGO
MODERN
CLASSIC

NUMBER

332

E. H. YOUNG

CELIA

WITH A NEW INTRODUCTION BY
LYNN KNIGHT

Virago

Published by VIRAGO PRESS Limited 1990
20–23 Mandela Street, Camden Town, London NW1 0HQ

First published in Great Britain by Jonathan Cape Ltd. 1937
Copyright © E. H. Young 1937

Introduction Copyright © Lynn Knight 1990

A CIP catalogue record for this book is available from the British Library

Printed by Cox and Wyman Ltd. Reading, Berks

Celia is not a comfortable novel. To admirers of E. H. Young this will be no surprise; newcomers to this writer should pause if they are anticipating a novel that will entertain but not trouble them, for *Celia* has a sting in its tail. En route there is wit, compassion, and E. H. Young's incomparable skill in laying bare the nuances of relationships. Here are squabbles and rivalries, hints of affairs (and the hope that affairs exist where they do not) and, most importantly, an array of bedraggled marriages. But the person who thinks that *Celia* will conclude with its marital creases nicely smoothed and ironed out will be mistaken. There is no room for complacency—the reader will not be let off the hook, nor will Celia herself.

Celia is the guide to and interpreter of the events that take place in a corner of Upper Radstowe, the area of Bristol through which all of E. H. Young's novels roam. This character who will lead the way through tangled paths of relationships, with all their hidden snares, is swiftly and dextrously sketched; within the novel's first pages she stands before us as a very real figure. She is supposed to be tidying the drawers of her bureau; instead she has sifted its papers and old pen nibs, discovered letters she simply must read and disappeared into the past with a bundle of photographs. Reminded of this plethora of mementoes she can't possibly discard, she has paused to gaze out of the window and reflect on the view she so loves. Immediately we like this woman who makes clear her ambivalence to housekeeping and is far more concerned with the content than the appearance of things.

She married on the eve of the First World War, but cannot conceive of Gerald as past hero and doubts that he has sufficient imagination to do so either. Nor has he excelled as an architect; the risks he has taken have not paid off and their cramped flat is a daily and bitter reminder of his curmudgeonly designs. In struggling to bring up two children on a restricted income, Celia's dissatisfactions have grown. She is now middle-aged and has had years in which to contemplate the shortcomings of her marriage while trying to conceal endless economies: 'She did not want Jimmy and Catherine to have among their hopes for the future, an unlimited supply of butter.'

i

What is surprising—and an instant cause for sympathy—is the unusual degree of honesty with which she admits her most intimate feelings for Gerald. Here is a woman boxed in (almost literally) by a man she feels oppressed by. The solemn, heavy furniture he has chosen stands sentinel over her, their bed, 'like a barbaric triumphal car which had lost its wheels', rebukes her physical repugnance of him. Never have sexual failure and incompatibility been so neatly—and so decorously— expressed. That simile will recur as a damning refrain and though more than half a century has passed since *Celia* was first published in 1937, and sexual intricacies have become common currency for the novelist, the ease with which its heroine acknowledges this truth is startling. The image is made bearable, but no less forceful, by the self-mockery of its announcement.

Self-pity is anathema to Celia, who is as quick to smile at her own deficiencies as she is to note those of others. She grumbles about her lot, then decides to list her blessings: a constant source of hot water is among them. As she is not a landlady enticing prospective tenants, her blessings—unlike the water—would seem to be in short supply. If Celia's own list is brief, there is another to be made for her. She is a loving, but not proprietorial mother, her adolescent daughter adores her laughter and her sensibility. They share jokes over the washing-up, for Celia does not change her tone when speaking to her children. Jimmy, too, feels he can confide in her and Celia is wise enough to know that his late-night confession will be regretted the following morning. As friend to Pauline Carey, she shows the same generous looseness of approach, never encroaching, always available. She is someone we would like to know.

We might not be so keen on her relatives, whose inquisitive ways are the axis on which the plot turns. At the very least, *Celia* strikes a note of warning to all those members of families who may be tempted to live in one another's pockets. Celia's family has lived in Upper Radstowe for generations, but their position in the social pecking order is undermined by the draper's shop on which their past security is founded: the novel is set at the edge of that awkward moment in history when 'retail trade' was still a phrase to be whispered rather than pronounced abroad. To Celia's brother John, who has inherited the thriving business, such snobberies are irrelevant. Smug in his success (and blind to the fact that much of it was handed to him on a plate), he is convinced of his 'right to decide the oughts and ought nots for other people' and disparaging of those such as Gerald, whose achievements are less glorious. His brother-in-law, Stephen, is a lawyer (thereby enhancing the family's respectability) and a man who 'collected examples of the unexpectedness in human nature and found his own vagaries the most interesting of all'. As she shares this curiosity herself, Celia enjoys Stephen's company more than that of any other relative.

For years, their respective wives, Julia and May, have been constant companions. In Julia, whose eyes 'were like two gossips who had simultaneously leapt to their windows at the hint of a scandal in the street', E. H. Young has created a superb portrait of an interfering woman. May, though less voracious in her fascination for other people's affairs, has willingly followed her lead. Like other well-heeled women of the 1930s, Julia and May have time on their hands. With servants at their bidding, they have ample leisure to count the household linen before parading the high street in search of new hats. Celia is distanced from these activities by financial constraints: her own hat has lasted two winters and she is wondering if her coat can manage a fourth. However, there are advantages to being the least wealthy of the circle—unable to afford a telephone, Celia is 'spared the invasion of family voices'.

She is also distanced by temperament. Her relatives are uncertain what to make of this woman whose oblique humour puzzles them and who has a tendency to drop apparently detached remarks into conversation. In short, those who do not understand Celia are tempted to believe in her stupidity. Despite this, she holds a central position in family affairs and though she does not beckon confidences, she receives them: in times of crisis its members knock on her door. She has cultivated this reputation for being far more absent-minded than she is and uses it to her advantage. Who better to confide in than someone who may not be paying full attention? But the veracity of her off-beat remarks rings in the ears of her visitors long after the door has closed on them. There is nothing detached about Celia's observations.

Stephen's sudden departure from home brings his marriage under immediate scrutiny. For Julia there can be only one explanation for a man to leave his wife and daughters; she is eager to bury the marriage before it has been pronounced dead and offers May an insulting sympathy she could well do without. As with all short-sighted people, she will be unable to comprehend why her behaviour should sever May's allegiance to her and will be oblivious to the faults in her own marriage until forced to confront them.

Shortly before his disappearance, and harking back to a childhood game, Stephen suggests to Celia that she find the 'monkey' in his 'puzzle'. Adept at interpreting slips between the lines, Celia will guess correctly. She will also see behind the consequences of these distressed relationships to their root. Even if she can't quite grasp with what inner resources May has created a home of such elegant serenity, she realises they belie the frothy disguise May wears and that Stephen must learn how to appreciate her. She knows, too, that John, who wanted a pretty and doll-like wife to parade on his arm, has got just that—and all the silliness that goes with it. If his marriage to Julia lacks respect, they have each unintentionally, but carefully, constructed it that way.

In the midst of these unravelling threads, Celia appears to be the still point. We are privy to her secret thoughts, but she keeps her own counsel and displays no hint of her own marital difficulties. Assured again and again of Celia's acuity in relation to others, we have faith that, regardless of the obvious differences between them, she and Gerald will muddle through without calamity. And, if that were not enough, there is the evidence of Gerald's frank pleasure in greeting her each evening and their friendly and relaxed relationship with their children. If Celia knows what Gerald's limitations are, her integrity and her reticence must surely enable her to hide her awareness of them.

But there is a monkey in Celia's puzzle too. Her mistake is in thinking it to be Richard Carey, whom she fell in love with more than twenty years earlier when Gerald was at the Front. Though she asks herself if the middle-aged man who now lives in France, and whom she sees so seldom, can still reciprocate that feeling, or if the love she cherishes is a delusion, it is Richard to whom Celia silently relates her dreams; Richard who is 'the imaginative centre of her life'.

It seems appropriate that E. H. Young should have created a heroine who is not quite what she seems, for her own public persona was at odds with her private one. For years she shared the home of a Dulwich head-master, Ralph Henderson, and his wife. She was in fact Henderson's lover, though the relationship was concealed from all but their closest friends. They had met through J. A. H. Daniell, the man E. H. Young married when she was twenty-two (more or less the same age as Celia when she married Gerald) and who was killed at Ypres. Though E. H. Young's family believe the marriage to have been a happy one, little is known of it. What is known is that it involved her in reduced financial circumstances and her relationship with Henderson almost certainly began before her husband's death.*

It can only be conjecture, but it is difficult not to draw comparisons between Celia and her creator. And, as there are parallels in their history, so for much of the novel Celia also shares E. H. Young's angle of vision— her acerbic humour, her unblinking clear sight, are also the characteristics which give E. H. Young's work its piquancy. Yet their apparent affinity is misleading. E. H. Young has often been compared to Jane Austen, and the novel *Celia* comes closest to is *Emma*. Like her literary forebear in that slippery fiction, E. H. Young reserves her sharpest revelations for her heroine. The tone of the novel shifts, Celia ceases to be arbiter and its moral truths become less palatable.

As Stephen's absence from May pushes their marriage into focus, Celia's absence from Gerald is also a catalyst. It is ironic that Gerald's mother, whom Celia dislikes and unaccountably holds responsible for the divisions between herself and her husband, should prove to be the vehicle for those divisions to be revealed, when Mrs Marston's illness requires Celia as nursemaid. Seeing how well the family manages without her, Celia realises for the first time that she is not its 'invisible but necessary cement' and reminds herself how 'self-satisfaction flourished on self-deception'. However, there are other, more serious ways in which Celia will be divested of her illusions.

E. H. Young has seized upon a common trait of human nature and fully exposed it. Much of Celia's charm—and she has lots of it—lies in the confident way she expresses her opinions and admits her failings. That honesty is revealed to be inadequate because it does not go far enough. In admitting a great deal, Celia thinks she has acknowledged everything; instead, paradoxically, she has constructed another mask for herself.

One of the disconcerting facets of *Celia* is the vicarious transference of that culpability. We too have been lulled into a false sense of security, a security dependent upon our empathy with Celia. Although we have seen, via Celia's own admission, that Gerald also has cause for grievance, we have taken her part. We too, like Celia's relatives, and like Celia herself,

---

*I am grateful to Sally Beauman's introduction to E. H. Young's *The Misses Mallet* for this biographical information.

have been willingly duped by appearances. How can she see Gerald for what he is when she is so absorbed in her own private world and so convinced of the superiority of her own judgements? The choreography of the novel is such that, though there have been vivid pointers all along, Celia's shocks are ours too. The effect is dramatic and only *just* stops short of tragedy.

Celia is about deceptions: those which are easy to identify and those which are more painful to confess—the elliptical deceits and self-dissemblings whose corrosiveness is unobtrusive but far more damaging in its cumulative effect. As with all of E. H. Young's novels, marriage is the arena which allows but also discloses them. In *Celia* each of her characters has assumed a knowledge of their partner they are ill-fitted to claim, and built their marriage upon it—only to discover they have fooled themselves and those to whom they have ascribed false identities. Pulled up short, they must learn forbearance. Hollowed, they are wiser for it; bruised but civilised. And Celia too will survive. Yet, as E. H. Young strips away the layers of camouflage which separate Stephen from May, John from Julia, her relentlessly sharp vision is harnessed to wry humour and lightness of touch. There are tears and recriminations and a pervasive sense of the awful limitations of humanity, but compassion is always in view. When she turns to Celia, that vision darkens. Perhaps Celia is a representation of the woman E. H. Young might have become if her husband had returned from war; perhaps the barrier between heroine and reader becomes too blurred and we are simply threatened by our own inadequacies.

E. H. Young belongs to that body of novelists whose fiction is described as domestic. The term is almost a disabling one: by definition it proclaims the small stage, the small spotlight. Detractors from the genre may scoff at its insularity. If they do so, they ignore the fact that home truths are the most disturbing of all.

Lynn Knight, London, 1989

CHAPTER I

CELIA MARSTON was standing on a wooden stool and looking
out of the high-set window. From the floor in this attic
flat, nothing could be seen through the window except the
sky and now it had the blue depth of a brilliant day at the
end of March. Little clouds moved across it, like white-clad
ladies of infinite leisure strolling on an azure lawn in the
first real warmth of the year. Celia loved the sun and she
loved the view from the top of this tall house, so she had
mounted the stool and saw, straight in front of her but a
long way off, the high ground above the village of Easterly
stretching, almost as level as a wall top, against the sky.
Only the tower of the church broke the horizontal line and
the tower looked, she thought, like a signpost that had lost
its directing arm and must, perforce, point heavenwards, as
indeed it should, when heaven was of such a colour. But
there were times when she thought it was more like a little
black exclamation mark on a big, blank page, making some
sly, malicious comment on itself and on all it had observed
from its place on the hill. The village was huddled, hardly
visible, in the folds of the fields which, steepening suddenly
near their crest, ran down at a gentler angle to what, from
her window, seemed to be the very edge of the docks.
There were the fields, bearing here and there a single elm
and dotted with the minute forms of sheep and cattle, and
then, without warning, there were cranes and warehouses
and a tangle of masts and funnels. Just so, a child might
have ambled happily down a grassy slope and stopped with
a start at the sight of something alien and unexpected. On
this side of the water the ground rose again, more sharply,
to the plateau on which Upper Radstowe was perched and

9

Celia looked down on a cascade of roofs and chimney pots and trees. She could see an almond tree in blossom; the buds of a chestnut, which had outgrown the plot of ground it stood in, were thickening day by day, sticky brown fists striving to unclench themselves. Soon they would succeed and hold out their fingers, like a class at school presenting them for inspection.

In the warmth of the sun, Celia shut her eyes, laid her arms on the narrow window-sill and rested her head on them. There was enough breeze to stir her hair, but not enough to remind her that there was a chill in it, that the wind was tolerantly allowing the sunshine to have its way for a few hours and, wisely, she took what came and would not spoil her present pleasure with the consciousness of its briefness. In this stillness of the air, all sounds reached her very clearly and yet with a dream-like quality. She could relate them to their causes while she felt detached from the world in which they happened. There was the clang of metal on metal, down by the docks, the passing of cars and carts in the road below the broad terrace after which this long row of houses had its name; she heard the swish and jingle of a bicycle, even the creaking of the errand boy's basket attached to it; there were voices and footsteps and then, gravely urgent on a low, sustained note, a steamer hooted as it took one of the river bends. It was a sound characteristic of the place and familiar to Celia since her babyhood. It came, according to the tides, by day or night and more often than not she missed it or slept through it, but when she heard it with complete awareness, she was always moved to a sense of vicarious adventure and experience. The siren told her of hardships and toil she would have hated, of courage she could not emulate, but her own nature was enriched by the knowledge of other people's qualities and, when the voice had the note of triumphant home-coming or solemn leave-taking, then it spoke for her, too, who was initiate, of that mixture of happiness and sorrow which is romance.

As she lifted her head in response to the sound, the door of the sitting-room was opened and she turned to see Miss Riggs looking sorrowfully at the litter on the floor, at the open drawers of the bureau only half-emptied of old letters, bills, photographs, penholders with the nibs corroded, stumps of pencils and scraps of much-used blotting-paper, the accumulations of an indifferent housewife.

'I did think . . .' she began.

'No, you didn't. You only hoped and, by this time, you ought to know better. Turn all the rest of the rubbish on to the floor and wash the drawers if you must and I'll sort it all out some time or other.'

'Some time's never,' said Miss Riggs. 'And where's the newspaper I gave you to save the carpet?' she asked in a quiet voice and the Radstowe accent. Her figure was ample and her eyes were soft, her mouth was bigger and more generously curved than Celia's own and she had hard work not to smile as she asked of her employer, who was her contemporary and seemed to her rather like a child, 'What are you doing on that stool, anyway?'

'Playing at Sister Anne.'

'Tut!' said Miss Riggs without discourtesy.

'Yes, much too early.   He can't come yet.'

'And we've half the spring cleaning to do and soon it'll be Miss Catherine's holidays and then where shall we be?'

'I don't think you have a proper sense of values,' Celia said. 'What's spring cleaning compared to a spring day?'

'Ah, I like cleaning when the sun's shining. Seems more sense in it.'

'And I don't like it ever.   And it isn't necessary . . .'

'But you've only to look,' said Miss Riggs, 'at what you've been keeping in your bureau.'

'It isn't necessary,' Celia continued, 'when I have you to keep me right.'

'And what can I do with only the two mornings a week?' Miss Riggs cried, and her passion for order and spotlessness was in her voice.

'Quite enough,' Celia said easily.

She stepped from the stool. At forty-five, the rounded slenderness of her youth was changing to a not unpleasing plumpness, but she stepped lightly, without looking where she set the feet which were still slim under ankles that had not thickened with middle age. 'I know,' she said reasonably, 'there's sometimes dirt in the corners and all my drawers are untidy, but nobody notices or knows, and I think this room is very pretty and that's what matters. Make the place where gods may dwell, beautiful, entire and clean! Yes, but if I also make myself into an ill-tempered nuisance, what's the good? There are not many people like you, Miss Riggs, dear,' she went on, opening wide the eyes which were usually veiled and drowsy and showing a dancing light in them, 'not many who can be perfect housewives and perfect angels. It's one of the arrangements for keeping us dissatisfied with this world and in hope of a better one to come.'

Miss Riggs, kneeling on the floor and neatly stacking Celia's belongings on a sheet of newspaper, made no reply. She pulled out a drawer and examined it carefully when she had tipped its contents on to another sheet. 'No worm,' she said. 'That's good. I'd not like any harm to come to it,' and she, who had so little time to spare, sat back on her heels and looked at the bureau.

Celia looked at it, too. It was quite unlike any other bureau she had ever seen, though in design it was conventional enough. Of pale wood, it was flecked with a faint indefinite pattern in colours which were the phantoms of fawn and pink and blue and perhaps time had mellowed into a charming fancy what might once have been absurd. It belonged to

Celia who had bought it, years ago, straight off the pavement outside a secondhand furniture shop, but Miss Riggs had her spiritual share in it. Her labour had removed its film of dirt, it was she who, gently and patiently, had rubbed the handles until they were revealed as knobs of carved ivory set in ebony. Solemnly, she had fetched Celia to view the miracle. 'It's like those bulbs,' she said, 'that look no better than onions and then, if you treat them right, you get a flower. So you see, you never know.'

'And do you think there's anything else in the house you can transform like that?' Celia had asked flippantly because she was moved by the thought of the man who had fashioned the piece of furniture and rewarded his own pains with those little handles, and there was no need for Miss Riggs to say, as she did, admonishingly, 'Just you be thankful. It doesn't do to want too much.'

Now, she said lovingly. 'It's a dainty little piece. And I have a fancy it would feel more itself if it was all neat inside.'

'Yes. All right, I'll do it. And I wonder how it feels to be neat inside.'

'You'll know better when you've finished this.'

'And I wonder still more,' Celia said, 'why your moral remarks don't vex me.'

Calmly, without any reply to words she may not have troubled to hear, Miss Riggs carried the drawers into the kitchen. She had a manner which might have been mistaken for self-satisfaction, but Celia knew that she was hardly concerned with herself at all. And she knew the answer to her own question. The advice of Miss Riggs, her reproofs, her little maxims, were the fruits of her experience; she uttered them as naturally as she would have given apples from a tree in full bearing and if she saw any virtue in the gift, it came of the tree's fecundity, not of the generous hand.

Presently she returned with soap, a bowl and a rag with which to wash the hollow interior of the desk. 'It'll be all dry

13

before you're ready,' she said, not without some dryness of her own, and it was Celia's turn to make no reply. Miss Riggs sighed silently. There was going to be last year's trouble over again. Last year, Mrs. Marston had undertaken to dust the books and there was hardly one of them that was not opened first and read in for a few minutes or, it might be, for half an hour. Now she was sitting on the floor, and Miss Riggs looked with affection at the dark head, at the broad cheek-bones which made the chin seem smaller than it was, and vaguely realized that the qualities she deplored in Mrs. Marston were part of her lazy charm, that the laziness itself was, to some extent, a disguise. She had found a bundle of letters written by her children on some of the rare occasions when she had been parted from them; she had found an envelope full of snapshot photographs and a portfolio bulging with professional efforts. There were photographs of family and school groups, of her father and mother, her brother and sisters, nephews and nieces, of school friends whose names she could hardly remember. There was one of herself with her hair curling to her shoulders and drawn from her forehead with a bow of ribbon; there was another with Catherine on her knee and Jimmy leaning against her in an attitude of affection which had plainly been inspired by the photographer. She was one of the bridesmaids in her sister May's wedding group, wearing an enormous feathered hat and tilting her head to keep the weight balanced.

'Funny, some of these,' she said, pushing them towards Miss Riggs and Miss Riggs weakly took the bait. She went through the pile with a real interest, recognizing many of Celia's relatives, but paying the same scrupulous attention to the strangers. She was considering each face on its own merits, without humour to spare for past fashions or out-dated postures, and she lingered longest over the picture of Celia's husband in the uniform of a soldier.

'Ah, there were lots of lads like him,' she said, looking at

14

this representation of a young man with ordinary features, a fair complexion and undoubtedly blue eyes which were shadowed and made serious by the peaked cap. 'And those caps did a lot of damage. Hid the shape of the head. Oh well, they deserved all they could get, poor things, and much more than most of them got when they came back.'

'Much more,' Celia agreed.

'And you can't blame the girls. The caps came off and the heads were smaller, very small, some of them, and the men looked different. They were, too. It's not in nature to remember, all the time, that they'd run the risk of having no head at all. Not all the time,' she repeated thoughtfully. 'The baby cries and the man gets vexed and, may be, the money's short. There's nothing that ever happened as big as what the little things mount up to as the years go by. Having words with each other or trying not to and that's worse, and this done and that undone. Oh, it's a mountain! And that's where I think I'm lucky. You never know what life'll do to you. Death's kinder, often. Anyway, it's left me with the Fred that went away. Very comical he was, too. He wouldn't laugh himself, but he'd make me, right enough, and that's the kind that makes you laugh most, isn't it? Often-times I laugh now, when I think of the things he'd say. But what if he'd come back and by this time there wasn't a smile between us?'

'But there would have been, there would have been,' Celia said in resentment for this acquiescence in loss, and remembering the photograph she had seen of Fred, his expression ironic with the peculiar irony of his class, she believed his humour would have survived and overcome misfortunes.

Miss Riggs shook her head. 'You can't tell. I know what I had when war started. I'll never know what I might have got with the peace.'

CHAPTER II

CELIA might have said, with truth, that the peace had brought back to her the man who had gone away, that in all these succeeding years, when the children had cried and money had been short and there had been what Miss Riggs called words, oftener restrained than uttered, he had remained very much what he was before and, if she had done nothing else, she had remembered with some consistency the risks he had run and the debt in which they had involved her. He had never referred to the risks or the debt. He had not the sort of imagination which could make him see himself as a hero. As a matter of course, he had gone to fight and it did not, she believed, occur to him that his part was a braver one than hers in bearing his son, rearing him on inadequate supplies and waiting for bad news. 'Poor boy,' she thought, as she took his photograph from Miss Riggs and added it to the pile of things she meant to keep. He would be pleased, perhaps, if she put it on the mantelshelf or, more intimately, on her dressing-table. She was sure Miss Riggs could see Fred's face from her bed, but then, unlike Celia, she had not the living man beside her, twenty years older, a good deal bulkier and occupying rather more than his share of space. Looking down at Gerald's clear eyes — and she well remembered how clear they had been, how about him, as about countless other young men, there had been an unconscious air of dedication which no cynicism of the new generation could change, for her, into false sentiment or unworthy purpose — she envied Miss Riggs her solitary room, her unshared bed. The art of living, the only one Celia tried to practise, was as exacting as any other: it might be that it was the most exacting, for no concessions could be made to the artist whose skill was in doing without them, and Celia's worst failures happened in that bedroom crowded with the heavy, carved furniture of Gerald's choice. And fortunately, the ghosts of them stayed there, grinning at her when she opened the wardrobe door and saw Gerald's coats alongside her dresses, peeping from under the bed which was like a barbaric triumphal car which had lost its wheels, hostile ghosts, expecting and hoping to see her fail again.

The artist in living has no medium except life itself, but he needs room enough to step back and look at his work and see if it is good. In quarters too close, the work, too, becomes cramped and distorted, unless the artist has genius and Celia laid no claim to that. Outside there was space and to spare and a permanent consciousness of great stretches of sky: indoors, she had to teach herself with difficulty that the mind need not be bounded by walls.

Hastily she turned over what remained of her litter on the floor. 'I suppose you haven't seen a newspaper cutting with the picture of a house on it?' she asked.

'You'll have screwed it up and thrown it in the waste-paper basket, I expect.'

'No, I've found it.' She smoothed it on her knee and she did not offer it for the inspection of Miss Riggs who now rose reluctantly, saying, 'I'll have to work double tides to catch up, but it's been a treat, looking at all those.'

'At home,' Celia said, 'when I was a child, there were albums of photographs in the drawing-room. I believe visitors were invited to look at them. There was a stereoscope too, and views of Roman ruins. Hymns after tea on Sundays and then the ruins. And we liked them!'

'I don't know about ruins,' said Miss Riggs, 'but hymns I do like. I like singing them, too, though I've no more voice than a rook. They make me feel very jolly, somehow, specially the sad ones. And as for faces, I can't tire of them.'

'Well, there's no lack of them.'

'And not two alike, barring twins now and then. Wonderful

17

I call it!' She looked at the clock. 'Quarter past twelve and I've hardly started on the stew!'

'Don't bother. We can have cold meat.'

'Yes, and Miss Catherine turning up her nose at it.'

'She can't help it, Miss Riggs. It's that kind of nose.'

'She can make it go a good bit higher than God ever meant.'

'You don't really believe he ever thought about Catherine's nose?'

'I can't see why not. It would be a lot easier than some of the things he's done.'

'You can't be sure of that and, judging by some of the noses one sees, it's rather a ticklish job.'

As usual when she was at a loss for the last word, Miss Riggs quietly retired and for some time Celia sat and contemplated the picture of what, for her, was the perfect house, the one in which personal perfection might be attained. It had been for sale when she cut the advertisement from the newspaper and she could not believe that everyone in the possession of three thousand pounds had not rushed to buy it. It was described as a Georgian country house of character, and its character, she decided, was one of wisdom and serenity. An exquisitely proportioned pediment rose above three of the five windows in the upper story; the outer pair of four flat pillars made a frame for these windows, for two of the four lower ones and the door. Each window was divided by wooden transoms into twelve little squares; what looked like a magnolia tree broke the severity of the façade and each end of the house was attached to a low wall which was pierced by a rounded doorway. She was not a person desirous of many possessions, but she had a sick longing for that house. With a bed in it, a bed of her own, a table and a few pots and pans, she believed she would be content. How still and cool the nights would be, as she lay beside an open window, surrounded by her own garden! To what long,

quiet days she would wake each morning! She wanted no
one else in the house, not even Catherine and Jimmy except
for visits, and, in the generosity of her happiness, Gerald
should come too, sometimes, but she knew the silence would
often be broken by the sound of uneven footsteps. But living
there would be no test of virtue. A better test would be to
live there with her family, a constant shortage of money,
the knowledge that Gerald was still designing hideous little
villas without the usual worldly reward for sin, yes, even with
Gerald's mother living just beyond the garden. Yet she knew
that she might be worse off in that lovely house. She would
be deprived of the comforting belief that she would be a
nicer woman in other circumstances: for her own content
she might be safer where she was and, after all, things were
well enough. She had a roof over her head, plenty to eat and
children who were healthy and satisfactory on the whole: she
was a citizen of no mean city, one which had never quite
succeeded in driving back the country: the true, unspoilt
country was just across the river and the river brought ships
into the heart of the town. Moreover, Miss Riggs was in the
kitchen and, whatever the other faults of the little flat, the
hot water was always hot.

Carefully, she folded her picture and put it in an envelope
on which she wrote in her straggling handwriting, 'My house.'
Some day, soon, perhaps, she would show it to Richard, just
show it without a word and he would put on his spectacles,
consider it gravely and say, 'Yes,' and for long after that she
would be very happy. He might say something much less
satisfactory, but no, she would not allow him to do that. She
would know in good time whether it were safe to show him
her little treasure. There had never been a time yet when
she could not have done it but, in half a minute, everything
might be changed. More than twenty years ago her whole
life had changed almost as quickly, and now every half
minute was a menace while it was a hope. She was forty-five

and she felt as though she were still a girl, for though she had borne two children, she had not known the emotions proper to their making; and she wondered whether, they had missed a better love than what she gave them. She did not know what quality hers had or lacked, but she was glad to hear her daughter opening the door of the flat, banging it back and flinging her school satchel on the floor.

For Catherine, there could be nothing in her mother's appearance to arouse any suspicion of her girlishness; it was impossible to imagine any happenings of much importance in a life which had advanced to middle-age, but with her drowsy eyes, her slow movements, the mouth which looked as though she had thought of something funny and then decided not to say it, Celia had her importance for her daughter. Under her tolerance she preserved her own standards, there was something enlivening in her silences and she was still the chief source of physical comfort though she was absent-minded in her housekeeping and unimaginative about food.

'One of Miss Riggs's days,' Catherine said. 'Good! There'll be something nice to eat.' Her neatly tilted nose was lifted in appreciation of a savoury smell. She had a square, school-girl's figure, she knocked the furniture when she passed it, not so much in actual clumsiness as in an overflowing of conscious health, but her head was charming and the close, light brown curls growing upwards from her round neck, cleverly matched the aspiring little nose. Some day she would be very attractive; at present, though she was seventeen, she was not in the least concerned with her physical possibilities. That, Celia thought loyally, was due to the influence of the school, the school to which she herself had gone from the age of nine until she was eighteen. For those nine years the school had been the chief part of her world, as it had been her sister Hester's and, almost in spite of herself, her sister May's. May's daughters and Catherine had carried on the tradition without any slackening of enthusiasm, but Celia doubted whether they could feel her pride, her sense of enlargement, when each morning at prayers, she read, on a board behind the headmistress's desk, these words printed in Gothic characters — 'Knowledge is now no more a fountain sealed.' She was near enough in time to the pioneers to feel some of the glow of their achievement; she did not forget that to them she owed the privilege of belonging to a big public school at a time when people in Upper Radstowe, who considered themselves gentlefolks, were still a little shy of this broader education. Some of them had not lost their shyness yet and feared the contamination of the butcher's and baker's daughters more than they desired their children's acquaintance with some of the longest established and most respected families in the place. Celia's own family was comparatively long established, a distinction somewhat marred, however, by their owning of a draper's shop. It was the best draper's shop in the city, but in Upper Radstowe there was a firm line drawn between wholesale and retail trade and the Fellows were on the wrong side of it. This disgrace had never troubled Celia: she did not believe it could trouble Catherine, but then Catherine was the daughter of an architect and May's daughters had a lawyer for a father. The pure draper blood was being diluted with that of the professions. The blot on the scutcheon was on the distaff side, except for the family of her brother who was still stubbornly a draper. He liked to call himself a tradesman, he expected his eldest son to follow in his footsteps and, after all, Celia thought, there were good thick carpets on the floor of John's shop; it ought to be easy-going and there might be much worse occupation for her own child than selling pretty things across a counter.

'But not,' she murmured, 'in what they call the haberdashery.'

When Miss Riggs was in the flat, Celia and Catherine had their midday meal in the dining-room. On other days they had it in the kitchen, a much pleasanter room than this one crowded with the carved oak which Gerald, in simple faith, believed must be antique and valuable if only it were black enough. It was a little touching, this simple faith, and, rather than disturb it, Celia silently endured the furniture, just as she made no adverse comments on the houses he designed with so much zest.

Catherine, eating heartily of the stew, ignored her mother's remark. She was hungry, she had her preoccupations, her own universe in which she was not a negligible figure, and Celia was apt to drop apparently detached remarks, while a show of polite interest, an encouraging inquiry, rarely produced a satisfactory reply, so Catherine ate her dinner and Celia continued to meditate aloud.

'No, not the haberdashery,' she repeated. 'The people who approach that counter know exactly what they want. Tape and hooks and eyes and shirt buttons and bootlaces. There can't be any opportunity for exercising persuasion or guiding taste. Hats would be the most fun, I should think, but I suppose no one can just spring straight into hats.'

Catherine looked up. The last word had reached her consciousness and half roused her slumbering femininity. 'Hats? What are you talking about, pet?'

'I was thinking about the shop and which department I should like to serve in.'

'That's a queer thing to think about. I'm sure they'd all be loathsome and I should even hate the hats.'

'Oh, would you?' Celia said. She was disappointed of a simple solution to a difficult problem.

CHAPTER III

IT was difficult, not because Catherine was without ability, but because so little could be done for her without money. However, she consoled herself, as she dressed to walk out in the afternoon sunshine, John's sense of duty towards his family was chiefly confined to criticism. It was not probable that he would find a place for Catherine in the shop and, from one point of view, he would be right. There would be suspicions of favouritism and privilege, and John, in consequence, would feel bound to badger his niece. It was a good thing to be spared the awkwardness of making a suggestion which would lay Gerald open to blame. John, who had inherited the shop from his father, who had inherited it from his, and never had any anxiety about his own future or his children's, was without much patience or sympathy for the poorer circumstances of a brother-in-law. He was inclined to point to his own success and say that what he had done, other men could do.

'And what has he done?' Celia asked of her reflection as she put on the hat she had worn for two winters and the coat she had worn for three and might wear for another. He had preserved and perhaps improved a business set on very firm foundations, one which, in the worst times, could hardly show a loss, while Gerald had started from nothing except his qualifications as an architect and his hope that the public would realize what they were. There were times when Celia feared they realized it all too well, more altruistic times when she was thankful that they did, for she had little faith in the firmness of the material foundations on which Gerald's houses rose, in the thickness of his walls or the tightness of his roofs. In imagination she suffered the rheumatism of the old people, the colds of the children who inhabited those villas planned by Gerald, with striking oddities of ornament and design, for a pushing firm of builders who wanted a quick return for the money they outlaid. In imagination she saw the yearly bills for repairs which must be paid by optimistic young couples proud of owning their own house. She hoped she suffered unnecessarily in this way. She suffered too much already from the actual evidences of Gerald's ingenuity and it was just one of the puzzles of life that, with more of this evidence of which she was ashamed, she need never have been ashamed to look the butcher in the face. She had been brought up by people who were scrupulous to pay their household bills punctually and when she had to keep the butcher waiting longer than a week for the small amount she owed him, she could not believe he did not cut the next joint for her with great reluctance; she fancied she was constantly in the thoughts which kept him awake at night; she felt rather uncomfortable when she passed a policeman. She had discarded many of the beliefs and values imposed on her in childhood, but this one, most inconveniently, remained. The clothes which would look so shabby in the sunshine were practical signs of her fear of debt.

There was no sunshine on the terrace when she stepped on to it. The tall houses cast their shadow on it and on the road below, but she could see where the sun was picking out bright objects far away, shining, here and there, on windows until they were like burnished shields, like huge signals flashing from one side of the city to the other, and she had only to turn leftwards into Barton Street and so to The Green and the suspension bridge and she would get all the sun there was until it sank behind the cliff.

She paid the toll. It was an extravagance when she might have stood for nothing on the little hill overlooking bridge and river, but nowhere else could she get this feeling of being poised, of hovering between earth and water. Though the structure was strong enough, no doubt, it looked as though it had been flung across the gulf by a light hand and when she stood on it, between the tall railings at the edge and the curved girder on the other side of the footpath, she liked to believe that a strong gust of wind might catch her up and fling her beyond these barriers and to know, meanwhile, that she was safe.

Slowly she walked across the bridge on the city side where some of the water was allowed to be a river still, the rest controlled by locks and gathered into basins for such ships as could take the shallow channel from the sea. Beyond these docks with their masts and funnels and cranes, beyond the warehouses standing like dumb creatures waiting to swallow what the ships brought them, beyond these and as far as she could see, except for the fields below Easterly, there were roofs and towers and spires, the roofs lying flat, like flower beds, the spires and towers like carefully trained trees, and always there was the sense of freedom given by the water coming from the sea and going back to it.

Now, she stood near the toll-keeper's little house and watched a great variety of cars go slowly across the bridge. Even the fastest, with drivers who thought their privileges rose with their horse power, were compelled to go at a walking pace; even Pauline Carey, in her big yellow car, was crawling with the rest, but she was not wearing the properly insulted expression at being hindered. She lay back in her low seat, her practised hands light on the wheel, her face rather set under the rakish little hat and the cosmetics which were used not to aid Nature but to produce a decorative effect. The face was set in the mould of a mood she need not trouble to conceal when all eyes were safely fixed in front of them, her eyebrows were raised in a question she did not seem able to answer, and Celia quickly looked away. She was taking her friend at a disadvantage, seeing without being seen, in a moment when Pauline had dropped her mask.

I suppose we all wear one, she thought.

25

She had crossed to the other side of the bridge and as she went with the Radstowe bound traffic she lingered to look at the river and the gorge, the bare cliffs steepened here beyond the possibility of harbouring more than ivy and an adventurous tree, and to see, farther off, just where the rocks began their ultimate submission to flat meadows, the chimneys of Pauline's own house, discernible to one who knew where to look for them, and the garden wall flush with the wall of the gorge. Then she hurried after the yellow car and, level with it, called Pauline's name.

'Oh!' The face changed. 'I'll wait for you on the other side.'

They made a contrast, these two women, as they sat together a few minutes later. From the back view, if she could have seen it, Celia would have been the first to say that she looked like some humble dependant of Pauline's, not quite the charwoman but, perhaps, the woman who did her household mending. This was a matter of clothes, their cut and the art of wearing them; from the front, though still differently circumstanced and probably different in tastes, they were socially equal and they had a common look of quiet pleasure as they sat in the stationary car which was drawn into a convenient curve of the road.

'I've just decided to go to Paris the day after to-morrow,' Pauline said. 'I shall fly if I can. Will you come?'

'Oh, of course! But why procrastinate? Why not to-morrow, What are you going for?'

'Clothes. Look at this weather.'

'You ought to support local industries. What's the matter with John Fellows & Son? All the new spring models. I've had the catalogue.'

'Are you tempted? You'd much better come with me.'

'I should be frightened,' Celia said.

'Then we won't fly.'

'Sea-sick.'

'Nonsense! We'll wait till the sea's like a lake.'

'Homesick, then.' Her mouth twitched but she remained grave. 'I've had my fill of foreign travel. I had a fortnight in Lucerne after my last term at school. We all had. Just the finishing touch, you know.' She remembered a wounded lion in stone, the sun sparkling on blue water, snow mountains against a bluer sky, coral and tortoiseshell ornaments in the shop windows and a thirsty longing for a wet day at home. 'Take me round the Downs, but slowly, and I shall be quite satisfied.'

Pauline started the car. She went slowly up the slight rise and across The Green, but when she saw The Avenue, wide and almost empty in front of her, she yielded to her passion for showing what the car could do in gathering speed. Celia put a hand to her hat; she saw the great elms not as separate trees but brought together by this swift passage into a gigantic fence, with hardly a chink between the posts. Pauline checked at the cross roads, long enough but not a second too long, saw her way clear and took the short, steep ascent to the Downs with the minimum of loss, with some effect of doing all this not only with the aid of her brain, but with her own body. Then she stopped with precision, a tiny click of the brake pulled home, and laid her hands on her knee.

'I'm full of admiration,' Celia said, 'but I knew all that before. I wanted to see the buds on the elms, I wanted to see them burgeoning. That's a good word. It doesn't sound too easy and I don't suppose it is.'

'And it isn't easy to drive a car properly.'

'It isn't easy to do anything properly. To fry eggs, for instance.'

'Or to be a friend, apparently. I think you're rather a poor one.'

'That's just it,' Celia said with a chuckle.

'But, if you won't come, may I take Catherine? It would do her good.'

27

'Heaps, but the term isn't over yet and you might lose her in Paris. One hears dreadful stories.'

'Oh rubbish! But of course you're talking rubbish on purpose. The fact is you won't take a single thing from me.'

'Nothing tangible, but so much that isn't.'

'It's horribly selfish.'

'Horribly, but it's one of my few indulgences.'

'I don't quite understand it,' Pauline said slowly.

'Oh, I think you do,' Celia said.

The ensuing silence was quite amicable. They acknowledged each other's right to keep their motives unexplained but, since Pauline had ventured on a comment, Celia asked a question.

'Was it pure kindness, or do you really want some one with you?'

With her hands behind her, she raised herself to see, above the wall and railings guarding the cliffs' edge, the pale hills far away across the sea. Sometimes they were blue, sometimes grey, never the colour of the grass on them, or the rocks or the slag heaps with which they might be blotched. She had a dim idea that she was looking at hills as they were in the mind of God and that the solution to puzzles, the rule for life, was to look beyond what men called facts and to see, if she could, the true reality, but those hills were a long way off and the facts of every day pressed very close, and as though these were too much for her, she dropped back into her seat and heard Pauline answering the question she had quite forgotten.

'Certainly not kindness. I don't believe in it. Half the mistakes we make come of thinking our idea of it must be what the other person wants.' Her thin eyebrows went up again, her mouth was curled ironically, and now Celia felt free to contemplate her, to wonder what had induced this bitter mood in the vivacious Mrs. Carey with her lively interest in books, music, pictures and the theatre, and enough intelligence, time and money to enjoy them fully. 'Kindness,' Pauline said, 'is another of the things that are not easy.'

'You are very clever,' Celia said gently.

'There's nothing clever in that. It's obvious.'

'Quite.'

'I see. I'm talking platitudes.'

'Not at all,' Celia said politely. 'I was thinking how clever you are to drive this — this flamboyant car and wear a hat like that and make your face like an artist's palette and yet...'

'Don't tell me I look like a lady.'

'But you do. I suppose breeding will out, though May thinks you look, as well as go, very fast.'

'At my age!'

'May is very stupid,' Celia explained soothingly, 'and she has to find a good reason for not being as friendly with you as she longs to be, and, it's just occurred to me, why don't you ask her to let Susan go with you to Paris? Susan would love it and, you know, she's charming. I can't understand how May begat her, or is it only men who beget? Anyhow, she's a sweet and I'm sure the noise of the engines will sound like soft music in her ears, after her mother's voice. Not that it's raucous. Just tiresome.'

'Shall I? I confess that I shouldn't like a refusal from May.'

'Now you are being stupid, too, but I suppose you don't realize that you are one of the social prizes, or how carefully I pretend not to know you very well. Already she and Julia suspect me a little.'

'How can they?' Pauline asked unguardedly, and when Celia answered, her voice was pitched a tone higher than usual; it sounded rather distant and the distance was for the implication in Pauline's question, not for the awkwardness of her own reply.

'Your husband is a flourishing architect, mine's not a very successful one. I think they imagine I am on the look out for pickings on his behalf.'

'I see. I hadn't thought of that. They don't know much about you, do they? It's I who've had to do all the running, you proud piece!'

'Not proud,' Celia said.

'What, then?'

'Indolent,' Celia replied, but she might have added that she was also cautious, for she had divined, though she had not experienced, in Pauline, something capricious and uncertain, even a little cruel, which might be roused by an unwary word or movement, and, for their friendship's sake, it was well to continue on their present easy terms, with Pauline seeking, rather than being sought.

'No, they don't know much about me,' Celia said. 'That low cunning is the only kind of intelligence they think I've got. Otherwise I'm very stupid, and yet they like me. At least they like being with me. I suppose they feel they can relax comfortably in my company. So they can. So they do.'

'You have a lot of patience.'

'No, I enjoy it. I'm very lucky in a taste for simple pleasures.'

'I think you make your own luck,' Pauline said.

CHAPTER IV

'I'll walk back and go at my own pace,' Celia said.

'No, I promise to creep. You shall look at all the buds you like.'

'But unfortunately,' Celia said, as, true to her word, Pauline went slowly up The Avenue, 'and please stop for a minute, unfortunately there's more than buds in view. That small black person, over there, in the mantle, she always wears a mantle, is my mother-in-law.'

'Well, she hasn't seen us.'

'But she will when we go past. Could you bear to stop and pick her up?'

'No,' Pauline said pleasantly, 'I could not.'

Celia sighed. 'Another bad mark against me!'

'And do you mind?'

'Not much, but they mount up.'

'Then we'll give her a little longer and dash past at about sixty miles an hour and, if these ruses are really necessary, you can be absorbed in the contents of your handbag.'

'Yes. Thank you,' Celia said meekly, 'but she'll see me, she sees everything. Dashing about, neglecting my home. . . .'

'Are you afraid of the woman?' Pauline asked impatiently.

'Not exactly. No, not of her, but I detest her emanations.'

'Camphor, I should think,' Pauline said, flashing past the black mantle. 'She looks camphorous.'

'She is, but that's fairly innocuous, I believe, except to moths. Why she couldn't stay in the Midlands where she belongs, I don't know. She stayed there mercifully and, I think, happily, until two years ago and it's absurd for a woman of her age to come and live here where she has no friends and can't possibly make them.'

'She must have wanted a daughter's love.'

'If only she had a daughter of her own! It would have been awful for the poor girl, but how nice for me!'

'Doesn't Gerald love her as he should?'

'I don't like to ask him,' Celia said.

'Better not, perhaps. If I see Richard, is there any message?'

'No.'

Pauline half laughed and raised her shoulders in a tiny shrug. 'Oh well, I suppose he will be coming, as usual, in the summer.' She brought the car alongside the flight of steps leading to The Terrace and suddenly, as Celia stood on the pavement to watch her turn and go, Pauline's sophisticated mouth drooped childishly.

'I've been to Brimley to-day,' she said, and the bright eyes of the alert and clever Mrs. Carey, who seemed to have all she wanted in this world, almost lost their human characteristics and darkened into those of an animal which, only through its eyes, could ask for help. And Celia could give none, but with the drooping of her own mouth, a laxness of her whole figure, she offered her dumb sympathy to this dumb appeal. Never before had she seen Pauline with all her defences down, and they were up again in a minute, raised by another, slightly different shrug of the shoulders, topped by a little flag of defiance as she lifted a hand in farewell.

Celia now understood her expression as she drove across the bridge, why she was rushing off to Paris, did not wish to be alone and received the suggestion of Susan's company with rather surprising willingness. Things at Brimley must have been worse than usual, she thought, or had she been stupidly blind to the fact that they were always as bad as this for Pauline? Well, the sight of Richard would comfort her, it would comfort anybody, Celia thought, and as she entered the hall of the house and looked up at the domed skylight above the staircase, the frosted glass seemed to disappear and, in the circular space, she fancied she saw an

32

aeroplane carrying away a Pauline restored to gaiety and a demurely excited Susan, both peering down for a last look at the man who, leaning on a stick, watched their departure. She felt a little spasm of envy and then denied it. Susan would not look back; youth looked forward; and she who was middle-aged, could look back as far and as long as she liked, wherever she might chance to be.

And she did look back for a few minutes before she began her ascent towards the skylight. Then she went up slowly, passing the doors of the drawing-room flat and the one above it, and resenting, as she always did, the mutilation of the nobly curving staircase. When Gerald converted this old house into flats, he had been constrained to rob each landing of enough space to make a separate entrance and now the stairs crawled upwards like something wounded. However, the flats were never empty. Gerald was proud of them and he had been paid fairly for his work, yet here was the same puzzle of gain and loss, more money for the family and a little less beauty in the world. But, she thought, making the best of it, there were no servants now, living in the underground vaults, no legs aching with going up and down these stairs, from basement to attics and attics to basement, no one carrying hot water to the bedrooms, loaded trays to the dining-room or tea to the drawing-room a flight still higher up. The gain wins, she thought, her own legs aching a little as she put her key in the door and heard, far below, the sound of heavy feet. They were not Catherine's, which were also quick and firm; these were the feet of Mrs. Marston coming, as it seemed to Celia, in slow, clumsy pursuit.

She shut the door very quietly. She wondered if she dared risk pretending to be out, but no, she could not tell how long her visitor might wait on the landing, listening for a betraying sound within. Mrs. Marston was not altogether lacking in imagination, and where poor, stupid May would go away, indignant at her unnecessary climb, and John's Julia would slip a card with a loving message on it, through the letter-box, Mrs. Marston, in her low-heeled boots, would keep as still as a cat at a mouse hole. She always wore boots, buttoned at the sides, and Celia thought those little shining knobs were like queerly placed extensions of her senses, giving her sharper sight and hearing. She wore the boots in her own home; her ankles needed the support, she said, but if she had been endowed with all apparent virtues, Celia would still have suspected some bad mental twist in a woman who could wear boots in the house.

Quickly she took off her own outdoor shoes, her hat and coat. She had a childish hope that Mrs. Marston had not seen her in Pauline's car. Everything connected with Pauline had a little gilding on it and she did not want it tarnished by the glance of Mrs. Marston's eyes. She heard the boots on the topmost flight; she heard them outside the door, and there was a considerable pause before the bell was rung, but Celia answered it at once, with a slow, sleepy smile for her mother-in-law. It had occurred to her that a suspicious mind must be an unhappy one.

'I called earlier,' Mrs. Marston said severely.

'Did you? Was I out?' Celia asked with pleasant vagueness.

'You know best,' Mrs. Marston said.

She had a small, spare body, which the weakest ankles might have supported without difficulty, but it was probably heavier than it looked. It was stiff, as though it were made of iron tubes that had grown rusty. The cloth mantle widened her shoulders; a little perched bonnet, fashionable nearly half a century ago and fastened under the chin with loose velvet strings, had no softening effect on a face which took cold wind and hot sun alike inhospitably, with red patches on nose and cheek-bones. Often Celia had scanned that face in fear of finding in it some likeness to Jimmy or Catherine, and rejoiced to see none. Gerald himself owed nothing to her

34

physical appearance and yet he had to pay for it. This was not fair. Celia was all too apt to trace the source of her dissatisfactions to this little woman in the buttoned boots, and she wondered whether she would have married Gerald, even in his uniform, in the peaked cap, and on the eve of going to war, if she had seen Mrs. Marston first.

'Poor boy,' she thought, still smiling at his mother.

'Having a nap, perhaps,' said Mrs. Marston, 'but you ought to take a turn in this fine weather.'

'It's a beautiful day.'

Celia had carefully steered her towards the dining-room. Fortunately it was the room Mrs. Marston liked, and the one containing the bureau, Celia's books and her little rocking chair, was spared the faint smell of camphor, the disapproval and suspicion diffused by Gerald's mother who was left to admire the baronial oak while Celia made the tea.

She did not hurry the kettle. Actually, she was a verbal match for her mother-in-law, and though there was a kind of enjoyment in being pleasantly obtuse, resistance was not natural to her; she liked life to move to a gracious rhythm and this was her weakness and her strength. Little jars and checks were so distasteful that she avoided problems which ought to have been faced, but she also avoided the state of mind which might produce them. Like the majority of people, she moved to a simple enough music, but she wanted to keep time and tune, Mrs. Marston was an alien and discordant, jerky instrument in her orchestra, and she must play it by herself for a while.

But after all, Celia found, it had not been wise to turn the gas so low under the kettle and to spread the butter so slowly on the bread, for Mrs. Marston, left like a patient in a doctor's waiting-room, had decided to assert her right to wander at will in her son's home. She appeared in the kitchen doorway to say, 'I wonder you don't put the kettle on before you go out or, as I should say, before you have your rest. Very low, you

35

can keep the gas, and then the water will boil as soon as you want it.'

'I generally wait for Catherine.'

'Oh then, I'm putting you out, I suppose. And when does she get back?'

'I never know.'

'Then I'd make sure if I were you.'

'But I don't mind. The only rule in this house is that there isn't one, for anybody.'

'I wasn't brought up that way.'

'Neither was I.'

'And I didn't bring up my boy that way either.'

'I thought'—Celia began gravely, 'but do you mind carrying the bread and butter and I'll bring the tray — I thought a different method might have better results.'

'And what's wrong with Gerald, pray?'

'Gerald? I was thinking of myself.'

'Ah yes, that's what a lot of people do. Well, you'll have her leave school soon and then she'll be able to help you in the house and we'll see what she thinks about regular hours for meals. One good thing, you'll save that woman's wages. I don't think she earns them.'

'She would be worth her weight in gold if she sat in the kitchen all day and did nothing.'

'Then she must weigh very light. There's dust in the carving on this beautiful old furniture.'

'Yes, it's part of its antiquity. I think it must have been there ever since the barons had it.'

'The who?' Mrs. Marston asked. 'I've never heard of them and they can't have been very house proud.'

'I don't think they were,' Celia said.

'Well, we can't all be alike.' She lifted her cup and the saucer with it. It was true that in pouring out the tea Celia had not been quite steady with her aim and there was a danger of drips, but Mrs. Marston's attachment to the saucer was not only caution for her dress or reproach for carelessness, it was the gesture of her amiability, of her desire to establish the proper, friendly relationship with her daughter-in-law, and Celia, recognizing the signs, prepared herself for defence.

'Yes, it will be nice for you to have Catherine home. She's been at school more than long enough, in my opinion, but of course you must do as you think best. I only wish I had a daughter of my own.'

'I wish you had,' Celia said.

'But I ought not to complain,' Mrs. Marston said bravely, and with a smile. Her teeth were her own, they were strong and they would last her lifetime, but in their length and the generous way in which they were spaced, they gave the impression of being perilously shaky and, during meals, Celia was always in fear of looking up and seeing that one of them was missing. 'It's lonely at times, of course. In fact,' her voice sharpened a little, 'it's lonely most of the time, to tell the truth. And many hands make light work and two incomes go a long way farther than one, even when one of them's as small as mine.'

'And three,' Celia said, slowly but with the air of making a discovery, 'would go farther still.'

'And where,' demanded Mrs. Marston, 'is the third to come from?'

Celia shook her head. 'I don't know. From the same place I suppose,' she mused, 'as the men who overtake each other in races, and the taps that fill cisterns at different speeds and when will the cistern overflow? And there's buying things at different prices on different days and how much does each apple cost? But that's easier — a little.'

Mrs. Marston put down her saucer and Celia felt sorry for her because she was bewildered, uncertain whether to be enraged or to consider her daughter-in-law half-witted. She could not have had one to suit her less. What she wanted was a hearty, gossiping creature, calling her mother, confiding in her and making her free of the little flat, or some one waspish with whom she could have lively quarrels, not a woman who, with concealed difficulty, was always courteous and therefore disconcerting, who would not take a hint or answer a question with directness.

'But Catherine will know. She's good at mathematics. I can hear her coming now,' Celia said, and she went to open the door for her. She knew Catherine's inability to control her expression when she was taken by surprise.

Mrs. Marston may have suspected the finger pointed in warning towards the dining-room and Catherine's answering grimace; or she may simply have extended her displeasure to Celia's daughter for she did not respond very cheerfully to Catherine when she said, 'Hullo, Grandmamma!' in the rather high and sprightly tones she kept for the people she disliked. She did nothing to aid the conversation and she soon took her departure.

CHAPTER V

'Do you like her?' Catherine asked.

'No,' Celia said penitently.

'What a mercy!'

'But sometimes, when I remember, I try to love her.'

'Hard work!' Catherine said. 'And I don't see how you can love what you don't like.'

'Oh, they are quite different feelings. I don't like worms but, in a distant sort of way, I can believe I love them. "He made their glowing colours, He made their tiny wings." When I'm in that kind of mood, when the sun's shining, when it's easy enough to feel charitable.'

'I don't think worms is at all a good comparison.'

'I didn't mean it to be exact,' Celia said gravely. 'I shouldn't dream of calling your grandmother a worm.'

'No, worms stay where they are put and they can't talk, not to us, anyhow. Oh well, I suppose people turn funny when they get old and we don't see her much. Quite enough, though.'

She went into her bedroom to do her homework. She did not suggest helping to wash the tea-things. Celia had said there were no rules in the house, but there were customs which were just as rigid and one of these was Catherine's regular disappearance, after tea, into her little slip of a room where she stayed until her work was done. She had been brought up to feel as free as Jimmy did from any obligation to help in the house. She could concentrate without any stirrings of conscience when she heard the rattling of crockery in the kitchen and, as she was a practical person, she found, when she did emerge, a real recreation among the pots and pans.

39

Slowly Celia removed the tea-things and laid the table for supper, and then, over the kitchen sink and the unfailingly hot water, she stood for some time, a little mop in her hand, the cups and saucers awaiting attention. With no particular desire to do anything else, she did not resent the number of hours she had to spend in preparing meals and dealing with the dishes afterwards. There were more of these hours than there need have been, because she refused to hurry, and there was always the final resource of leaving a good deal undone. A certain amount of dirt, as she had told Miss Riggs, was better than a flushed and fussy woman, and, while she often wondered why ordinary people like herself should live at all and have ordinary children who, in their turn, would feel this strangely imperative necessity to preserve existence and reproduce it for no obvious purpose, she felt that, for her part, in accepting life and giving it to Catherine and Jimmy, she had to make it as seemly as she could. In absentmindedness, she might burn the soup, but she served it without a sign of her anxious efforts to disguise an unmistakable flavour.

She was troubled now by Mrs. Marston's determined loneliness and economic hints. There was a threat in them, a call for kindness and a practical solution of difficulties, without any realization of the far vaster difficulties involved, and men were very stupid in their reasonableness. If, to their minds, a thing were sensible or convenient, it immediately became possible and the psychological effects either counted for nothing, because they counted for so little with them, or must be combated, by someone else. She had learnt the hard lesson of not approaching a subject when her mind was full of it; she knew, too, that a threat might remain a threat, but she distrusted Mrs. Marston's pathos. As she went down the stairs, she had looked up at Celia who leaned over the banisters to watch her go.

'Tell Gerald,' she said and her chin trembled slightly in

the foreshortened face, 'tell him his mother would like to see him, now and then, when you can spare him.'

Celia opened her lips and shut them without speaking. She had a strong belief in Mrs. Marston's malice and some faith in Gerald's truthfulness, yet this seemed a strange message for a son who had been to see his mother only the night before. But she put the matter from her mind. It was one she had no right to ponder over, for what, essentially, was the difference between Gerald's excursions in the body, she knew not where, and her own secret journeys of the spirit where she would not allow him to follow her? She claimed her own privacy and she gave him his, and he had not said anything definite; he had simply given her an impression which, after all, might be the true one.

She emptied her bowl of the water that had gone cold while she took one of these little journeys, not far in distance, only to Pauline's garden at the edge of the cliff, but a long way off in time, when Jimmy was a baby crawling on the grass and Gerald was in France and Pauline's brother lay in a long chair and frowned while he tried to knit. She had always hoped, and not in vain, that he would drop his stitches or get the wool into a tangle, and then she would have to help him. Perhaps he had pretended to be clumsier than he was — she had never asked him that — but at last he had become more skilful than she was herself.

'What are you smiling at?' Catherine inquired.

'Why aren't you in your bedroom?'

'I've finished. Not much to-night and very easy. What shall I do and what's the joke?' Catherine asked, peering into the pots on the stove and turning up her sleeves. 'Did you put any salt in the potatoes?'

'I forget.'

'Then I'll put some in for luck.' She took and dried the cups her mother was putting on the draining-board. 'Do you know what I think you ought to have been?'

41

'Born with more sense.'

'Oh no, you have plenty of sense, of your own kind, but you ought to have had heaps of servants and sat in a pretty room. . . .'

'I do sit in a pretty room.'

'Yes, but a much grander one, and wear a beautiful dress with yards of stuff in the skirt spreading round you.'

'I should certainly need yards. I should get fat.'

'And otherwise,' Catherine went on, 'be exactly like you are.'

'And what may that be?'

'Comfortable.'

'Is that all?'

'But it means a lot. Comfortable,' she repeated, savouring the word and all it meant for her. 'Now look at Aunt May — and thank goodness, we can't.'

'But I like looking at her. She's very handsome.'

'Is she? I can't see her through the noise she makes. But she's a good manager and she needn't manage. She could sit in a pretty room. . . .'

'She can. All her rooms are lovely. I don't know how she does it. Not by taking thought, because that's beyond her. It's just an instinct. And they have serenity, too. That's what's so strange. But we don't know. Perhaps, under the froth she has a stillness of her own.'

'Not much good to other people, though. When Jimmy goes there, Susan leaves the garden door unlocked and he can get up to the nursery without seeing Aunt May. You can always hear where she is, so it's easy to dodge her. And the nursery's a long way up,' Catherine said with a chuckle, and then, as Celia was silent and looked with unnatural interest at the simmering potatoes, she added defensively, 'Well, they must have somewhere peaceful to play chess in, mustn't they?'

'Chess? Oh yes, yes. All the peace in the world I should think.'

'For a minute', Catherine confessed, 'I thought you were being shocked at deceiving poor old May, but I suppose you were only half-listening, as usual.'

There were advantages, Celia reflected, in this reputation for being so much more absent-minded than she was. Her vagueness was for practical affairs; for personal ones she had, though she did not wear buttoned boots, her own extensions of the senses. She might and did deliberately look away and shut her ears, that was part of her policy, but, at need, she was quick enough. Sometimes, in spite of herself, she was quicker than she wished to be and yet she had not known that Jimmy played chess with Susan.

'I must be very stupid,' she said, and she felt vexed with Jimmy for not sparing her the little anxieties she felt when he went out at night without a word of explanation, but already she had realized that his withholding of an explanation so simple was the sign of its importance for him.

'All the same,' Catherine went on, 'I think it's a pity Priscilla knows. It was she who told me and she's too young.'

'What for?'

'To know people have to run away from her mother. She's too much with grown-up people. They ought not to have had her so long after Prudence and Susan.'

Celia smiled to herself as she tried to imagine the effect on her own mother if, at Catherine's age, she had made such a comment, but she could never have brought herself to make it. There was still, in her young days, a tendency to be embarrassed, when among older people, by any reference to babies until they were a few days old, and a corresponding tendency to discuss the subject a good deal among her contemporaries, but now she could say, without discomfort, to her own daughter, 'I don't think they meant to have her. She's spoilt, but she's a lovely child. May simply can't make an aesthetic mistake.'

43

'Never mind, she makes heaps of others, and Jimmy and I aren't too awful, are we? Lucky, I think, considering Grandmamma!'

'Hush!' Celia said, for she heard Gerald at the door, and a moment later, she turned to greet him and offer her cheek for his kiss. She experienced her usual surprise at finding his own cheek less moist than it looked, her usual regret that, while he smiled at her with frank pleasure, she could never see him without covert criticism of his appearance, his thickening figure, and his round, softly stubborn chin in a face that was eminently kind, and she was the more regretful because she knew how rare true kindness was.

'We've had Grandmamma to tea,' Catherine said.

'Why Grandmamma?'

'Because she came,' Catherine replied with a world of suggestion under her apparent innocence.

'Supper's ready,' Celia said, and Gerald picked up the loaded tray and carried it to the dining-room.

'I mean,' he said, 'it's a silly thing to call her. Why not Grandmother or Granny?'

'I've forgotten the water,' said Celia. 'Get it, Catherine, please,' and Catherine, responding to more in her mother's voice than this simple request, relinquished with a slight grimace, the answer she might have made to her father's question.

'Do you forget things on purpose?' he inquired.

'No,' she said truthfully, but she was a little startled. She was always inclined to believe him rather dull of sight and hearing. 'No, I'm not so clever as that and we don't often need to be tactful, do we?'

'But when we do, it might be better not to try. You won't teach Catherine to be respectful by sending her on errands. Much better let her be as rude as she likes and then tell her what you think of her.'

'I'm not so sure,' Celia said. 'And respectful?' she added

thoughtfully, as though the word were strange to her. 'You can't teach respectfulness. You can only cause it.'

'And my mother doesn't?'

This was half a statement, half a question, and the whole was a rebuke, but she said tolerantly, giving Mrs. Marston every chance, 'Oh, don't you think so? And she gave me a message for you. I was to tell you she'd like to see you now and then.'

She had omitted the last part of Mrs. Marston's message. She did not add that Gerald was to go when she could spare him, for the irony she heard in the words might reach him in his present mood. He was not a moody person, and while she served the food and ate it, made little noises in response to Catherine's chatter, heard Jimmy, late as usual, open the front door and turn on the hot water in the bathroom and knew he would leave the usual tidemark of dirt from his engineering shop, she felt an interest in Gerald which was inspired entirely by this mood: she saw at what a disadvantage the good-natured person places himself. Gerald cheerful, was more or less ignored; in this state of mild irritation, which would have been placidity itself in some fathers of families, he became of more importance, she wanted to make him happy.

'The meek shall inherit the earth,' she said suddenly, 'but I wonder how long they have to wait for it. Jimmy was a very good baby and played by himself for hours.'

She saw him again on the grass in Pauline's garden and something sentimentally reminiscent in the droop of her eyelids and the curve of her lips made Catherine say mockingly, 'I'm sure he was sweet, but I don't see what he has to do with the conversation.'

'Or why he should be late for every meal,' Gerald said.

'It's his way of being punctual. And Catherine demanded attention all the time and so she got it.'

'I'm not getting it now.'

45

'Ah, but you aren't asking for it.'

'Have I to ask? All right.' She turned to her father. 'We have to ask for it,' she said.

'And shall we get it?' His eyes, looking at Celia steadily, were those of the young soldier in the peaked cap who had asked for what he wanted with so little selfish urgency, saying nothing of his claim to kindness at that hour, and now, with a smile, she forced herself to pay some of the debt she owed him.

'I'm sorry. You mustn't let me talk to myself. It's a bad habit,' she said lightly. It was also a dangerous one. It had led her into almost making a promise and she doubted whether she could keep it.

CHAPTER VI

SHE leant over the bath — her sleeves turned up — and removed Jimmy's nightly tidemark, so that the bath should be clean for the family in the morning. The steam from the hot water made a congenial mist about her, like a mantle for her thoughts, an insulator which made them safe from reaching other people, and what she thought was that her relationship with Gerald was very much like her relationship with the little flat, but infinitely harder. By neglecting some of the duties of a good housewife, she stored the energy necessary for avoiding friction; by avoiding, as much as possible, Gerald's demonstrations of affection, and she had almost perfected her technique, she could give him the friendship and the kindness which vanished when more was asked of her. He lost everything when he tried to take all and yet his desires were natural, their absence would have reproached her womanhood which was alive enough, though not for him. She blamed herself for a lack of generosity, for a narrowness of the spirit which ought to have been so big that the merely physical incidents were negligible pin-points, but for her the spirit and the body were not separable and one could not enclose the other. They were entangled and, with her spirit far away, she could not keep a complaisant body here. And yet, she thought, pausing in her labours and staring in front of her as though dimly, through the steam, she could see a light which would make all things clear if her own sight were stronger, Catherine who was conceived in horrified reluctance was now a precious possession, a treasure she would have refused if she could have had her way. It seemed as though wisdom lay in giving as much as possible and taking everything that was offered, but it was all a mystery, for she had refused part of

47

Richard's offering and, through that refusal, he had become a sort of father to this same Catherine. She liked that thought, but aloud she murmured, 'What a muddle and a mess!'

'Yes,' Jimmy said, 'I ought to have gone in for a cleaner trade.'

She turned and seated herself on the edge of the bath. 'I don't mind. I like dabbling in hot water, and yes, I like that tie better than the one you wore at supper.'

He touched it as though he had forgotten which it was, as though he had not been considering himself critically in his bedroom; then he went to the washing basin and scrubbed his nails and, examining them carefully, he asked, 'Why didn't you make me into a little gentleman?' He held out his hands. 'Awful, aren't they?'

'Honest toil,' Celia said, guessing that he saw them poised above a chessboard. She stretched towards the shelf overhanging the bath and brought down a little pot of cream. 'Have some of this.'

'All right. Shove up.' He sat beside her and solemnly they rubbed the cream into their hands. 'Pity to spoil yours,' he said at length. 'I'd like to see Aunt May cleaning a bath! If I were a nice helpful lad, I'd do it myself. Yes, give me a rag and a bit of soap or whatever it is you use, and I'll wipe the dirt off myself before it has time to stick. Never thought of that before. Save heaps of time and labour. Put the weapons on a tin plate or something under the bath and I'll know where to find them, but don't,' he begged, 'keep changing the place for them.'

'You wrong me,' Celia said. 'I'm not in the least concerned with what happens under the bath. They'll be left where they are.'

'Not if old Riggs finds them.'

'I'll tell her.'

He gave her a rough kiss. 'Good night.'

'Are you going to be late?'

'I don't suppose so. And does it matter? You never wait up, do you?'

'No,' she said, and she did not tell him that though she never waited for him, she never slept until she heard his key in the lock.

He went away, but he was back in a moment. 'Quite harmlessly employed,' he assured her with a grin.

Yes, the game was harmless enough, she thought, but what of the girl on the other side of the chessboard. Would she be harmless for Jimmy, even if she loved him? She pictured the two in the old nursery, whence the toys had all gone or been hidden away, though the childish pictures were still hanging and the families of china animals were still on the mantelshelf and Susan's doll's house stood on a sturdy table against the wall. She had never shared it with Prudence or allowed Priscilla, when her time came, to play with it. Its front, which swung back on hinges, to give access to the rooms, could be and, unless Susan was busy with the house, always was firmly locked, and Celia remembered her own shocked surprise when she saw a little girl of twelve years old turning the key in the tiny padlock and putting it in her pocket. All the other grown-up people assembled for the birthday party had exchanged glances and raised eyebrows at this unnatural gesture, and Julia, John's wife, who made a study of the youthful mind, was more distressed than anybody else in discovering indications of bad character and foreseeing disastrous habits of secrecy and acquisitiveness. Prettily, very gently, for all children must be handled tenderly, she had promised Susan her choice of furniture for two of those empty rooms on condition that Prudence should play with the house when she chose, and Susan had refused, gravely and politely. This doll's house, as Celia had soon come to understand, was not a toy. It was a little world Susan was going to create and she knew it was work

49

for a single mind and purpose. It was a world, too, which could not get beyond control. She could change it with her own changing conceptions of beauty and there were no wilful human beings in it to upset her plans. There was no semblance of a human being in it. She had never had a cook in the kitchen or a lady and gentleman sitting woodenly in armchairs, beside an empty grate. Its only inhabitants were Susan's thoughts, the experience and developments in her few years, and it seemed to Celia that the thought of Jimmy would be alien in it. She wondered if the doll's house had ever been unlocked for him. It would be interesting to know that, and suddenly, she felt an unreasonable anger against the niece she loved, because, in her vision of the nursery, she saw that doll's house secretly enclosing the real Susan while Jimmy thought she was playing chess with him. No, Celia could be fairly sure he had not been allowed to look inside. He would want to put electric light into it, he would want to set up a cistern and bring pipes from it into a bathroom, he would misunderstand the whole conception. And that might be just as well and the sooner the better, Celia thought. Susan was his cousin and that was a disadvantage in itself and chess could hardly provide enough sympathy on which to build a life together.

'But this is too fast, too fast,' she said, admonishing herself.

She recovered her normal rhythm and slowly gathering up the clean silver from the kitchen table, she carried it to the dining-room and put it away in the sideboard drawer, but the drawer would not run easily and the contents rattled.

Gerald looked up from the plans spread out before him. 'Coax it,' he advised.

'That's what I'm doing and it simply gibbers at me. It's the kind of drawer I might have made myself. Bad workmanship.'

'Bad workmanship? Look at the carving!'

'Yes, I know, but I like things to be smooth. Dogs with smooth coats and drawers that run and silk underclothes.'

'Your brother has his windows full of those,' Gerald said rather grimly. 'Do you know what he's doing to the shop?'

'No, I haven't seen him lately.'

'Putting in a new frontage — acres of plate glass. I saw the scaffolding as I came by to-night. He might have given me the chance of making a design.'

'Yes, he might,' she said loyally, 'but he seems to be completely without imagination.' It occurred to her, as she spoke, that John might think Gerald had too much, and she looked down at the elevations of his little houses.

'I'd have been glad of the money,' he muttered. 'But never mind. Things may be better in the summer. There'll be people getting married and wanting houses and when that begins,' he tapped the plans in front of him, 'more of these will go up.' He hesitated. 'There's been some talk about our going to live there. There couldn't be a better advertisement than an architect living in his own house, and you'd like that, wouldn't you? Plenty of fresh air. You'd have a bit of garden. And look, these new houses are very simple and you like plain things. No ornament on them, you see. Big windows.' He looked about him. 'And no sloping ceilings.'

'No,' Celia said. A child with half a dozen bricks could have reproduced Gerald's variations in the arrangement of rectangular blocks. On a large scale, their mass would have had a certain grandeur: on this small one, they were absurd and she saw them springing up amid the unmade roads like fungoid growths on a blighted stretch of country.

'And labour-saving,' he said contentedly.

'Yes, that sounds very attractive,' she said, but from experience she knew it meant little more than a serving hatch from kitchen to dining-room and a complete absence of cupboards. 'But we're very cosy here, and it would be a long way out for the children.'

'Oh well, Catherine will be leaving school soon. There's no reason why she shouldn't leave at the end of this summer term, and you'll save Miss Riggs's wages.'

Celia moved from her place beside his chair. 'Did you see your mother last night?' she asked, for he seemed to be echoing his mother's words and she hoped they were indeed only an echo and not a sign that his mind naturally worked as her's did.

'No.' There was just a hint of defiance in his direct stare. 'Why do you ask?'

'Because I hoped you had.'

'Has she been badgering you about me?'

'Oh no, but you are saying just what she said about Catherine. She's only seventeen. I want her to have another year at school. We all stayed at school until we were eighteen.'

'I daresay. Your father happened to be a rich draper.'

'And after that,' Celia went on with the firmness which came so hardly to her, 'she must be trained to earn her living. There's my thousand pounds.'

He laughed. 'That was a fine legacy, wasn't it? Your father seems to have had no more imagination than your brother.'

'He had old-fashioned ideas about a husband's duty to support his wife.'

'And that,' said Gerald, turning red, 'is the worst thing you have ever said to me. Haven't I done my best?'

'Yes, yes, poor boy.' She put a hand on his shoulder and then her cheek against his. 'And your best has been very good.'

He pulled her to his knee. 'You mean that?'

She shut her eyes and nodded and, while he kissed her eyelids, she thought she was justified in her mental reservations about the sad material results of all his conscientious labour.

'Well, if you mean that . . .' he said, and, hearing the emotion he tried to keep out of his voice, she was moved to a realization of all she had left undone and unsaid, she shrank from the thought of all, in mere kindness, she must say and do. 'If you think that, we'll manage somehow. But there's not nearly a thousand pounds. A lot of it went for Jimmy's articles, you know.'

'Yes, I know, but we must keep the rest for Catherine.'

'Yes, we must,' he agreed. 'We will. And then,' he said, laughing a little, 'she'll marry at once and our nest egg will be gone.'

'I don't want her to do that.'

'It's what you did yourself.'

'She might not be so lucky as I was,' she said, and she, too, laughed a little. Her eyes were still shut, but she could feel him trying to interpret that laughter. It might have meant content or faint derision and, though she was not contented, she knew she had no right to deride anyone except herself and, for his reassurance, she touched him lightly on the cheek. But when she left him to say good night to Catherine, she stood for a minute in the passage with her clenched hands against her mouth. Then she dropped them. She had no choice. Here was a human being who depended on her more than she had cared to believe. She could not deny him what measure of happiness it was in her power to give.

CHAPTER VII

GERALD was asleep. He snored with a gentle whistling sound which ascended slowly and ended with a determined downward puff. The noise was not loud, but it was regular, and each puff took shape for her in the darkness, dun-coloured, circular, a bubble that would not break, and she was oppressed by their increasing number; she fancied they would soon fill the room and smother her unless she could persuade them to go out by the window. Carefully she freed herself from his heavy arm and slipped out of the bed. He stirred, the sounds ceased for a moment and then began again on a lower note and she thought the puffballs were a little darker, a little bigger.

Here, as in the sitting-room, there was a stool under the window. Standing on it, she pulled back the curtains and looked out at the view she had seen that morning in the sunshine. No moon was visible, but there was pale light on the crowded roofs and she could distinguish the fields rising to Easterly; there was no wind and, for a few moments, not a sound reached her from outside. The place was under some enchantment of stillness and she was held less by its beauty than by its look of defencelessness in the quiet night and by the thought of the defencelessness against fate of all the hidden people and the meek trust with which they laid themselves down to sleep and took the supreme blessing of oblivion. From how many women, she wondered, had this precious gift been kept by worse trumpetings than Gerald's? And suddenly, mocking these human noises, there came through the stillness the loud hooting of a ship's siren. It did not break the stillness: it was like a level trough of sound with peace on either side of it and, when it came again, it brought her youth with it. She felt the happiness of those days when a whole world was at war, when it was filled with tortured minds and bodies and the chief part of her own suffering was her shameless ability to forget those griefs. Then the hooting of the sirens had not reached her as a sound of mourning. She, unlike countless other women, did not hear it as a scream of pain: everything, all sights and sounds, were ministers to her content. There was no future, no reckoning to be made, and when, after what might have been years or a single day, the reckoning had to be faced, she refused to do the sum. What was the use of adding and subtracting and cancelling out when she already knew the answer? She had ignored it, but she had known it all the time. 'And yet,' she told the night, as she had told Mrs. Marston, 'I was never very good at mathematics.' But she had to pay her debts, to fulfil her obligations and she could not comfort herself with a sense of noble renunciation. She acted according to her nature and, though she suffered, she would have suffered more in acting otherwise. She was waiting for Gerald when he came home without a scratch, but her youth was not there to meet him. Had he missed it? Did he think it had gone with the ruin of so much else? It was intact. All her capacities for love and gaiety were unchipped, unfrayed, and though she was cynic enough to tell herself that this might be because they had been safely laid away, like sentimentally kept relics of girlhood, a dance programme or a dress worn in some happy hour, and like them would seem foolish or out of date if they were brought forth again, she still believed she could produce them in all their freshness, in spite of her two children, in spite of Gerald in the barbaric bed. And she never would, not those particular capacities, but she had others which better served her present turn, and remembering Miss Riggs's sense of secure possession in her loss, she believed that she, too, was fortunate in having her unspoilt memories.

She shivered, standing there in her nightgown, and left

her perch. Gerald turned in his sleep and the snoring ceased; then as he settled his head into the pillow with an impatient, childish movement, he let out a long sigh. Where did it come from? she wondered. Perhaps it came from some region he had not consciously explored but found in his sleep and felt its bitter loneliness, and pity for him overcame her physical repugnance, her cruel desire for cleansing. Or perhaps he had his happy secret places, as she had hers and, in that case, he had no right to her but, more likely still, she thought, the sigh was only caused by some readjustment of his breathing.

She had her knee on the bed when she heard someone stirring in the passage and when she opened the door she saw Jimmy in his pyjamas, his hair ruffled, his mouth stretched in a yawn.

'Hungry,' he said.

'Wait a minute.' She put on her dressing-gown and slippers and found him where she had left him and looking about three years old. 'I'll make some tea,' she said, and by the gas fire in the dining-room they drank it and ate biscuits.

'Mustn't forget to clean our teeth,' he said. His own were strong and regular. 'Biscuit crumbs play the deuce with them.'

'Haven't you been to sleep? I thought you might have had a nightmare. You used to, when you were little, and I rather liked it when you did. You became so affectionate and I became so important, and then, the next morning, it was disappointing, you were quite self-sufficient again.'

He paid no apparent attention to these reminiscences. Catherine would have kissed her and told her she was important still: frowning a little, Jimmy sent his tongue prying among his teeth and she knew he had no curiosity about her as a person with a life apart from his. He did not wonder why she was awake and what might be happening in her mind any more than she had wondered about her own mother whose ordered life had seemed limited to the interests of her children and her husband. It had never occurred to Celia that there might be indecorous desire, or even criticism of the man she had married, in that Victorian matron, but towards the end of her life, when discreet behaviour had become less imperative as an example, she had sometimes displayed a dry kind of humour, as though she were leaving a door ajar for anyone who chose to enter. But if that invitation had been accepted, she might have expected another in return and Celia had not been willing to give it. She, too, had presented herself as a matron of discretion, and now, wishing her son would see her as more than that, she regretted her refusal.

'Such a lot of loose ends,' she said. 'I hope we're allowed to pick them up in another world.'

'Don't believe there is one,' Jimmy said.

'No, but you'll hope there is when you come to my age.'

'What's the matter with this one?'

'Loose ends,' she said again. 'I'd like to make them into something satisfactory.'

He gave his grin of amusement. 'You won't be any tidier than you are now. I'm going to tie up my ends while I'm here.'

'I'm glad you can,' she said demurely.

'You've only got to know what you want and want it hard enough.'

'And smash everything that gets in your way. Yes,' she said encouragingly, and, looking at his sturdy face, his broad, strong hands, she knew he would not be daunted, as she was, by the evidences of a crash.

'And what I'd like to smash at this moment,' he said, 'is my Aunt May's face.'

'She's very nice looking,' she protested.

'She's stupid. I don't know,' this was the first compliment

57

he had ever paid her, 'I don't know how you managed to have a sister like that.'

'Or how she managed to have her daughters.'

'H'm, Priscilla takes after her all right. She wants spanking, that kid.'

'The family seems to be in disgrace.'

'No, I am.'

'Oh Jimmy, what a bother!'

'Yes, you'll hear all about it, so I'll tell you first.'

Feeling immensely flattered by this rare confidence, she listened, not too eagerly, to the story she knew in part already, the garden door left open for him, the chess with Susan in the nursery.

'And I'm sure it was that kid who told.'

'I don't like that word.'

'I don't like the kid. And up came old May and told me I was an ill-mannered boy, getting into her house on the sly. I'd have been much more ill-mannered if I'd told her why. And then she made some damn vulgar insinuations.' And now, in his eyes, darker and softer than usual because he was troubled, she found some likeness to the little boy in the clutches of a nightmare. 'In front of Susan!'

'And they were all false?' To that he made no direct reply, and Celia said, 'I shouldn't let them keep you awake at night.'

'I can't forget the look on Susan's face,' he said simply.

'I'm sure she must have been very much annoyed with her mother.'

'Oh! You think it would only be that?'

'And ashamed of her, perhaps. It's terrible to be ashamed of a parent.'

'Oh!' he said again. 'I was afraid — well, we may get some more chess, after all.'

'Why not?' Celia asked lightly.

'Putting ideas into her head,' he muttered.

58

Celia smiled secretly. She doubted May's ability to put any ideas into Susan's neat and knowing head and Susan had probably realized where Jimmy was long before he suspected it himself. He was not the only young man in Upper Radstowe and she was both touched and vexed that he should dower Susan with such innocence. She said sensibly, 'Don't worry about it. With another girl it might be awkward; with a cousin it doesn't matter. She's practically a sister,' she said and pretended not to see a tightening of his lips which reminded her unwillingly of Gerald. 'You can laugh at poor old May together and you'll have your chess again.'

'Chess?' he said slowly. 'Yes, let's call it chess. One name's sometimes better than another, and as for the game, tiddly-winks would suit me just as well. But as for laughing,' his voice rose a little, 'it isn't funny. It's true! But you see, Susan didn't know. I didn't want her to know. Not yet. I have to give myself a chance. If she guesses now, she'll turn me down.'

'Is that your experience of girls?'

'Susan's different,' he said.

It was his profession of faith, the faith of every man when he first falls in love. Susan was different, not prone to the temptation of accepting adoration she could not return and persuading herself that it would do no harm, but in fairness to Susan, if she needed fairness, Celia remembered that no girl, physically inexperienced, quite understood the strength of the forces with which she played. She measured it by her own mild excitement and the mental pleasure of watching her own skill in approaches and retreats. Oh bother! she thought. I suppose I shall have to explain all that to Catherine, before long.

'Perhaps,' she ventured aloud, 'the chief difference is that she's a cousin.'

'You needn't say it again. I didn't miss it the first time

59

you emphasized the cousinship. And practically a sister! Do I want to spend my evenings with Catherine?'

'No, it wasn't very adroit,' she agreed. 'I'm not very adroit, Jimmy. I just want to spare you pain.'

'But why,' he asked, 'should I have to have it?'

'Because we all do,' she said.

He was silent for a moment. After all, she had made him see her as a person and now she hoped he would not look too far and, either in chivalry for her or unwillingness to know more, he looked away and said, 'But there are different kinds of pain. I don't see why mine should come from Susan.'

'Perhaps it won't. Oh dear! I thought I'd finished long ago with the nursery fireguard, but I've had to bring it out again. There are different ways of getting burnt! You are tall enough now to reach over it, but at least I've made a show of protecting you. Go to bed. You have to be up so early in the morning.'

'So have you.'

'I can go to sleep in the afternoon.'

'You can't! You'll have old May stumping up the stairs.'

'I shall get some fun out of that. Sleep or laughter, it doesn't much matter which. Good night.'

'Good night. Thanks for the tea.'

This, as she knew, was as near as he could get to thanking her for what was more important and he would be rather gruffer than usual in the morning, regretful of his confidences and a little suspicious of her future dealings with him. But he had nothing to fear. She did not expect to go on from the point they had reached to-night. She would slip back meekly into her proper place, just as she had to slip back into her bed. She had chosen it and she had to lie on it, and she was lucky to have one at all, but for a long time she did not fall asleep in it. She was troubled and puzzled by a feeling of enmity towards Susan for whom she had always had a special fondness. Was she more possessively maternal than she had believed and ready to be jealous of the girl's love or indignant at her indifference? She could not answer that question, but, profoundly and unreasonably, she wished there were no such person. And if she goes to Paris with Pauline, I hope she'll stay there, she thought absurdly.

CHAPTER VIII

CONTRARY to all likelihood, Jimmy mentioned her while he was having his breakfast and because the rest of the household was still asleep, for he had to be at his work very early, it seemed as though last night's conversation had not been broken.

'I've never noticed it before,' he said, 'but you're rather like her to look at. Not the face exactly. I think it must be the way you move and the shape of you.'

'I never move unless I must and I'm twice her size,' Celia said, and Jimmy replied without distress, 'Oh, she'll catch you up when she's your age.'

Yes, the hips, so slim now under the trim plumpness above, would probably grow a good deal wider, but the feet would not grow smaller and they were already bigger than Celia's. They were the big feet of Susan's generation, but they were not unshapely. She had been cast in a good mould; she was comely and she knew, another characteristic of her generation, how to give an impression of beauty. They were fortunate, these girls of the moment. Celia's own hair waved naturally, but she could remember the stoically endured lank locks of some of her contemporaries in her youth, the pale cheeks and lips and eyelashes which had to be accepted as a cross in the name of respectability, while to-day, such disadvantages were a challenge to skill and courage, a blank canvas waiting for a picture.

'There it is again!' she exclaimed and Jimmy looked up inquiringly. 'The profit and loss account,' she said. 'I'm beginning to think they really do adjust themselves to keep a balance. Ugly machinery spoiling the world on one side and definitely prettier people on the other.'

'No efficient machinery can be ugly,' he said coldly.

'A machine is beautiful when it fulfils its purpose with the least possible waste of energy.'

He was right. She was on the point of saying that the pretty people fulfilled their purpose, too, though with rather more labour than was necessary, but, with her hands clasped in front of her, she decided to remain meek and silent under his reproof. This was the best turned sentence she had ever heard from him; she liked his air of authority and she was surprised by her feminine pleasure in being scolded.

'There's nothing wrong with good machinery,' he went on. 'I'm not guilty of spoiling any of your world.' He gave a backward jerk of his head. 'What about his houses?'

Her own head went up. 'They've fed and clothed you,' she said severely. Then, more gently, she added, 'Don't be unkind about them. He likes them.'

'All right, all right, but just tell me this. Do you like them yourself?'

'No,' she said sadly.

'Then why on earth didn't you tell him, long ago, before they grew into a habit?'

It was a more searching question than he knew. The answer involved the whole history of her divided loyalties. There had been a satisfaction, hardly recognized until this minute, a justification of herself, another reason for detachment, in despising Gerald's creations, and now Jimmy was making her responsible for the very things she had disowned.

'But would it have made any difference?' she asked, and she thought the young were very cruel and he was typically masculine when he said briskly, 'Heaps, I should think. But for goodness' sake, don't say anything. It's too late, now, and he would feel very sore if he found you'd been hating them all the time. That would give him a nasty knock.'

He hurried away and she heard him running down the stairs, careless of the nasty knock he had given her. Men, she

63

thought, always had this resource of attributing their failures to their women, and though Gerald, unaware of failure, was not put to this necessity, his son was laying the blame in the appointed place.

'Must we do everything?' she asked herself angrily, as she looked with distaste at Jimmy's breakfast plate. 'Bear their children and bring them up, manage the money, do without nearly everything we want and pretend we don't want anything, keep the peace, be polite to their horrid mothers, and do half their work as well? Where do they think we are going to get the energy?'

Life was easier now when, as Jimmy said, it was too late, but when the children were small she had worked much harder than Gerald had, doing up buttons and undoing them, tying strings, washing and ironing and sewing, answering questions, persuading and commanding, pushing perambulators or, much more wearyingly, adapting her pace to shorter legs and her patience to the delays incident to an intense curiosity about a world full of wonders. Those afternoon walks, every day for weeks and months and years, when she was tired and sleepy and longed for a sofa and a book, were among her most heroic achievements. Now, when she saw mothers with young children and no nurses, she was deeply thankful for middle-age and a son and daughter who could manage their own buttons and find their way about the streets. And yet, actually, there was and could be no end to her care of them although Jimmy had reached the age when he could question her dealings with his father. But her indignation passed with her rare indulgence of it; she had an honest mind and she knew she had no right to feel ashamed of Gerald.

It was in pure penitence that she burnt his breakfast bacon, a mishap which had its germ in a mistake made more than twenty years ago and her realization of the continuity of events was at once a despair and a hope. The past was for ever chasing the present and overtaking it, but the future must outstrip them both and in that determination she helped Gerald into his overcoat, kissed him, and watched him go down the stairs. The smile with which she sped him was partly for her fear that the exuberance of his spirits might lead him to some regrettable singularity of design, but she could not now deny him kindness because, long ago, she had denied him counsel.

She regretted her failures, but she returned cheerfully to the little flat, for she was faced with a whole long morning to herself. There was no critic of her leisurely way of going about her affairs, no one to see her standing on the stool and looking at the spread city or taking a book from the shelf she should be dusting. She refused to spoil her precious solitude by anticipating May's angry advent and in this she was wise, for when she opened the door that afternoon, in answer to an imperious push of the bell, she saw signs of satisfaction, not of anger, on her sister's face. Behind her, less satisfied, but prettily polite, was Julia.

'Two of you!' Celia exclaimed.

'We happened to meet,' said May, marching in.

'How lucky you are!' Celia said, for they met nearly every day and always made a point of the fortuitous nature of their encounters, as though each was unwilling to admit a pleasure in the other's company.

Julia, playfully serious, shook her head. 'I don't believe in luck.'

She looked absurdly young to be the mother of a large family. Her big blue eyes were still the childish ones which had enchanted John into the one hasty action of his life. In anyone else he would have scoffed at so headlong a wooing and marriage and foretold disaster, and there were many people who foretold it for him, but they were wrong. He might rage at her, he might think she was a fool and tell her so, but the enchantment held. The great eyes, the little nose with its fluttering nostrils could still move him to passionate tenderness and the violence of his tempers and his love had not marked her small pointed face. She must have had some stubbornness of character to preserve her and also some imperishable individuality, for though she was dressed, unwillingly, from the shop she hated and in the height of fashion according to the house of Fellows, she gave the impression of wearing a poke bonnet and girlish fripperies of frills and ribbons belonging to another day.

'Not lucky to meet May!' Celia exclaimed. 'Then you must be dogged by misfortune.'

'You are very naughty,' Julia said. 'May I sit in this darling little rocking-chair? I believe these things are arranged for us.'

'It's Mrs. Carey,' said May, 'who is making all the arrangements.' She had taken up a position in a corner of the sofa and she sat there, solid, handsome, grander than usual in manner and less voluble. She had the eyes of an ox and in the heavy silences which punctuated her flow of talk, she seemed to ruminate with all time at her disposal. She was in Celia's sitting-room, but somehow she transformed it into a meadow rich with buttercups and daisies.

'For Julia?'

May stopped chewing the cud for a moment, as though she had noticed some disquieting object in the field. 'Julia has nothing to do with it.'

'Certainly not!' Julia said with agitation of the invisible ribbons. 'John wouldn't think of allowing a daughter of ours to go off to Paris with a woman who is practically a stranger.'

'Stranger to you but not to me,' May said.

'And I can only hope no harm will come of it.'

'These things are arranged for us,' Celia said.

'But,' Julia shook her head again, 'we have to use our judgment.'

'Not much use. Just confusing. Like somebody taking our

66

railway tickets for a journey and booking the seats, without letting us know, so we crowd unnecessarily into third-class carriages with sticky babies.'

'First class, of course,' said May.

'I'd rather be with the babies,' Julia said, and, smiling and symbolic, she set the chair rocking, the mother type with arms and a heart for every baby. 'And I agree with John, I could never care for a woman who deserts her own child.'

'Pooh! I don't believe that old story.'

'You believed it yesterday, May,' Julia said gently.

'And John's jealous for his old shop. He can't approve of anyone who doesn't spend half her income there, and Mrs. Carey gets her clothes in Paris. That's why she's going. She told me so, this morning.' She turned to Celia who seemed half asleep in the other corner of the sofa. 'Mrs. Carey!' she said, in the slow, clear tone used for the partially deaf.

'Where?' Celia inquired with a start.

'Haven't you been listening? What's the good of coming to see you? She's flying to Paris the day after to-morrow and taking Susan with her.'

'Oh yes, yes,' Celia said carelessly. 'I know all about that. It was my idea, really. She asked me to go, but I can't leave home and she wanted Catherine, but I wouldn't let her miss school, so I suggested Susan. I'm so glad she can go. Now, go on entertaining each other and I'll get some tea.'

Slowly she went out of the room, leaving silence behind her, knowing that she had temporarily united these two, who, oddly dependent on each other, were generally at war, and this truce was not long-lived; as she returned with the tea-tray, she heard Julia's voice raised to a plaintively quarrelsome note.

'It's a terrible disadvantage,' she was saying, 'for me and for the children. Why, even their school uniform has to be

67

bought at the shop! It's yours, far more than it's mine; my family never had any connection with trade, but you married a professional man and changed your name and half the people in Upper Radstowe forget who you really are. How would you like seeing your name in huge letters over a shop or in the local papers, advertising corsets? That does seem to me so unnecessary.'

'But you are so slim,' Celia said sweetly. 'And you forget that we were born seeing our name over the shop.'

'Yes, I suppose so,' Julia said with superiority, 'but my children, well, my children are particularly sensitive. One doesn't know how their whole lives may be affected.'

'Rubbish!' said May. She was very cross.

'And I know what you are going to say,' Julia said to Celia with gentle reproach. 'But the things arranged for us are only arranged so that we can turn them to their best use. And there's nothing to be done with John! Only the other day,' she said, and her nostrils fluttered in distress, 'when I was with him in a tramcar, he looked at a woman who was sitting quite near us and said, "Five and a half guineas and very good value". That sort of thing!'

'Just to tease you.'

'But it isn't kind. I'm afraid to go with him to a party in case he tells me somebody's dress hasn't been paid for.'

'I once went to a party,' Celia said, 'years and years ago, long before the War, with John and Hester, and there was a girl there with the shop label still pinned to her sleeve. Sent home in a hurry, I suppose. It disappeared later in the evening and I've always wondered what she did with it. Ate it, I expect, or put it in a flower-pot. There were always flower-pots about, in those days.'

'I can't eat the whole shop,' Julia sighed.

May did not laugh; she did not hear. A new idea had passed across her field of vision, her eyes had the bluish film of concentration.

'I don't believe it's true,' she said, 'about Mrs. Carey. Why should she ask you to go with her? Or Catherine?'

'Why indeed?' Celia said.

'And anyhow,' said May, 'if she really had asked you and you couldn't go, you wouldn't be likely to suggest anyone else. I've been thinking it out. I generally get to the bottom of things if I'm given time. And I suppose you would have gone on letting me believe it. But I'm not so stupid as people think, and that's what I told Jimmy, last night. However . . .', she dismissed Jimmy who was not of much importance now, 'all's well that ends well, but you shouldn't tell lies, Celia, even in fun. Other people might take them seriously.'

'I always insist on truth from my children,' said Julia, crestfallen, but authoritative in her particular sphere.

'Ah,' said May, 'I've never needed to do that with mine.'

CHAPTER IX

SHE was telling the truth herself. Her children seemed to have been born amiable and honest and though Priscilla was a little spoilt and precocious, her character was sound enough. They had been spared the tender curiosity which Julia's children met glibly with the replies they knew she wanted, and it occurred to Celia that it might be a positive advantage to have a mother like May, a better warning than those texts, wreathed in flowers, which had hung disregarded over the beds of the older generation. And May herself was probably the least unhappy person in the world. To have called her happy would have been to credit her with qualities she seemed not to possess, capacities for judgment, acceptance or refusal, for suffering and vision. And yet, Celia thought, as from the landing, she watched her visitors descend, of these three middle-aged women on the staircase, all with that intense interest in themselves which is the chief preservative of life, she herself might well be considered the dullest by an impartial observer. She was congratulating herself on a superior wit because these two had supplied her with so much unintentional amusement, but she knew she had supplied them with something they valued more than laughter, an opportunity for criticism and disapproval. She envied them their companionship. She had many acquaintances in this place where she had lived all her life, and Pauline was her friend in the half-detached way peculiar to her, but she missed her sister Hester who was rooted in the same soil and who, if she had a fault, was a little too quick in detecting undertones. She would have enjoyed this tea-party. She and Celia would have had their own companionship of criticism and comment. Hester would have known with what a lively sense of the blessings

70

she had made for herself Julia would rush up to her nursery and insist on hearing her children's adventures of the afternoon, finding under their simple stories the subtler adventures of the spirit; how her lips would be parted while they talked, almost framing the words for them in the perfection of her sympathy, how her eyes would widen with the required astonishment or half shut in a disappointment shared. But Hester would not laugh as, in imagination, she followed May to her home. She might, indeed, refuse to follow her. Her pleasure in contemplating May stopped at the doorstep of the big cream-coloured house, a house of no particular style or date, but pleasant in its solid plainness. And inside there was an air of peace and comfort strangely created by May in the choice of colours and shapes and the disposal of her possessions. She had money to spend, but no money could have made her rooms seem cool on a hot day, warm on a cold one, and no one could fairly deny her praise for an accomplishment which she herself took for granted.

Celia, picturing those rooms, almost doubted her considered estimate of May's abilities, and then, seeing her in them, and still more, seeing Stephen there with the consistent courtesy which was like a bearing rein on a horse, she doubted no longer. May was a stupid woman accidentally gifted with an unerring eye, and Stephen, that trusted family lawyer with a large experience of men and women, had married her before he had experience enough to doubt his own eye's judgment. She had been a lovely girl and he had known her since he first went to Radstowe School with John, but she had been a silent person in her youth and could have been suspected of profundity by a young man who found her appearance charming. And, after all, what had made him grave might have made her voluble. Somewhere, only half-known to herself, there might be an emptiness she had to fill.

71

It was presumptuous to judge anyone, Celia thought, going back to the sitting-room, gathering up the tea-things and removing the crumbs May had scattered on the floor. May was a scatterer. When she read the newspaper she disordered all the sheets; they billowed round her like waves breaking against a rock, and Prudence and Susan quietly stemmed the tide, yet she had the power, often evident in otherwise stupid people, of ordering her household well and inspiring conscientious and even affectionate domestic service. Stephen would return to a good dinner, three fair daughters and a wife rather less talkative than usual. John's dinner would not be so good, for Julia's determination to treat her servants as sensitive human beings had unfortunate effects on the food, but his wife would be eager to hear about his day, even though it had been spent in the shameful shop, there would be pretty good-night ceremonies with the children and consolingly acid remarks about Mrs. Carey. Celia did not know what Gerald would find when he came home or what he expected, beyond a meal he had had many times before and eaten uncomplainingly, but she thought she knew what he hoped for, the kindness she had to remind herself to give and he acknowledged with so much more ardour than she could accept with grace and, hearing quick steps which were not Catherine's on the stairs as she went through the passage, she thought he must be returning early for an extra hour of her company.

She opened the door and waited, ready with a wifely smile, but it changed to one of a different kind when she saw, not Gerald, a little hot with the ascent, but Stephen, thin and desiccated, in shape a tall dead tree of a man. The mouth, the chin, the grey hair, and a pleasantly grave demeanour were as good guarantees of his probity as anyone could expect, but his eyes were what persuaded his clients to unnecessary confidences and confessions, they were what changed the character of Celia's smile; they also saved his

wife from feeling an awe which would have had its comfort
for him. They were not the right eyes for the rest of his face.
They should have been serious and steady, but they were
very quick. There was the slightest possible cast in one of
them and rather than a physical defect, it seemed to be a
mental peculiarity, another kind of vision turned first upon
himself and so giving him the power to see what was not
obvious in other people, assuring them that, much to his
humorous regret, he, too, was a potential fool or cheat.

'You've just missed May,' Celia said. 'May and Julia.
They've been to tea. Will you have some?'

'Yes please.'

It was not the answer she wanted or expected, but he
followed her into the kitchen and sat contentedly at a corner
of the table without a cloth.

'I've always wanted meals in a kitchen,' he said.

'It's quite easily managed.'

She had given him the loaf and the butter in its rough
state and, leaning against the other side of the table, she
suddenly became more feminine, softening her mouth,
conscious of the round white arms from which she had
rolled up her sleeves. She wanted the luxury of being
attractive in perfect safety and, with his odd glance, he
seemed to take this in, with as little disturbance and as
much enjoyment as she felt herself.

'Get found out,' she said, 'and ruined, and these will be
your daily pleasures.'

'Jail first, though. That would spoil my taste for simplicity.'

'They'd let you off,' she said half-scornfully. 'You'd look
so noble and bowed down with grief.'

'But you see, our English law ...' he began solemnly,
and she cried, 'Oh, now you're going to be like Jimmy
with his machinery! Quite perfect. I agree beforehand.
You didn't come here to tell me about the law.'

'No.'

'Or even to be brotherly.'

'Yes, decidedly brotherly.'

'I don't like that, I don't like that,' she said, for brotherliness was chiefly connected in her mind with scoldings for her faults and failures or those of her family, and, hearing an unusual note in her voice, Stephen looked up quickly.

'You sound like Hester,' he said.

'And Jimmy says I look like Susan.'

'I don't see the resemblance.'

'I suppose you wouldn't.' He loved Susan but, not being in love with her, he was unreceptive to fleeting likenesses of face or voice. 'But it's a compliment.'

'Yes, I think it is.'

'To Susan?'

'Oh yes, yes,' he said quickly, but she knew he had not been thinking about his daughter, and, with his eyes on his plate, she thought the rest of him looked tired and old.

'It's all wrong,' he said. 'It's wrong for me to have so much, for John to have so much, and for you to have so little.'

'Meals in the kitchen,' she reminded him and then, more seriously, with a touch of anger, 'How do you know how much I have? What weights and measures do you use for my possessions?'

'It's not right,' he persisted. 'Your father made a bad will. I'm glad I had nothing to do with it. Luckily, he didn't employ his son-in-law. I couldn't have said much. It would have looked as though I wanted to feather my own nest. And I have plenty of feathers.'

'We don't all build with the same materials, but we can be just as cosy in our own way. Why worry about it at this time of day?'

'How much does John allow Hester?'

'I don't know. He had to give her what he considered a reasonable amount to live on until she married.'

'Yes, at his own discretion! It's iniquitous!'

'Then it's been iniquitous for ten years and more.'

'Just enough', Stephen said, 'to make a less spirited creature go and live under his thumb. And that's what he wanted. I wonder he didn't give Gerald that new work on the shop, just to have a chance of bullying him.'

'I'm glad he didn't. And I thought you were so fond of him.'

'You know I'm fond of him, always have been and always shall be. Fond enough to tell him what I think. He ought to give you girls a regular income from the business. He does the work and he must have the lion's share, but he might remember that he didn't bring down the game. Your grandfather did that.'

'And John's cubs will benefit and not ours. Yes, it's unfair. It's so unfair that I won't think about it and I'd rather do anything than fight. It's John's money by law. He would give us a share as charity. No, Stephen, he'd think he had the right to know how we spent every penny and I'm surprised he hasn't thought of that himself. It would be worth quite a lot of money to him.'

'He isn't particularly fond of money. In his way, he's a generous man. If I got into difficulties, he'd get me out of them at the price of all he had, and never say another word about it.'

'But you are a man,' Celia said.

'Yes, he's rather stupid.'

'Ah,' she said, 'there's a lot of stupidity in our family,' and wished her words unsaid for he must surely hear in them some reference to May and she had uttered them in the childish hope of hearing herself praised. She could get praise from Gerald, but, with its sincerity, there was always the prejudice in favour of what belonged to him and the ease with which he gave it spoilt its flavour. Moreover, she had no faith in his judgment; she feared his admiration classed

75

her with his little houses and she wanted to be recognized by a connoisseur, as something rather rare. It would not be true but it would be pleasant, better than a holiday, and meeting Stephen's eyes with their queer obliqueness which actually made him see straighter than other people, she wondered if he, too, had reached the point of craving for something new, something exciting, a point when he could feel young again if someone else would forget his age; she wondered whether he knew that this was the point she had reached herself and so had come to find her like an animal going towards water. And then, with the acknowledgment of her own state, she felt the doubt which often assailed her and which she always resisted because she could not live with it. How much of her love for Richard was a fairy story with which she beguiled herself? It had been true once, it might have continued and grown in his company, but could it be true still? She had always had a secret pride in its intangible persistence, its difference from a love nourished by the senses, and a more secret fear that what gave it life was its dream-like quality. A lonely child would tell itself, night after night, just such a continued story and create a happy world of success and recognition, yet, when she saw him, she had no doubts. But she saw him so seldom, and here was Stephen, suddenly attractive, and frankly, shamelessly, she wished he would kiss her. She would not be sorry afterwards, not in the least, and an indication of a desire to kiss her would do almost as well.

'Champagne,' she said vaguely. 'That was all it would be, though there's always the danger of getting a taste for it.'

'And how long is it since you've had champagne?'

'More than twenty years and very little of it.'

'Oh, later than that. There was John's wedding.'

'Well,' she said, looking away, 'wasn't that twenty years ago?'

'No, twenty years ago, John was in France and didn't

76

know Julia existed. I was there too and so was Gerald. I'm surprised you've forgotten that.'

'I haven't forgotten it.' She looked at him now and gave him, perhaps for the first time, the full gaze of her eyes, more grey than blue. 'No, I can't forget that, but Stephen, you can, can't you?'

'Easily,' he said, 'but for my private comfort, I shall remember.'

'How will it comfort you?'

'It will go into my collection and sometimes I'll take it out and have a look at it. I've got a very interesting collection.'

'I don't want to be one of your specimens.'

'You can't help yourself. But there are no two quite alike and most of them are consoling to a man's sense of frailty.'

'I wish I hadn't told you.'

'And what have you told me?' he asked suavely.

She laughed. 'That I'm very bad at dates.'

'That's what I shall put on your ticket. Bad at dates.'

He did kiss her now, kindly, as a brother should and now that was all she wanted. 'But you didn't come to collect a specimen,' she said. 'That was just luck. I believe you came to show me one.'

'Perhaps I did. Do you remember those puzzles we used to get in Christmas crackers? "Find the monkey!" And if you twisted the paper about, you found him in a tree or mixed up with somebody's boot? Well, find the monkey!'

'I expect I shall,' she said.

CHAPTER X

HE had eaten a great deal of her butter. He was one of those lean men who consume large quantities of fat and still look as though every joint needs oiling. She did not grudge him the butter, it would do her no harm to go short and she was thankful that his consciousness of her comparative poverty — and this was a moderate way of describing the difference between his worldly state and hers — had not made him chary of taking what she could give him, but of course he would not realize that she had to be as careful as she was. Her own children did not realize it, and when she remembered the household in which Stephen was brought up, she was sure that such small stringencies had been concealed from him too. There was nothing cramping to the spirit in being denied big things. For the young, they were always just beyond the horizon, to be reached some day by their own efforts, but the tiny economies were her concern. She did not want Jimmy and Catherine to have among their hopes for the future, an unlimited supply of butter. Julia, she knew, would agree with her about the psychological dangers of an early preoccupation with food, and Stephen's aunt, who brought him up, though innocent of theories, had the old-fashioned pride of a gentlewoman in matters of money.

Celia remembered her very well in the little house crowded with furniture and the curiosities sent by Stephen's parents from the strange countries where they worked as missionaries. Miss Grey was nearly as tall as Stephen grew to be; in shape she was like a board, without a curve at back or front and, above this flatness on which her clothes seemed to hang precariously, her narrow face, with an endearing sprinkling of freckles across the nose, was enlivened by a humorous

mouth and made almost beautiful by eyes of a wonderful
dark blue. To her entire care Stephen was soon committed
for both his parents died during his first year at Radstowe
School, not, as the young Fellows were disappointed to learn,
at the hands of hungry heathen, but of some kind of fever.
This lesser honour was still great enough to make Stephen
a romantic figure; it was impossible not to believe that he,
too, had some special nobility of character. What with
his parents dying so young, for the sake of black people
who could not really matter. What with his aunt who
was rigid where Mrs. Fellows was careless or indifferent,
and frank where she was discreet, and the foreign shells,
the bits of embroidery, the beads and cunningly contrived
boxes, the strange weapons, spears and shields, that
clattered against the wall of the passage when the front
door was opened, Stephen belonged to a different, a more
exciting world than the one to which the young Fellows
were native. And some of that distinction had always clung
to him for Celia, though he had betrayed her view of him
when he married May. If Miss Grey had lived longer he
might not have married her, but there was no knowing what
beauty could do; it could make Miss Grey seem foolish and
May wise; but he might have turned to Celia herself and
in that Miss Grey would have encouraged him, while Celia,
half asleep, would have acquiesced. At that time, and she
was young for her years, being loved was all she expected of
life, and the man who found her desirable was likely, unless
he was positively distasteful, to become the one she ought to
marry. But, for herself, she did not regret his choice. She
had always liked him and never better than to-day when she
had seen him from a new angle, the angle of her wish to
attract him, and found in him a taste which might have been
inherited from his parents who, in going forth to convert the
heathen, were possibly impelled by a force less altruistic.
They had collected converts; Stephen collected examples of

the unexpectedness in human nature and found his own vagaries the most interesting of all. That was natural; what surprised her was that he would have shown it to her if she had not diverted him by that slip of her tongue about her past. But was it a slip? She was not sure. She thought that both he and she, and it was a little alarming and pathetic, were defying their age and what, from one view, was a lessening of opportunities, by trying to impress each other, to prove that they were not exactly what they seemed, and next time they met, they would be a little ashamed and resume their old casual relationship.

She thought of Gerald with new appreciation. He did not make up fairy stories in the belief that he was too good for his conditions. He was simple in his ideas of himself and though outwardly he had no air of dignity and looked, as he was, a humdrum, middle-aged man growing rather too stout for his well-worn clothes and easily bedewed with little beads of perspiration, she could not deny him the inner dignity of an adult human being who was free of all pretence. Often, that she might feel less disloyal, she had wished he would give her some real cause for complaint, by bad temper or self-indulgence or niggardliness, but he had not obliged her. It was the only thing within his power he had not done to please her, and she did not really want to salve her conscience at the price of an unhappy home. As marriage went, she knew she was fortunate. There was no dish for which one had an appetite at every meal and, given only one kind of food, a homely one was best.

'Rice pudding, rice pudding,' she said and heard a voice behind her crying tragically, 'Oh, not again! You haven't many ideas, have you?'

'Heaps,' Celia said, 'but you have to adjust them to your materials.'

'Then get some different materials.'

'I don't think they are worth the price.'

Behind Catherine, she was aware of Gerald, not as a shape but as a slight movement in the passage. She had not heard his arrival nor Catherine's, though her ear was tuned to every step on the stairs, to each different manner of turning the key in the lock and opening and shutting the door. These comings and goings were the chief events in her daily life, they marked the time for her and controlled her movements, but she had forgotten the time and she did not believe she had moved at all.

Now she saw Catherine looking resignedly amused as she took the tea-things towards the sink, and she said calmly, 'Don't interfere. And don't look as though you think I've been neglecting my duties. Go and attend to your own.'

'Yes, I'm going, but I've something to tell you first. Susan's going to Paris! With Mrs. Carey! Flying! Priscilla told me this afternoon.'

'Have they informed the newspapers? We might be living at the back of beyond and Paris might be in the moon! Your Aunt May came to tell me this afternoon, I expect Susan herself will come to-night and Prudence will come with her, in case it's the last chance she'll ever have. Mercifully, your Uncle Stephen didn't know — he's been here, too — and I took care not to tell him.'

'Well, I think it's very exciting.'

'Yes, for Susan, but not for the whole world.'

'You're in a funny mood,' Catherine said as she went away.

'And what did Stephen come for?' Gerald inquired, entering the kitchen and sparing her his usual kiss. 'Yes, I've been listening, just outside the door. I didn't mean to be eavesdropping, though I suppose it comes to that, but I suddenly thought how queer it is that we never see the people we know best except when they know we're looking at them.'

'Only one facet of the diamond,' Celia said sententiously.

'Yes, and reckoning back, I don't believe I've ever seen

you before when I haven't been with you, and I haven't seen Catherine since she was a baby and we used to watch her through a crack in the door. And you haven't seen me, when you're not there, at least, I suppose not.'

'No, it's rather a dreadful thought. And I hope it was worth your while to-night.'

'Yes. I think you go too easily with Catherine. She talks to you,' he said indignantly, 'as though you are a friend!'

'Oh Gerald! It certainly wasn't what I did with my own mother and don't you wish you could do it with yours?'

His lips tightened. 'There are other ways as good. I've just been to see her.' And again he asked insistently, 'What did Stephen come for?'

'I really don't know.' What had he come for? He had begun by talking about the money and the subject had been dropped in their sudden, half-spurious interest in each other. She ought to have made him promise to do nothing about the money, for, in one respect, her loyalty to Gerald was complete. She would not suffer criticism from outside; she had developed an instinct for knowing whence, however indirectly, it might arrive and she locked her doors against it when she could. On the other hand, she had a loyalty to the honour of her family. She would dislike his criticism of that almost as much as she disliked the family's criticism of him and she did not tell him what Stephen had said about the money.

'He may have come,' she said, 'for pleasure, or as a duty or out of curiosity.'

'Curiosity?'

'Well,' she said meekly, 'he may think I'm an interesting character. You never know. And that would account for the curiosity and the pleasure, but, as I'm very modest, I'm afraid it must have been as duty.'

'And what duty can he think he has towards you?'

'I don't know,' she said again.

'I'm beginning to think,' he said, 'that the things you care about are the ones you never talk of.'

'But, at their best, or worst, they are such little things,' she said, 'and all the time, such awful ones are happening to other people, everywhere.'

'What's that got to do with us?'

'Nothing. That's just it. There they are, but they have nothing to do with us, we don't care, and we know so little about real suffering, we live so much on the top of life, that we have to make trouble for ourselves, to get a sort of re-flection of real happiness.'

'We may starve yet,' he said darkly.

'Well, don't let's worry until we do. Supper's ready.'

But he had something else to say.

'You're so secretive,' he complained. 'It shakes one's con-fidence.'

'No, no, Gerald, somebody else has done that for you. What has your mother been saying?'

He answered with sulky determination. 'You don't treat her as you should. You don't make her feel welcome. And she's lonely. I know what she means. You're so dammed evasive. Why couldn't you tell her, yesterday, that you'd been out in Mrs. Carey's car? Anyhow, she saw you in it. And why didn't you tell me? I'd have been glad to know you'd been enjoying yourself. It looks as if you wanted to hide something.' That was his mother speaking, but it was himself when he said plaintively, 'Or just — just to shut me out. But you've always been like that about Mrs. Carey, as though she was God, as though the rest of us weren't fit to know her. And why's your precious friend taking Susan and not you?'

'She knows I can't leave home.'

'Mother would have come and looked after us.'

'Where could she sleep?'

'Oh, Jimmy and I could have doubled up.'

'Horrid for both of you!'

'It's true that we haven't enough room in this little place,' he said, and he looked at her more kindly and with a sort of question.

She heard the danger in it, with its echo of Mrs. Marston, and, like a person on a fragile raft likely to be swamped, she threw overboard all unnecessary possessions, her pride and her anger and some of her honesty.

'What's the matter with us both?' she said gently, and she put her hands on his shoulders.

He softened at once and she thought this was pathetic and unconsciously reproachful. 'Oh, I'm tired, I think, and a bit worried, but everything's all right when we are friends.'

CHAPTER XI

CELIA went up the dim, cool staircase with a bunch of primroses in her hand. They were like a bowl of cream she was carrying to the top shelf of this tall larder, or a full moon she was kindly assisting on its journey, but she did not develop this simile. She could never remember what she had been told about the movements of the heavenly bodies and she was rather sceptical of its truth. The stars did just as well, or better, for her when she thought of them as friendly little candles and not as vast, distant suns which, by comparison, reduced the world she lived on to a handful of dust and herself to the smallest speck in it, of no importance now or hereafter. Her acquaintance with the man in the moon who grinned at her reassuringly, was much more real than a belief in a great body rolling round another which, in its turn, pursued its ceaseless course round something else, and though she knew that, essentially, she understood as little about the primroses, they seemed more comprehensible because she could touch them; she could choose between picking them and leaving them in their green nests under the hedges. And why compare them to anything else when she loved them for their innocent faces, their slim, delicately hairy stalks just flushed with pink and the comic sturdiness of their leaves, mocking the frailness of the flowers?

She had been a long way to get them and she was tired and hot, yet she felt cool-minded and refreshed. She was reduced to nothing when she attempted any comprehension of the whole universe, but in this yearly procession of the spring, in her own tiny corner of the world, the one manifestation in her experience which never disappointed or lost its wonder, she became of real importance, though it might only be as a spectator. She could and did find the old moral in the young green on trees that stood almost knee-deep in the leaves of many autumns; here was the eternal cycle of birth and death and resurrection. She saw it when she had crossed the bridge, and followed the upper edge of the woods clothing that side of the gorge, but the leaves were still sparse enough to make a lattice against the opposite cliffs and she could see miniature figures leaning against the railings; she could hear, when she silenced her own footsteps, the sound of oars in rowlocks far below and it was a good sound, like nearly all the noises with man power behind them. Hearty hammering, the splash and scrape of bricks being mortared, a roller being dragged over damp gravel, the oars in the rowlocks, all these have the slight irregularity which speaks of the mind and the mood, as well as the muscles, of the person making them and gives a sense of harmony even in discord, but the cars, passing swiftly now and then, on the road behind her, had an inhuman pulse and when she had moved on and crossed another, wider road where the cars went faster, tearing after each other as though they were in pursuit of thieves, she was glad to find peace in the familiar fields where grey ewes and white lambs lived in an enviably simple relationship of give and take.

No young ram distressed his mother with the surliness peculiar to the thwarted male of the human species: the girl lambs were supplied with adequate clothing and suitable mates would be found for them; the father or fathers of this nursery, no longer wanted, had disappeared, and, in the green meadow, there was a minimum of demand and a singleness of purpose.

She realized that the perfect unit was composed of both parents and their children but, when she looked for it among her acquaintances, she did not find it. The tie was too close and it was knotted with the conventions that had grown round it. The happiest home she had known was one with no parents in it, the one Miss Grey had made for Stephen, where affection was not expected but had grown out of unexpected sympathies. The best marriage in her experience was that of Pauline with her Reginald where there were no children in the house. She could almost have forgotten that these two had a child elsewhere, for Pauline had definitely the look of a childless woman. It was not the look of a spinster but of a woman who had known passion and failed to fulfil its purpose, or refused it. She had the restless energy for which Nature had intended its own uses; she seemed to be happily, if over-busily, absorbed in the many interests which excluded ordinary social intercourse, but Celia knew she was not so indifferent to people and their opinions as she seemed, and her air of detachment was partly due to her habit of seeing herself with the shocked eyes of other mothers who had not hidden their children, who had no need to hide them.

Pauline's son was the child of an ecstatic reunion when the War was over, an almost exact contemporary of Catherine who was the child of another reunion in which there had been no ecstasy for Celia, and he had been a lovely baby, large and fair and placid. He looked as though his whole life were already planned and settled and to see him as he lay in his crib was to see him in all his future stages, as a schoolboy not noticeably cleverer than his fellows, as a young man twice the size of his mother, without his father's artistic ability but able enough, the kind of young man who would inevitably take some administrative post abroad and act with the good sense, the instinct for justice of his class and nation. And indeed, his whole life was already planned and settled, for the eyes which looked so wisely contemplative in infancy were never lighted, as he grew older, by curiosity or recognition, and those of his parents, watching with such careful carelessness for signs of the intelligence they both had in abundance, met, at last, in acknowledgment of the truth,

87

in pity for each other, in bewilderment that happiness should produce this sorrow.

Celia, who knew it had to come, was the unwilling witness of that look, and, fortunate in her drooping eyelids, she had pretended not to see it, but she had longed to run away, to push Catherine, laughing in her perambulator, out of sight. She was ashamed to possess this lively creature she had not wanted. And then Pauline had shown her quality and her quickness. She had been specially appreciative of Catherine, thus consoling her friend for being richer than she was herself. Celia had never been able to decide why the child had been sent away and she had not been told, but she did not criticize her friend; she knew too well the complexity of human motives and the difficulties of choice.

'Lucky sheep!' she sighed, remembering Pauline's face as she drove across the bridge and the childish droop of her painted mouth when they parted, a few days ago, at The Terrace steps, wondering why she had betrayed herself then, after so many years without a sign.

Celia stopped in the field and looked down at the intricacies of grass and leaves and mosses for which she had no name, and she thought the whole of life was just as intricate and as full of things she did not understand, a very absorbing puzzle; but she saw it less as one to be solved for the discovery of God's purposes than as an endless preoccupation for herself, an entertainment both humorous and bitter, but for her there was more humour than bitterness and she strolled contentedly across the fields, finding fences where she had been free to wander in her youth but overcoming them with determination, until she was beyond the sound of traffic and stood, a little later, at the edge of the spinney which, to the Monks' Pool in the hollow, was like eyelashes to an eye. Today the eye was almost blue for though the trees were reflected in it, only the Scotch firs offered much resistance to the sky. When the leaves thickened, the eye would change to hazel and in the autumn, when the leaves lay on the still water, it would be dull and nearly blind; it would seem to use what sight it had for some sort of communion with the old carp in the pool.

It was a mysterious spot, though, at one end, ducks were quacking and fussing, quarrelling and repeating themselves tirelessly. They reminded Celia of busy women preparing for some festivity at the chapel to which her father, faithful though really indifferent, as John still was, to his noncon- formity, had marched his family, Sunday by Sunday. Meta- phorically, the ducks had put on their aprons and rolled up their sleeves. With practised hands they were slapping the butter on the bread, halving the buns, cutting up the cake, filling sugar basins and milk jugs, disapproving of each other's methods with pleasant acrimony and endearments, refusing the responsibility for mistakes and taking all the credit for success.

Celia had not been to the chapel since she was married there. That binding ceremony had given her other freedoms, but she would not have exchanged her memory of the services, the extemporary prayer and the varnished pews, for that of an older and lovelier ritual. She might have felt nearer God in another church — though she would not have heard him addressed with so much familiarity — but she would have missed something both homely and spicy, rather vulgar and yet lovable, of which she had been conscious since her early years when she sat beside her mother in the family pew, hearing the persistent, slight hiss of her silk petticoat, and saw her father, leaning a little forward, intensely critical and looking as though he might interrupt the proceedings at any minute and set the minister right. No surpliced choir and exquisite singing could have given her the enjoyment she had found in the mixed voices fluting and booming from the gallery at the back of the building and as she was most happily placed in a pew at right angles to it, she was able to watch the singers without danger of reproof. She could see the men in their frock coats, the basses pressing their chins against their collars, the tenors revealing their Adam's apples and wearing that expression of disdain apparently necessary to tenors: she could see the wagging heads of the women and the glinting of their eyeglasses and how some of them, the quavering sopranos, bending their elbows and turning up their wrists, held their hymn-books in a daintily sacred manner, while others, the bolder ones, held their music at arms' length and seemed to shout at it. She had felt an immense respect for these important people. On Sundays they were translated from the ordinary human beings she met in the streets or saw behind the counters of shops, into a kind of hierarchy, but at the same time, she had another feeling which was not respect, a warm glow of satisfaction, as though she were eating something she liked very much and knew there was plenty more of it. As a matter of fact, she was storing up what she was too young to recognize or to use, but as she grew older, increasing her store while she fed from it, she understood that her pleasure came from an insatiable interest in men and women and an eye for the ludicrous, the pathetic and the incongruous which she was always ready to turn against herself.

'No,' she said solemnly and aloud, 'I wouldn't have missed all that for anything.'

BEYOND that hollow, out in the open, on a bank edging a sloping field, she found the primroses. She stooped for them under a canopy of larch branches which, though they were held out like supplicating arms, had triumph in the shrill green of the draperies. It was not enough to call that green a colour. It was a cry, a bugle blown for spring, and as she sat under the trees and looked down at the furrows which seemed almost bare, because there was so little growth on them, but, in the distance, became misted over with pale green; as she looked at the rough lane below and the rising ground beyond, where the trees held frail gilt cups against the sky, she accepted all this beauty as a gift and carried much more than her primroses up the stairs, a feeling that the spring had made her temporarily immune from her own small frets. Carrying her primroses, she had a feeling of immunity from the smaller frets and of ability to bear disasters if they came.

She heard lively voices when she opened the door and found Catherine and Susan in the sitting-room and saw that Susan was wearing a new hat.

'French or Fellows?' Celia inquired, offering a cheek, and Catherine said, 'It's funny how you never kiss people. You just let them kiss you.'

'I know. I live in the passive voice.'

'And how much,' Catherine asked in her indulgent way, 'do you know about the passive voice.'

'I went to your own school. They did their best for me.'

'I'm rather glad they didn't do any better. It suits you to be like you are.'

'But,' said Susan indignantly, 'she's very wise!'

'You are the first person to say so and I do feel rather wise to-day. I've been picking primroses. But how dreadful that sounds! So pretty! Like a lady posing against a herbaceous border and pretending the flowers had grown because they loved her. No, the primroses happened to be there and there were plenty of them, so I picked some.'

'Nice.' Catherine said with her nose in them as they lay on Celia's knee and her own fair head on its young neck was like a flower on its stalk, a flower livelier than a primrose, but a more prejudiced mother than Celia would not have found anything flower-like in the rest of her, except for the fragrance of youth and health. Moving clumsily, she seated herself on the sofa beside her cousin who was disposed there in a pretty attitude, and Susan's figure rose a little as the springs bounced and sank as they subsided, without losing its poise.

Catherine said, rather reproachfully, 'You haven't asked any questions,' and she looked with admiration at the traveller safely returned from perils.

'Yes, Susan, tell us all about it. Were you sick when you flew? But of course you wouldn't be. I don't suppose you were ever sick in your life.'

'Oh yes, Aunt Celia, when I was little.'

'We often were,' Celia said reminiscently. 'And there was a special little basin, with blue flowers on it, kept for the purpose. Easy to hold, you know. I wonder what happened to it.'

'They were an hour late, coming home, in a fog,' Catherine said.

'Cornflowers,' said Celia.

'I think,' Catherine said, addressing Susan, 'perhaps she might pay more attention to the hat.'

'I saw it at once. It's very pretty.'

'Ah, but there's another,' Catherine said and stretching over the back of the sofa, she brought up a gay band-box. 'It's for you!' She put the box on Susan's knee and said encouragingly, 'Give it to her! Give it to her!'

'For me?' Celia said again.

'Yes, it's for you,' Catherine said again, and tapped her toes impatiently.

Smiling and fingering the string, Susan said, 'I thought it looked just like you when I saw it in the shop.'

'Then, Susan dear, it must be a strangely dowdy hat to come from Paris.'

'No,' Susan said, and by this time the lid was off, 'it's beautifully simple, but it has an air. You'll have to get a dress to go with it.'

'Of course!' Celia agreed enthusiastically, while she wondered what sort of air her home-made dress would have. 'Oh yes, Susan, it's exactly right.' She looked at herself in the mirror above the mantelpiece and, seeing her face, broad in the region of the cheekbones, the oval chin, the big mouth and sleepy eyes all much enhanced by the good lines of the hat and the soft velvet ribbon on it, she said simply, 'I look almost pretty.'

'Not almost. Quite,' Catherine said, standing beside her, flinging a rough arm round her waist and looking at the face in the glass. 'Wasn't that a nice surprise for you?'

'Lovely.'

'It will be grand for the school garden party.'

'Perfect. Thank you, Susan.'

'But it's not only from me,' Susan said. 'It's from all of us.'

'All of you?'

'Yes. Mrs. Carey and Mr. Milligan and me.'

'Mr. Milligan?'

'Yes, you know him. A nice little man! And do you know, Aunt Celia, he said the best thing anyone's ever said to me. He said I reminded him of you.'

'I don't see it,' Catherine said, looking from her mother to her cousin, while Celia watched herself slowly raising both hands to the hat. She took it off and laid it down, feeling the kind of anger which can only express itself in

93

very gentle and delicate movement. She detested the hat. What had Richard been thinking of? Not, surely, of her, and she had a clear vision of a middle-aged man a little excited by the presence of a charming girl whose appearance sentimentally reminded him of his old, frustrated romance, excited to the point of losing the fine restraint, the determination not to make things harder for her, which, hitherto, had forbidden him to give her the simplest present, even to write her a letter. She could see them all, very merry, in the hat shop, after a good luncheon, a little freer and livelier than they would have been after a good luncheon in their own country and she sincerely hoped that Richard had not been funny and tried on any of the hats. And what was he doing in Paris? she asked herself, while she heard Susan saying, 'Oh, Aunt Celia, don't you like it, after all?'

'She's not thinking about it,' Catherine said reassuringly. 'She gets like this sometimes. Often. One thing seems to make her think of something else and then she gets sort of lost. Don't you, pet?'

'Yes, terribly lost. It's a lovely hat, Susan. Let's put it back in its box.'

'You'll have to show it to the others when they come home.'

'But somebody might sit on it. It will be safer in the box. And now tell us some of the things you did. You went up the Eiffel Tower, of course.'

'Oh no!'

'No? But you sent Jimmy a picture of it on a postcard. One of those very shiny ones.'

'And he wasn't much pleased with it either,' Catherine said.

'Well — ' Susan began, and Celia said, 'I know. It was the first one you picked up.'

'Well — ' Susan said again, faintly mutinous, 'we always seemed to be in such a rush.'

'Poor Mr. Milligan can't have rushed much. Susan says

he only has one leg. I hate the idea of that! I do like people to be whole.'

'Yes,' Celia said drily, 'but you might not have been whole yourself, if he hadn't been willing to lose a leg for you.'

'Me? I wasn't born!'

'No, it's true that you weren't born,' Celia said slowly. 'But Jimmy was. There might have been no Jimmy for the Eiffel Tower and no Eiffel Tower for Jimmy!'

'That wouldn't have been much loss. The Tower, I mean. But Mr. Milligan's leg — what I want to know is how he got into the aeroplane.'

'Don't be absurd,' Susan said. 'It's quite easy to get into them. And you can hardly tell there's anything wrong with him.'

'Then I wish you hadn't told me. I hope I shall never see him. Things like that give me the creeps.'

'But he's so nice. Isn't he, Aunt Celia?'

'Yes, I suppose you might call him nice.'

'And when Mrs. Carey was having her dresses fitted, and she seemed to be getting dozens, it was lovely to have him to take me about. He's very amusing.'

'Jocular with the funny foreigners?' Celia suggested, meanly punishing him for amusing Susan.

'Oh, not as crude as that!'

Then, thought Celia, perhaps he had not tried on any of the hats. 'Pauline didn't tell me he was going, too,' she said.

'I don't think she knew. When he met us at the station, he told us he'd booked a seat for himself.'

Then he had booked his seat before he set eyes on Susan, and Celia's tightened muscles suddenly relaxed and left her aching. But where was her boasted immunity? Where was her wisdom? She had actually been spiteful about the post-card and, indeed, it was a careless sop to throw poor Jimmy who had been sadly bad-tempered during the last week. But it was not maternal loyalty that made her doubt whether

95

she would ever again feel quite the old affection for Susan; it was Richard's unfortunate discovery of the resemblance which was also apparent to Jimmy who loved this girl.

'They are very fond of each other, aren't they?' Susan said. 'They made me wish I had a brother.'

'Depends on the brother,' Catherine grunted. 'Jimmy's not much good to me.'

'Well,' said Susan, 'how much good are you to him? You'll be better friends when you're both older.'

'Yes, I expect so. I'd hate to be old now but, by the time I am, I don't suppose I'll mind. Nothing will matter so much then, will it?'

'I don't know about that, but perhaps we shall have more sense.'

'Shall we?' Catherine asked, appealing to her mother. 'Shall we have more sense when we're older?'

'What? Oh yes, yes, much more sense.' She smiled. She wanted to say, 'But you won't be any better able to use it. You'll be more vulnerable, not less. You won't draw the reins so tight, but your secret grip on them will be just as firm. You'll be very wise until you're hurt.'

But how absurd she was to be hurt! Susan could not be the first young woman to whom Richard had been pleasant during all these years. She did not suppose, nor did she hope, that he had been physically faithful to her. He knew she could not be faithful in that way to him. And she was not troubled by the thought of the unknown women with whom he might have trafficked. It was strange how little they mattered. That was because she had not seen them, while Susan was visible in the charming flesh, young and softly rounded, without a line on her face, and her little air of sophistication, her way of wearing her clothes, took none of the freshness from her youth and could not spoil the impression she gave of an inner inviolability. She was like her own doll's house: people could look at it through the windows, but she still kept the key, and Celia, searching for the likeness he had discovered, missed the possibility that he had found it in some quality of the mind or spirit. That thought might have been more disturbing than any other. The one that possessed her now was the necessity to protect herself from pain, to adapt herself to conditions not caused by Susan but by time, and she said aloud and half-defiantly, 'I shall certainly wear the hat!'

'Why yes, Aunt Celia, that's what it's for!' What else could you do with it?'

'I might hoard it. I'm inclined to hoard things. But it's a great mistake. When you take them out and look at them, with some one else's eyes, you find that they are quite old-fashioned, not worn out — that's the worst of it — but slightly ludicrous. We mustn't on any account be ludicrous, but I'm glad other people so often are. Let me put the hat on again. I'm going to wear it for the rest of the day, just to get into the habit of it. Yes, I look nice. Sensible, too, I think. The rest of me doesn't match and it's a pity my shoes are muddy, but I can take those off.'

She nodded at herself with unnatural energy and Catherine said, 'How sort of brisk and practical you sound.'

'Yes,' said her mother, 'I'm going to be different. I'm going to live up to the hat.'

'I'd rather you didn't,' Catherine said. 'The place won't feel like home.'

CHAPTER XIII

THE first reward of her good intentions, the first effect of the hat, was the kind of kiss from Gerald which she particularly disliked.

'Sweet,' he said, with his mouth on hers and, drawing away from him, and keeping her eyes lowered, she gave an impression of provocative shyness which made him laugh and kiss her again. 'You look like a girl!'

'But I'm trying to grow up.'

'Stay as you are.'

'I expect I shall,' she answered.

She would stay as she was, feeling fond of him and wanting to make him happy, while she shrivelled inwardly under his possessive caresses. If she could have told him how much she hated them, the hatred might have vanished, but the truth was too devastating, too cruel: it was not worth the relief it would give her, so she simply smiled and said, 'You've brought up some letters?'

'Yes, one from John — what's he writing to you for? — and one from Hester.'

When the postman was tired or out of temper he would not always climb to the top flat, unless he also had something for the one below, to make the journey worth his pains. He left the letters in the letter-box attached to the front door of the house and hoped they would reach their owners. Sooner or later, somebody found them. This was one of the easy ways of the household. No one had much correspondence except Gerald and his went to his office; no one grumbled at the postman. The baker and the milkman were more obliging, but then, although she did not know it, Celia repaid them well. She was incapable of limiting her interest in anyone to the use he had for her and the grave baker, with his reddish vandyke beard, and the jaunty young milkman who stood on her threshold and exchanged their goods for money and their greetings for hers, conscious of being persons for her, toiled cheerfully up the stairs. The postman, trudging along the streets and up and down the stairs, was a mere instrument of fate as he dropped his messages of good or evil, heard them thud on the floor and turned away, ignorant of the nature of his gifts, seldom seeing the people to whom he brought them and so, dealing with the most intimate matters, he remained impersonal, little more than a footstep and a knock.

'What's John writing to you for?' Gerald repeated.

'How do I know? I haven't read the letter.'

'And aren't you going to?'

'Yes,' she said patiently, but she wished he would not hover so close, she wished she might have a letter to herself. In the narrow passage his bulk oppressed her and she was vexed because he extended his marital rights to a share in her correspondence. The little flat seemed to be full of people and to have no place where she could be free of interruption.

'Count your blessings,' she said primly, but with a dry twist to her mouth.

'I do, but your brother John isn't one of them.'

'You never know,' she said, and she slit the envelope. Whatever its contents, Gerald would have to know them and at least they might divert him from any interest in Hester's letter. 'It's only asking me to go and see him to-morrow.'

'H'm. He might give himself the trouble to come and see you.'

'Oh, I like the shop,' she said, 'and he's always nicer there than anywhere else.'

He lifted his shoulders. 'You're all so damned grateful when John behaves like a decent human being.'

'It's the way we were brought up. He was always so much more important, in the family, than the rest of us and, somehow or other, men do seem able to impose their moods on

99

other people more heavily than women can.' She thought of Jimmy, during this last week of Susan's absence, as dark and threatening as a thunder-cloud. 'Perhaps,' she said, 'it's a real superiority. But you are an exception. You are not like that.'

'Inferior, then.'

'Oh no, no, much more unselfish.'

'I don't believe it pays,' he said thoughtfully.

She looked up quickly. 'Haven't you been paid?' she asked.

'No one but you can tell me that,' he said. 'I suppose it all depends on what I'm worth.' He kissed her again. 'Not much, perhaps.'

'You used not to talk like this,' she said gently.

'I used to be young,' he replied.

'Things don't get easier,' she agreed, yet she was hurt that he should find them harder. He had his rights, but she had hers and one of them was to seem perfect in his eyes, in spite of anything she did or left undone, and instinctively, almost imperceptibly to herself — she did not know whether or not it was perceptible to him — she looked at him oftener than usual, she smiled at him across the table and made two groups of the little party, Gerald and herself in one, and Susan, who had stayed to supper, with Jimmy and Catherine in the other. Whatever she felt, she had no doubt about what he ought to feel, and her claim to it became more insistent, his value or rather, the value of his admiration increased, when he showed an absence of his usual pathetic response to her small kindnesses.

In the middle of the night, she started up in bed. 'What impudence!' she cried aloud and Gerald, naturally a heavy sleeper, woke with the words which came surprisingly from his placid wife.

'What is it? What's impudence?' he asked.

She bowed her head on her knees, then slipped under the

bedclothes and lay flat. 'Sort of nightmare,' she muttered vaguely. Across her dreams she had remembered Susan's description of Richard. A nice little man, she had called him and Celia, who hardly had a temper, did not know how to contain an anger that made her want to cry.

'I thought,' Gerald said, 'you might have been thinking of your present from Paris. I wasn't too pleased about that myself. A slight error in taste, I call it.'

Celia was silent because he was right and Richard wrong, but perhaps Richard really had nothing to do with it; perhaps he had acquiesced because to do so was less marked than a refusal would have been. 'Oh,' she said wearily, thinking how small her life was or how small she made it, 'it doesn't matter very much.'

'No,' he said with a chuckle, 'not when you think of the awful things happening to the other people everywhere. You remember? And people sleeping six in a bed no bigger than this. Count your blessings!'

'But when I said that to-night,' she told him, and her voice seemed to be muffled by the darkness of the room with its one high pitched window, the ceiling sloping over the bed, the wardrobe like some large animal which had slipped out of its cover in the jungle to listen to these alien sounds and try to understand them, 'When I said that about the blessings, I was talking to myself, not to you.'

'I know,' he said quietly. 'I haven't lived with you for twenty years without learning something about you and how much oftener you talk to yourself than to anybody else. No, it's not quite twenty. There were the war years.'

'Yes — poor boy.'

'No,' he said lightly, 'it was the best time I ever had.'

She lay quite still and now the short, thick bed-posts, like smaller animals, had stolen from their hiding-places and also listened to what these strange, recumbent figures might have to say to one another. Celia said nothing, and as though he heard the reproach in his words and wished to soften it, he added, 'Life is so simple when you know exactly what you ought to do.'

'Yes. And you did it.'

'Tried to, anyhow.'

'And now,' she half-questioned, 'it's not so simple.'

She heard the lift of a sigh, but he was careful not to lower it noisily. 'Is it as simple for you?'

'It has always been the same for me.'

'Dull?'

'Not in the least,' she said in a livelier tone. 'How could it be?'

'Easily. Same old things day after day.'

'But they are never quite the same. Except, I'm afraid,' she added, 'the things you get to eat. There are so few edible animals. And there's so much of nearly everything else.'

'What else?'

'People and the things that happen to them. To their minds. It's very interesting. I suppose we ought to try to go to sleep. And much more interesting to be getting old than to be young.'

'Yes, interesting, certainly,' Gerald said a little drily.

It was interesting, for instance, though it was a little agitating, to wonder why John wished to see her the next morning. It was a day when Miss Riggs came to the flat and therefore the day started well, yet she seemed a little less serene than usual, and when, for she took pleasure in such little services, she went to open the door for Celia's departure, she pursed her lips, raised her eyebrows and seemed inclined to bar the way.

'Does this mean that there's something the matter with me?' Celia asked. 'I hope not. I've taken special pains with myself. I have to do my best when I'm going to the shop. The young ladies are so alarming.'

'You've no need to care what anybody thinks. No, it's just something on my mind, but it'll keep.'

'I'm disappointed. I always thought you were the one person in the world who never had anything on your mind.'

'I can't help it if some one else goes and puts it there, can I?' Miss Riggs demanded.

'It's a way they have,' Celia said gravely.

'Yes. It's Fred's friend. He's lost his wife. Silly, I call it.'

'Could he help it?'

'Though I will say,' Miss Riggs went on, refusing to hear that flippancy, 'it'll be two years since, come the summer. And he's Fred's friend. Carpenter by trade and, Fred being a plumber, they'd planned to set up together when they came back from France. Two steady fellows and they never had a wrong word! I reckon they'd have had a tidy little business by now. And it seems as if, one way of looking at it, it'd be like me doing it for Fred.'

'But then, Miss Riggs, you don't happen to be a plumber.'

'And,' said Miss Riggs, ignoring, as usual, any remark for which she had not an immediate answer, 'I wouldn't wonder whether Fred wouldn't be better pleased than not.'

'And as you can't find out,' Celia said with the utmost gentleness, 'don't you think you'd better please yourself?'

'But that's just it,' Miss Riggs replied, and, for the first time in Celia's acquaintance with her, she looked thoroughly bewildered and doubtful. 'What do I want with marrying? But there'll be no pleasing myself, either way, because I believe the man needs looking after.'

'Then you're lost,' Celia said. 'Unless you remember that there are thousands of other men who need it too.'

'Yes, but Jo's the only one that's come my way,' Miss Riggs said simply. 'And he was a good friend to Fred.' She opened the door as though, the matter being settled, Celia could now depart.

'Then you are going to desert me,' Celia said, from the landing.

'Pooh!' said Miss Riggs, following her out, 'I could manage

his little place with one hand and still have the other one for you.'

Celia went down a few stairs, then stopped and looked up. Miss Riggs was leaning over the banisters and, under the dome of the skylight, a few grey hairs were visible among the dark ones on her smooth head. Her mouth had settled into its contented curves, a white apron enwrapped her ample figure, she looked like a wise, competent mother who watched a daughter setting off for a day's work, but this maternal aspect did not prevent Celia from asking, 'What sort of woman was Jo's wife?'

'Scraggy,' said Miss Riggs with a good deal of satisfaction.

Celia gave a little nod. She was pleased that a primitive femininity should lie under Miss Riggs's desire to serve, under her immediate response to anyone who needed her and the sort of loyalty to Fred which could identify him with his friend.

'But you may regret it,' she called warningly from the next landing.

'Well, and if I do,' said Miss Riggs, leaning further over the railing, 'Jo'll never know anything about it.'

Again Celia nodded. That was the difference between Miss Riggs and herself. If Miss Riggs made a mistake, no one else would suffer for it. Jo might be duller than Gerald but, with the sharpest wits in the world, he would learn nothing Miss Riggs did not wish him to know.

CHAPTER XIV

I⟶ was a warm, sunny morning. The primroses which she had seen as buds yesterday would be full blown by now and, on the trees, the narrow gilded cups would be opening into shallow bowls, more green than yellow. In the streets, too, there were signs of spring. Shutting her eyes for a minute, Celia believed she could have named the season from the smell in the air and distinguished the sounds from those she heard at other times of the year. These were not the slurred footsteps of summer or the heavy ones of autumn; they had the quickness of winter ones but far more lightness, as though the sun, pulling things out of the earth and from the branches with a confident, warm hand, was also lifting human beings from the flat of their feet to their toes.

Once more, as she left the shops and crossed Albert Square and made towards Nunnery Road, past gardens where the flowering trees were beginning to blossom, she registered her thankfulness for living in this place and no other. She supposed, without regret, that she revealed her limitations in the simple pleasure she found in the sight of familiar places and people. She had spoken the truth when she told Gerald she did not tire of the daily round. Some little thing was always happening and the thought of Miss Riggs, giving herself in marriage and giving up her blessedly solitary bed, was as absorbing as any other affair in which motives and feelings and character could be traced.

But she had a feeling that, after years of personal uneventfulness since the War ended, all the middle-aged people who made the chief part of her world, who had reached the age at which Catherine believed that nothing could matter very much, were aware of some yeasty element working in them, as it used to work in the bread made in her mother's kitchen.

She could remember the smooth heap of the mixture in a pan set before the fire and how, for some time, it was a mild-looking quiescent lump, and then it slowly rose under a hidden ferment, to be popped into an oven of the right heat and brought out as wholesome food. She was not sure what would have happened to the mixture if it had not been baked. She supposed it would have grown some unpleasant kind of fungus and been wasted, and she thought it might be well for human beings of a certain age to experience some healthy emotional fires. But she did not want them for herself, she decided as she reached Nunnery Road and stood still for a minute to watch the tramcars go up and down. They were like toys in their bright colours; they had the earnest, determined appearance of toys which had been wound up and made to go and the man with one gloved hand on the control and the other ready to drop a palm on the warning bell, was like a painted tin figure, fixed by a peg into its appointed slot. And the passengers, too, were pegged into their positions. It was odd, when the tramcar stopped, to see them rise, and straighten themselves from their seated postures but, from one point of view, it was all odd — this wide space which was the meeting-place of many roads, the concert hall on her left with its Greek façade and surrounding of British shrubs, the bronze soldier for ever on his stone pedestal, the men and women all hurrying on their separate errands, the motor cars rushing, the tramcars swaying and jangling and, over it all, the feeling that there was no real need to hurry in this place. It was following the fashion for speed, but it could never rid itself of the presence of the quiet country across the river, subject only to the seasons and the weather.

And now, some way off, she saw two figures which did not conform to this affected mania for speed. May and Julia were taking their daily promenade; as usual, they had happened to meet, and Celia had a suspicion that they would

106

soon slip into some shop, and continue their disagreements and rivalries over cups of creamy coffee and rich cakes. She was tempted to wait for them and the amusement they would give her, but John would be cross if she was late: she did not linger and she soon reached the family shop which now occupied almost the whole of a short stretch of street. Doubtless Julia would cross the road in good time and pretend not to see it, but Celia took a long look at the pink underclothes in the corner window and at the lady who smiled bravely above the restrictions of a corset. She found the main entrance impassable. Workmen were still busy on the new windows and she had to enter by a modest door farther down the street. Here she found herself among the lace curtains and the bedspreads. From this department her own household linen had been supplied in generous quantity when she was married, and she could testify to its quality. Much of it was still in use, but she wished she could have taken a seat at one of the counters and caused a young man to produce his best sheets and table linen for her choice. She could pass the dresses and the hats, the lace and the silk stockings with no more than a mild desire for them, but household linen was a secret, unlikely passion, and even tea-cloths and dusters, though she used them without enthusiasm, touched some tender spot in her when she saw them in their virgin state.

However, she had found that one of the less difficult lessons was learning to do without material things, and she dropped her desires as she went up the wide, carpeted stairs and through a short corridor where gay silk petticoats hung on stands and looked like the petals of great drooping flowers, and so to the holy of holies where Mr. John, as he was still called, held all the threads of the business in his hands. And he seemed to hold them easily. There was nothing harassed or hurried about him and, in his grey tweed suit and coloured shirt, he looked as though he had driven in his dog-cart from a country home beyond the river.

He kissed her affectionately. She knew he was fond of her and for him she had that rooted family affection which is not really shaken by differences of opinion or quarrels or disapproval.

'What do you think of my new windows?' was his first remark.

She raised her eyebrows but not her eyes. Anybody else with a brother-in-law in need of all the work he could get would have avoided mentioning what he so easily might have had, but John had the obtuseness of the man who has never had a doubt about the wisdom or the justice of his actions.

'I should think you'll have a lot of fun with them,' she said. 'You'll be able to arrange a complete tea-party in one of them — afternoon frocks — and a happy day by the sea — bathing dresses — in the other. Is business bad?' she added kindly.

It was to the credit of his honesty, but also to the same obtuseness, that he answered at once, 'No, it's very good.'

'So few people in the shop.'

'The shop's never crowded, even at sale time. That's one of its charms. Plenty of room, plenty of assistants, and twenty women spending a few shillings may look very fine, but they're not so useful to me as one woman spending twenty pounds.'

Much more intelligent looking than May, much more alert, he had, nevertheless, some of her self-complacency, and Celia felt a spiteful little desire to disturb it.

'And so much nicer for Julia!' she said sympathetically.

'Of course it's nicer. When I benefit, so does she.'

'I meant, as she would say, psychologically. I'm sure the thought of women snatching for bargains must distress her.'

'Oh rubbish!' John said impatiently. 'Don't you worry about Julia.'

'I don't,' Celia said softly. 'I don't worry about anybody.'

'Then you're lucky. I worry about the whole lot of you.

Of course Hester never condescends to write to me, but I suppose you hear from her sometimes, don't you?'

'Sometimes,' Celia said with caution.

'And what's her latest prank?'

'Prank? She's earning her living, taking people's dogs for walks in the parks, getting a commission on picking up bargains in old shops, doing a little secretarial work when she can get it.'

'Well, I call it disgraceful! Making an errand boy of herself and feeling that she's got a grievance, I suppose.'

'I shouldn't think so.' Hester was much too proud a person to harbour one, even in secret, but there had been a hint of weariness in her letter, of dissatisfaction with this amusing, scrambling existence by which she kept her independence of her brother, and a suggestion of her readiness to do something practical to settle herself in life, or wildly imprudent for the sake of excitement and experience, and these remarks had been followed by the exclamation marks with which women attempt to modify their readers' impressions or to indicate their own humour.

'Well, if Hester hasn't one, Stephen has, and you, too, it seems. What's the matter with Stephen, anyway? Does he think he's dying or what? He said he couldn't rest until he'd told me what was on his mind. He didn't say rest in his grave, but that's what it sounded like.'

'And what was on his mind?' Celia inquired.

'He says you girls haven't been treated fairly and, upon my word, if he wasn't Stephen, I should think he was in difficulties himself and wanted to make sure of something for May. But, mind you, he didn't mention her.'

Celia was not surprised. She realized, on consideration, how seldom that name was on on his lips.

'But,' John went on, 'what applies to one of you applies to the others. You must all be treated alike, fairly or unfairly! Now, I don't know what you've been grumbling about, but

I've always taken my stand by my father's will and his known wishes. Hester's doing just what he meant to prevent her from doing — living her own life, as silly women call it. She can live in my house, as she knows, with every comfort and plenty of pocket money, and I won't be a party to anything else. And as for you, my dear . . .'

'No,' Celia said, 'leave me out of it.'

'But Stephen didn't.'

'That's Stephen's business and I wish he hadn't interfered with mine.' Slowly she rose and pulled on her gloves. She kept her look of lazy imperturbability. It was her best defence against attack or any sign of her emotions. 'I shall go and have a look at your spring display. Wasn't it rather silly of you to have those windows done just when you have so many things to show?'

This was a successful diversion, but only a temporary one. In the shop and at home he was used to a submissive audience and when he had explained the wisdom of his action and how its inconvenience was outweighed by its advertisement of the shop's increasing prosperity, he said genially, 'And when I've finished what I'm going to say, you shall get yourself a new frock, a new coat, anything you like.

CHAPTER XV

SHE did not look at the spring display and she did not accept John's offer. She left the shop, slightly sick, her head aching under her determination to forget some of the things he had said or hinted. She had pretended not to hear all their significance but, foolish as he thought her, she could not hope he believed her to be as dense as she tried to appear.

At those points where stupidity became useless, she hoped she had been properly loyal to Gerald for, indeed, she felt it, and she had managed to laugh at John instead of showing her anger. How smug he was in the safety of his position, how respectable in the chapel-going which meant nothing except stubbornness in abiding by the faith of his fathers lest he should be suspected of leaving it for worldly reasons, how thoroughly he represented the environment from which he sprang! He had been educated outside it, his friends were not in it, but he had kept all its prejudices, its inelasticity, its right to decide the oughts and ought nots for other people, and though she absolved him from all vulgarity in connection with money, the possession of it had for him, as for most people, its subtle, unconscious influence. She doubted whether he would feel any uneasiness because she had refused his present and, if he did, whether he would not see in her refusal a sign of a grievance she wished to keep, rather than an indication of her independence and resentment. And already the resentment had nearly gone, though the lump in the throat and the aching head remained.

She stood at the edge of the pavement and she might have been standing beside a river, hearing but not heeding the rushing water. Behind her there were footsteps and voices and the sounds made by the workmen at the shop windows:

in front of her the cars and the carts went by and gradually she became soothed by the ceaseless noise and its complete indifference to her and her affairs, as people are calmed who take their troubles to flowing water.

Let them go! she thought, as though she actually saw on the river the little straws and sticks and the scum gathered against the banks. These were less than nothing to a stream urgent to reach the sea. It was folly to concentrate on the straws and scum and miss the beauty because there were some flecks on it, to dwell, as everybody was inclined to do, on the qualities they dislike in people instead of on those worthy of admiration. Nevertheless, she felt she had a score to settle with Stephen whose good qualities had caused her present distresses and, as household matters were in the safe keeping of Miss Riggs, she decided to go and see him and turned from her contemplation on the kerbstone to make her way down the Slope and so to the side street where he had his office.

Considering the neighbourhood of a cake-shop it was not surprising to meet May and Julia still coming up as she went down, and she thought they looked like cats who had been lapping cream, a large, smooth tabby of mature age and a fluffy little kitten, but, on a nearer view, May's bovine appearance was stronger than her look of feline content. Even in its drowsiest moments, a cat seems to have some age-old secret and rather dreadful knowledge, and May was more like a handsome steer being driven through the streets and not actively puzzled by the conditions in which it found itself. The sight of Celia, however, was like the sight of the farm-yard gate. This was familiar, she knew all about this, and her glance sharpened as she asked what her sister was doing abroad at this time of the day.

'When I want you to come and see me, you're always too busy, though what you find to do in that little flat I can't think. I know I often envy you, with all the people I have to care for and the house I have to manage. And here you are, prancing about in the middle of the morning!'

'Because I have so little to do,' Celia said amiably.

'Then why does everybody talk as though you were scrubbing floors all day long? If I dare to say a word about you to Susan . . . '

'Only one word?' Celia asked with surprise.

'Oh, I'd say much more if I had the chance, but she's up in arms at once. And so is Stephen. But nowadays I can't say anything to Stephen. At least, I never get an answer. I don't know whether he's getting deaf or just bad tempered.'

'Not bad tempered!' Julia begged for justice. 'So gentle!' She smiled and sighed. Her patient thoughts went towards her husband who wreaked on her all the mishaps, caused by other people, of his days. 'Worried, perhaps,' she said.

'What can he have to worry him? And, if there's anything, surely I'm the one to help him. I'm used to it. There are the servants, there are the children, all coming to me with their troubles and difficulties. It's natural. I don't complain, I suppose that's what I'm for.'

'What all women are for,' Julia murmured.

'And Prudence and Susan,' May went on, 'are out from morning till night and I never know where they're going or what they're doing. When we were young, Celia, we had to tell our parents if we went to the pillar box.'

'Yes, and wasn't it a bore! But then, we were very docile. We weren't posting any letters we didn't want them to see.'

'And who says my girls are doing that? But I shouldn't wonder. Prudence is a great anxiety to me. So mysterious. Won't tell me anything. For all I know she may be carrying on with some terribly unsuitable young man. It would be just my luck to have something happen like that, and if you know anything, if Susan's told you, for she wouldn't tell me, then you ought to let me know.'

'But I don't know anything,' Celia cried. 'I don't suspect anything! What a muddle-head you've got, poor May!'

'And you'd be muddle-headed if you had my family to deal with.'

'I imagined Susan must be perfect since her journey to Paris,' Celia said slyly and Julia, relaxing her self-discipline of generosity and kindness, permitted herself to smile slyly too.

'Mrs. Carey didn't bring her home,' May said with annoyance. 'She stayed in London with her brother and never suggested that Susan should stay, too. Just made use of her when she wanted her, it seems to me, and I shouldn't be surprised if we see nothing more of her.'

'I warned you about that, dear,' Julia said.

'Yes, but you're not proved right, yet,' May said sharply. 'And I shall have to ask her to dinner.'

'She won't come,' Celia said consolingly.

'Then she'll be very rude,' said May. 'But I'm sure I don't know who I could ask to meet her.'

This was Celia's opportunity for escape. She laughed and went on, anxious to test Stephen's hearing for herself and she wondered whether she was going to find the monkey in the puzzle and whether she would be sorry when she saw it.

What she actually saw was a familiar Stephen who looked tired, but not furtively apprehensive or suspiciously free from care, and it seemed a long time before he could extend himself to his full length when he rose from his revolving chair. His desk was strewn with bundles of documents encircled by tape of an offensive pink and they were all in varying degrees of dustiness. Against the walls were ranged the usual tin boxes, initialled or named in white; there was a bookcase full of drearily bound volumes and the whole room was impoverished and yet redeemed by a chair with a noble spread of seat, a high back and winged sides.

She said, 'That's May, of course.'

'Yes, I haven't had it long. Excellent for embarrassed clients. I put it against the light and they can huddle under the wings.' His queer eyes twinkled. 'You'd better sit in it.'

She stayed where she was, trying to see the hidden May who lived somewhere under her stupidity and her capacity for making Stephen deaf. The chair stood there like a witness to that sense of beauty which seemed unrelated to anything else in her life and, as she considered it, Celia remembered that all the furniture of her sister's choosing had definite character with its beauty. She was never caught by flimsy grace. The chairs, the tables, the chests of drawers, were like wise, quiet people, outwardly rather grave, but possessed of a serenity impossible without an inner sense of gaiety.

'Poor May!' she said very softly, and Stephen's hearing must have been unimpaired for, slightly on the defensive, he asked quickly, 'Why?'

'I don't quite know,' Celia said. Suddenly, for a minute, she felt an unreasonable dislike for him. He could hardly avoid a consciousness of his intellectual superiority to his wife, but he ought to have known how not to waste her. He need not have created an atmosphere in which she could not see her way and had to signal by constant shouting. And then, remorsefully, she remembered Gerald's little houses and Jimmy's reproachful question.

'Oh, we're all in the same boat,' she said, as she sat in the chair. 'I came feeling rather unfriendly. You've got me into trouble with John and I was vexed because I spend most of my life in dodging trouble and then you go and make it for me out of kindness. I suppose it was out of kindness.'

'What has he been saying?'

'You needn't ask that. He must have said it all to you. What you really want to know is how much of it he left out with me. And I expect he thinks it was a good deal. He must be capable in his business — look at his new windows — but he's very heavy handed when he tries diplomacy. I could have done it for him so much better. He took such a sudden interest in our domestic affairs, even asking how we all spent our evenings! The kind brother, the kind uncle, but particularly, the kind brother-in-law! Never mind!' She put her hands to her forehead, then swept them apart. 'It's gone. But he's anxious about you, too. He seemed to think there was something ominous in your attempt to help us, as though you wanted to get things straight before you took your departure.'

'Departure?' Stephen asked. He had been drawing on his blotting-paper, but now he dropped the pencil and looked up.

'For another world,' Celia said.

'Oh, I see.' He looked down again. 'Well, you never know. I seem to have done more harm than good, but I had to try. I might as well have battered my head against a wall. There's not the smallest crack in his solid belief in himself and everything he does. No doubts. He must be amazingly happy and I believe he is. That's what's the matter with him. Julia ought to run off with someone for the sake of John's immortal soul.'

'Heavens! Who would run off with Julia? She's pretty enough, but she's just a dainty little book of moral maxims.'

'Suitable for the bedside table?'

'For the table. Exactly!' Celia said dryly.

'Then another member of the family must oblige.' He directed his faintly oblique glance at her. 'What about you?'

She shook her head. 'Much too lazy. And you needn't worry about John's soul. Sooner or later, he'll get his share of misery. And he'll be bewildered. He won't understand why he should be punished.'

'Do you understand why you are?'

'I'm not,' she said, 'but I expect I shall be.'

'And will you understand?'

'No, but I hope I shall believe that I'm getting off more lightly than I deserve.'

'What submission!'

'Easier than rebellion and, after all, if we make mistakes, we must pay for them.'

'Honest mistakes?'

'Yes, that's the mystery. A few pence wrong in our accounts seems to mount up to quite a lot of money in twenty years. Compound interest, whatever that may be. But I suppose there must be mystery where there's life.'

'It's true about the accounts,' he muttered.

CHAPTER XVI

THE garden behind the Greys' house kept to the exact width of the ground in front of it, but it was a good deal longer than it was wide and, at the farther end, beyond the smooth lawn which was flanked by paths and broad flower beds, there was another path, parallel to the house, and a rough patch of grass where a few neglected apple trees spread their twisted limbs, adorned them in the spring with scanty blossom and then, as though enraged, cast down their small, hard apples in the autumn. In a corner made by the containing walls and screened by the trees, there was a somewhat dilapidated summer-house, cobwebby and dark, furnished with a rickety table and a fixed bench following the curve of the little building. It was like thousands of other summer-houses in suburban gardens, commonplace in the day-time, sinister and not willingly entered at night, but the old apple trees gave importance to this one. Even in the day-time it could be turned into a witch's hovel and at night it was the hiding-place of everything Prudence and Susan feared when they were children. Burglars waited there until all the lights in the house were out; a snake, escaped from the Zoological Gardens, whence the roaring of the lions could be plainly heard, and taking refuge in the garden, would uncoil itself from the legs of the rickety table and climb by a water-pipe to the bedroom window in the deadest hour of the night; then, too, the witch became a reality. And there were fears much less definite, strange and ugly metamorphoses of familiar faces, a sense of vague danger, impossibilities which become almost inevitable to imaginative children in the dark. Yet, in the morning, there was never any expectation of finding the snake in the summer-house, the witch came or went at their bidding, her hovel could be changed into a palace or into the home of an ordinary lady who was entertaining another to tea. And there were endless happy possibilities for adventure in that piece of ground, untouched by the gardener until the grass grew too rank and never invaded by their mother or her friends. Priscilla had missed this privilege of privacy and imagination. By the time she was old enough to escape from her watchful nurse, she would find her sisters there, still in possession, reading or sewing now, instead of playing, and though this was interesting and romantic in its way, it was not the way Prudence and Susan had known. And Priscilla might not have used such opportunities, even with a sister or brother nearer her own age. She was born into a world where people outside fairy tales could fly; where the turn of a knob brought voices from thousands of miles across the sea, and the seven leagued boots had been outdone. But her imagination and her wits were used freely and acutely on the actual people she knew and if, on this warm May night, she had been looking out of her bedroom window instead of sleeping peacefully after her usual cunning or coaxing attempts to stay up as late as everybody else, she would have found reasons, practical or dramatic, according to her mood, for her father's solitary pacing of the gravel path between the smooth lawn and the rough grass.

It was Susan who saw him as she knelt at the window in her nightgown, smelling all the scents of leaves and grass and flowers which seemed to be released at night. They did not rush forth tumultuously; they came slowly, furtively, as though the door were only opened by a few inches and the prisoners must steal out one by one.

'Smoking a cigar,' she said softly. She could see the glow of it like a tiny brazier in the darkness. 'He doesn't often do that.'

'High days and holidays,' Prudence said from her bed.

'Then why to-night?' Susan asked, with her lips against the hands resting on the sill.

'We shall have thousands of moths in this room in a minute,' Prudence said, glancing up from the careful filing of her nails.

'There don't seem to be any,' said Susan, but she blew a kiss to the figure at the bottom of the garden who must be able to see her dark head against the light, and then she drew the curtains.

She felt rather envious of her sister. In the first place, she admired her looks which were less dependent on attention than her own. Prudence's hair, a true brown with no black in it and with a faint lacquering of gold, dropped against the nape of her neck in curls which needed no more persuasion than a twist of her fingers. Her eyes, brown too, were enlivened by a hint of green and the intelligence thus given to them reduced the sensuousness of her naturally red mouth. Some day she might be as massive as her mother, but now her limbs, protruding from the wisp of pale yellow nightgown, were at their round perfection and the skin had the subdued glow which was her physical characteristic. But what Susan really envied was her apparent ability to immunize herself from the feelings, the sympathies and antipathies in the household and to feel no curiosity about them. In spite of what her mother said, she lived in her home with grace and a good deal of patience. This was due to her conception of good manners and to the proud pleasure, which is derived from the exercise of self-control, but while Susan knelt at the window and wondered, rather anxiously, why her father stayed out there so late, Prudence trimmed her nails and hoped no moths would enter. Whether this was wisdom or indifference, Susan did not know but, when the light was out, she lay awake, thinking the frightening thoughts of childhood. There might be someone hiding in the summer-house who would do her father an injury. He was almost perfect in her eyes, but she could believe that he might be faulty for someone else, and lately he had not been his equable self. He had been a little short in the temper and less ready than usual to identify himself with the doings of his family, and Susan, who had imagination, could understand that, in his fifty odd years of life, there might be troubling incidents to remember or events which, like forgotten seeds, suddenly lifted surprising heads from the soil.

She was relieved when she heard his footsteps approaching the house, the distant sounds of doors being bolted, then his light tread on the landing and the click of the switch as he turned off the light, and just as the snake and the burglar were forgotten in the morning, long ago, her anxieties disappeared and she could laugh at herself when she knew he was safe under his own roof.

She gave a little sigh and turned over to sleep, but a voice came from the other bed.

'What are you going to do about Jimmy?'

Susan was surprised and there was a pause before she put a question of her own. 'What are you going to do about several people?'

'That's different. That's fun and we all know it, but poor old Jimmy isn't having fun. He's in earnest.'

'But what about?'

'You are not really stupid,' Prudence remarked politely.

Susan turned on to her other side. Plainly, though Prudence seemed to be detached, she was not unobservant, and she was exercising an elder sister's privilege in uttering a warning, but she was the elder by so little and Susan had always believed that it was she who had the greater share of wisdom, because she was by nature calmer. There was a suggestion of possible excess in Prudence who had surely been wrongly named, excess of feeling, extravagance of action, and the very possibility almost made her guilty in Susan's eyes. She rather resented this warning. It creased the smoothness of her mind in relation to herself. She took, as her natural burden, the family affairs, willingly carrying her anxiety when she saw her father looking weary, enduring her mother's inconsequence, her chatter and contradictory orders, doing her duty towards the precocious and beloved Priscilla, but her secret self had to be kept unruffled and now Prudence had ruffled it. Susan had to question herself and she disliked all problems. She was faced with the knowledge that nothing could be done and no life could be lived in isolation. Each person was like a little island, apparently separate but actually connected, under the sea, with the mainland; the sea was constantly bringing to it and taking from it, pebbles and sand and seaweed and the flotsam cast up on either shore, and it was useless to assign responsibility to one side or the other. Causes might be unalterable but effects had to be dealt with and, if Prudence was right, an intellectual and impersonal game of chess was going to involve her in emotions she did not want.

'I've always treated him,' she said, 'exactly as though he were a brother.'

'If you'd ever had a brother, you would know better,' Prudence replied. 'Of course,' she said on a higher note, 'I may be wrong. He may feel like a brother towards you and be rather worried by suspecting that you don't feel like a sister to him.'

'Oh, that's absurd!'

'Not absurd,' said Prudence, 'but annoying, for some reason or other. I don't know why women should have to feel more humiliated than men do when their love is unrequited! It makes men seem rather noble and women just poor things.'

'Well, I'm not a poor thing. I'm not in love with Jimmy.'

'No, but you're a little more in love with him than you

were before I spoke. I've made him more interesting for you. That was a mistake. It's always a mistake to interfere.'

'It doesn't matter,' Susan said.

She lay facing the window. The curtains had been drawn back again when the light was put out and she could see a segment of the sky bending to enclose the poplars in a neighbouring garden. It seemed to dip on purpose to keep them in their black rigidity. They made the sky look pale and she thought it was like a greenish bowl of glass, such as she had seen in old-fashioned parlours, inverted to protect some representation of fruit or flowers. She, too, was within the bowl, but Jimmy was outside it. He was just beyond the semi-transparent glass and she believed there would always be that sort of dimness between them. Physically, she could imagine him clearly, lying in bed in his little room, and as she pictured him asleep, his hair disordered on the pillow, his blunt features composed into a rather pathetic childishness, she realized that this dimness did not emanate from him and that he was probably unaware of it. She created it herself, though she had nothing to hide, because it was necessary to her nature. There were no secrets in her doll's house, but no one was allowed to meddle with it and suddenly she remembered how she had once found Jimmy in the nursery, standing in front of the doll's house, his hands in his pockets, and because he did not turn at once, as was proper, to look at her, she knew he was absorbed in exercising his particular talent on that interior, as though it were a human habitation. But he had said nothing. He had simply set out the chessmen with the roughened hands which moved with such surprising precision, and she thought she had found the reason for the content she always had in his company. He was able to see her as a person, without reference to himself. She did not know that this was the rarest attribute of lovers, this acceptance of what was, without the demand for a merging which can never be complete and, in its incompleteness, is perpetually troubling, but she knew he would allow her to be a little island. Neither he nor she could control the tides and their effects, or cut the hidden communications, but he would abide by the old definition they had both learnt in childhood. He would admit that an island was a piece of land entirely surrounded by water and he would not insist on a permanent bridge or a regular service of steamers.

Who else would be like that? she asked herself, and aloud, careless of whether Prudence waked or slept, she said, 'Well, I suppose we shall have to marry somebody.'

'Why?' Prudence asked.

It was a reasonable question and the only reasonable answer was one which Susan was not prepared to make. She had the healthy young woman's desire to provoke love in innumerable people, but giving it to one person in perpetuity was another matter.

'I wish,' she said, in a tone of exasperation, 'it was the custom, in our world, to arrange suitable marriages for daughters. Then we'd have no responsibility.'

'I expect they'd be as good as any others, in the long run,' Prudence said, 'but you might have to do a lot of running first and most likely it would be uphill. Anyhow, they'd never arrange one with a cousin.'

'No, that would be the convenience of the custom,' Susan said.

CHAPTER XVII

THERE was no fear of waking May; she gave herself to sleep like a child, but when Stephen entered the room he shared with her, he did not turn on the light. She, too, had drawn back her curtains, so that a faint illumination came from the street lamp beyond the garden and, as he stood against the door, the room seemed to him like one presented on a stage, unfamiliar, holding the spectator taut for what might happen in it. Slowly, the two beds, the tallboy facing them, the bow-fronted dressing-table, took shape and meaning. They seemed to wait in the knowledge of what word or movement would begin the drama, for they had been at all the rehearsals, while he did not know whether comedy or tragedy were to be enacted here. Then he shook his head, stepped quickly to the window and looked out.

The broad road, very white where the shadows did not fall on it, the white houses, set in their gardens, across the way, the tall lamps holding the steady lights, renewed his impression of looking at the setting for a play. The night and the silence gave to this ordinary road inhabited by ordinary citizens, much more significance than it ever had by day and much more beauty. Everything was so still, so black and white, that it seemed to be held by frost, yet the air was warm and what looked like rime on the grass below the window was a mass of May-flowering tulips, just past their prime, their colour lost in the night. The scene had the quality of suspense. It seemed as though figures must emerge from the opposite houses to play their parts, and already he saw them in fancy, the women in full, silken skirts, the men with swords at their sides, all voiceless, but eloquent in gestures of love or hatred, people in the actions and the costumes of an earlier day, long prior to the raising of these houses. But they disappeared at the sound of an approaching footstep. Slowly, on his rubber soles, a large policeman came into sight, halted for a time under a tree on the opposite pavement and then marched on. During his passage he broke the spell lying on the place but, though the actors did not return, it settled down again when he had gone. Perhaps, Stephen thought, the spell was created not so much by the night itself and the lamplight and the immobile shadows as by the general pervasiveness of sleep. Among the many thousands of people in Upper Radstowe, only a negligible number would be waking at this hour, so many dreams and so much oblivion could not be powerless of effect, and with that thought he became actively conscious of May in the bed behind him.

He turned on the bedside light and, shielding the glare from her face, he looked at it with remorseful tenderness, blaming himself for the failures towards her which were very present to his mind and absent, he hoped, from hers. Withdrawn as she was by sleep, she had none of the unreachable remoteness of death, the majesty of an experience no one looking at her had known. Nevertheless, she was mysterious in this living stillness, for the experiences of her dreams, try as she might and would, could never be properly transmitted to another. That was true of all experiences, but over the sleeping ones she had no control. She was assailable by the truths which, for all he knew, she evaded, rather than missed through stupidity, in the day-time. With her hair tied back in a ribbon, as she had tied it since her schooldays, and the dark lashes on the faintly flushed cheeks, she looked almost as young as she had been on their marriage night when he had found her fast asleep. He remembered that he had been hurt to get no welcome and then touched by the simplicity of her faith in him and her confidence in the future they were to share. He was touched now, by the same faith, as she lay there, defenceless, for how did she know he would not take the pillows from his own bed and play Othello? Ah well, he had no inclination to do that, but what harm had he already done and what might he yet do? He shrank from the thought of Susan or Prudence given into the keeping of any man, but with what assurance he had taken May into his own!

He shook his head again and, putting out the light, he went into the adjoining dressing-room and shut the door. Everything here was in perfect order. When he opened the cupboard, he knew he would find his bag in its proper corner; his handkerchiefs were neatly piled in one drawer; in another his underclothes were arranged according to their kind and thickness, and if May's own hands had not set them in their places, she had seen that it was done. And yet, this very evening, he had walked out of the drawing-room because he could not bear the creaking of the news-paper as she turned it and the sight of the sheets scattered on the floor. But why, he asked himself, should he expect or want consistency from her? Inconsistency was one of the qualities he looked for in his collection of interesting specimens, but then, he had never classified May or put a label on her. He might, he supposed, have told her long ago that this trick offended him. Why had he not done that? Kneeling beside his open bag, he realized that, in all these years, they had never quarrelled, there had been none of the sharp retorts and wearisome complaints usually incident to marriage, and as though he must run at once from this thought, instead of dwelling on it with pleasure, he packed his bag hastily, undressed and slipped into bed.

May had not stirred. While he was awake, and that was for a long time, he did not hear her move, and he felt all the superiority of the bad sleeper in the presence of a good one, but when he woke it was to find that his greater sensibility had not prevented him from sleeping through the arrival of the morning tea and his wife's movements as she dressed. He opened his eyes to see her arranging her thick, dark hair. The sleeves of her pale wrap had fallen back and her raised arms were black against the window. This essentially feminine attitude, the unusual stealth of her gestures, lest she should wake him, the careful laying down of her comb and choosing of a hairpin, gave him a surprising sense of home and of being cared for, and he wished he might stay in bed indefinitely, without any compunction to rise and act, speaking to no one, hearing only the sounds made in a house where someone is lying ill and the impersonal ones of tradespeople going to and fro and the click of the neighbours' gates. And now, through the mirror, she saw that he was awake and she gave him the bright, encouraging smile offered to invalids and babies.

He would not respond at once. 'I'm terribly tired,' he said.

'Tired, after that lovely sleep?'

'It wasn't a very long one.'

'Then that's your own fault, Stephen. You stay up far too late. It's all a matter of habit. I expect to be asleep soon after eleven and I always am. It isn't', she said unexpectedly, 'that you have to tell yourself to go to sleep. You've got to tell sleep it's time it came and then it comes.'

'And what does it look like?' he inquired.

'Look like? If you could see it it wouldn't be there.'

'I thought,' he said hopefully, almost persuasively, 'you might see it in some shape or other. You can't evoke anything, can you, without giving it form in your mind? Now, I see it, very conventionally, no doubt, as a woman's figure, veiled from head to foot, of course, in some filmy stuff — what do you call it — chiffon? The colour of the bloom on grapes.

'Grapes?'

'Yes, I think that's the colour of sleep — the bloom on them,' he said, and she, who had changed her dressing-gown for a neat morning frock while he talked, came to the table between the beds and made a note on the writing-pad that lay there.

'What are you writing?' he asked.

'I've a very bad memory,' she said, 'and so much to think of.'

'Well?'

She was sitting on the edge of her bed and he thought she was very comely with the clear complexion on which she used nothing except good soap and water, the strong hair brushed back and arranged without regard for fashion, the white muslin collar and cuffs on the dark blue dress, and he promised himself that, if she gave a sign not of affection — for that, he knew, she had — but of some sort of response to what he had been saying, foolish though it was, he would not run away this morning.

'I must see the greengrocer myself. Cook takes in any rubbish he likes to send and if you hadn't mentioned grapes I might have forgotten.'

'What did I say about grapes?'

'I don't know. I just caught the word when I was putting my head through my dress. And you are going to be late for breakfast.'

He sprang out of bed. 'I'm going to lose my train!'

'Oh, a train? What a bother! Susan had better drive you to the station.'

'No, I've ordered a cab.'

'I call that very wasteful,' she said.

The waste was not excessive, he thought, splashing in his bath; at much greater cost, he would have chosen to be driven by a hireling and not by his own daughter, but he knew he was not to have his way without some difficulty, and, when he went downstairs, just in time to kiss Priscilla before she set off for school, he could hear argument from the dining-room.

'He always has a good reason for what he does,' Susan was saying.

'Well, you may think that pampering you is a good reason, but I don't. He's simply afraid of hurrying you over your breakfast or preventing you from doing some unimportant little thing for yourself.'

'Oh, Mother dear!' Susan begged.

'And,' May went on, 'he wouldn't feel like that unless you'd trained him to it. It isn't natural. When I was a girl I was on tenterhooks till your grandfather had gone to business and on them again as soon as he came back. I don't know what you're laughing at. He had a very quick temper and it wasn't at all funny.'

Silently, Stephen joined in the laughter and he heard Prudence ask, 'What were they like?'

'Who?'

'The tenterhooks. I've always wondered.'

There was a pause before May said slowly, 'I don't think that's funny, either, and anyhow, Susan, engagements or no engagements, you must meet your father to-night, or this afternoon or whenever he wants you.'

'Not to-day,' Stephen said lightly. 'Coffee, quickly, please. The cab will be here in a few minutes.'

'Not to-day?' she said. 'To-morrow, then?'

'I don't know,' he said quietly.

'Are you going on business?'

'No, not on business.'

Prudence quietly removed her mother's hand from the coffee-pot and he had a feeling of brutality in face of his wife's bewilderment, of a cruel understanding with these girls from which she was shut out, yet it was not as definite as an understanding. They knew no more of his mind than he did of theirs, but they took him on trust as he took them and, seeing to his immediate needs, could preserve their curiosity for a more leisured moment.

'Call it a whim,' he said.

'But you don't have whims!' she exclaimed. 'And what about your luggage? Susan . . . Prudence . . .' A gesture, imperilling her cup, bade them rush upstairs and do the packing.

'No, no,' he said. 'I packed my little bag last night.'

'I can't make it out,' she said, 'like this, all of a sudden.' She raised her voice and the ox-like eyes had a momentary gleam of panic. 'What's the matter, Stephen? You've never been away without me before, not on a holiday! Is it a holiday?'

'I hope it will be. If I'm not called back. But I shall get a day, at least, or two days, somewhere. I'm tired,' he said. 'I want to be alone,' and he spoke with irritation because he was sorry for her, dissatisfied with himself and determined to have his way. 'I only decided definitely last night and when I meant to tell you, you were asleep. I believe the weather's going to be fine,' now he spoke with a gay defiance, conscious that his daughters had shifted their position a little nearer to their mother's, 'and if I'm lucky I shall sleep for hours, out of doors, beside running water.'

'Where?' May demanded.

'I don't know. That's the fun of it.'

'You must have your mackintosh. Get it, Susan. But,' she added for, as she said herself, she could work things out when she was given time, 'how can you be sent for if you don't know where you're going to be?'

'Because,' he said, laughing a little, kissing her and Prudence and Susan, 'I'll send an address as soon as I get one. I may have to sleep under a haystack. I may come back to-morrow.'

'Then where's the sense in going at all?' she asked plaintively.

'Oh, I'm not making any claim to sense,' he responded mildly.

CHAPTER XVIII

MAY, who had been standing on the steps to watch his departure, turned into the house. Prudence and Susan walked slowly up the broad path from the gate and felt the early sunshine already warm on their bare heads.

'What a day to spend in a train,' Prudence said.

'Rather nice, I think, just doing nothing and looking at the country. Very shiny, it all is, at this time of year. It will do him good.'

'I hope so,' Prudence said.

They looked at each other for a minute, both ready to speak, and simultaneously both decided not to do so. They mounted the steps side by side and paused, like bathers drawing a breath before the plunge.

'I haven't finished my breakfast,' Prudence said.

'Neither have I.'

'Then we'll have some fresh coffee and take our time over it. After all, there hasn't been a sudden death in the house.'

'No,' Susan agreed, but there was that in her voice which made Prudence take her firmly by the arm and lead her into the dining-room.

'Don't be a ministering angel,' she begged, 'not more than usual, anyhow. That would be a mistake.'

'But where is she?'

'Telling Aunt Julia all about it on the telephone, I expect.'

'I hope she won't do that,' Susan said.

Prudence laughed. 'Oh, there'll be a lot of excitement in the family because father suddenly decides to have a few days to himself!'

'Yes, it's absurd,' Susan said, making a pretence of eating her toast and keeping her ear turned towards the door.

'I think,' said Prudence, 'it was a very wise thing to do.

We ought all to get out of our rut sometimes. It's a comfortable one and smooth as ruts go, but it makes such a violent impression when anyone moves out of it.'

'Yes,' Susan said.

'If we often did sudden things they wouldn't seem so sudden.'

'No, they wouldn't,' said Susan.

'And perhaps this will break the family holiday habit.'

'Yes, I think it may.'

Prudence was doing her best. She was trying to make this occurrence seem an ordinary one and so, in some households, it might have been, but not in this one, and Susan, remembering her fears of the night before, wondered if they had been in the nature of premonitions.

'And didn't I tell you,' Prudence asked brightly, 'that a cigar meant a high day or holiday? But,' she added grimly, 'it isn't going to be a high day for us,' and knowing that their father must have foreseen the kind of trouble he was leaving behind him, they felt that his urgency must have been great and yet could be very easily explained. 'We'll have our turn when he comes back. We'll be hearty young women and go off with packs on our backs.'

'Yes, let's,' Susan said cheerfully.

'And we won't leave an address.'

'How could we?' Susan replied.

They rose from the table, a little uneasy at the silence in the house. This was the hour when their mother's voice could be heard from the kitchen. She had the excellent habit of looking into the larder every day, for she combined thrift with a certain lavishness, and when she had planned the day's food with the cook, she had long talks by telephone with the tradespeople. But she was not making a sound and with their father vanished towards some unknown destination and their mother mute, the girls had a feeling of being stranded, left high and dry when the essential life of the house had ebbed, a fleeting impression of being orphans.

And, apparently, their mother felt that she was widowed. She was sitting in the drawing-room, her hands folded, as though she were ready to receive condolences, but she was not merely patient or rebellious under the decree of Providence. Death was a happening for which no one could blame her; this was a much more complicated affair, involving her pride and her position. She was worse than a widow, she was a deserted wife, puzzled to find a reason for her husband's astonishing behaviour.

If there had been a fire in the grate, that help in moments of embarrassment, Susan would have poked it. She went, instead, to the french windows and pushed them back, while Prudence opened the piano and ran up and down a scale.

'Dust on the keys,' she said, stopping to flick her fingers.

'Then ring for Harriet. I wonder how often I've told her about the piano. No,' she said, as Prudence went towards the bell, 'go first and telephone to your Aunt Julia and tell her I shan't be out this morning. She doesn't seem able to buy a yard of tape without me to choose it for her, but she must manage to do her shopping alone to-day. And Susan, find out what Cook wants, and as you may want the telephone Julia will have to wait.'

'It's such a lovely morning,' Prudence said, 'isn't it a pity not to go out?'

'I don't want to see your aunt.'

'Can't you go out without seeing her?'

'Yes, but where could I go?' May asked with annoyance.

'Round the hill, over the bridge, I'll take you somewhere in the car.'

'I can't understand why your father ordered a cab.'

'Because, as you said yourself,' Prudence replied, 'he's always so much afraid of giving trouble.'

'Oh, then, if it's a trouble to take me out, I certainly shan't come.'

'Now, Mother, that's silly!'

'Silly!' May exclaimed, and Prudence turned from the sight of the tears in her eyes. She had never seen them there before, the young do not know what to do for the grief of their elders, and while Prudence believed that she had twice the wisdom of the mother who had twice her years, she recognized her own ignorance of the past, the relationship between her parents and the real character of both, and at the back of her mind, she was troubled. Bad things could happen on sunny mornings to nice people in charming houses; there was no absolute security, and laughing at an absurd fuss over nothing might be as wrong as dwelling on possible disaster.

'I'm hurt,' May explained on a checked sob, 'and Julia will be so kind and tell me how unhappy she would be if John treated her like this.'

'And he never would,' Prudence said, and May retorted sharply, 'It's not for you to criticize your father.'

'Uncle John wouldn't,' Prudence said perseveringly, 'because he couldn't trust her to understand his feelings, a sort of bursting feeling, as though he must run away and forget his business for a time. I don't suppose father would have gone at all if he hadn't done it on the spur of the moment. Making arrangements would have spoilt the whole thing.'

'Not making them has spoilt everything for me,' said May. 'And he likes his business.'

'Yes, but you always say yourself that you enjoy staying in an hotel because you haven't to think about the meals.'

'Your father never has to think about the meals. I've always seen to every detail of the house myself, and that's more than Julia does. John has to have his finger in every pie. Oh!' The bluish film of her concentration dulled the eyes which had been bright with tears and indignation.

'Oh! I see what you mean. Yes, but I'd never run off like that myself. And you're quite right about Julia. The fact is she's just as simple as she was when your uncle first saw her, in spite of all the grand books she says she reads, and she knows just as little about men. I really do sometimes wonder that John doesn't get a little sick of her. You needn't telephone. And where's Susan? I'll see Cook myself before I go out.'

Prudence was saddened by this little triumph of her tact. It showed her clearly, what indeed she knew already, that in distresses of her own she would find no true comfort where it would be natural to seek it, while her little ruse had been so cruelly easy, that she half-expected her mother to return, in one of her shrewd moments, full of resentment for having been treated like a child. But she did not come back. She ousted Susan from the kitchen and scolded Harriet about the piano keys: she spent some time at the telephone, discussing prices and quantities with the butcher and the fishmonger, deciding in each case to postpone her choice until her arrival at the shop. Then Fanny, the elderly parlourmaid who had served the family for years and was always where she was wanted, performed the daily task of opening the door for her mistress and shutting it behind her, and the earlier sense of having lost both parents changed for Prudence and Susan to one of temporary freedom. Prudence could practise now, without fear of interruption; Susan could read or sew. For a few hours they were safe from being sent on foolish messages or given tasks there was no need to do and when Harriet had dealt apologetically with the piano keys, Prudence sat down to play. Though she was no brilliant performer, she found a great satisfaction in the discipline imposed by precision. Everything that was sturdy and sane in her character appreciated the logical sequence in severe music and her young emotions found appeasement and, at the same time, justification, when she tried to interpret those which had been perpetuated in lovely sound.

Susan was less fortunate. She had no occupation in which she could both forget and enlarge herself. She could not be for ever rearranging her doll's house and her actual world was composed of people who would not behave as she would have them, who talked when they should be silent, disappeared suddenly and rather mysteriously, in hired cabs and, in their loving, which was a proper tribute, created a feeling that some sort of return was obligatory, and this was an inconvenience.

'So,' she said, entering the drawing-room with her hat on, 'I shall go and see Aunt Celia.'

'So . . .?' Prudence asked, and managed not to frown at this interruption.

'Because she's soothing. Because we're rather alike. Funny little Mr. Milligan said we were and I've been thinking about it and it's true. She wants life to be smooth.'

'Who doesn't?'

'Hardly anyone. They want other things more. Their own way.'

'Well, what's your way?'

Susan thought for a moment. 'A nice, grassy lane,' she said, 'in high country, with great swooping views on each side, but with good strong walls to it, so that I needn't keep wondering if there are bulls in the fields.'

'It's just possible that there might be a bull in the lane.'

'There'd still be the walls to climb over.'

'If you were quick enough.'

'There'd be plenty of time. There wouldn't be any corners in my lane. I should be able to see a long way ahead.'

'But,' said Prudence, 'if that's your idea of life, you ought not to climb the wall. If you expect to live without a struggle, you ought to allow the bull to gore you if he wants to. But I don't think even Aunt Celia would do that. And you have to think of the mess that someone else would find.'

'Yes,' Susan agreed, drawing on her gloves, 'there's that to be thought of. I suppose there's always someone else.'

CHAPTER XIX

She forgot the heaviness of this responsibility as soon as she was outside the house. The quality of the sunshine, the sight of the flowering trees overhanging the pavements, assured her youth that, on this day of early summer, the world had been planned for her pleasure and her little worries had no real existence. Like everybody else of her years, she trusted the future to give her what she wanted, and, as she could not picture herself with a face wrinkled or with the flesh sagging under her clothes, so she had no conception of the corresponding marks made on the mind, as ineradicable as the others though, like them with cosmetics, they might be partially overlaid by that high courage which grows harder to evoke with the increased need for it. She had it now, in reserve, but she had no use for it when the sun shone and she could sniff all the scents from the gardens as she went down the road. On either side of it there were houses, like her own home, of a certain spaciousness, an air of leisure and of belief that the outward graces of life must be permanent because they were good, and, a little farther on, the buildings and playing-fields of Radstowe School proclaimed the same faith. It was implicit in the trees neatly overhanging their own shadows in the Close, in a glimpse of a gowned figure passing from one classroom to another, in the leathershod horse, attached to a roller for the cricket pitch, and for a few minutes, Susan stood beside the railings and savoured the peace of the green fields, the smell of newly-cut grass, the sight of the old horse, relaxed, hanging his head, waiting indifferently, drowsily, for his next order. She had a sense of possession in the place, as strong as the one she felt for her own school, and more romantic, for on these fields her father had played, he had moved among these buildings, and the thought of him, here, all the years ago before she had known him, with bony wrists probably protruding from his coat sleeves, was somehow touching and a little mysterious, for though the school was a modern foundation, it had adopted the traditions of an older one and each member of it was enriched and enlarged by a sense of continuity which could be found again in that part of Upper Radstowe towards which she went.

She strolled on towards the aunt who, with less practical orderliness than her own, had the same desire for a slow and unruffled way through life, but when she reached The Terrace and looked into the roadway below, she found evidence of someone who, though her taste might be for smoothness, was certainly for speed. This was Mrs. Carey's low-built, yellow car, untenanted and looking, in its immobility, like a strong, swift animal which had been killed instantaneously by a master shot and was stiffening where it dropped. This indication that Mrs. Carey was with her aunt gave Susan pause. She doubted whether she would herself be welcome. When she was alone with Celia it was like being with a wiser contemporary, but she knew this pair of middle-aged women who were friends would force on her the embarrassing certainty of their combined knowledge rather than of their wisdom, that knowledge of the experienced and the initiated which, though it may be tender and respectful towards the young, cannot altogether rid itself of a humorous pity for the novice who has to meet the treachery of the future and continue to live as though it had been faithful. Moreover, she had a quick social sense, surprising in her mother's daughter, which warned her that a friendship could not always be picked up at the place where it had been left. Mrs. Carey, in Paris, had been a delightful companion, in a holiday mood admitting of little freedoms, but since then she had shown no desire for more of Susan's company and Susan had been disappointed and fearful of having failed in some small matter which was of great importance to the fastidious. How was she to adjust her behaviour to fit her grateful memory of the gay days with Pauline and her brother and yet show her realization that they had established no permanent claim on her hosts? Concerned with this little problem and her possible crudenesses, she frowned slightly. Then, as she lived again and criticized herself through that adventure, the frown vanished, her mouth softened, for though it was good to satisfy a critical woman and perhaps she had not done it, there was another, more primitive pleasure in enlivening a far less critical man, even a maimed, middle-aged man who had to adjust his spectacles before he could read the menu in a restaurant. She had been happy with him, especially when Mrs. Carey was occupied with her dressmakers; she had been careful to be like a bright, intelligent niece, just as he had been like a kind uncle, but she had always been conscious of the fact that he was no uncle at all, and then she had been inspired to move more lightly, to hold her head higher, to vary the quality of her smiles. It was the natural reaction to a stranger of another sex and it had definitely involved a brightening of the sunshine, a sharpening of sounds, a keener appreciation of what she was expected to admire. Nice, funny little man, she thought, remembering how his spectacles would slip down his nose and he would look at her over them, with a rather childish hope of her laughter at his dry absurdities. She thought he was an unlikely brother for Mrs. Carey who was as quick and sharp as a rapier and could be as daunting, and, remembering that, she took her hand from the rail of the banisters and her foot from the first stair. Then, from far up, under the skylight, she heard the opening of a door and decided that she need not retreat if Mrs. Carey was about to do so. She expected to hear voices calling to each other in farewell, but the only sound was the quick and rather heavy one of descending feet, and of more than two feet, for the sounds overlapped each other and, looking up, she saw that Celia was accompanying Mrs. Carey. The stairs were wide, the two walked abreast without touching, there was an odd effect of finality in their silence and, as they approached the bottom of the stairs and Susan could see their faces, she knew they were absorbed by the same thought but thinking about it differently. They looked as though they had quarrelled with an intensity which made a union of their disagreement and, no more than happy lovers, would they willingly be parted.

Susan stepped back into the well of the staircase to give them a clear passage, for now she saw these two women, Mrs. Carey in her distinguished, slightly exaggerated clothes, Celia in her old overall, as the front rank of a determined army which would surely sweep everything out of its way, but this was the impression of a moment. The sight of her arrested them. They both greeted her with vague kindness, with the air of recognizing an acquaintance, but forgetting exactly who she was.

'You're sure you've got Hester's address?' Celia asked, and Pauline gave a nod of assent and leave-taking. Alone she passed through the hall and out on to The Terrace and Celia stood quite still, her hands loosely clasped in front of her, her head turned sideways, until the triumphant roar of Mrs. Carey's yellow monster, restored to life, was lost in distance, and as though it had been a devouring animal going after its prey, these two, at the foot of the staircase, seemed to remain motionless under the awe of their own escape.

'About three hours, if she doesn't have an accident,' Celia said in a dull tone which caused Susan to cry, 'Oh, Aunt Celia, what is it? Has something happened to Aunt Hester?'

'Hester? Why Hester?' But now she became properly

aware of Susan and of herself and, after a pause, she said quietly, 'No, it's Pauline's brother. He's very ill.'

'And she's so fond of him!' Susan exclaimed.

'Yes, that's rather the point,' Celia said, with a touch of irony.

'Of course.' Susan felt she had been foolish. 'Is he in danger?'

'I suppose pneumonia's always dangerous.'

'And specially,' said Susan, 'for old people. I mean, not young ones. How old do you think he can be?'

'Ah, I wonder,' Celia said.

'About fifty, I should think. He's got that nutty look. Not a Brazil, with a hard shell, but a filbert with the green sheath still round it.'

She was pleased with this description. It suited the dry aspect and the fresh kindliness of Mr. Milligan, but when she met her aunt's glance, though it was veiled and drowsy as usual, she thought she detected criticism in it, faintly scornful, almost inimical, and, accusing herself of frivolity, hastening to be grave at this grave moment she said earnestly, 'I'm truly sorry for Mrs. Carey, but perhaps it will be all right. Things don't always go wrong, do they?'

'Things?' Celia said. She turned and led the way upstairs. She went slowly, her hand on the narrow mahogany rail of the banisters, and Susan, following meekly, at a much greater distance than that of the few feet between them, heard her saying impatiently, 'What are called the Acts of God are, presumably, all they should be, and the others we are responsible for ourselves.'

'But who,' Susan inquired, 'can be responsible for Mr. Milligan's pneumonia?'

'Well,' said Celia, pausing by the open door of the flat, 'it's just conceivable that I might be.'

'But that's fantastic! When do you ever see him?'

Celia laughed. 'It's a remote possibility, of course. But

we don't know. Something we've said, something we've done, ages ago, may make some other person eventually get pneumonia. Something we haven't done,' she added.

'Then, if that's true, you might as well say it's my fault,' Susan exclaimed.

'Might I?' Celia said softly, smiling a little and feeling an immense scorn for this girl's ignorance and presumption.

CHAPTER XX

THERE was a slight tinkling sound within the flat and Miss Riggs appeared in the doorway, bearing glasses on a tray. 'Ah,' she said, at the sight of Susan, 'one goes and another comes,' and the words had the double significance she managed to impart to so many of her simple utterances. 'I might have known I'd be too late for Mrs. Carey. She can't settle, any more than a fly, and she needed her strength keeping up. It's a funny thing,' she went on, looking at the yellow mixture in the tumblers, 'the more you beat the eggs the better, and, doing my best, I've missed her altogether.'

'Not funny,' Celia said. 'Well yes, funny, perhaps, but just what you ought to expect at your time of life. Don't you know that's what always happens to good intentions?'

'Anyway, there's no sense in standing on the landing,' was all Miss Riggs said in reply. 'I'll take these to the sitting-room and it'll do Miss Susan no harm to drink Mrs. Carey's share.'

'You can't be sure of that,' Celia said, 'and you've been making very free with my eggs,' but Miss Riggs marched off, deposited her burden and, meeting Celia and Susan in the passage on her return, went by with the air of a nurse who silently shows her disapproval of her naughty charges, and such was its power that Susan, picking up the glass and wrinkling her nose at it, said with meek annoyance, 'Need I really drink this stuff?'

Celia did not answer. She stood, looking at the room consideringly, like a person who plans some change in the disposition of the furniture, and Susan, sipping her egg and milk with distaste, held herself in readiness to help when her aunt made a movement, but Celia did not move and Susan said wisely, 'I believe you're worrying. You mustn't. She'll be all right, but do you think one of us ought to have gone with her? But I didn't know, you see, and anyhow I wouldn't have dared to suggest it, and you couldn't have gone very well, could you?'

'Not very well,' Celia agreed.

Her only conscious emotion was one of dull surprise at her lack of any other feeling, yet she did take a certain pleasure in answering Susan's question, answering it with truth and in an altogether different sense from the one Susan accepted and it was a relief to discover, in her emptiness, a capacity for irritation at the child's assumption that she would have made as fit a companion as Celia herself for Pauline Carey. Pauline had not come in search of company, though she had half-expected it. At the cost of an hour's precious time, she had given Celia her chance to soothe the sick or share the last moments of the dying and Celia had not taken it, for she perceived the irony in rushing to Richard now, when the misery of the body must have complete charge of a mind which, for all she knew, had long ago learnt to manage comfortably without her.

'I'll come if he asks for me,' she had said, sure that if he was capable of remembering her at all, he would also remember, as he had done all through the years, not to embarrass her with difficult demands. And now the old question returned to her. Was her love for him more than the fairy tale in which she — foolish old woman — was the captive princess? For surely, if it were more, she ought to have ignored discretion, she ought to have longed to perform the services she had willingly delegated to Hester.

'There will be nurses, of course,' she said aloud, 'but Hester can make herself useful, buying hot-water bottles and that sort of thing.'

'And there will be plenty of that sort of thing,' Susan said. 'I wish you'd drink this, Aunt Celia. You'll only get into trouble if you don't. I should think the first thing they'll want to do will be to get rid of the frowsty curtains and carpet. It looked to me as though they had years of dust in them.'

'To you?'

'We went to his rooms, you know, while he packed his bag when he decided to go to Paris with us.'

'No, I didn't know,' Celia said.

'Yes. Everything a dark, sage green and a blear-eyed sort of ex-butler man to look after him. The chairs were comfortable — men like comfort, don't they? — but they felt very gritty.'

Celia looked down at the hands she was careful not to squeeze together. She was enraged beyond all her experience and, for a moment, she was too much pre-occupied with this new sensation to find its cause in the fact that Susan could instruct her in details of Richard's life. But she had never taken her chances, she thought wildly, and now perhaps they had gone for ever. It might have been she who had seen the blear-eyed butler and sat — how uncritically — on the gritty chairs, she who had walked with Richard in the Paris streets, under the spring sunlight, the spring night, and Susan, to whom she had given the opportunity, was the visible reminder of other people who must have accepted what she had resigned, the visible reminder for him, too, perhaps, of other women who had pleased him and thus, by some irrational transmutation, she actually became for Celia, at this moment, a hateful, bodily instance of his faithlessness. For what did she know of his real mind? She would not have believed she could ever feel enmity towards this girl who was saying coolly, 'I'm surprised Mrs. Carey lets him go on living there.'

'Lets him? Do you think he can't manage his own affairs?'

'Yes, the ones that matter, if there are any and I shouldn't think there are. I'm sure he'd never struggle for the others.

Like you, Aunt Celia! Like me! He said I was like you, you know, and we are both like him! I expect that's what made him so easy to get on with. Makes him,' she added, apologetically and superstitiously changing the tense, but the past tense pleased Celia better. She would much rather have him dead and safely her own, as Miss Riggs had her Fred, than know that he and she were members of a trio in which Susan was the third, Susan who dared to speak with such authority about Richard and the unimportance of his affairs — while his really important affair sat here with all her usual appearance of laxness though every muscle was painfully tightened. But she lifted her head at the sound of the opening door, and then, seeing Miss Riggs, gave her a rare, full glance and a lovely smile of welcome, for here, in a white apron, was sanity, sweet reasonableness, the kind and homely virtues, able to dispel the miasma in the room, and it was high time they came.

But, for once, Miss Riggs's perceptions were at fault. She misunderstood her welcome. She looked severe and said, 'No, you won't get over me with smiling that way. You've not drunk a drop.'

'I tried to make her,' Susan said quickly.

'But I'll stand over her till she does.'

'And that's what you like doing, isn't it? That's why you're going to be married. You pretend you want to look after the poor man and you are really going to indulge your favourite vice. It's just an opportunity for bullying — as a good many marriages are. But you shan't have any encouragement from me. I'm going to be good!' She drained the glass and put it down. 'It's much more comfortable, it's much less trouble. Much less trouble,' she repeated, 'much more comfortable but, unfortunately, you have to be wicked before you can find that out.'

'Then how do you know about it?' Susan inquired.

Miss Riggs picked up the tray. 'H'm,' she said, for she

was always inclined to disparage the moral discoveries of other people, 'Must have read it in a book somewhere. And it's a funny thing, the way folks will tell the young ones they were wicked themselves — once. When they say that you can make pretty sure they never dared.'

'She's quite right,' Celia said, when the door was shut. 'She nearly always is — within her limits. I suppose there's a difference between feeling evilly and doing wicked things. One needs less courage than the other! But then, what is real wickedness?'

'You see,' Susan said triumphantly, 'you don't know!'

'Who does?' Celia answered, but it occurred to her as she looked at Susan and looked, now, without animosity, with affection and with pleasure in her prettiness, that one of the real sins might be the withholding of knowledge. It was easy for older people to tell the young the results of their experiences and it was gratifying to seem wise, but did they ever tell more than could be found somewhere in a book? The generous gift and the hard one would be to relate the experiences themselves, leaving out none of the mean and sordid details one might be anxious to forget. This was the knowledge which might be of use to someone else, but there were more difficulties than the breaking down of personal reserve. Technically, in the matter of her love, Celia had not sinned, but if she had translated into action what she had imagined with enough intensity to make it more real than reality, and if, for the instruction of another, she had told the story of the shifts and deceptions inherent in the situation, she would still not be telling all the truth. She would be emphasizing what was ugly to the exclusion of the beauty when the two were hopelessly intermixed and one could not have existed without the other. In fairness, she would have to remind her hearer that sea and sky owed to impurities those colours of which poets sang, which painters tried to reproduce, which made countless human beings happy.

And, if she spoke of her renunciation, she would have to own that while it was the only conclusion possible to her, she had been moved less by a distinction between right and wrong, than by her own weakness and by a loyalty which had been false for she had repudiated it, in another manner, ever since. She was as guilty in her innocence as she might have been innocent in her guilt. And there could not be a purely personal story. Would her own, barren of incident but full of implication, be honest dealing towards Gerald and the children? Fortunately, she had no present impulse to tell it, but she said, aloud, 'It can't be done — ever. There's always someone else.'

She heard Susan draw a breath. 'How lovely of you to say that!' she exclaimed. 'It's why I came to see you.'

It took Celia a few seconds to realize that Susan might be occupied by her own affairs and that they might be of importance to Jimmy; then, raising herself from the corner of the sofa in which she had been sunk, she crossed the room to the little rocking chair and sat in that. Very gently, she set it going and its small, steady movement, irritating though it might be to the observer, restored her own sense of rhythm, until she could say to Susan, encouragingly, 'Someone else?'

'Oh, no one in particular,' Susan said quickly, and she fixed on Celia the unnaturally candid gaze of the person who wishes to conceal a thought. 'I was just in the mood when I thought I'd like to see you. I often am,' she said simply, and she added thankfully, 'You are so peaceful. I don't believe you'd get excited if there was an earthquake.'

'No. But then I shouldn't mind very much. I should accept the Act of God! Especially if I knew Catherine was safe — and Jimmy. I should certainly prefer that,' she said dryly.

'Well anyhow, you wouldn't make it worse for everybody else.'

This seemed to be the moment for a direct question and Celia asked it. 'What's the matter?'

Susan hesitated for a second. 'What do you think about father?'

'I'm very fond of him.'

'Oh, that's nothing. I don't see how you could help that. I mean, do you think he's been looking well lately?'

'Rather tired.'

'That's what I think and he must be, because he's gone away, all of a sudden, for a holiday. That's very sensible, but . . .' she hesitated; she seemed to make careful choice of her qualification, 'he says he may sleep under a haystack! Suppose,' here was a useful cause for the anxiety she knew she had not altogether concealed, 'suppose he gets pneumonia too?'

'But why a haystack? Very tickly.'

'Because he doesn't know where he's going.'

'What fun for him,' Celia said, and then she lifted a hand, calling attention to the sound of voices in the passage.

CHAPTER XXI

'EVERY room,' Susan said quickly, pulling nervously at the gloves she held and sitting forward in her chair, 'ought to have at least two doors.'

'Things are certainly easier on the stage,' Celia admitted. This criticism of May, though it was tacit, was the first she had ever heard Susan make, and it must have sounded strange in Susan's own ears, for she added, 'Aunt Julia is such a bore. I do hate being understood, don't you?'

There was no need to rise hospitably, yet. May would have plenty to say to Miss Riggs who could be trusted to draw the fire as long as possible and Celia went on rocking.

'I was a Victorian child,' she said. 'It was late Victorian, but even so I ought to have been misunderstood and to be suffering now from my repressions. It's the fashion to talk as though we all crept about in terror of our lives but, actually, how splendidly free we were! Our movements were restricted, unbearably, you would think, but we were allowed to keep our minds to ourselves, and our troubles. My mind to me a kingdom was.'

'And still is?'

'Well, it's not a very rich one but, in a poor way, I think it's self-supporting. Yes, we were lucky.'

'Oh, I don't know,' Susan said. 'I don't suppose you had a really satisfactory aunt,' and with a little mocking grimace she mitigated this bare-faced flattery.

'No, but your father had one and she was a kind of aunt to me — and to Hester. Doesn't he talk about her?'

'He doesn't talk much about anything,' Susan murmured, and she flushed a little for her mother's voice could be plainly heard.

'We'll find our own way,' May was saying to Miss Riggs,

but Miss Riggs had her own view of what was proper and she announced the visitors with dignity.

'Ridiculous!' May said. What she expected from her own parlourmaid was almost an insult from the woman who worked twice a week in her sister's little flat. 'Your charwoman,' she said, 'gives herself too many airs.'

'My Miss Riggs,' Celia replied with emphasis, 'doesn't give herself very much. She spends what she has on other people, but her manners she has from God and I don't think he would like her to reject them.'

Any answer May might have made was arrested at the sight of Susan. How long had she been there? Had she nothing useful to do at home, where, to-day of all days, she might have stayed? Did she not realize that her aunt might be busy in the morning? And why had not Susan told her where she was going? 'Nobody tells me anything,' she said.

'Do sit down and rest, dear,' Julia begged, lightly laying a hand on May's arm.

Quite clearly, Julia was in command of the situation. Though she looked like a toy shepherdess accustomed to the docility of sheep, she was able, in an emergency, to manage a larger animal, and with patience, coaxing and occasional feints with a stick she could drive this bewildered steer into the best shelter the circumstances allowed. May meekly sat down and Julia, standing behind her, looking from Celia to Susan and nodding significantly, said gaily, 'We've been buying a hat!'

'Couldn't you have had one apiece?' Celia asked.

The nodding of Julia's head changed to a shaking. She pursed her lips and frowned warningly and now she was like a nurse appealing for tactful help with her patient. 'We thought it would be so nice to be wearing it when Stephen comes back.'

'You'll need a lot of practice,' Celia said. 'It won't be easy to tip it from May's head to yours quickly enough to give the impression that you're both wearing it. And I don't see how you're going to do it as neither of you was apprenticed to a juggler from the nursery.'

'How absurd you are!' Julia purred happily. 'Of course it's May's hat. May's hat,' she repeated in accents such as those with which she had unnecessarily reassured her babies in their cradles.

'Of course it's mine,' May said with some impatience. 'But I don't need it and I don't know when I'm going to wear it.'

'Soon, we hope,' Julia said, 'and, in the meantime, we must just live from day to day.'

'Don't be silly,' May retorted with sturdy common sense. 'You know we couldn't do anything else if we tried.'

'I mean we must live bravely.'

Susan laughed. The sound came in a little burst of merriment but it trailed to a weak ending and a catch of the breath, as though she had been enjoying a joke until she realized that it was directed against herself. These, it seemed to say, are divertingly ridiculous women, but how I wish they belonged to someone else's family! It was the sort of sound which first impels a silence and then gives importance to it and no one spoke until Celia asked, 'Where did you get the hat?'

'Not in Paris!' May said with emphasis on each word. 'I think nothing of the one Susan got there for herself and I can't believe you'll look anything but silly in the one she brought for you. We've just seen Mrs. Carey with an outrageous little affair on her head and going through the streets as if she was a royal procession and no one else had a right to the road.'

Julia gave a vague murmur of universal love and condonement and Celia stopped rocking. Out of the corner of her eye she had seen Susan make a movement, but it was not followed by the quick words of protest and explanation she had expected. The girl had perceptions, Celia told herself. She knew there was a higher loyalty than eager justifications; there was the reserve the accused person would value more, and between the aunt and the niece there passed a slow look and the suggestion of a smile.

Susan contented herself with saying, 'She drives very fast, but quite safely. Good-bye, Aunt Celia.'

'You're not going!' May exclaimed. 'I don't understand it. I simply don't understand it. I never know where you are and as soon as I find you, you move off. Nobody would think we lived in the same house, and though I don't ask for much, I did think your first thought would be for me to-day.'

'But it will soon be lunch time and Priscilla will be back from school and somebody ought to be there.'

'That's what I say,' said May. 'And what', she inquired, with the control of a person prepared to hear of any enormity, 'is Prudence doing all this time?'

'She was practising when I came out.'

'And that was a really sensible thing to do,' Julia said warmly. 'No, dear May, you must let me speak. Much more sensible than some of us would have expected, but people always rise to the occasion. Prudence will be able to turn her gift for music to a good purpose. I'm sure she saw that at once and wasted no time in setting to work. She's going to show us what she's made of. She's going to be the real head of the family.'

'She's going to be nothing of the sort,' May said acidly.

'Under you, dear, of course. Run along, Susan, and try to keep Priscilla happy. I'm going to take your mother back to lunch with me, she'll like being with the children, and then she can have a good rest before I bring her home to you.'

'We're going to a tennis party, Prudence and I, this afternoon.'

'Well, why not? I think it would be a mistake to give it up.'

'It would be extremely rude,' said Susan. 'You are very mysterious, Aunt Julia. What's the matter with you?' she asked, and Celia would have felt no surprise if she had taken her aunt by the shoulders and shaken her. It was what Celia would have liked to do herself, for there was a sort of glee in Julia's tender, practical solicitude and May must at last have become aware of it, for she said sharply, 'There's nothing the matter with her, except nonsense.' She stood up, flushed and handsome, the bovine eyes enlivened by her annoyance. 'The fact is, she knows nothing about men, nothing. She'd be scared to death if John went off for a little holiday by himself. She'd imagine all the things she's trying to make us believe. And poor John,' she went on weightily, while Celia, ignorant of Prudence's suggestions, listened in wonder and amusement, 'poor John daren't do it, although I expect he wants to. He couldn't trust her to understand that he might want to get away from everything and everybody, yes, everybody, for a little while. I'm not going back with you, Julia. I'm going home with Susan. And I don't want to see your children. Nor,' she added, with the acuteness which occasionally forced its way up, like a bubble in some viscous substance, through the clotted surface of her mind, 'do I wish to see how perfectly you manage them. I've seen that before, often, and I think you'd better give it up. You'll just put nasty ideas into their heads. You've been trying to put them into mine.' She passed her hand across her forehead and the bewildered dignity of the gesture was an admission of Julia's temporary success. 'Of course, I know why you made me buy that hat. Nothing else would have kept me so quiet, while you went off, pretending to buy stockings.'

'I did buy them! I don't tell lies!' Julia sobbed. There were tears on her long lashes and slowly they dripped on to her cheeks. Her nostrils quivered, her mouth drooped and the weeping which would have disfigured most women, simply increased her already absurdly youthful look. Why, Celia asked herself, should John trouble to keep his temper when it had results like these? It gave him the power to change the mother of his family into a girl of eighteen and folly combined with beauty seemed capable of perpetuating a romance.

'But you didn't want the stockings and you can send them back to-morrow,' May said.

'No, I shouldn't consider that honest,' Julia said nobly.

'Why not? It's your own shop.'

Julia's eyelids fluttered; she bit her lips with the exaggeration of a poor actress who means the audience to understand how she is feeling. 'I meant not honest towards you.'

'Oh, rubbish!' May said.

They were her last words. She made no comment to Celia, in the passage, or so much as expressed an opinion with a look, as though she had been warned, by the instinct which guided her in matters of the eye, not to lower her high sense of injury by an appeal for sympathy.

And now, from the head of the stairs, Celia watched two women going down as, an hour ago and from the bottom, Susan had watched another pair, and again there was silence during the descent and, in the observer, a consciousness of two minds absorbed, from different aspects, in the same affair. And there were, there must be, as many aspects as there were minds. Celia, cautiously taking a middle view, ready to remember or to discount the signs of unrest she had seen in Stephen, to nod her head wisely at her own foresight or to laugh at everybody else, found herself actually more concerned with May and what depth of affection might lie under the habit of ignoring all Stephen's needs except the material ones, and what reserves she had of the good sense she could sometimes show. Still standing on the landing, she was making these interesting reflections and

157

forgetting about Julia, when she was interrupted by Miss Riggs.

'If Mrs. John is staying to dinner, there's only the mutton hash,' she said.

'And what will there be if she isn't?' Celia asked flippantly. 'Ducklings?'

Julia had dried all her tears. 'Wasn't she horrid about the shop?' she said. 'You know I never go into it. When I see someone I know at a counter, I feel as if I ought to thank her! I have everything sent up and all my fittings in my own bedroom, so you can imagine whether I was pleasing myself when I took May in, this morning, but I had to see John, I had to tell him. He's been worried for a long time about Stephen and now this has happened!'

'What?' Celia asked.

'Oh, if we only knew!' Julia cried. 'If it's money troubles, he may have thrown himself out of the train and if it isn't, we may wish he had! And who but May would be to blame? He may be lying dead at this moment.'

'I hope it isn't money troubles.'

'One can care too much about money, dear. It would be the making of those girls to earn their own livings.'

'I think they are very nice as they are. No, I can't see any positive advantage in having them harassed and badly dressed. I don't think Providence is going to afflict a lot of trustful old ladies in order to discipline Prudence and Susan.'

Julia was aware of failure in complete benevolence. 'But,' she said, 'we know that all things work together for good.'

'Then why worry?'

'I thought May ought to be prepared for — for what might seem evil to us. To our finite minds,' she added, and she smiled as though for her, at least, a crack of light showed in a dark sky.

'Then you've done your duty. But you won't try to prepare anyone else, will you? You see, Stephen may be sitting in a first class carriage, smoking a cigar, or sleeping the sleep of innocence.'

'May be, yes, but tell me what you would think if Gerald suddenly went off like that.'

'I should be green with envy. It's what I have so often longed to do myself. However, I should make the very best of having sole possession of my bed. Because', she added, for there was a change in the expression of Julia's eyes and she thought their pupils were like two gossips who had simultaneously leapt to their windows at the hint of a scandal in the street, 'because it's rather a small one.'

'Then why don't you get another? Or get two? Not that I really approve of two. They are often the first little rift in married life. And Stephen and May . . .'

'It would be a very small rift in my case. There wouldn't be an inch between the beds.'

'Ah, but I mean it's a sort of symbol and I think symbols are so important. I always try to remember that with the children.'. She caught her lip again and this time it was an entirely natural gesture. 'Wasn't she dreadful,' she whispered, 'about the children? How can I put nasty thoughts into their heads when I haven't any of my own?'

Celia patted her arm. 'You needn't worry. I don't suppose you put any ideas into them at all, good or bad. I believe there's a special apparatus for keeping them out. Undesirable aliens. The children have their own business to attend to and that dull, stubborn look they put on, that glazing of the eyes, isn't stupidity. In fact,' Celia went on with some enjoyment, 'I've often noticed that very stupid people often have very lively eyes. No, it's just their way of shutting the gates, raising the drawbridge.'

'But,' said Julia, 'I've never seen such a look on my children's faces. They are so eager and receptive.'

'I'm sure they are very clever,' Celia said.

'Yes,' said Julia modestly, 'but is it altogether an advantage? Does it make for happiness?'

'You know that better than I do,' Celia said.

'Oh, you mustn't say that,' Julia responded, with a little laugh. 'But just look at the clock! Here I am, starting on my favourite subject, and by this time poor John may know the worst. He ought to be able to find me if he needs me. He said he would go to Stephen's office and see if everything was in order there, and we must hope for the best.'

'Yes, we're all doing that,' said Celia, 'but do we know what it is?'

CHAPTER XXII

'WHAT's that thing that the king has, every so often?' Miss Riggs inquired.

She was peeling potatoes at the sink and she did it with the economy she would have used if the potatoes had been her own, the skins falling away in thin brown streamers.

'A rest?' Celia suggested, and she leaned against the kitchen table.

'No, no, poor chap, he never gets that, but anyway, it's what you've been having this morning and I hope Mrs. John's the last of them.'

'Oh, a levée.'

'That's it,' said Miss Riggs, 'and soon we'll have Miss Catherine whooping all over the place.'

'I shan't mind that. I shall like it.'

She knew she was not meant to take the word too literally. She understood it as a description of Catherine's enthusiasm and cheerful energy, the noise of her school satchel dropped to the floor, her careless way of throwing her hat on to the nearest chair, her healthy interest in her food and her hurry to be done with it and back again in the place where her real life was lived. She might sometimes be exhausting, but so was a long walk on a windy day, and a walk in a high wind was what Celia wanted; her visitors had left her with the feeling that she needed something definite to push against.

Through the high window she could see the sky, a clear blue without a moving cloud to betray a breeze, but it was unnecessary to look for one. Up there, under the roof, she could always hear whatever wind there was. The row of tall houses forming the terrace was like a sister ridge to the opposite heights of Easterly and what stirred the rough grasses there made a whispering here, among the chimney-pots.

In a westerly gale, when the tower of Easterly church might have been the broken mast of a ship almost submerged in a rising wave, the tops of the houses swayed a little, the wind roared along the crest and battered viciously at the skylight above the staircase. But now there was no creaking of doors or window panes; the curtains hardly stirred and the sunny stillness which had meant reassurance for Susan was utter callousness for Celia, a reminder of the vast indifference of the universe to her small affairs.

'She'll be getting near London now, poor thing,' said Miss Riggs to whom Pauline had told her trouble as soon as the door of the flat was opened. 'But she seemed, didn't she, more vexed than worried? That's the way her kind takes grief. She's too thin. There's nothing on her that trouble can bounce off of. But things always even up,' she went on serenely, 'and the more Mrs. Carey's vexed, the more she'll make a fight of it. And I fancy she likes a fight. Now, you and me, we'd do all we could, but in our minds we'd give up and perhaps we'd think more of ourselves for taking whatever comes and making out it must be best — and so it may be — but it's the easy way of doing, none the less. But Mrs. Carey likes a fight,' Miss Riggs said again, and Celia wondered whether in this pugnacity, some explanation could be found of Pauline's unlikely dealings with her son. Far too proud to have been moved by the fear of pity, too generous to grudge time and attention, she might have been unbearably tortured by her helplessness in the face of her child's sweet vacuity.

'So we won't worry,' said Miss Riggs, uniting herself, quite inoffensively, with the interested persons.

'Ah, we shan't have any difficulty,' Celia said cynically. Already, in her mind, as Miss Riggs said, she had given up and, after all, how much was she resigning? For him perhaps, she had long been what he might soon be for her, a memory, not the chief reason for existence. And if so, he was right. No man could feel otherwise, in his circumstances, without conscientious effort or overmuch femininity in his nature. He owed her nothing except a decent tenderness towards the past and some gratitude for instruction in the art of knitting. Her own debt was greater. She felt she could never give enough for the days in Pauline's garden, for having been loved, if it was only for a time, in just that fashion, with such exquisite thrift in the expression of a boundless generosity.

Death, she thought, defying it, could not take all this from her, but, at that moment, a steamer hooted in the river and the first low, mournful sound rose and swelled into a sustained note like the call of an unearthly trumpet, and with a hand at her throat, she stared at Miss Riggs with wide, questioning eyes.

Miss Riggs, after a moment's pause in which she met and calmly estimated the meaning of that look, did not fail to give the proper answer. 'No,' she said firmly. 'Certainly not.' Nevertheless, she looked at the bland face of the kitchen clock. 'We heard that yesterday and we'll hear it to-morrow.'

Celia smiled feebly. 'Yes, but it was rather startling — just then,' she said, and she was glad to have learnt that her love was not etherealized beyond human fears.

Yet, as she set about preparing the table for the midday meal and dragged at the ill-fitting drawers in Gerald's massive sideboard and heard the silver rattling within, she wondered whether death could be the real clue to life, for what was her own life but the doing of things so insignificant that when, as this morning, she left them undone to entertain her relatives no one was a whit the poorer? And perhaps the Heaven of her grandparents, a glittering splendour combined with the peaceful cosiness they wanted, was actually a state in which everything was understood.

'And in the meantime,' she said, as she pulled and pushed the drawers, 'we must just go blundering on.'

She heard Catherine's heavy step on the last flight of stairs and, prepared for the breezy entrance of a young person without afterthoughts, suspicions or doubts she was surprised to discover anger, not light-heartedness, in the flinging aside of Catherine's hat and to see disdain, not a welcome for the mutton hash, in the exaggerated tilt of her nose.

'I came back,' she said in severe tones, 'with Mary Sanders.'

'That wasn't my fault, darling,' Celia protested mildly. 'There! I've forgotten the tablespoons and I don't feel fit for another wrestling match. Your ways lie together, don't they?'

'Yes and I wish they didn't.' She opened the sideboard drawer with comparative ease and produced the spoons. 'She lives at the end of the Terrace, in a whole house, not a flat, and they have heaps of servants and things like that.'

'What a dreadful worry for her mother. She ought not to have married a man who deals in foodstuffs even when they are wholesale. It's fatal to domestic peace. There's too much of everything and it simply gets in the way.'

'But they keep it in the house,' Catherine said. 'It doesn't sit just outside their door and eat things, crumby things, out of a paper bag. I'm not a snob!' she cried in defiance of her fear, 'but I did feel awful when I saw my grandmother doing that. So I pretended she wasn't there and, luckily, Mary was showing me her home work and her head was down.'

'And do you think your grandmother saw you?'

'Of course she did.'

'Shall I go and ask her to come up?'

'Certainly not! That would be petting her and she ought to be punished.'

'Yes, perhaps, but who's to do it?'

'You are so indefinite!' Catherine complained. 'If only you would say it was awful, too, I shouldn't mind so much. And now, every day, I shall have to dodge going home with Mary, and I like her.'

'We shall have to ask the town council to move the seat. I'm afraid they haven't powers to remove your grandmother as well.'

Catherine rewarded her with a clumsy hug. 'That's better! Couldn't we have a really good talk about her and make the very worst of her instead of trying to be kind? I shouldn't have been nearly so much ashamed of a tramp. There might be something rather grand about a tramp. I don't think I should mind so much if she was terribly noisy and vulgar. What I hate — oh well,' she said, at a loss, 'what I hate is just everything she is. And she's the biggest shadow on my life.'

'But it will pass away, like the rest of them! And,' Celia said, serving the hash from a dish attractively decorated by Miss Riggs with garnishings of chopped carrot and cabbage, 'I don't know that Mary Sanders could produce anything much better in the way of grandmothers. Ask your uncle John. He knows everything about everybody, and no wonder. He remembers our grandfather very well and his memory went a long way back. He was always ready to draw on it, too, and so was our own father on his. All the men of the family have been gossips and it's not surprising in people who can see so many women in the street and tell you everything they're wearing. John will know all about Mary Sanders's forebears, if they are Radstowe born.'

'But I never see him.'

'There's the permanent invitation for us all to go to tea on Sundays.'

'Yes, with Aunt Julia almost telling us how we ought to eat and drink and trying to make us feel at home in a place so much grander than ours, though it isn't half so pretty, and sort of hinting that we may not be used to such good food. Well, we're not, but the last time I went, I only had bread and butter just to show her, and there really were some gorgeous cakes.'

'That was noble of you, but quite useless. She would just twist it into some reason to please herself, and most likely it was biliousness on your part, owing to your mother's injudicious meals. That's what she told your Aunt May when they went shopping the next morning. So, next time, eat anything you like, and then she'll say it's quite evident that you're underfed. There's no more satisfaction in trying to outwit Julia than there is in smacking a cat. She goes back into the same shape.'

'And altogether,' Catherine said, 'I don't think much of our relations. Aunt Hester's the only really nice one and we never see her. Why don't we? Why doesn't she come here for her holidays?'

'She has her holidays in bits and pieces, that is to say when she's out of work. And then, we haven't room for her here.'

'Plenty of rooms at Aunt Julia's.'

'Plenty of rooms, but no room.'

'There's Aunt May's.'

'Yes, there's Aunt May's,' Celia agreed, and she lowered her eyelids, an action equivalent to a raising of the eyebrows in other people, and Catherine gave a chuckle of pleasure in in a parent who did not indulge in hypocritical praise of elders whose age was their only claim to respect, but Celia suddenly remembered how May had passed her hand across her forehead and gone down the stairs in silence.

'Poor May,' she said almost tenderly.

'What's the matter with her?'

'Nothing, I hope, except what you know already. And perhaps,' she added, 'it isn't really as much as that.'

'But far too much if it keeps my only good aunt away.'

Now Miss Riggs brought in the rice pudding, a humble dish, but it had been slowly cooked in good country milk and the brown skin glowed, each grain was swollen to a pearly fatness.

'And,' said Miss Riggs, 'I wouldn't have been sorry for

Mrs. John to see it. It's not everybody can make a rice pudding like that.'

'No one but you, of course,' said Celia.

'Aunt Julia? Has she been here? Then that was nearly as bad as having Grandmamma on the seat. I believe,' she said thoughtfully, 'it was gingerbread she was eating. Stale. Been kept in the tin for a long time. The paper bag hadn't the look of belonging to the cake. It was crumpled.'

'I know. Its neck was wrung several days ago, when there were eggs in it. You saw a good deal considering you were pretending not to.'

'Ah, but I saw a lot before I realized who it was, before I recognized the bonnet. I wish there was a back door to this house, but perhaps she will have gone before I go back to school. Why should she have been eating gingerbread just when she ought to have been having a proper meal?'

'You mean when she ought to have been sharing ours.'

'Perhaps, that's why she was sitting there — waiting to be asked,' Catherine said without regret.

'Oh dear!' Celia sighed. Her horror of unkindness was as great as her dislike of Gerald's mother, and entertaining her would have been easier, in the long run, than neglecting her. 'I suppose it's too late,' she said.

'Much,' Catherine answered with satisfaction. 'Besides, that would be confessing that I'd seen her.'

'True,' Celia said. 'Life's a network of complications. It's hardly safe to breathe.'

'And,' said Catherine after a pause, 'I don't want to know about Mary Sanders's grandmothers. I should feel mean if they turned out to be the kind she'd rather I didn't know about and, if she can be proud of them, it will only be worse for me. So don't say anything to Uncle John when you see him.'

'And when will that be?' Celia inquired.

CHAPTER XXIII

She had every expectation of seeing him that day. He would come, she believed, either in distress or in curiosity, not really hopeful of help or information, but simply in obedience to a sort of homing instinct towards a person of his own blood. He was incapable of discretion in his dealings with Julia, no doubt he would tell her everything he felt and thought, but it would all be influenced, lessened or increased, by the knowledge that his hearer was an alien in the clan. Her past, short as it had been before he met her, was not the one he had shared with his sisters and with Stephen. He would be suspicious of her criticism and searching for it while he was delivering his own, and though hers might be identical with his, it would have an irritating, faintly foreign flavour. A sister, especially one whom he considered rather stupid, would better meet his needs when there was trouble or mystery in the family, and what a comment it was on the narrowness of the family's outlook, that a man could not take a sudden holiday without this fluttering in the dovecots. And perhaps, for Stephen, the chief part of his holiday was simply in knowing that he had created a disturbance for the first time in his life. She could imagine that he might get a rather malicious satisfaction out of that, but while she spared this thought for him and awaited John's arrival, neither had anything to do with her feeling of nausea as she sat in her rocking-chair and strongly, but not very neatly, darned the men's socks, and more neatly, in feminine favouritism, darned Catherine's stockings. The slight creaking of her chair was the only sound in the flat. Catherine had returned to school, Miss Riggs had gone. Celia was alone, and suddenly she found that she was weeping, not only in anxiety and self-pity, but because Richard only had one leg and it was intolerable, now that he was ill, to think of him in bed without the other, his maimed condition evident to those who tended him. And she allowed herself to cry, with choking sobs and shaking lips and the healing, astringent taste of her own tears. It was years since she had cried. The impulse always came at the moment when it had to be repressed. Often she could have wept bitterly in the barbaric bed and eased her pain by giving it to a bewildered Gerald, but now she could indulge herself freely, knowing it was indulgence and urging herself on at a sign of slackening, until at last, remembering John, remembering the baker, she went to the bathroom and bathed her face, sniffing a little as she leaned over the basin and holding her hands for a long time in the comforting hot water. But it was impossible to remove all traces of the disturbance and John gave her a keen glance when she opened the door to him.

'So you've heard the news. Thought you would have. Ridiculous!'

'Is there any?'

'Haven't you seen May or Julia?'

'Both of them.'

'Well, then, they must have told you about Stephen.'

'Oh, that!' she said, and led the way into the sitting-room.

'Oh that!' he mimicked as he followed her.

'Yes, as you say, ridiculous!'

'Enough to make you cry, though, or was it something else?'

She went to the mirror over the mantelpiece. 'Do I look as if I have been crying? Yes, I do. There's nothing like inhaling, though it's unbecoming, for a cold. I've been steaming over the washing basin.'

'You've no business to have a cold in this weather. Draughty place this, though, I should think. That's a very flimsy partition between you and the staircase.'

'That's what's so nice. No caller can ever take me by surprise.'

'But it must work both ways. It's no good pretending to be out when a sneeze will give the show away.'

Celia wiped a dry nose with a wet handkerchief. 'Not a bit,' she agreed, thinking of her mother-in-law who might, at any moment, be standing out there in her buttoned boots, her cotton-gloved hands clasping the long handle of her umbrella. And it occurred to Celia, for dislike has the acute vision of love, that Mrs. Marston might stand there, she might often have stood there, with no intention of knocking unless she was discovered, giving herself a perverted pleasure out of a sense of exile.

'What's the matter?' John asked. 'Somebody coming now?'

'No. No. I was just thinking about boot buttons. They always look so horribly knowing, don't they.'

'Never see them nowadays.'

'Ah, you're lucky. Not even in the haberdashery? All eyes and ears and yet not a single feature among them. It's queer.'

'It's you that's queer, I think. Have you got a temperature?'

'No, it's only the excitement of seeing you. You come so seldom. It's gone to my head,' she said and she smiled at him with a slight exaggeration of affection.

'I thought you might be worried.'

'Not at all. Delighted.'

With his legs crossed, he waggled the upper foot, a sign of annoyance inherited from his father. She could see that he was approaching his subject cautiously. He had jeered at the visit of May and Julia and how could he tell her that his own was more than a brotherly call? It was difficult for him and it amused her to make it harder. She would not give him the opening he wanted, the one which would enable him to tell her she was a fool while he tried to discover whether, in fact, she was one. She was determined that he should risk being proved a fool himself.

'Lovely weather,' she said pleasantly. 'Do you still play golf on Saturdays?'

'Yes, and it's a pity Gerald doesn't.'

'Yes, isn't it?' she said. It was a pity, too, she thought, that entrance fees and subscriptions and golf balls were so expensive, and she looked at John in his well-cut grey tweed suit and thought, with remorse, of Gerald's shiny trousers and wondered why the virtues should command less love than the tone of a voice or some chance trick of facial muscles.

'Getting fat,' John said.

'Are you? I haven't noticed it.'

'I'm talking about Gerald.'

'Oh! Yes, he's spreading a little. So am I.'

'You ought to be careful about your diet.'

'I am, very.'

Conscious of her reddened eyelids and swollen nose, to which she remembered to apply a handkerchief, she looked at John and laughed and decided that she liked him, though he had the stupidity of his self-satisfaction and a complete inability to put himself in another person's place.

'I'm very careful to avoid anything in the nature of rich food,' she said solemnly, and she watched to see whether he would take her meaning and picture her with a shopping basket on her arm, choosing the most economical joints and rejecting the little luxuries to which her indolence of body was naturally sympathetic.

'Quite right! We live very plainly too,' he said heartily, but she knew there would be a little sherry in his ascetic-looking clear soup, a little port in the gravy accompanying the best English meat and a good deal of cream in the after-dinner coffee. 'I never give a second thought to my food.'

'Neither do I. I like to forget it as soon as possible. Just a minute! I think that's the baker.'

'At this time of day?'

'Yes. He leaves me to the last, but he's a nice man. Plays the harmonium.'

In the passage, she seized each hand in turn and held it

tight. It was half-past five, the baker's hour, but this might not be the baker. This might be one of those boys who spend their lives in carrying messages of joy or sorrow, who take them from their jaunty pouches and then wait, whistling, for an answer or the slow shutting of the door. But this was indeed the baker and she was glad to see him for his own sake. Though possibly of a cheerful habit at home, he looked, when he reached the top of the stairs, like a man who had known sorrow; he handled the loaves with the tenderness due from wisdom and experience to anything connected with humanity and though he accepted money in exchange for them, he seemed to be humbly dispensing alms and feeling grateful to the receiver. It was the effect of his melancholy brown eyes, his pointed brown beard, the harmony of colour made by these with his faded hat and coat and his burden of brown and yellow, and Celia felt soothed as she carried the loaves to the kitchen; the brown and yellow colour scheme was completed, something was accomplished, when she dropped the bread into the earthenware crock with its glazed lining.

'Well,' said John, 'I'd change my custom if I couldn't be better served. It's what I should expect of my own customers.'

'Ah but, you see, you don't deliver the goods in person. That makes all the difference. Nobody would mind having their hats at ten o'clock at night if you brought them yourself. They'd like it.'

'You talk a lot of rubbish, don't you? I don't know where the brains went to, with you girls.'

'Nature is very thrifty,' she replied. 'She may have decided that it was better to concentrate what there was on you, than to give us all a sprinkling. They are not so much use to women, are they?'

'They don't need many, but they need a few,' he said.

'Just enough to make them companions for their husbands?'

'Ah,' he detected mockery here, 'you think you're very funny, but if they don't get companionship in the proper place, they'll look for it in another.'

'Yes, it seems to be a way they have.'

'I'm glad you've realized it,' John said sharply, and, quite unreasonably, the words were a dull blow on her heart, but she knew she had laid herself open to attack when she allowed herself to tease him.

'Oh yes, I realize it,' she said lightly, 'but it's strange that we hear so little about women who need companionship. Why is that, I wonder? Must we assume that they can always get it from their husbands? I don't think they do, and perhaps poor old May is yearning for it. An inferior quality is still a quality and some people really prefer the kind of cake you can get at the grocer's.'

He stared at her in frank amazement. 'May!' he said at last. 'Don't be so silly. I'm serious.'

'Yes, and so fortunate, because Julia is serious too. So am I, as it happens. Not serious, no, no, but fortunate.'

'Julia,' he said, waggling his foot, 'can certainly be trusted to take serious things seriously.'

'I'm glad,' Celia said simply, 'but who decides on the seriousness? You said it was ridiculous to come here with her news to-day, so there doesn't seem to be perfect unanimity.'

'Ridiculous because she'd, they'd, got the wrong end of the stick and ought to have waited till I'd shown them the right one. Of course, they jumped to the conclusion that there was something wrong with Stephen's affairs, and I believe you did too. Not a sign of it! Everything quite normal, as I expected, in the office. I went in on business of my own. There was no need to ask for Stephen and they took for granted that I knew he was away. Well,' he rose to end this somewhat unsatisfactory interview, 'I can only hope he is alone.'

'How unkind of you!'

'Don't be foolish! If he was going away with a man, wouldn't he have said so? And what man is there?'

'What woman? You are an old woman yourself, John, dressed up to look like a prosperous business man. You've known Stephen all your life but you're showing yourself a poor sort of friend.'

'I'm a brother, too,' he said nobly. 'I've my duties as a brother and I'll pop in on my way home and cheer May up.'

'I don't advise you to do any popping. Can't you see that cheering her up will be a worry if it isn't an insult? She's had enough of that from Julia already.'

'Now, just leave Julia alone,' he said warningly.

'But I do, I promise you. It's I who seem to have such an attraction for her.' She patted his sleeve. 'As I seem to have for you!' she said, lightly brushing her cheek against his shoulder.

Mollified, he returned the pat. 'I believe, after all, you're a bit of a dark horse,' he said. 'And don't come out on to the stairs with that cold. Take care of yourself.'

'Yes,' she said meekly, but she followed him and, leaning over the banister rail, as she had done so often to watch the arrival or departure of friends and children, husband and lover, she heard a quick step, a gay whistling, and John and the telegraph boy met on the middle flight of stairs.

John paused, then followed him upwards. 'Any news?'

'No answer,' she told the boy, and at John she shook her head. 'Some one who wants an address,' she said.

'H'm, must be in a hurry for it,' he growled, and he stumped down again, looking, as she noticed even at this moment, exactly like his father when he considered himself ignored.

Then she went into the flat and smoothed out the flimsy paper she had crushed against John's curiosity. 'Not hopeless,' the message said, 'but can't get hold of Hester.'

CHAPTER XXIV

'It's no good,' Jimmy said. 'You're not thinking about the game.'

'No,' said Susan, 'I don't think I like playing chess in the summer. I like it when there's a fire and the curtains are drawn. Now,' she said, and she went to the window, 'everything outside seems to be peering in and somehow interfering.'

The nursery, like her bedroom, looked on to the garden and it seemed a long time since last night when she had seen her father pacing to and fro, but now, in the clear, pale light, there was no lurking malignancy down there where the apple trees grew in the rough grass and the summer-house huddled against the wall. It was the place which had been her playground and, turning to the room again, she saw that, too, almost unchanged since her childhood. The doll's house was still in its place and it was still locked; the shelves flanking the fireplace held the books which marked her progress from words of one syllable to Caesar's *Gallic Wars*; the high nursery guard protected the empty grate and families of china animals which she and Prudence had once collected with passion, were in their old places on the mantelpiece, the mother cat permanently bored with her kittens, the terriers for ever expectant of a hunt and a group of goats, a rare find, this, modelled to suggest playfulness and now somewhat damaged about the horns, wearing an air of communal pessimism.

'You mean,' said Jimmy, his eyes on the chessboard, 'I needn't come any more?'

'You'd be bored, wouldn't you, if we didn't play?'

'But why shouldn't we play?' he asked stubbornly.

'The world's so lovely,' she said.

'Oh yes,' he muttered and he looked up, now, at his own lovely world, for she had lifted and turned her neat head and she gazed at the tops of the poplars with an effect of motion, of flight, like that of the trees, in her stillness.

'When we were little,' she said, 'we did hate having the nursery at the back of the house. I suppose we were meant to appreciate the garden and to get the freshest air and all the time we were longing for the organ grinders and the errand boys and the lighted lamps in the evenings. I do love the shadows of the trees when the lamps are lighted. They seem — sort of enchanted. But we never told anyone about it.'

'Why didn't you?'

'I don't know. I'm sure we could have had what we wanted, we were rather spoilt, but it was a secret. We wanted it so much that it seemed as if we couldn't ask. I think we felt it would be telling grown-up people too much about ourselves. The lamps would have made us feel so safe when we were in bed. Perhaps that was the most important, the most secret thing.' She laughed a little. 'They would still make me feel safe.'

'So you went without,' Jimmy said.

His rough, scrubbed hands rested on the table as though they had been dropped there and while they exactly fitted the rest of his appearance, they looked detached; he seemed to wonder how they had come there.

'Yes, we went without,' Susan said.

'Because you didn't ask.'

'And now it doesn't matter a bit. I expect that's always the way.'

'But you can't tell,' Jimmy said, 'what you've missed.' With his unexpected deftness, he put the chessmen into their box. 'And there aren't any grown-up people here.'

'Aren't we grown up?'

'Not to each other.'

'No. How old were we when we first met? I suppose we were in long clothes and we've kept together ever since. It's a nice relationship, ours.'

'What's nice about it?'

'Being such comfortable friends.'

Under the bookshelves there was a cupboard still containing a few toys too dear to be given away, and into it Jimmy put the chessboard and the box. Then, straightening himself, he ran his eye up the shelves, from the baby books and the Christmas annuals to the evidence of the point Susan's scholarship had reached.

'You know perfectly well,' he said, 'that all this time,' and he gestured toward the books, 'we never took the slightest notice of each other.' He grinned, showing his even teeth. 'We were only childhood playmates when we were forced together at family parties. I'm sure you thought I was an ill-mannered kid and then a clumsy lout and you would have been a bit ashamed to own me except at Christmas parties with the grandparents and that kind of thing.'

'I wouldn't! I couldn't feel like that about anyone belonging to Aunt Celia!'

'But you would have been right. And I always hoped I shouldn't meet you.'

'How hateful of you!'

'When I was with anyone belonging to the school.'

'Was I so dreadful? I thought we always looked rather nice.'

'You were a girl,' Jimmy explained, 'and then when we were older and I was beginning to be interested in girls, you looked so grand.'

'Grand? In my school clothes!'

'You might have been in rags for all I knew. No, you had your nose in the air and looked so damned earnest, upholding the school traditions, getting knowledge, in the sixth!'

'Yes, I daresay I was a bit of a prig. And I didn't know you were ever interested in girls.'

'Oh, wasn't I! Common ones. I was frightened of the others, frightened of all of them, really, but I used to meet them after dark.'

'Oh Jimmy, how nasty! In the streets?'

'Where else?'

She was frowning a little. She could not adjust her idea of Jimmy's simplicity, of Jimmy as a rough but valuable diamond without a moral flaw, to this new vision of him in which he giggled with girls at street corners.

'I didn't know,' she said slowly, 'that people like us did things like that.'

'All sorts of queer things,' Jimmy said.

'But you don't do it now, do you?'

'Good Lord, no! And I wasn't a success. Tried very hard but never knew what to say. Couldn't bear their beastly accents and felt a fool. But I suppose I thought I was a bit of a dog and hoped I'd improve in time, but long before I'd shown any sign of that I'd given it up.'

'I call it very messy.'

'So are lots of kids' complaints.'

'And I wish you hadn't told me.'

He grinned again. 'Then you shouldn't have pretended we were childhood playmates. Until about a year ago I hardly knew the difference between you and Prudence.'

'She's better looking.'

'Yes,' Jimmy said simply.

'But,' Susan said, comforting herself and encouraging him, 'I'm supposed to be rather like Aunt Celia.'

'Yes, you are, rather.'

'But how, exactly?'

'Oh, I don't know,' he said casually.

There was an impatient lift of her shoulders. 'Didn't she give you a message for me?'

'She didn't know I was coming.'

'And did she know when you went to meet those girls?'

'I hope not,' Jimmy said. 'I was much too awkward to come to any harm, but it might have worried her.'

'And didn't you want her to know, either, that you were coming here?'

'I didn't care one way or the other.'

'You're still rather awkward, aren't you?' Susan said pleasantly.

'I'm not the only one.'

'Do you mean that I am?'

'No, I wasn't thinking about you. Look here, let's go out. Let's go for a walk.'

'In this frock?'

'What's the matter with it? It's all right, isn't it? But there seems to be something wrong with houses to-night and you said the world was lovely. Let's go and look at it.'

'Yes, it's lovely,' she said, and again she looked into the garden and saw, with her mind's eye, the beauty that was spread beyond it, the high Downs, the cliffs and the river, the distant view of hills across the channel, and she knew, and resented the knowledge that, being what she was, she would be half-blind to the soul of beauty until some one looked for it with her, and she was sure that person could not be Jimmy who was half-blind himself to her pretty beflowered frock matching the creaminess of her skin and the aided rose in her cheeks and who told her things she did not want to know. He had betrayed a murkiness in human nature which her young pride disdained and feared to find in others she had trusted, for if he had been saved, only by his own clumsiness, from gross commerce with people he despised, what might not happen to men and women who were more adroit? He seemed to have opened a door giving on to underground, twisting passages and, though she had known they existed, he had opened the door on the wrong day, when her Aunt Julia had already been fumbling at the handle.

'I could show you all sorts of places you've never seen,' Jimmy said, and, when he saw her curled lip, he added, 'Oh yes, I could.'

'I'm not doubting you,' she said.

'All right, if you don't want to come, but how often have you been across the river?'

'Hundreds of times.'

'Yes, across the bridge, but there are other ways, the ferries and the locks. I like to go by ferry when it's dark. It's a good noise the oars make, a dull thud in the rowlocks and then a soft dip as though they were going into something a little thinner than treacle, and the turn of the chaps' wrists when they row, if you can call it rowing, the way their bodies balance as they stand, the utmost effect with the least waste of energy, well, it's like a machine running to perfection.' He paused, considering the mechanical beauty with which he spent his days, but it seemed that he had not altogether deserted his night scene by the docks. 'And I like to see the oars smashing up the lights.'

'The lights?'

'The ones, the reflections, straggling across the water. And if it wasn't for the lights, you'd think there was a forest on each side of the river, the masts and the funnels and the warehouses. Or you can think they're the camp-fires of people watching, not friendly, waiting to pounce, hundreds of them, all the way up the hill, above the forest on the Radstowe side, and just an outpost, here and there, on the other. You've never seen that, have you? Very late, when nearly all the din has stopped for the night, and what there is has nothing to do with the watchers. They are just waiting, they don't understand. Puzzled, uneasy.' He looked up and met her steady and, as it seemed to him, slightly ironic gaze.

'Sorry!' he said. 'Reminiscences of boyhood! Must have read something like that in a book when I was a kid and used to hang about the docks. It was grand, not having a nurse! It's one of the things I'm thankful for. I could slip out . . .'

'After dark?' Susan asked.

'Yes,' he said innocently, 'when I was lucky.'

'You horrid little boy! You must have worried Aunt Celia to death.'

'She didn't mind.'

'Of course she minded.'

'Then why didn't she say so?'

'And you've lived with her all these years!' Susan exclaimed.

'Well, yes,' he said after a moment, 'I suppose you're right. But she wouldn't mind now, so come and let me show you.'

'It won't be dark for hours.'

'All the better. There's plenty to see while it's light.'

'But my own mother would mind. Father's away you know.'

'Is he? I can't see what difference that makes.'

'Anyone would think you were an orphan,' Susan said scornfully. 'A family isn't several separate persons. It's a lot of — of dismembered people. Somebody has your head and another one has your hands and you have bits of all the others fastened on to you. You don't belong to yourself, but then, they, poor things, don't belong to themselves either. But you're a man and men are not expected to pool everything like that. It's because they have their work to do and it's why they do it so well.'

'And what,' Jimmy asked practically, 'are you supposed to be doing now?'

'Just being here,' Susan replied.

'I can't see the sense in it.'

'I don't think there is any.'

'Then don't do it.'

She shook her head. 'You don't understand. I can't just live as I like. I have to do the things other people expect, and now, as it happens, I'm pleasing myself, too. Some day I should love to see your forest and the camp-fires. To-night . . .' She made a little gesture. She could not tell him that she had her own watch to keep here, in the house, and her vague feeling of suspense and expectation, which her reason denied, drifted across the tree-tops to her Aunt Celia whose friend was in definite trouble: it went farther, east-wards, across the country, to that friend herself and the man who had been her own friend for a little while.

'I wish you'd told Aunt Celia you were coming. There might have been a message. Has she heard do you know, but it's too soon, I'm afraid, from Mrs. Carey?'

'Yes, she'd had a telegram.'

'Well? How is he?'

'Rather ill, I think.'

'Of course he's rather ill! I know that.'

'And I rather wished he was dead to-night, at supper. We had him with each course. But there were only two. Lucky again, you see! If there'd been soup and a savoury, the row would have lasted longer. Oh, it wasn't a bad one, but bad for us, because we live peaceably as a rule. All Catherine's fault, irritating the old man. And he'd met our good Uncle John on the doorstep and they hate the sight of each other, so that was a bad start for the family reunion round the supper table.'

'Had he been to see Aunt Celia?' Susan asked quickly.

'That's the conclusion to be drawn when he's found on our doorstep, isn't it? Yes, he'd put himself to the trouble of climbing up. First time in years, I should think.'

'I wonder why?'

'Absorbed in great affairs.'

'No, I mean why to-day?'

'Just to add to our difficulties.'

'What difficulties, Jimmy?'

'Oh, nothing, nothing.'

He was vexed with himself for bringing that unnecessary anxiety into her voice and such small domestic matters to her notice, and, looking at her now, he saw not only the Susan he loved but the trappings that enclosed her, the soft fall of the flowery frock, the sleeves slipping back to show the rounded arms, the bracelet on her wrist, the toe of a pale slipper, and he thought she was rightly remote and should be kept remote from common cares and such stupid wrangling, to the accompaniment of plates filled and passed and carried to the kitchen, the mustard missing and someone lacking a spoon, as had been enacted in his home that night. Only beautiful things should touch her, yet, without scruple or consciousness of inconsistency, he would have carried her into poverty if she had been willing to come; happily he would have seen her washing his dishes, roughening her hands, and being harassed by a hundred little cares, for deep in his mind, though it had its humility towards her, he believed in the compensating splendour of his love, the romance to be found in dishes which were his.

'You're not deceiving me, are you?' Susan asked.

'Why on earth should I? They were just little things that weren't worth telling.'

'I've always trusted you,' she reminded him gravely, but, quite evidently, this remark had no embarrassment for his conscience.

He nodded. 'I should hope so. And if you won't come, I'm going for a walk by myself, into the country.'

'By one of the ferries?'

'No.' For to-night, at least, the ferries were hers. 'By the bridge. I feel as if I could walk for twenty miles and perhaps I shall.'

'But don't be too late. Aunt Celia won't go to sleep till you get back.'

'Don't you believe it! She's never waited up for me in her life.'

'I really think I know more about her than you do. But I wish I knew what was in that telegram, because I like Mr. Milligan very much. You could hardly have him for every course without hearing something about him.'

'I heard that he'd lost a leg. That was the trouble. Catherine pretending to be sick at the thought and the parent telling her she ought to be ashamed of herself for feeling like that about a man maimed in the War. And did we realize what his generation had done for ours? And he was quite right, but I'd never heard him talk like that before. And Catherine was pretty pert. Needs spanking.' He shrugged his shoulders in tolerant amusement and went towards the door, but he came back. 'I know what it was. Something about an address Mrs. Carey wanted.'

'Aunt Hester's? But Aunt Celia asked Mrs. Carey if she was sure she had it. I heard her.'

'Well, I don't know. Mother didn't say anything about Aunt Hester.'

'NOT very tactful,' Celia said that night, offering her cheek for her daughter's good-night kiss.

'But need I be, at my age?' Catherine asked, and she looked young enough to be excused the effort. She had been working in her bedroom and her hair was ruffled where her hands had been running through it, but the curls at the nape of her neck had kept their tightness and, except in the matter of size, her head was that of her babyhood, her mouth was mutinous under the defiant little nose.

'It would be good practice for the future.'

'And in my own home?'

'It's the home of three other people as well.'

'But it ought to be the one place where I can say what I think.'

'And the world ought to be a place where no one ever gets vexed with anyone else, but, you see, it isn't.'

'Yes, pet, I know, but I do think the elders ought to set a good example. They've had longer to learn.'

'And more time to get tired in.'

'You always have an answer,' Catherine sighed. 'Are you tired yourself? Because you generally manage to stop me when I'm going too far and to-night you didn't, so perhaps I had a feeling that it was all right.'

'Yes, I think I must be tired.'

'Then why don't you go to bed?'

'I shall, soon.'

She glanced at the clock. The night nurse would be on duty by this time, moving competently and quietly under the shaded light, and Pauline might be preparing a make-shift bed for herself in the dingy sitting-room. The day nurse would be stepping through the streets towards her own bed or her own affairs and it seemed to Celia that, as she passed, the roar of the traffic must take on another note, a tone of apology for the necessity of pursuing business alien to the vital one in which this woman was concerned. And where, in that huge city, had Hester hidden herself? And where was Stephen? Where, to come nearer home and to a question more easily answered, had Gerald gone and Jimmy? There was nothing unusual and nothing she much regretted in their absence but, to-night, she felt it like a comment on her mismanagement. She had driven her team badly. Normally, a light hand on the reins would keep it on the road with the horses well enough in step, but she had dropped the reins altogether and though the horses had not bolted, they had shown ill-temper, snapping at each other as they tossed their heads. And if Gerald had gone to see his mother, he would not return in a serener mood. The trouble had really begun with John on the doorstep and she had not had time to arrange her thoughts, her reserve or frankness, before Gerald was in the flat, bristling at an encounter with an enemy on his own terrain. John had told him of Celia's cold and blamed him and his draughty flat for it; told him there was a telegram for Celia and she seemed upset. Was she upset? Where was the telegram? She had not kept it, she told him, and he asked who had sent it, and why. Was somebody in trouble? Yes, Mrs. Carey's brother was very ill; and what, he asked, could Celia do about that?

'Nothing,' she said with truth. She was cautious, not for herself, but for Hester, perhaps for Stephen. She acted on a surmise which was vague, but had its strength, and she was careful for all the loyalties which Gerald, no more than Julia, could be expected to share.

'Nothing,' she said, 'but Pauline thought I knew of some one who might help her, not a nurse, some one to run errands, and I don't.'

'I can't see why that should upset you.'

She found it easy to laugh. 'John, naturally, wouldn't think he had done it himself. He had to find a reason.'

'And what has he been saying to worry you?' Gerald demanded.

'Oh, you know it isn't what he says. And you know he'll turn a sniff, which, of course, was unmannerly to begin with, into a serious cold if he can blame some one else for it.'

'Blame me, you mean?'

'As it happens. He's a great fault finder, yet I believe he is charming to the assistants in his shop.'

'That's because he's got them under his thumb.'

'And he hasn't got us there.'

The pronoun pleased him and the pleasure hurt her. She saw that she was within a short distance of making one person permanently happy, an achievement, after all, worthy of endeavour, yet she could not force her step across the space, and, no one was to blame, not Richard, not herself, and Gerald least of all. He was not responsible for his appearance, attractive in his youth when his body was lean and hard with training, not uncomely now, but plump, domestic, suggesting a permanent state of warmth and woollen underclothes, without any charm for her eye to make mental differences much more negligible and physical contact more endurable. It was a shame, she thought contritely — but it was an important factor in her life. She could not change it: she could only try to hide its influence — and when she heard him return she followed him to the dining-room.

'Working?' she said with kind remonstrance when she found him poring over the plans he had spread on the table.

'Trying to,' he said. He threw down the pencil and looked at her, his face coarsened with its flush, and she thought it was pathetic to be middle-aged, when even a worthy emotion had an unbecoming mode of expression. 'And it isn't easy when I'm thoroughly upset. I went to see my mother and found her crying. Crying!' he repeated heavily.

187

It was on the tip of Celia's tongue to say that she must have heard him coming. Instead, she said weakly, 'How — how painful,' and she pictured Mrs. Marston in her sitting-room with the stiff lace curtains at the windows, the barrel-shaped biscuit-box on the sideboard, the ferns in pots, the neat emptiness surrounding a person who read nothing but the local newspaper and, when the housework was done, made crochet edgings for her nightgowns. She saw Mrs. Marston wielding a large, clean handkerchief, a cotton one for which there could be no excuse; she saw the feet in their kid boots, the buttons taking an interested share in the interview, the eyes twinkling intelligently, the ears cocked and, almost imperceptibly, she shook her head, denying Mrs. Marston any virtues.

'Your mother ought not to have let you see her doing that,' she said. 'I wouldn't let my son see me cry.'

'You wait till your son's married,' he said roughly.

She sat down at the other end of the table, shading her eyes with a hand, and she knew she was not going to be very patient, she no longer wished to be.

'So,' she said, 'it's something to do with us, is it? I hoped, rather meanly, your mother had just been quarrelling with the little servant again.'

'No, she's hurt by the behaviour of some one who ought to know, better than the little servant, how to behave. Your daughter.'

She was glad he gave her the sole ownership of Catherine, and she said, 'Then I know all about it and my sympathies are with Catherine. And so would yours be, if she hadn't irritated you already, to-night. I've talked to her about that, but your mother has no business to eat gingerbread out of a paper bag just outside our door. I'm sure she didn't tell you she was doing that.'

He had a moment's hesitation and then he said stubbornly, 'I can't see any harm in it. If your precious Mrs. Carey did something of the sort, you'd think it was very funny.'

'I should indeed, yet she could do it safely.'

'Because she has plenty of money and needn't.'

'Oh Gerald, you're not going to tell me your mother can't afford a decent meal. She's fond of food and, as a matter of fact, she eats a lot of it. But isn't all this rather stupid? Does it matter very much?'

'It matters that she should be lonely and neglected. She tells me she was sitting on that seat for hours. She knows she's not welcome here, but she was hoping to get a word with you or Catherine and Catherine wouldn't give her one and neither did your niece, or your sister or your sister-in-law.'

'I don't suppose they saw her.'

'They didn't want to.'

'But even if they'd seen her,' she said, 'I don't believe they would have known who she was.'

'And whose fault's that? You've never tried to bring my mother into your circle.'

'No, it never occurred to me that she would like it. I don't like it very much myself, and it's hardly a circle. Semicircle, perhaps. Was she there all the afternoon, too? Did she see John?'

'No, she did not, and it's clear that I should have heard nothing about him if I hadn't met him, or about the rest of your visitors. You say you don't like them, but they seem to be too sacred to be mentioned!'

'It never occurred to me . . .' Celia began again, and he interrupted her to ask, 'When does it ever occur to you to tell me anything? I come home and there's a meal ready for me, but there's very little else.'

'And there's very little else to tell you. What do you suppose I'm doing all day?'

'I often wonder.'

'No, your mother does. I don't pretend to work very hard. I take care not to, but I'm always here, for you or the children, when I'm wanted.'

189

'Part of you,' Gerald said, and in these words, which silenced her for a time, she heard Gerald, not his mother, the quicker, subtler Gerald who sometimes spoke, who might see more than she knew, who might even, she feared, see his own houses clearly.

'But,' she said at last, 'I don't talk much to anyone,' and as he gave her an odd smile, she realized that, on this occasion, she had not been happy in her choice of pronoun.

'No, you are not talkative,' he said, and, picking up his pencil, seemed to dismiss both her and the subject.

It was the way to make her stay, though if she had credited him with that intention, she would have gone. In the most instinctive part of her nature she was a failure when he did not want her, and, though she would have drawn deep breaths of freedom if he had willingly resigned all his claims to her person and her thoughts, how dry the air she breathed would be, too dry and harsh for the encouragement of any green or lovely thing. What she knew she wanted and knew it, to her surprise, at this hour when Richard might be dying, was what most women want from every lover except the one on whom their hearts are set, love which made no claims, desire which persisted though it was not satisfied, a mirror which simply gave back an enchanting picture of herself.

'We're not quarrelling, are we?' she asked, putting out a hand. 'We've never done it. Don't let us begin.'

'No, we've always been polite, I think,' he said dryly.

'Courteous,' she said.

'What's wrong with my word? Isn't it up to your standard?'

'I think mine means more. We're polite, I think, to those who serve us. And courteous to the people we like and live with.'

'Ah, thank you very much, I didn't know, but then you don't expect me to know that kind of thing, do you?'

She felt properly rebuked for her instruction and she saw that his loyalty to his mother had been severely strained, that he suffered because she represented a mode of living, an attitude of mind, a self-satisfied ignorance and affected gentility which were repugnant to Celia's world, simple though that was, to her upbringing and her education. There were no words which would put him right with himself or her, and she had to put him right, for she had the pity of her insufficient love, but later, when she thought he was asleep, she cried for the second time that day and, this time, very stealthily.

CHAPTER XXVI

WHILE Jimmy was making his way downstairs, Susan followed quietly to the next landing and went into her mother's bedroom. She was at the window when he banged the door and she watched him as he went slowly down the broad path to the gate. She was astonished to find herself in the position of a curious housemaid and, to change it into one of dignity and frankness, she knelt where the window was thrown open at the bottom and rested her arms on the sill. She wanted to see him as the somewhat detached person he had rather disconcertingly shown himself to be. Prudence was wrong. There was nothing to be done about Jimmy and that was a great relief, yet it left her feeling curiously suspended, as though, from standing on firm ground, she had been lifted to swing just clear of it, and her toes kept stretching downwards to learn how far they were from the familiar earth.

He liked his game of chess, she thought, looking down at his bare head; deprived of chess, he could solace himself with a long walk. Evidently he had to be doing something; he could not be content to sit idly in the nursery with a friend. If Prudence had been right, he would have done that or he would have gone with dramatic haste, to walk blindly through the night, but he was strolling down the path, pausing to look, with his hands in his pockets, at the roses in the beds. He did not smell one, he did not touch one, he looked at them critically, like a farmer considering the beasts in his field, and she was surprised that he looked at them at all. But then, he had seen the lights of Radstowe like watch fires and the masts and the funnels like great trees edging a strange river, and he might have other fancies when he walked in the country to-night and she would not be there to hear of them.

'Jimmy!' she said in a soft voice, testing her desire to bid. him wait, and before she could call again more loudly, another young man had appeared at the other side of the gate and the two exchanged greetings: they provided a contrast. The new-comer's hair was sleek and Jimmy's was of a stubborn nature; the other looked debonair in his evening clothes, with a tie a little broader than was usual, a suggestion that this slight exaggeration was due to the music he held under his arm, but Susan liked Jimmy better in his loose coat and flannel trousers; she commended his little changing expression in comparison with the other's vivacity. Prudence's young men were always inclined to indulge in a play of feature when they did not set their faces in an interesting melancholy, and this one, she remembered now, was coming to sing to Prudence's accompaniment.

At the moment, he was talking to Jimmy about football, for though it was an unseasonable subject, it had always been Jimmy's game, and it was as odd to hear it discussed by the young man in the large tie as it would have been to hear Jimmy showing a knowledge of music. And why should he not? He had already shown her that people were not always what they seemed and, still kneeling there, while he went his way with firm steps down the road and the visitor approached the door with light, quick ones, she had a fleeting, unhappy feeling that she was in a world peopled by strangers. Downstairs, her mother was probably rattling the newspaper and would continue to rattle it during the young man's songs, but what her thoughts were, what they had been since the episode in Celia's flat, she could make no likely guess. She did not know towards which point of the compass her father had steered, and, refusing to be anxious, to admit any ideas approaching those of her Aunt Julia, she had to feel angry with him for the only lapse she could remember in thoughtfulness for his family. And Jimmy had marched off into the country. It been a long day, she thought, and a puzzling one, and it was not ended yet. No day was ended in that house until Priscilla had been coaxed or coerced into her bed and Susan rose to set about that task.

Priscilla, most unexpectedly, was in her bedroom, a neat, straight-legged figure in her knickerbockers, and Susan, from the doorway, exclaimed gladly, 'Good girl! Shall I turn on the bath water?'

'I'm not going to bed, dear.' Priscilla explained gently. 'I'm just changing my frock for the party.'

Susan moved swiftly into the room. The chiffon folds of her skirt spread and fluttered with her steps; when she sat down they subsided meekly, without a sound, and while she wondered how she was going to manage this young person, she had no idea that Priscilla was heartily admiring her, thinking she was like a full-petalled flower as she walked and a flower folding itself for sleep when she sat, finding her mysterious, feeling what she could not say in words, that here was poetry made flesh.

'What party?' Susan asked, and her voice was faint with the certainty of defeat.

'Downstairs. In the drawing-room. Not,' she added, 'that I'm thinking of it as a party. I'm thinking of it as education for me.'

'In that case, your school tunic would be quite suitable. You're certainly not going to dress up in anything else. And, if you want to please me . . .'

'But I don't. Not particularly. I think it's more important to learn all I can.'

'I see,' Susan said gravely. 'Then I suggest that you do without your bath, though I'm sure you need one, and pop into bed and leave your door open. I'll leave the drawing-room door open too, and you'll be able to listen in peace.'

Susan's tone was sympathetic, but she knew Priscilla did not want to listen. She wanted to appear and be appreciated as a charming and intelligent child responsive to the influence of the arts. She wanted, naturally and without precocity, to have her share in the life of the house from which her age alone debarred her, and, suddenly, Susan saw her point of view, her possible loneliness and, putting out a hand, she said, 'Come here. Come and sit beside me.'

'Why?' asked Priscilla, suspicious of persuasion.

'Just, truly, to be friends.'

Priscilla, unhesitatingly, on past experience, accepted that statement. She had never discovered either of her sisters in a false one or known them break a promise and she sat close to Susan and Susan's arm went round her waist.

'How sweet you smell,' she said. 'Like roses.'

From the end of the bed where they sat they could see tree-tops and the upper windows of the houses on the other side of the wide road. Above the roofs, the sky, as though wearied by its ardent blue during the day, was almost colourless, resting before it could absorb the darker colour of night, but there was already the beginning of twilight in Priscilla's bedroom and this made her companionship with Susan more secure and more important, while, from below, there came the sound of a few chords on the piano, a few bars, and then a silence before piano and voice together seemed to come floating up the stairs for the special delight of these two on the bed.

'It's better here, really,' Priscilla whispered, 'the music is.' She sighed lightly. 'Is he in love with Prudence?'

'I don't know. I don't think so. They could quite easily just be friends, you know.'

'Like you and Jimmy?'

Susan nodded. She wondered where he was but, wherever it might be, it was really better, as Priscilla said, to be here, and not only for the music, the tenor voice now rising in plaintive, somewhat throaty, passion, but because she felt a great tenderness for the child whose thin waist she clasped and a desire to do more for her than see that she was tidy and punctual for school and as little spoilt as possible in the household. She was ready to take all responsibility for her and, inspired by the music to a noble melancholy, she saw herself refusing personal happiness to find it in a life of service.

'Music for Prudence like chess for you,' Priscilla said. 'But he might be in love with her, mightn't he?' she asked hopefully. 'And if he is, it's lucky it's Prudence and not you. Lucky for him.'

'Is it?' Priscilla, she thought, ought still to be playing with dolls, indulging her maternal instinct in complete indifference to any antecedent feelings and processes: she ought to be at a boarding school where crude facts coarsely told would probably be less harmful than this sentimental interest in courtship.

'Because,' Priscilla said, 'she doesn't see him when he's singing and you would. He makes such awful faces. That thing in his throat, that lump, looks as if it will come through his skin. That's partly why I wanted to be here, to watch it,' she said, and Susan thought, this is better, this is more childlike, and her little squeeze of appreciation encouraged Priscilla to proceed. 'He can't get his highest notes without grinning — you know the way they do. Being brave though it hurts. Up here it's not such fun. Just now and then it's a little bit as though he's going to be sick, but not much, but all the same I like it here. You forget who's doing it. It seems to be a thing all by itself.'

'Yes,' said Susan, envying Prudence and the young man whose personalities could be lost in their performance, in something much greater than themselves, and she thought there must surely, unless the universe were senseless, be something greater than self for everybody if they could but find it, some aspect of beauty that could be created though it might not be crystallized into forms to be seen or heard.

'Yes,' she said again, 'it seems to be by itself now, but a man made it and he was unhappy and ill and very poor and no one even knows where he is buried. So you see . . .'

'I don't,' Priscilla said contentedly, 'but it doesn't matter.' She had her head, now, on Susan's shoulder and she was much too comfortable to invite disturbing information or moral maxims, and Susan, who had been talking chiefly to herself, pursued her thoughts in silence. Thus, to May, who came unnoticed up the stairs, and discovered, through the open doorway, the clasped figures silhouetted against the window-pane, there must have been something strange and discomforting in the stillness and in a posture which could be interpreted as one of a shared sorrow.

Either to dissolve this vision or for a purely practical purpose, she switched on the light and sat, rather heavily, on the nearest chair while her daughters, disengaging each other, swung round to face her.

'I couldn't stay there any longer,' she said, 'all by myself. I didn't know where you were both hiding. I don't like the noise they're making, I don't like it at all, and as far as I can see, they won't stop for hours. I don't know how we're going to sleep. You ought to be in bed, Priscilla, and if you keep your door shut perhaps you won't hear much. Why didn't you come and say good night? I'm very fond of music, but I do like it to have a tune every now and then. Of course, I know that's old-fashioned and all wrong, but there it is. So I'm going to bed myself.' She looked at Priscilla who was lying on her stomach and kicking up her heels and said, with less than her usual assurance, 'Would you like to come and sleep in the bed next to mine?'

To gain time, Priscilla put a question of her own. 'Was his Adam's apple wobbling much?'

'I was too vexed to look,' May said, and Priscilla laughed and gave an extra flourish with her heels.

'Shall I have morning tea? All right, I'll come,' she said,

and she picked up her pyjamas and towels and went into the bathroom.

'You shouldn't have let her stay up,' May said.

'The difficulty was to prevent her from going down.'

'It wouldn't have done any harm, once in a way.'

'I'll change the sheets,' Susan said, beginning to strip Priscilla's bed.

'Ring the bell. There's no need for you to do it.'

'I don't mind. It's rather a shame to disturb the kitchen.'

'Now,' said May, 'you're making me seem selfish and inconsiderate, but', her lips trembled a little, 'I'm not used to being alone. I'd like to have the child near me.'

Susan, standing in front of her with her arms full of linen, wisely restrained a sentimental impulse to bend down and kiss her.

'And why shouldn't you?' she asked cheerfully. 'It will be fun for Priscilla and nothing else would have got her to bed with so little trouble.'

She carried her bundle down the passage and found herself, to her own illumination, regretting that her father could not see her mother when he was not there.

CHAPTER XXVII

No one truly successful in the chosen profession need suffer very acutely from a suspicion of failure in another sphere, and Julia, hurrying homewards, from Celia's flat, tried to fix her mind on the fact that, first and foremost, she was a mother. Next, in slightly less perfection, she was a wife and a long way after that she was sister-in-law, aunt and friend. Gladly, therefore, she hastened towards her children and the expression of her fullest self.

She went across The Green and down The Avenue where the broad walk was roofed with the young leaves of the elms and in this pattern of leaf and twig, the blue of the sky had its part, for the whole was like a flattened dome of glass stained to a shimmering green and steady blue and set in the light firm clasp of iron wrought by a master. Issuing from this and without slackening her pace, she mounted the steep rise to the Downs, conscious of a slimness and speed remarkable in the mother of a family but explicable to herself as the physical counterpart of her mental and spiritual fitness for her function. Whether to have suffered protracted agonies in giving birth to her six children or to have accomplished it easily and gaily, was a difficult decision to make, and she never made it, for it was not really necessary. There were many ways of suggesting reminiscence and, as occasion and her company served, she could smile over a bitten lip of intense recollection, assume an expression of dedication to motherhood which brought its own serenity, or gallantly dismiss these experiences as her natural share in the battles which must be fought. And characteristically, when she topped the rise, she hardly saw the hawthorn bushes in flower and scattered in scores, like white haycocks of all sizes, on the Downs. They had a sweet, warm smell in the quiet air and if she had not been alone Julia would have gazed and sniffed with ecstasy. Accompanied by her children, she would have had many pretty fancies about the heaps of blossom and with loving fingers she would have separated the flowers in the clusters to display the pale pink on their petals and offered to the young minds and senses that beauty on which she believed they should be fed. She had not time or attention for this beauty now. She was like the artist who works subconsciously when he is not in actual touch with his medium and towards her medium she was hurrying, hoping, it is true, that acquaintances would recognize her for what she was and whither she went so eagerly.

Her home, the one in which part of John's youth had been spent, stood with its back to the houses facing the Downs and the garden ran down the farther slope and spread beyond it. At the level of the Downs a short carriage drive led to the front door; half-way down the hill there was an entrance to the garden and Julia often gave herself the trouble of descending and then returning for the sake of reaching home in this less formal manner, for the sake of the little people who might be at the nursery window and would see their mother coming towards them between the flower beds or across the lawn. Moreover, she liked her garden, she liked talking to the gardener and she had a real sense of home when she saw the solid, bow-windowed house looking down at her as she approached. Built by John's father, it was the fruit of the drapery business and even Julia's imagination could do very little for it with its short existence, but at least no other family had lived in it and everything must have a beginning. Her own father's home, half farm, half manor house, had been young two centuries ago, and he, too, and his forebears had bought and sold, though not across a counter. He had looked and smelt and often spoken like the neighbouring farmers, and he worked, at need, as they did, but always he carried with him a sense of the past, in his own place, on his own soil. He had not been pleased by John's impetuous courtship of his daughter; he put a literal meaning on a stake in the country but, with his eye on a second wife hardly older than Julia, he grudgingly dropped his opposition and now he was dead, of injuries at the horns of his own bull, and Julia's half-brother reigned in his stead and would soon be marrying and rearing his sons to the old calling. Two hundred years hence this house, built to last, would be venerable though it could not be beautiful. Thousands of meals cooked and eaten in it, births and deaths and marriages happening in it, all the emotions of its inhabitants, would go to enriching it and, by that time, the family of Fellows might be reckoned among the peerage, if John's descendants were less convinced than he was that charity began and remained at home. But Julia was living in the present and she had to find present reasons for liking this house of unmellowed brick, faced with decorative panels in yellow stone, and she found them in the knowledge that within these walls she was alternately scolded and adored by John, that here she adored her children though she could not be said to scold them, that here, most potent reason of all, she faced the future. She would have said she had no fear of it and, indeed, she did not think of it except in terms of happiness. Its only real shadow was the shop and in its shade she could have most of the things she wanted, but the future waited, unknown, capricious, as full of danger as a strange country possessed by savages and beasts of prey. The fortunate, the wary, might escape: the best of people, and Julia quite simply, saw herself among them, might fall to a poisoned arrow or the blow of a great paw and she feared that on poor May who had been fortunate but who was neither wary nor particularly good, a blow had fallen already. She did not remember that there were poisons which were not necessarily mortal and that they could be administered by a friendly hand. She told herself she must be tolerant of May's unfairness and for an hour, while she sat at the head of the table and dealt with meat and vegetables and a milk pudding which would certainly have evoked Miss Riggs's scorn, while she chatted encouragingly when there was a silence and wished the children were less sensitively reserved, or listened eagerly when they talked, she forgot May altogether.

Of her six children only four were at home, Robert and Sybil staying at school for their midday meal, and only the youngest, now five years old, was entirely frank in his desires and demands. The others had, at times, a sort of discretion, a means of communication among themselves, seen in children who are with people or in situations they do not entirely trust, and then Julia was like a person admitted into a society of familiar friends and anxious, by appreciation of their jokes and adoption of their catchwords, to show herself worthy of full membership.

Of this company there was Christopher, fair and handsome, too stout and tall for his age and a little backward at his books, but entering Radstowe School next term: there was Rachel, her pretty likeness to her mother spoilt by protruding teeth which gave her a permanently deprecating expression: there was Mary, a solemn child, a greedy reader and an advanced one for her years, apt to hide herself in corners with a book and not, her mother feared, a natural sharer, and there was Paul, still clumsy with his spoon and fork and likely to besmear his bib.

Julia loved these evidences of babyhood. A stern sense of duty alone persuaded her to correct and aid and as she looked at him and saw him a little more skilful than he was yesterday, she told herself with a sort of desperation that she must have another child, a creature utterly helpless and dependent on her, without speech which puzzled oftener than it explained, with appetites and no elusive thoughts.

'How,' she asked brightly, for she believed in a mitigated candour in these matters, 'would you like a baby brother, or a baby sister?'

'Hate it,' said Christopher.

Rachel said nothing, but she gave a series of little nods, her teeth were tightened on her lip, her bright blue eyes had a fixed gleam. Mary and Paul ignored the question altogether and Julia left it where it was, in her own mind as a practical proposition, in Rachel's as a dream which might come true. And a more immediate matter now occupied Julia's attention. Something must be done about Rachel's teeth. All her emotions, and she was still held by her dream, seemed to emphasize their salience. They were strong and healthy, as such teeth usually are, but how would they affect her future? Psychologically, in the long run, would she suffer more through having them controlled by a disfiguring gold band or through keeping them in their present position for the rest of her life? May was constantly saying the child's teeth should receive attention and this had stiffened Julia into inactivity, but her little failure that morning had had its effect. In the shaking of her self-confidence, some of the mistiness with which she surrounded herself had been dispersed and very clearly she saw Rachel's teeth and Christopher's roughness; she almost saw the separate world in which the children lived, almost admitted her half-fear of Robert, an adolescent with his father's temper disguised as sulkiness, and her consciousness of Sybil's foresight in resisting an affection which, encouraged, would have demanded a knowledge of her secret mind. But Julia created her own mist, and it settled down again when she had kissed the children before they went off to the occupations of the afternoon and she went to the telephone to speak to John.

She was kept waiting for some time before John sharply asked her what she wanted.

'Just to help you, if you need me, John.'

'Ah, thank you very much. I'm going into some rather complicated figures at the moment.'

'Stephen's?'

She could hear the vexed sound of his tongue against his teeth. 'Stephen's?' he said. 'I'm a draper, not an accountant.'

He always, she reminded herself, stressed the nature of his business when he was cross with her, and he was always cross with her when someone else had angered him.

'But you're worried, darling.'

'Yes, I'm worried,' he said grimly.

'Tell me, please.'

'Better not.'

'But you know I always want to share.'

'Well, then, if you must have it, I'm worried because you've interrupted me at a very inconvenient moment.'

'About Stephen?'

'Stephen! Stephen! Stephen's having a holiday and I wish I could have one, too.'

'Then,' she said, and in her voice there was a note of disappointment as well as one of suffering at this harshness, 'then, isn't there anything wrong?'

'Not that I know of. Why should there be? You've too much imagination, my dear,' he said, finishing the conversation.

This remark, meant as a reproach, was something of a solace. It was not, however, enough of one to quell her indignation. It was just like John to repudiate his judgment when he found it faulty and to blame her for the very ideas he had put into her head. This was not a new experience, but small wrongs are more powerful in their accumulation than they are negligible in their familiarity, and she sat beside the telephone, biting her lip and looking very much like Rachel, indulging herself in a lively hatred of John, his impatience, his unfairness, and that tenderness which he considered compensation enough for all the rest. And she decided that she would not have another of his children. What were they, she asked, enjoying her bitterness and remembering the unresponsive brood at the dinner table, but posts of varying sizes in this fence which went by the name of marriage? Another one, as she recognized, would hardly strengthen what was already too strong to break, but she was in no mood to drive it in at her own choice. She was enraged by John's masculine belief in the sufficiency of his lasting passion for her, his primitive conviction that she was honoured by it and for its sake must gladly endure his faults of character and his intolerance of her own. In this rarely candid moment, she searched her mind for any other reason why she should like him and could not find one, but he was a habit and she would have been lost without him. There was nothing tangible, within his means, he would not give her. This little sitting-room, hung and studded with photographs of the children, where she wrote her letters and tried to keep her accounts, read all the newest novels and laid her psychological treatises in prominent positions, was evidence of his lavishness from the hand-made letter paper on her writing-table to the hand-woven carpet on which her small feet were pressed. But, her heart cried, she wanted more than that, more than caresses; she wanted the respect of a man who was friend as well as lover and John could not be the friend she needed until he recognized her quality.

'I don't like him,' she whispered sadly. 'I suppose I love him, but I don't like him.'

Then the telephone bell rang and she heard his voice, loving, apologetic, asking forgiveness for his roughness, and she knew that, with all his faults, she liked as well as loved him, that here was the person on whom she could ultimately depend. She was more wife than mother in that moment, and if she had been honest with herself, she would have attributed most of her late dissatisfaction to another cause than John, to the fear that, after all, she was not to have the pleasure of pitying May.

CHAPTER XXVIII

THE possibility of losing May altogether as a person to pity or to envy, with whom to gossip or gently quarrel, did not occur to Julia until the next morning when she awaited the usual message and received none. Since the days when she was a young wife and inexperienced housekeeper, a girl without a friend in the place to which marriage had brought her, May had telephoned every morning, ready, at first, to offer assistance, advice or company, and thereafter, though the relationship of the two had slowly changed, the custom had persisted. It was part of the daily ritual, like telephoning to the butcher. Celia had often wondered what direction their lives would have taken without the influence of this means of communication, and she, who was apt to count her blessings, found one of them in the poverty which denied her the possession of this instrument and spared her the invasion of family voices.

This morning, Julia was restless under May's silence. She might have been conscience-stricken if John, bearing flowers as a peace-offering on his return last night and still scornful of any suspicion about Stephen's professional affairs, had not sadly excited her with suspicions of another kind.

'You've only to listen to May,' he said, justifying himself. Julia shook her head wisely. 'I know,' she sighed.

'Not,' John continued, 'that it's an excuse, though it might be a reason. There is no excuse for that sort of thing. Plenty of reasons, of course.'

A little uneasy at this remark but, with one of his roses in her belt, tactfully letting it go, she said she was afraid May had never tried to be a companion to Stephen.

'And a good thing too! That kind of woman's the worst of all. Trying to understand when, obviously, she can't.

That's very boring. What I like about you is that you're a wife and don't pretend to be anything else.'

'I'm a mother, too,' she said.

'And that's just part of being a wife,' he said, little knowing how his complacency sharpened the wits he did not like in a woman.

Was he abysmally dull, she asked her gently smiling self, in having missed the careful thought, the actual study she had given to the training of their children? It was this insensibility, the impossibility of getting on to equal terms with him, which made May's society so desirable. She was stupid but, like John, she was a habit, and the stupidest woman has some feminine perception wherein the chief value is its difference from the masculine variety. She does not expect or want any logical sequence of ideas; she can leap the conversational ditches by which a man is baffled: she may criticize and quarrel and though she will dismiss opinions as worthless, she maintains an ardent interest in the person who forms them and an untiring curiosity. It was, perhaps, curiosity which Julia most missed in John, and it was a strange lack in a man who made the family affairs so much his own and could even feel aggrieved because Celia had not let him read her telegram.

'Crumpled it up in her hand,' he told Julia, 'as though she was afraid I'd try to take it from her. What made her do that, d'you think? It's not as if I ever try to interfere with anybody.'

He would speculate about such little matters, yet, finding Julia in a muse or sensitively fluttering her eyelashes, would never ask her what she was thinking of, what she was feeling.

Now it was half-past ten, long after May must have finished with the tradespeople, and Julia was able to wait no longer, but it was Susan who answered the telephone call and her cool voice had courteous surprise in it when her aunt asked if there were any news.

'Then', said Julia, 'may I speak to your mother?'

'I don't like to bring her down,' Susan said. 'She's in the linen cupboard, very busy. Can I give her a message.'

'No,' Julia said. 'Just my love, dear, and keep her occupied. It's the best thing for her. Good girls! And if I'm wanted, I'll come at once.'

But she knew she would not be wanted, and no one, at the moment, wanted her at home. All the children were at school except Paul and he was taking the air with a nurse who found it fresher on the Downs than in the garden and, with an eye on her mistress's weakness, thought a larger world was better for the child's development than the confines of his home. Whatever the inspiration of these opinions, they were right. The Downs were a good place for anyone and particularly for a child. Vastly greater than himself, belonging to him no more than to anybody else, they gave him an opportunity, which Julia hoped and believed he took, for exercising his imagination, and the most stolid child, the one most resistant to impressions, could hardly escape the sight and smell of the hawthorn, a sense of space, high skies and pageantry, for here, people on horses, people sitting or strolling under the old trees, humdrum people, sober matrons, children shouting as they played, tired, shabby folk taking what ease they could on the hard seats, even the nursemaids and the babies in perambulators, contributed to a whole which became fixed in the mind, though the details might be forgotten, with the permanent significance of a fine picture depicting a scene of no apparent significance at all. Almost, it might have been a scene set on a stage, for though, on one side, the Downs slipped easily into a suburb of outer Radstowe, on all the others they were lifted above the level of their surroundings and the consciousness of this elevation was strongest where the Downs met the cliff edge without any masking of the sheer drop by the trees and bushes which, farther southward, concealed the gorge. Here, close to Pauline Carey's garden but on a higher level, a low wall topped by railings secured the public and gave it the safe contemplation of river, ships, gulls, the woods on the other, gentler side of the water, and a far view of ghostly hills beyond the channel. It was here, farthest from the city, nearest to the sea, poised hundreds of feet above the river and the road bordering it, that design was manifest, the scene set, the picture composed. The sheep, though they were dull grey lumps, had their place in it; the riders, though they might bump in their saddles and the horses hardly needed reins, so well they knew where a path crossed the grass or a road stopped it, provided an air of gallantry; their movements seemed to fit those of the high clouds; the thud of hooves, creak of leather and jingle of steel were complementary to the wind in the branches and to the sound, sometimes a call, sometimes a comment, of a steamer hooting at the river bends.

All this was part of young Paul's daily fare, but Julia wished he were in the garden. She felt, indeed, and without pretence, very lonely this morning. John, as usual, had given her a hearty kiss before he drove off to his shop, but whom had he been kissing? Whom had the children, all but Robert, kissed? Robert had gone to the school he secretly loved and dreaded leaving, but he seemed to go unwillingly, to be sullenly enduring his lot. He was a stranger and had been one for years. He had reached an age when he was almost beyond any care she could give him and when, therefore, she could admit that he had faults. They were surface ones, no doubt, usual at his time of life, but as a member of the family he made no contribution of affection and gave no sign of any enthusiasms. Was this a phase through which Christopher and Paul would have to go? It was against all her instincts to make any complaints about the children to John, or to ask for counsel, and May, the silent May, who must not be disturbed this morning, had no experience of sons. Julia rejoiced in this dispensation of Providence, for May's son might have been affectionate, confiding, one of those sons who are almost like young lovers to their mothers. Her son would certainly, for so things happened, have taken his brains from his father; he would have gone to the university and then, perhaps, to the Bar, or been faithful to his father's branch of the profession, while Robert who was no scholar, whose father saw no value in any privilege he had not enjoyed himself, was doomed to the shop, not, immediately, to the family establishment, but to some equally big one in another town where he could learn the trade. How was she going to announce that to her acquaintances? In this matter she failed in her conviction that all things worked together for good. She ardently wished that Robert would have a serious call to the ministry, in the Church of England. It would be well worth his father's fury, yet she knew that in this still half-feudal place, though Robert became a bishop, the old families in the neighbourhood and the haughty ones whose fortunes flourished on wholesale trade, though they had probably had beginnings as humble as John's grandfather's little shop, would never forgive the draper for the sake of the bishop. They would merely be sorry for the dignitary of the Church and nervous for the Church's dignity.

Thinking of these difficulties and turning slowly into the house to fetch her gloves, for a larger world would help her as well as Paul, she began to wonder whether some of Robert's sullenness could be for the fate awaiting him, whether it was her duty to conquer her unacknowledged fear of him and promise her support in any future he desired. Perhaps dumbly, all the time, he was longing for the word that would unloose his tongue and a series of pictures immediately flashed past her mental eye. She was comforting Robert, she was braving John; she was very unhappy in the dissension with her husband, but she was marvellously sustained in her gentle inflexibility. And, at the actual moment, she was inspirited with purpose. She forgot the loneliness which, almost without her knowledge, had been slowly impelling her towards May, persuading her that her own pride must be subdued and consolation enforced. She was glad, now, to be alone with her thoughts, her plan of campaign, her prospect of victory, and when she left the garden by the lower gate and turned upwards towards the Downs, she might have neglected her usual glance at Mrs. Carey's winding drive if a familiar figure had not emerged at that moment through the gate.

It was Celia, unfortunately without Mrs. Carey, but carrying as spoils a great armful of early roses. She wore a rather faded dark blue cotton frock; her hat, like all her hats except the famous French one, was of the simple shape which can be worn, without peculiarity, for years. It was evident that this one had been so worn and yet Julia, coming on her unexpectedly and before she had time to check the thought, had told herself that Celia looked almost beautiful and like the lady of the manor who chooses to do her gardening in her old clothes or can safely ignore them altogether. She had a calm air of indifference to what anyone might think of her, not because she was herself indifferent to people, but because while she was interested in herself, as any intelligent person must be, she did not expect or wish to arouse interest in others, she had no apologies to make for what she was not, or explanations of what she was.

Something of this kind Julia divined in the moment before Celia raised her head and saw her sister-in-law, a little person dressed with the studied simplicity of one of the ladies in John's summer catalogue, but producing her usual effect of ribbons, reticules and mittens.

'How lovely!' Julia said, referring to the roses. 'We can't

grow them like that. Too many trees, but I'd rather have the trees. Wouldn't you?'

'Yes. In your garden!'

'In any garden.'

In honesty, she ought to have excepted Mrs. Carey's. She had only had glimpses of it from the cliff wall and very unsatisfactory ones, for though there were no forest trees in it, there were small ones and flowering shrubs cunningly arranged to act as screens.

'The roots of your trees would pull Mrs. Carey's terraces to pieces,' Celia said, 'but she has roses for half the year.'

'And she has been very generous with them to-day.'

'Oh, I helped myself.'

'I shouldn't have liked that. I should have been afraid to take what I really wanted. I should have felt very awkward,' Julia said delicately.

'So did I. I couldn't find the garden scissors where they're always kept and I couldn't find the gardener, so I had to borrow a kitchen knife and I wasn't very clever with it. There's something very grand about snipping roses with a pair of scissors, but I felt rather a butcher with the knife.'

'But wasn't Mrs. Carey with you?'

'No, she's away.'

'Oh, I see. And she said you might have the flowers.'

'No. I just took them.'

'But Celia . . .' Julia began gently.

They had mounted the slight slope and with their backs to the few houses facing the Downs, they had a view at once pastoral and sophisticated. The grass and trees, browsing sheep and playing children were changeless things: the cars moving on the white roads, here, close to the cliff wall and farther off, much diminished, were like toys set going on a vast nursery floor, varying in design, bound, like other toys, to fall out of fashion, and they were of no more real importance to the essence of the picture than a mode of dress discarded centuries ago.

'But Celia dear,' Julia said, 'do you think that was a wise thing to do?'

'It was a nice one.'

'For the moment, yes.'

'And one must live in the moment.'

'How I wish I could!' Julia sighed, but, seeing no curiosity in Celia's face and feeling a good deal of her own, she postponed the problem of Robert's future. 'I mean . . . Oh, but perhaps Mr. Carey was there?'

'No,' Celia said, and she looked, as Julia thought afterwards, a little sly.

'But the servants will tell her when she comes back, won't they?'

'I expect so. I hadn't thought of that. Shall I go and ask them not to? How much do you think their silence would cost? Much more than I can afford, I'm afraid. And I can't put the roses back, can I?'

Julia gave a half-playful shake of her head which could be interpreted either as reproof or as appreciation of Celia's fun. 'Did you know Mrs. Carey was away?'

'Of course. That's why I took my chance.'

'I don't know how you dared!'

'I'm rather a desperate character,' Celia said mildly. 'Which way were you going? But wait a minute. I want to look at the river.'

Julia followed her to the railings. 'Very beautiful,' she said, and having paid her hasty tribute, she pronounced Celia's name again in the tone she used towards her children when she knew they would not be happy until they had cleared themselves of suspicion or confessed their faults.

'Celia, how did you know where the garden scissors were kept?'

'How', asked Celia, 'do burglars know where the diamonds are? It's a sixth sense.'

'In the house?'

'No, no,' Celia said. 'I'm not going to tell you. I may be a hardened criminal myself, but I've never put temptation in the way of innocence.'

'What a tease you are. I believe you've been teasing me all the time, because you'd never really go and pick anybody's flowers like that. What would Catherine think of it? What would Gerald say?'

'What would Catherine say? What would Gerald think? I wonder. Yes, how right you are!' Nimbly, in spite of her burden, she stepped on to the low wall, leaned over the railings, and let the roses fall. 'Now,' she asked from her perch, 'are you satisfied? Out of sight, out of mind, but there's one, a lovely one, caught on a spike of rock.'

'It won't stay there long,' Julia said. 'Well, you've done your best, but we can never get rid of the past altogether, can we?'

'No, thank goodness, and it looks fairly firmly fixed,' Celia said, peering down. 'I think it will stay there until it dies.'

'But what a waste!' Julia exclaimed. 'It would have been better to take them back to the house and have made some sort of excuse about them.'

'Would you have come with me'? Celia asked, giving her an odd glance.

Julia looked brave. 'Yes. I should have felt very uncomfortable, but I would have done it.'

'And I believe you,' Celia said heartily.

CHAPTER XXIX

THEY separated affectionately as people will when they have served each other well. Celia had had her amusement and Julia had made her influence felt and this had strengthened her for a sterner battle.

'I must get back for the children's dinner. We're never free, we mothers,' Julia said brightly.

'No, it's most unfortunate for the children,' Celia replied, but Julia fancied she was beginning to understand her sister-in-law and looked suitably roguish before she tripped off towards her home, while Celia, in spite of her fear that she had left a kettle, which must be dry by this time, on the gas, went slowly in the other direction, without her roses.

She was glad she had let them go, glad, too, that one of them had remained in sight, refusing to be quite cast away. She was free of everything in Pauline's garden, but she ought to have left them blooming on their trees. Good news and Richard's love ought to have been enough for her, but, she supposed, as she had often been told in childhood, the more she had, the more she wanted. A long telegram from Pauline, who never omitted her prepositions in these missives or left anything economically vague, had sent Celia over the Downs on some small errands and to await a telephone message in comfort. The errands were not important: they were a thoughtful pretext for getting her to the house and hearing the details she must be wanting. It had been an anxious night, but Richard was much better, almost within sight of safety and he sent his love. Was that only another proof of Pauline's thoughtfulness? 'No, I must have it, I must have it,' Celia said to herself, and she thought it was like the rose caught on a spike of rock, a lovely remnant of what she might have had. It had been an anxious night,

Pauline said. Had he been in pain, or beyond the power of feeling it? She did not know what turns such illness took but, at least, she had suffered too and she had wept while, perhaps, as he fancied himself near death, the past appeared to him as it is said to rise before a drowning man. And then, in the morning, with the past far more real than the future, he had sent his love. She wished, now, that she had given him more to remember, yet she believed that, in their restraint, they had given themselves, as it were, a scaffolding on which memory could build wonders, and she had gone thus far in her thoughts and not very far across the Downs, when she heard her name called again. It was a pretty name, but Julia used it too often, and now, a little out of breath with her pursuit, she repeated it.

'Celia! I never asked you about Stephen!'

'About Stephen?'

'Yes, what you think of him.'

'I like him very much.'

'I didn't ask you what you felt. I asked you what you thought,' Julia exclaimed with surprising sharpness.

'True, but how feminine of me!'

'Yes.' Julia immediately looked romantically sad. 'And it's possible to go on loving people in spite of everything.'

'What's John been doing?' Celia inquired.

Again Julia hesitated. This was difficult, for while it was interesting to be unhappy, and John was indeed a frequent trial, being unhappy in marriage might suggest some failure in herself, so, with one of her many varieties of headshake, she denied any preoccupation with her own affairs. 'I'm thinking, all the time, of poor dear May.'

'Why aren't you with her?' Celia asked with smiling spite. 'You don't often miss your morning promenade.'

Julia blushed a little. 'I don't think she wants to leave the house. But I shall call this afternoon. Just to be there. Of course I shan't mention anything unpleasant . . .'

'No.' Suddenly Celia felt a desire to tell the truth to this little person who never knew whether or not she was telling the truth herself. 'You did enough of that yesterday.'

The ready tears sprang to Julia's eyes. 'But I wanted to prepare her! I wanted to help!' she pleaded.

'I know, I know. Such a mistake.'

'But what else are we here for?' Julia cried.

'To mind our own business,' Celia said, and, as Julia's lips parted to emit familiar quotations, she slowly lifted a hand. 'Yes, I know all that, too, but it's the spirit that matters, not the letter. And you see, I'm just as bad as you are! Being helpful, giving advice! Forget it.'

'You haven't given any advice I'm likely to take,' Julia said with dignity, 'but I shan't be able to forget that you've been unkind. For the first time.'

'Well, that isn't a bad record, is it? But it wasn't a good day to choose. It caught me on the rebound, I suppose. It's always dangerous to feel happy.'

'Happy!' Julia exclaimed. She was affronted by this callousness. 'How can you feel happy?'

'By the exercise of a rigid economy,' Celia explained gravely.

'And wasting those lovely roses after you'd stolen them!' Julia said, and her pertly defiant expression, that of a schoolgirl quarrelling with another, that of a meek maidservant suddenly turning on her mistress, startled Celia a little with the possibilities it suggested.

'Run home, my dear,' she said coolly, 'and as you go you can make up a little parable about the roses to give the children with their dinner. I don't quite see the moral at the moment, but I expect you'll find one. And if I don't hurry, Catherine won't have a dinner at all, let alone any sauce with it.'

In Julia's mind, the idea of Celia's good-natured stupidity had gone for ever. It was a loss which had to be replaced and, as though by a miracle, the void was filled, for there

218

was the sound of a car in Mrs. Carey's drive and though it was not the yellow one of which both Julia and May deplored the vulgarity and Julia felt a pang of disappointment, she was more than restored by the sight of a much more modest car, driven much more slowly by Mr. Carey who had a red rose in his coat.

He did not know her, nor did he seem to see her as he turned carefully into the road. She blushed for the rose he wore, a match to some of those Celia had carried, and she thought astutely, with excitement, that if they had not been valuable to Celia or if Mrs. Carey had presented them, she would not have thrown them away. Celia was a wolf in sheep's clothing and what made it worse was that the fleece was particularly white and soft. But Julia was generous. She recognized that a wolf, in his own opinion, had the right to live and the right, for that purpose, to use his wits, and how could she tell to what straits Celia had been put, to what she had been forced? And before she reached home, Julia had developed Gerald into a bully who drove his wife to the cajolery of the man who could help him.

It was a dramatic story and she enjoyed it, but it had its weakness for, in that case, surely Celia would have carried home the proof of her pitiful endeavours. No, it would not do, and Julia was brought to the conclusion that Celia was not a hungry wolf but a playful one. She would not believe it was anything worse than that, but how dangerous it was and how pathetic in an ageing woman, and she ran up the stairs of her home and into her big sunny bedroom and saw herself, clad in pale pink, slim hipped, with big blue eyes shaded by dark lashes, the mother of six children and looking like a girl.

But she was very quiet at the midday meal, a little absent-minded, and she did not notice that the children were more talkative than usual. They knew she was temporarily safe in her own universe and only Rachel wondered

what she saw there. She waited until the others had left
the room before she approached her mother with her air
of apprehension and the offering of her damp little kiss,
and Julia, receiving this, was reminded of the problem of
the child's teeth and so to that of Robert's future, John's
indifference to the first and inevitable violence about the
second.

'Are you thinking about that baby?' Rachel inquired.

Julia never told her children a lie, but she never missed
an opportunity of tightening natural bonds and, putting an
arm round Rachel's narrow waist, she sighed,

'I'm not sure that we can have one, darling.'

'Is that why you're sad?'

'Sad? Mother's never sad!' She enumerated some of the
many causes she and Rachel had for happiness, but the
child's only response was a fiercer clutching of her lower lip.
Then she released it and said stubbornly, 'I want the baby.
And it was a sort of promise.'

'But darling, how could I promise a thing like that?'

This was a question Rachel's knowledge did not enable
her to answer. She shook her head rapidly, choked down a
sob and rushed out of the room, leaving Julia with the horrid
fear that the child's maternal instincts might be permanently
injured.

CHAPTER XXX

BUT, on the other hand, she thought, for there was always another hand with Julia, this frustration, if such it proved to be, might be the very best thing for Rachel's character, best, in the end, for Rachel's own children, and without exactly following her own mental processes which were the courtship and marriage of this child, she decided that she really must make an appointment with the dentist. This decision was possibly strengthened by the sight of herself as she stood in her petticoat in front of the long glass. She was not vain but she could not help knowing she was pretty. Her dressing-table was bright with glass and silver; she had all the usual pots and bottles and all of them were empty, for her lips and cheeks and eyes needed no assistance and she was thankful that Heaven had spared her the temptation of supplying its omissions and the discomfort of perpetrating a fraud.

She reached for a more formal frock than the one she had taken off, then dropped an empty hand. She did not know and would not decide until much later, whether it was her good sense, her delicacy, her instinct, her wisdom, discretion or generosity towards Celia, that persuaded her not to visit May that afternoon, not to tell her a little story which might distress more than it interested her. It was certainly delicacy which rejected the grander dress and donned another simple one, a pale blue linen with white collar and cuffs, and it was as a form of offering the other cheek that she determined to take Celia the best flowers in the garden. It was more than that, for if Celia had any fine perceptions, she would read a message in the homely innocence of the bunch which was to replace the one she had thrown away. The best flowers were not very good, but the whole point of her errand would be lost if she bought better ones from a shop. This was just to be a posy from the garden where Celia's nephews and nieces played. She glanced down at the lawn but again there was no child there, and Julia sighed. Too much of the larger world was as bad as too little of it. There was rest for young minds in the peace of the garden and she would have to speak to nurse about it, but she was a formidable woman and, in one of her unguarded moments, it occurred to Julia that her house was strangely full of people of that kind. Her cook, without the excuse of being an accomplished one, would hardly allow Julia in the kitchen; the middle-aged parlourmaid was inclined to be condescendingly instructive about the customs of really good society; the pretty housemaid, clicking about the house in her ridiculously high-heeled shoes, wore on her face as clearly as though it were emblazoned on a banner, a warning against any kind of interference. Julia had always wanted her servants to be happy and she had not the least doubt that they were, yet May's seemed to be happy too, though she did not try to understand them, demanded much more of them and had free access to her larder every morning. She simply saw that they were well fed, had comfortable beds and a reasonable amount of leisure and ignored the moods to which Julia was so sensitive.

With patient ruefulness, Julia lifted her eyebrows at her mirrored reflection. She knew she would never conquer her desire to understand, to put things right, to make people happy, and in complete sincerity, as far as this aspect of herself was concerned, she arrived at the Terrace with her bouquet. There, on the stone staircase of Celia's house, she overtook Celia herself, accompanied in her ascent by a little woman in buttoned boots who held to the rail of the banisters with one hand and grasped an umbrella in the other.

Celia turned at the sound of footsteps and there was less

surprise in her smile than Julia felt at seeing it. 'I thought you might come,' she said. 'Mrs. Marston, this is my brother's wife, and Julia, this is Gerald's mother.'

Mrs. Marston nodded stiffly in answer to Julia's tender look of pleasure, then marched laboriously ahead.

'These stairs must be too much for her,' Julia said with commiseration.

'No,' said Celia. 'She can hop up and down very quickly and almost silently when she likes. This difficulty is only an expression of her feelings.'

'Unwilling?' Julia queried hopefully.

'Yes and no,' Celia replied for though no one likes being deprived of a grievance, there is compensation in the hope of finding another and Celia knew this was what had changed into acceptance Mrs. Marston's refusal to come to tea. Wishing to please Gerald, to make amends for Catherine's behaviour yesterday, to return thanks for blessings received, Celia had called at the little house round the corner and found her mother-in-law sitting with folded hands in the parlour which seemed cold even on this warm day and, still more chilled by the fan of white paper in the grate. No doubt she had seen Celia's arrival, for the window was close to the front door and had taken up that attitude of loneliness and desertion, but for Celia this increased rather than lessened the pathos of an existence which was dependent for its happiness on a pretence of misery, and so with coaxings which went very much against the grain, she had induced Mrs. Marston to put on her bonnet and her silk mantle, her boots she wore already, and have her tea under her son's roof.

'I'm so devoted to old people,' Julia remarked, hastening after Mrs. Marston who was already near Celia's door and who, even to Julia's enthusiastic eye, could hardly have the attributes proper to an old lady. She had not a grey hair on her head, she looked as though she had been cast in iron: she

223

was fixed permanently at the age when she found that life had disappointed her; she would never reach the age when less rigid people begin to wonder how they have failed life.

'So strange,' Julia was saying while Celia turned the key, 'that we have never met before.'

'Not at all,' said Mrs. Marston.

'But,' said Julia, gaily adapting her remark to the standard of her hearer, 'it's better late than never.'

Mrs. Marston gave a wry smile, hardly more than a reluctant determination not to contradict, and carried her umbrella into the sitting-room.

Julia lingered in the passage. 'Not very well, perhaps?' she suggested.

'Perfectly. She enjoys rude health,' Celia said, but Julia missed the little jest. She was determined to make Mrs. Marston happy and, tripping after her, she showed her the simple bunch of flowers and Mrs. Marston obediently looked, but she said nothing.

'I brought them for Celia. Celia,' she paused, 'I brought them for you. I know they are very ordinary little things but I thought you might like them.'

'I do, very much.'

'And after all, if they were as rare as orchids, we should think they were just as beautiful. We get so used to everyday things and forget how lovely they are. Sunsets, for instance. Didn't somebody say we should appreciate them much more if we had to pay for them? And I'm afraid it's true.'

Mrs. Marston, perhaps by accident, gave a slight thump with the point of her umbrella. Repeated, the sound could have been taken for applause; alone, it evoked in Celia a mild spasm of affection for her mother-in-law.

'But children,' Julia continued, merely thinking it was a pity Mrs. Marston had not left her umbrella in the passage, 'they see the beauty of a little daisy on the lawn.'

'And yet it's a disgrace to your gardener,' Celia said. 'Queer, isn't it?'

'And these flowers,' said Mrs. Marston, moved by an unfortunate association of ideas, 'would be all the better for a drop of water.'

'They are going to have it,' Celia said, and carried them to the kitchen.

She had a good deal of pleasure in leaving her visitors to entertain each other, Mrs. Marston with her natural dislike for anyone who had more of this world's goods than she had herself, and Julia who always knew how to find compensations for the unfortunate. What she did not suspect was that these two could meet happily in discussion of herself, with the kind of enthusiasm on Julia's part which leaves all the important things unsaid, or suggested and immediately regretted as uncharitable, with appeals for their being forgotten and hopes of their being mistaken, an excellent opening for Mrs. Marston's grief at losing a son and gaining so little in exchange.

Celia did her duty by the flowers, trying not to treat them as she would have enjoyed treating Julia, but she did not take them to the sitting-room until the tea-tray was equipped. Her thoughts, as she moved slowly about the kitchen, travelled in a small circle but went much faster than she did. They leapt from the little flat to London, and lingered there, returned to wonder why Jimmy had come home so late last night, long after she had finished crying with her mouth pressed against her pillow: they went swiftly to Stephen's unknown destination and carefully looked for Hester in a different place: they darted to Gerald but did not stay there, flickered, a little troubled, between Jimmy and Susan and rested, in temporary content, on Catherine. Celia's was a narrow world, but what more was the greater world than a container of personalities and the pain and happiness they could bestow on their fellows? Here, in little, were most of the emotions, preoccupations and duties common to mankind—love, dislike, anxiety and doubt and the perpetual problem of right and wrong, the need to earn bread and eat it, to flavour it with humour and a little malice, to be temperate and forbearing, to keep the peace if it could be kept with honour.

She suspected that there was malice without humour in the sitting-room but she was quite equal to dealing with it. She would keep the peace with Mrs. Marston who, as she observed on her return, had laid aside her umbrella, a sure sign of a relaxed mood, while Julia leapt up eagerly to be helpful with the tray and blamed herself for allowing Celia to do all the work.

'And where shall I put the flowers?' she asked. 'On the bureau?'

'No,' Celia said, a little sharply. She would certainly not have Julia's moral lesson on her favourite piece of furniture.

'Perhaps,' Julia said playfully, 'you would like to throw them out of the window!'

'What an idea! Why should she?' Mrs. Marston demanded. 'Such pretty flowers!' They had definitely gained in beauty during the last quarter of an hour. 'I'm sure she ought to be grateful.'

'Just a little joke,' Julia said. 'On the mantelpiece, in front of the mirror? Then you'll get them twice. I always think this is such a pretty room.'

'But it's hot,' said Mrs. Marston, pushing her chin clear of her bonnet strings and unclasping the neck of her mantle.

'Nothing to what it will be,' Celia said, putting three lumps of sugar in Mrs. Marston's cup and despising her taste in this as in every other matter.

'It's hot and not healthy in the summer and it's cold in the winter,' Mrs. Marston informed Julia. 'What they want is a nice little house with a bit of garden, but my daughter-in-law prefers it here, so here they all are. Not that the men are in it much. I don't know how it is, but it's not a place that men will stay in if they can help it. Jimmy goes out every night. I've never been told where. And my son comes to see me or else he goes back to his office. And he oughtn't to do that. I never knew my husband, he was a lawyer, go back to his office after hours.'

In the absence of Julia, Celia might have suggested that the late Mr. Marston was not in the possession of an office key, for to call him a lawyer was a slight exaggeration on his widow's part. He had been a lawyer's clerk and Mrs. Marston's income was inherited from her father, an astonishingly thrifty man, with an eye for an occasional speculation, who had dealt in small quantities of coal, but this legend about Gerald's father did very well for Julia, and Mrs. Marston, bringing it with her from his native town, had come to believe in it for practical purposes herself.

Julia turned to Celia. 'Then you must be very lonely in the evening.'

'No, I'm never lonely,' Celia said. 'What chance have I, with Catherine always about and Jimmy out and in and Gerald with his plans in the dining-room, unless he's playing billiards somewhere? And very often I haven't washed the supper things and cleaned Jimmy's bath until nine o'clock. There's not much evening left.'

Somehow, without discourtesy, she had eliminated Mrs. Marston and her statements. Mrs. Marston was holding her saucer near her chin to catch any errant drops, and the cup was half-way to her lips; her face, always reddened by weather, was flushed to the forehead with anger, yet she seemed to have been brushed away, like a fly, with a flick of a hand, and it was a consciousness of this power, a still stronger taste of what she had experienced in the morning, more than a natural sympathy with Mrs. Marston, which made Julia very sceptical about Celia's labours.

'But think of your afternoons,' she said. 'You don't go

227

out much, do you? At least, I never see you anywhere, and there must be hours and hours when you have nothing to do in a tiny place like this. I know I often envy you your leisure. Unless,' this was an inspiration, 'that's when you have all sorts of visitors that we know nothing about.'

'Not many visitors,' Celia said amiably.

'But there's someone at the door now,' Julia said, for while Celia spoke there had been a ring and then a knock.

It was too early for the baker, the sounds were too imperative to be his, and neither Mrs. Marston nor Julia missed a careful steadying of Celia's lowered eyelids.

CHAPTER XXXI

'SOMEBODY in a hurry,' said Mrs. Marston.

'Perhaps it's another telegram.'

'And who's sending her telegrams, pray?'

'I'm afraid,' Julia said with reserve, 'I know very little about Celia's affairs.'

'Then,' said Mrs. Marston, 'you're just like me.'

'But it's not a telegram,' Julia said. 'It seems to be a visitor,' and Mrs. Marston at once got rid of her cup and a few crumbs.

'No,' she said, regretting these preparations, 'it's not a visitor. It sounded like a gentleman to me.'

Julia laughed and, undaunted by the glassy eye Mrs. Marston turned on her, said gaily, 'And why shouldn't Celia have a caller who is a gentleman, too?'

'Oh, I daresay I'm very old-fashioned,' Mrs. Marston said.

'But, as a matter of fact, of course you're right. She wouldn't take a caller into the dining-room and shut the door. That would be a very odd thing to do, when tea is ready here. It must be somebody on business.'

She glanced at the window, thinking how much more satisfactory it would be if Celia lived, as Mrs. Marston suggested, in a little house with a view of the garden gate. Looking out of this window, after mounting the stool placed for that purpose, would be like looking down a perpendicular cliff and The Terrace itself made a shelf under which a car could lie hidden in the road.

'One feels terribly shut in,' she said.

'That's what I say. It gives you a very funny feeling, having your front door inside the house.'

'But I suppose it has its advantages. I mean — well — all

the neighbours would know if a policeman called at your little house, Mrs. Marston.'

'My little house is just the size I want.'

'I wish I could have a little one myself. But I was going to say that when the policeman came in by the main entrance here, no one would know which flat he wanted.'

'It's no good trying to stuff me up with a policeman in the dining-room and I'm not in the habit of having them in my own house, either. What would he come for?'

'Well, they come and break the news when people are run over, don't they? Things like that. But that was only a sort of example. I don't really think it's a policeman. Policemen are very nice men.'

'I can't say I know much about them myself,' said Mrs. Marston, and Julia realized the difficulty of dealing subtly with people of this kind, while Mrs. Marston hardened towards the woman who had been listening so sympathetically to her woes a little while ago. If she was not silly, she was impudent with her talk about policemen. She was one of those people who take an ell when they have been given an inch and Mrs. Marston wished she could get her inch back again, yet, a few minutes later, these two were reunited in surprise, curiosity and disapproval, for Celia entered, wearing her hat and carrying a coat over her arm.

'I'm very sorry,' she said, 'but I have to go out at once. Do you mind looking after each other?'

She glanced round the room in what seemed a bewildered manner, but was actually an effort after swift and thorough concentration. Was there anything in her desk, in her bedroom, in any part of the house, she would not like Mrs. Marston to see? Or rather, for there was nothing which would not suffer from her leisured inspection, was there anything of which she could make use? Had Catherine or Jimmy any little secrets to be guarded? Catherine, she believed, had none, but she pretended to no certainty about Jimmy.

230

'I must just write a note,' she said, going to her desk.

She wrote two notes, one for Gerald and one for Catherine and she put them in envelopes which she fastened up.

'I shall put these on the table in the hall,' she said 'and they'll find them as soon as they come in. They'll be able to look after themselves. They'll manage quite well.'

'They certainly will not!' Mrs. Marston cried. 'Not while Gerald has a mother! Where are you going? When will you get back? What am I going to tell him?'

'I haven't the least idea,' Celia said, picking up her coat. 'I'm sorry to rush off like this, but it can't be helped.'

'H'm,' said Mrs. Marston, 'she can move quick enough when she likes. Now what do you make of that?'

Julia held up a finger until the front door was shut and the sound of descending footsteps had died away. Then she went to the window, mounted the stool and leaned out, and what she saw was entirely satisfactory to her belief in her instinct and perspicacity, but it was a sad thing to have to report to Gerald's mother and it was some time before she yielded to her pressure.

'I think everybody has gone mad,' she said, thinking of Stephen, too, but deciding not to mention him at present. 'But I'm sure it's only temporary. I expect she will be back before long.'

'So do I,' said Mrs. Marston grimly, for she had no faith in her good luck, and Julia, taking this remark, this grimness, for reproach, hastened to discover and produce plenty of good reasons why Mr. Carey should carry Celia off in his car.

'They must have arranged it this morning,' she said brightly.

'This morning! Then why did she ask me to tea? And what do you know about them, this morning?'

'Only', said Julia meekly, 'that I happen to know she was in the Careys' garden!'

'I'm not surprised. I only wonder she wasn't rampaging about in Mrs. Carey's car.'

'Mrs. Carey is away,' Julia said softly.

'Oh, is she? Well, the tea's cold by this time and I think I'll make another pot.'

Julia did not stay for the second brew. A little puzzled by Mrs. Marston's variations in sympathy, she left her in sole possession, and for the first time, of her son's home.

It was of her, prowling about, probably opening drawers, the buttons on her boots twinkling with suggestions, that Celia thought when Reginald Carey said gratefully, 'You're a good friend. I knew you'd come.'

'Well of course,' Celia said, 'but it's always a mistake, I've proved it over and over again, to do a good deed. Oh, I'm not thinking of this. A good deed is always something you don't want to do. I asked my mamma-in-law to tea and I've left her in the flat.'

'Does it matter? What will she do to it?' he asked, trying to be interested, keeping his eye on the road, wishing he could drive safely at his wife's speed.

'Just poison it,' Celia said calmly. 'It won't be right again until we get a good strong wind. And her clothes smell of camphor, but that's a minor evil.'

She watched him as he sat very straight, like a beginner, with both hands on the wheel and his head rigid. He had driven for years but he would never do it with ease. He was in constant expectation of some strange trick on the part of the car and he treated it as though it were an animal of uncertain temper; he slowed down from his very moderate pace at the sight of a child hundreds of yards away. She had often noticed that habit of special caution and liked him for it; to-day it made her heart ache and, as she looked at him, she saw in his face a vulnerability she had missed in it hitherto, but now she was looking at him with an eye which had been instructed during those few minutes in the flat.

He was a colourless man, rather sallow, with a big, flexible, thin-lipped mouth and a short, somewhat flattened nose; he was as inconspicuous as Pauline was vivid, but, close at hand as Celia was now, the fine grain of his skin, the small, well-placed lines at the corners of his eyes and mouth, seemed to match and to account for his fastidious choice of material for his buildings and the economy, without affected severity, of their design. She saw a dead rose in his coat and longed to remove it for she thought it was like an evil omen, but she knew he would be quick enough to understand why she wanted to take it from him.

They drew up at the entrance to the bridge and it was Celia who paid the toll: the toll-keeper had to ask the gentleman to drive on. He obeyed with a jerk, and said, 'I think I ought to have telephoned. I know I ought to have done it, but I couldn't.'

'I'll do it, I'll speak to her when we get there,' Celia said.

'I mean I wouldn't,' he said.

She made no response to that. Her object was to be as little noticeable as possible. He was like a man who had had too much to drink and was ready to make confidences at which he would shudder in a sober moment. It might be kind but it was not fair to encourage him and she tried to wrench her mind from him and his affairs, but she was not very successful.

As they went slowly, perforce, over the bridge, she thought it was an airy structure for carrying heavy hearts; she remembered how, in March, she had watched Pauline crossing the bridge, coming from her son as they were now going towards him, when, with her mask dropped, she was wearing an expression Celia had never seen before. Then, the trees had been mockingly putting out new leaves; to-day, fully clothed, they were still youthfully attired. In their yearly cycle they were a little older than Catherine; like her, they looked fresh and lovely with the promise of a

233

luxuriant maturity and a rich harvest, and Catherine and Meredith Carey were contemporaries, but his was an abortive growth. The trunk of him and the branches increased with his years; the first green shoots neither fell nor renewed themselves; they were tiny, almost invisible, minutely grotesque on a normal structure. In those woods covering the farther side of the gorge, such a tree would have been cut because it was occupying space and taking air and light which were needed for the healthy, but Meredith was carefully preserved, as though his rarity had a special value.

'Because,' said Reginald Carey, continuing the thought he had begun at the other end of the bridge, 'I have the first right.'

'But,' said Celia, looking down at the water which to-day, could not refuse the sky's insistence on giving it colour, at the fields, mounting towards Easterly, where the big elms were not yet heavily enough draped to look, as they would look later, like elderly widows, at the city spreading beyond the intricate waterways, at the sparkle, here and there, where the sun touched glass or metal. 'But,' she said, 'you wouldn't, you couldn't have waited for her, and you would still have been hours ahead of her.'

'Hours? Years!' he said, and the quiet vehemence in his voice, the stored resentment she heard in it, made a strange contrast with his stiff pose, his unrelaxing carefulness at the wheel and with her memory of him in his own home as a charming host, a kind, unobtrusive friend, living graciously in gracious surroundings. It seemed as though, under the feet of nearly every human being there was a gulf as deep as the one they had now crossed. She had not suspected one threatening Reginald and Pauline, she did not want to see what lay at the bottom of it. It was not fair to have Reginald alone as guide, but without brutality, unforgivable at the moment, she could not stop him. Luckily it was she and not

Julia who sat beside him and learnt how Pauline, who could not endure humiliation, whose passion for efficiency and success was mortified by her supreme failure in her son, had spared herself the daily pain of seeing him.

'And how could I insist on her suffering? How could I?' he demanded, slackening speed to allow a hen to cross the road. 'And yet I can't forgive her.'

'No, not to-day,' Celia said quietly. 'But you could yesterday and you will to-morrow. It's a presumptuous act, anyhow, on the part of us poor mortals.'

'She never speaks of him, never sees him. He might be dead. And perhaps he is!' he cried with a kind of triumph.

'But do you talk about him yourself?'

'How can I? But I see him.'

'So does she.'

'But not so often,' he said possessively, childishly, and Celia felt a sort of horror of him and an immense pity for a man fearing the loss of a treasure to which he had been secretly adding year by year.

'Richard . . . yes, she's good to him,' he said. 'He's not complete either, but that's different. That's to his credit and to hers through him. Otherwise, I don't know. She loves beauty. Well, don't I? Haven't I proved it?'

'Yes, yes,' she said, but he would not be silenced, and she thought this journey, along roads overhung by trees with leaves like satin and edged by fields full of polished butter-cups, would have been much less of a nightmare if he had once made a gesture to fit his state, but he sat like a tin figure on a tin toy, his hands permanently on the wheel and his head motionless. Sentiments and emotions issuing from that figure were fantastic, they were part of the clockwork inside it, but at the same time she knew he was a living man, and with her pity and comprehension there was impatience, because he could not take his trouble silently.

They had not more than twenty miles to go, but they seemed very long ones and when the car stopped in front of a house, benign and peaceful in its garden, her legs were aching with the control she was trying to give to him.

CHAPTER XXXII

HE made lovely buildings, she thought, as she climbed up the stairs to her flat. He was incapable of any mixture of styles which would offend a critical eye. If such a mixture happened to be necessary, he would know how to lead one style into the other, like a natural growth, but she was sure no intelligent woman, though she might make no claim to being an artist, would have changed her mood and manner with a jerk as violent as his when, after some hours of uncertainty, he was assured that Meredith was no nearer the point of death than was the brother whom Pauline tended. With her mood changed and the cause of it removed, a woman would continue to trail some melancholy wisps of her earlier emotion, to justify it and for the sake of sequence, before she assumed a livelier garb. Reginald Carey had dropped his rags and tatters in a moment and revealed himself as the courteous, reserved person she had always known, and while this was touching in its simplicity, it was also irritating in the demand it made on her adaptability and complaisance. But the demand was not made in vain. Her habitual air of placidity could conceal one kind of feeling as well as another and as she listened to him talking quietly about Pauline and Richard's illness, she almost believed his earlier manner which had been like that of someone chattering in delirium, had only existed in her imagination. Had he forgotten it, or did he think she had forgotten? She admired and despised this masculine assumption that her mental condition must march with his, this pretence that the smouldering volcano she had neighboured on the outward journey had not rumbled and emitted smoke, smearing her innocent belief in the happiness, increased by a shared sorrow, of her two friends.

Coming back through the peaceful summer evening, a bluer, cleaner smoke rising steadily from the cottage chimneys and smelling of burning wood, the trees overhanging the road more passively now, subduing their ardent life in preparation for another day of brilliant, shimmering green, the fields, with their colour dimmed, looking like quilts drawn over the earth for the night, it seemed to Celia that all violent emotions must be false and foolish, and Reginald Carey, hoping all the children were in bed by this time and all the hens gone to roost, drove a little faster and talked more slowly, about his garden and Pauline's skill with it.

'Everything grows for her,' he said, and, for a few seconds, they both listened to the irony in those words.

'And I'd better confess,' Celia said, not too quickly, 'that I stole a lot of your roses this morning. You may miss them to-morrow. I believe you know them all by name.'

'This morning? I was there for a few minutes, at about twelve o'clock.'

'Then we must just have missed each other. How did we, I wonder? I walked straight up to the Downs from your gate.'

'I went back that way, but I came in from the other side. I hadn't been to town. I'd been looking at a house and I thought there might be a later message from Pauline than the one I had at breakfast, but actually, of course, she would have sent it to the office. And nobody told me you'd been there.'

'It's an extraordinarily discreet household,' Celia said.

A few hours ago she would have given him Pauline's latest report; now she decided to be discreet too and merely told him that Pauline had asked her to do some small commissions for her.

'And I suppose,' she said, 'you didn't see my sister-in-law anywhere near your domains?'

'I don't know her, do I? he asked.

'No, that's part of the trouble,' Celia said dryly.

'Trouble?' he said vaguely. He had too much of his own to be interested in Julia's. 'No, I didn't notice anybody. I don't notice much when I'm driving.'

'And anyhow,' said Celia, 'she's not quite real. I just thought you might have seen her, very pretty, in a pink frock. I told her I'd taken your roses and she was worried about it. She's afraid the servants will tell Pauline when she comes back.'

'And I wonder when that will be? You told her, didn't you, there was no need?'

'I told her exactly what the doctor said.'

'Thank you.' He thanked her again when he stopped the car below The Terrace. 'You see,' he explained, 'I wanted to make sure there was nothing left undone, the things women think of and men don't. I think they are very kind to him, don't you?'

'I'm sure they are,' she said, and indeed she had been impressed by the true tenderness of Meredith's nurses. She hoped Reginald had noticed enough of it to comfort and not enough to mark the difference between this hireling service and that of the boy's mother. And she wished it had not been her own voice that told Pauline not to come. In answer to its emphatic reassurances she had felt, across the distance, a vibration of unfriendliness in Pauline. There was no reason for it and perhaps she had imagined it, but altogether it had not been a good day, she thought, taking her latchkey from her bag and forgetting her happiness of the morning, and when she found her family in the kitchen and saw Gerald very slowly and gravely drying a dish, she was thankful to be at home. She leant against him for a moment when he kissed her, for he seemed human, ordinary and kind.

'We've been having a frightful time!' Catherine cried cheerfully from the sink.

'And somebody's locked my top drawer and I can't find the key. I never lock that drawer and I want a clean collar.'

Celia made a movement towards her bag, but checked it. Jimmy was collarless now and in his shirt sleeves and he might have been any decent working lad, not yet fully dressed for his evening relaxation, but how strong he looked and intelligent and independent! And how naturally they told her their own stories and expressed their own needs before they asked what hers might be!

'Have you had anything to eat?' This was Gerald's question.

'No, I don't think so. No, I haven't. I'll have some tea in a minute. I must see about Jimmy's collar.'

'No hurry. I'm not going out. Too late. Our domestic duties have been a bit prolonged. What is home without a mother?'

'But there wasn't much to do. The cold meat, the salad — And I suppose I'd better have some.'

'Nothing left but the bone,' Catherine said, looking over her shoulder and seeming, for some reason, pleased to give this news.

'And I thought there might be enough for to-morrow,' Celia said, making a rapid calculation of the butcher's bill and a much longer survey of the back of Catherine's head and the curls at the nape of her neck.

'There's heaps of meat, pet,' Catherine said, drying her hands on the roller towel, 'only we can't eat it, to-day or to-morrow.' She tightened her lips before she opened them to say neatly, 'Curried. Out of kindness. And wasn't it lucky that we all loathe it? I should have pretended to, anyhow.'

'Now Catherine . . .' Gerald began.

'Now Papa, don't begin to be a father just because Mother's come home. Don't spoil the evening. You were splendid over the eggs and bacon. And everything else,' she added, and as Celia saw Gerald trying to frown down his gratification, it occurred to her that the fortunate children might be those who only had one parent, the fortunate parents those who had lost their partners and were in sole possession. Reginald Carey was trying to convince himself of his solitary claim, even with such a child as Meredith and, at the thought of that youth who was still a baby without a baby's charm, Celia sank a little lower in the chair she had taken beside the kitchen table.

'Go and take off your things,' Gerald said, 'and we'll bring your tray into the sitting-room.'

She went first to Jimmy's room and she heard Catherine saying, 'But, you know, she can't eat curry either.' and Gerald, his words indistinguishable, replying with calm resourcefulness. There was no doubt he had flourished exceedingly during her absence.

'Here's your key,' she said to Jimmy. He was shaving, as usual, to save time in the morning. 'I knew you kept letters in that drawer, so I wouldn't run any risks.'

'Thank you very much, but there weren't any risks to run and it would have been jolly awkward if I'd wanted to go out. What else did you lock up?'

'Nothing. There are not many keys, to begin with. I always lose them or forget which belongs to what. And I never have a letter I want to keep, so I get rid of them all. There wasn't much time, anyhow. I had to rush off and leave everything to its fate, including the cold meat. I suppose the curry was meant as a reproach and, after all, it wasn't much of an outing for me, but then she didn't know that.'

'She doesn't know now. Catherine wouldn't tell and she must have riled the old man pretty badly because he seems to have been mute, too. But most of the fun was over by the time I got back and the enemy was making a strategic retreat.'

'I hope some one told her we all hate curry.'

'You can bet Catherine didn't miss a chance like that. How's the boy?'

'Better.'

'Oh, bad luck.'

'Is it? Jimmy,' she sat on his bed, 'do you think I'm a difficult person to live with, a repressing sort of person?'

He wiped the soap from his face and thoughtfully felt his chin and lip. 'No,' he said, 'no, certainly not. Easy, in some ways, but critical — my word!'

'I never criticize.'

'Don't be simple,' he begged. 'And I'm not worried by it. I'm used to it, and the fools probably don't know.'

'And it doesn't matter about the fools.'

'Not a bit,' he said.

But Gerald, she thought, taking off her hat, smoothing her hair, holding her hands under the comforting hot water, was not a fool, and Jimmy was used to her and Catherine, quarrelling with her grandmother and cooking with her father, looked as gay as Celia had ever seen her. They had not missed her for a moment; they had felt they were having a holiday; her own view of herself as the invisible but necessary cement in the house, was as mistaken as her belief in the perfect accord existing between Pauline and Reginald. She had made a point, and quietly taken a good deal of credit for it, of being at home when the family returned from its daily business, of preserving a sort of haphazard order and beauty in the place, and they were happier without her and Gerald and Catherine had found friendship over the eggs and bacon. And for this, she thought, working herself up, she had denied herself hundreds of little pleasures, she had foregone that journey to Paris and mortified herself by letting Susan go instead. But no, not going to Paris was perhaps only one of the cases in which her unselfishness was at least partly dependent on her lack of money. And as for Susan, her holiday with Richard, her acquaintance with his home, it was not to her that he had sent his love and, startled by all the thoughts behind that unpremeditated boast, she had to confess to a possessiveness she had always believed she disdained. It was extraordinary how self-satisfaction flourished on self-deception, and again she owned to a little pang of jealousy when Gerald entered with the tray and Catherine followed him, with a lavish use of the first person plural and a great deal of praise for her father's inventiveness in the making of sandwiches.

'It's always a mistake to do a good deed,' she said once more. She knew she was being ridiculous and unfair, but she was sure that horrid old woman had indirectly robbed her of Catherine's entire allegiance.

'But they're lovely sandwiches!' Catherine cried. 'Orange and lettuce and cheese and all sorts of surprises.'

'Yes, you've been very clever, both of you,' she said, 'but I wasn't thinking of the sandwiches.'

'Oh, you mean — was it awful? Did you have to see him? I couldn't have borne that.'

'Go to bed,' Gerald said sharply. 'You don't know what you may have to bear yet.'

'There's all my homework to start with.'

'Oh, Catherine!'

'I couldn't help it.' She turned to her father. 'Could I help it?'

'No, I don't see how any of us could.' He waited until the door was shut before he said, 'She ought never to have come here.'

'I asked her to tea.'

'Did you? She didn't tell me that. I mean she ought not to have come to live near us. I suppose you won't believe it, but she was a good mother to me.'

'I don't know what a good mother is, but I do believe it. I know I'm the fly in the ointment.'

'In the amber,' he said, surprising her, 'and my mother can't get at you, she doesn't know how you got there and amber's rather mysterious in itself. And isn't it very nearly a precious stone?'

'A long way off that, I think.'

'You know best, but it's rare enough to be beyond some people's reach.'

There was no warmth in his voice, he spoke more slowly and quietly than usual and though his face was still flushed by his efforts in the kitchen and his old trousers were stretched across his thighs, he managed to look, as well as to sound, very little like his mother's son. He was rather like a doctor she did not know very well, describing the nature of a disease, or a lawyer, explaining some mystery of the law, and it was strange to think that he was the father of her children, the sharer of the barbaric bed. It was this relationship, unwilling on her part, unsatisfied on his, which really put the distance between them, and she remembered that she had cried last night when she thought he was asleep.

'I wonder, but I think I can guess, what your mother has been saying.'

She spoke lightly and he answered quietly, 'I don't want to talk about it.'

'But do you believe it?'

'Not a word. I don't think she does herself.'

'No, that's what makes it all so hopeless. I didn't explain where I was going. I couldn't give her and Julia — Julia was here too — that information to play with, not possibly, and you and Catherine, thank you both, felt just as I did, Jimmy says.'

'Are you surprised?'

'No, but I'm grateful. It would have been hateful to have her or Julia wagging their tongues and their heads over Meredith Carey.'

'Because he's Meredith Carey?'

'Because he's my friend's child, but I think I should feel the same about any child like that. And so would you.'

'He's just about Catherine's age, isn't he?'

'Just about. Like her,' she gave Gerald a quick, uncertain smile, 'he was the child of peace.'

CHAPTER XXXIII

To do Julia justice, she would have been ready to suspect a little intrigue in any other woman of her acquaintance who did what Celia had done, and urged by the human desire to share her pleasures, she decided to call on May on the way home, for she was sure no slight estrangement would survive this news, these fears and a necessary exchange of counsel, but she was mistaken, for May, in an arm-chair beside the drawing-room window, merely said, 'Pooh! I don't believe a word of it.'

She looked solid and handsome, secure in established circumstances and maturity. No one would have believed that, yesterday morning, she had seen herself as worse than a widow and since the arrival of Stephen's telegram, announcing his return, she was anxious to forget that absurd distress, but Julia, entering with animation, without embarrassment, served to remind her of it and acted as a precipitator, in large quantities, of that common sense which normally was almost negligible in solution. She looked at Julia with a cool, calculating eye, the corners of her mouth expressively turned down.

'You're always making things up,' she said.

'And what else,' Julia asked, her nostrils fluttering, 'have I made up?' and she thought this was a clever question and one which May might have some difficulty in answering, but May said carelessly, 'Oh, I don't know. You talk a lot of nonsense and I'm very glad the girls are out.'

'Out again!' Julia exclaimed softly, and, getting no response to this sympathy for May's usual grievance, she added in a matronly manner. 'But of course I shouldn't have said a word about all this if they had been at home.'

'I should hope not!' said May. 'They are ready enough to

think we are out of date. You mustn't let them laugh at you too much.'

'Laugh! At me?' Julia cried.

'Why yes. Didn't you know? And when your own daughters are grown up, they'll laugh too, I expect. Didn't we laugh at our own mothers?'

'I never knew my mother. That's why I do so much for my own children. I want to give them all I missed.'

'But you don't know what that is. She might have been very unpleasant.'

'Her memory is sacred!' Julia said indignantly.

'Well, that's another thing you must have made up because you've just said you never knew her. Anyhow, mothers aren't sacred as long as they're alive and a good thing too. You're very old-fashioned, Julia. Oh, I know you get all those books out of the library and leave them about and it looks very clever and all that, and I daresay you read a page here and there, but novelettes are really much more in your line. Coming to me with stories about Celia! It doesn't matter in the family, because nobody will believe you, but you'd better be careful anywhere else. You'll be telling me next that Stephen and Mrs. Carey have gone off together,' she said impatiently, and turning her head and looking at the peaceful garden, she missed the sudden brightness behind Julia's tears, like sun on raindrops. 'It's so common,' she said calmly.

'Very,' Julia agreed, rising to go and her eyes were still bright though the tears had disappeared. 'But what else can you expect?'

May did not answer, she had done a good deal of thinking during the last few hours and she had no patience with these silly speculations.

She tried to put them from her mind. She and Celia had both arrived at the comfortable age which was beyond the temptation to indulge in indiscretions and should have been

247

beyond suspicion of them. She was glad to be at that age and to be sitting in this room which was a complete, though almost unconscious, satisfaction to the eye, and her rupture with Julia was not much more to her than the casting of a warm petticoat she had worn for years and suddenly found was an unnecessary encumbrance. She could do very well without it, but she was shrewd enough to see how the story about Celia applied, in Julia's mind, to her own case, and the consequent additional pleasure there had been in telling it, but one was as absurd as the other. He was coming home to-morrow and she was very glad. It seemed a long time since yesterday morning, when he went. He could not be compared to the unnecessary petticoat. His presence, the habit of him, the sense of safety he gave her, were almost as much a part of her as her own skin and it was this feeling and not the tact it might have been, which gave the quality to her welcome the next day. Her pleasure at his arrival had not the excess of her bewilderment at his departure. Here he was, she thought, and here, she knew, he would always be, and this was a certainty he experienced himself when he carried his little bag into the hall and saw her standing by the drawing-room door.

At the sight of her there was no quickening of his senses, no solace or stimulus for his mind, no hope that her serene silence would endure, but he was too old for change. In two long railway journeys and one long day out of doors, he had tested the limits of his vagrancy and found them very narrow. He was glad to be at home, to feel the soft grey carpet under his feet and see it carried by the stairs to the landing where a charming daughter might appear. He liked the pale walls, the polish on the semicircular table, the peaceful aspect which May, oddly enough, had created. An ugly wall-paper, a painfully patterned carpet, a hat and umbrella-stand ful-filling its functions and contracting a narrow passage, a faint smell of cooking and no expectation of adequate reward,

248

would no doubt have weakened his conviction that he ought to want no more than he had already and that he had more than he deserved. But this was his conviction as he bent to kiss her and he wondered, as Celia had done before him, whether in May there was not some mental or spiritual correspondence to the dignity she could produce by means of material objects, whether it was not his own personality which, somehow, had stunted or buried it.

'I believe you're sunburnt,' she said, patting his shoulder.

'Well, I had one day in the sun, but most of this is dirt, I fancy. It was a slow train for part of the way and not a clean one for any of it. But I enjoyed it. I like the long waits at the little stations and the porters and passengers asking after each other's families. I was told a good deal about the passengers' families myself.'

'But,' she knew his fastidious habits, 'weren't you in a first class carriage?'

'No,' he said dryly, and he looked at her with the half-squint of his whimsical or thoughtful moments, 'I went first class in an express train and came back third class by a slow one.'

That, for him, was a summary of his little holiday and he waited for the comment or the question which ought to have been evoked by his tone.

'I think it was rather silly of you,' May said, and he laughed and went upstairs. When he had mounted a few steps, he looked back. 'And I went to the station in a cab, but Susan brought me back.'

'Yes,' said May, 'I was very cross with her about that.'

He laughed again, and Susan, entering the hall after putting the car away, saw her long-legged father near the top of the stairs, her mother following him in silence, one hand on the banisters, the other holding up the front of her dress, and she stood for a minute, looking at them, seeing a certain pathos in this small procession but getting a glimpse of some permanency beyond her own experience, some deeply rooted loyalty, and against her will she had a vision of herself, years hence, when she would not be so slim or swift as she was now, going rather heavily up a staircase and pursued by some faithful soul. She had changed the relative positions of her mother and herself, but she did not notice that. She was in too great a hurry to shut out the vision.

Stephen, too, was touched and surprised at being followed and though May did not unpack his bag or put away his things or turn on the water for his bath, but sat with her hands folded while he wandered between the bedroom and the dressing-room, she was doing a sufficiently wifely part in giving him her company. He would have been embarrassed by more fervent attentions and he would have enjoyed her stillness more if he had not wondered what it covered.

'You are very quiet,' he said at last.

'You're doing all the talking yourself.'

'Have I been talking?'

'Yes, when you weren't humming.'

'I apologize for the humming.'

'I like to hear you. I don't notice when people are out of tune. The holiday has done you good. I'm glad you went, but you ought to have stayed longer.'

'Long enough,' he said.

'Did you go to the office on your way back? Or call on John?'

'No, the only familiar thing I saw was Mrs. Carey's car flashing past. And I can live quite happily without John for some time yet.'

'Are you sure it was Mrs. Carey's car? I thought she was away.'

'So did Susan. But there she was.'

'Well,' May said slowly, for though she had not seen the pleased alertness in Julia's eyes, she remembered her own scornful words, 'if you see Julia or John don't tell them Mrs. Carey was in Radstowe to-day.'

'I'm not likely to talk about her.'

'No, but they are. Which way did you say she was going?'

'She seemed to be streaking out of town as fast as the traffic would let her — and a bit faster. And I thought you had no secrets from Julia.'

'H'm,' said May. 'They wouldn't be safe. But I've never had any.' She raised the eyes of a puzzled ox to the tall figure leaning against the door of the dressing-room. 'Until now,' she said. 'And they are not secrets, exactly. They are just Julia's tales.'

'And I thought you enjoyed her tales.'

'Not,' May said simply, 'when they are about you and me and Celia.'

'Ah,' he said, sitting down and gathering the skirts of his dressing-gown about him, 'they should be interesting. Let's have them.'

It amused him and touched him again to see that she felt some awkwardness in speaking of Julia's suggestions about himself. She was much more voluble and repetitive in telling him about Celia, and this reappearance of the May he knew so well had its consolatory effect.

'Yes,' he said, 'she's a mischievous little piece.'

'And you see,' May said with renewed difficulty, 'if she knew Mrs. Carey was at home . . .'

'It would ruin the romance she has made for Celia.'

'No, I didn't mean that. I may have put the idea into her head myself, when I was making fun of her. And so she might think it very queer that you and Mrs. Carey both came home on the same day. I hardly spoke the whole time she was here and then I said the very thing I shouldn't. I said she'd be telling me next that you'd gone off with Mrs. Carey.'

He shook his head gravely. 'No, I didn't do that. I'd never do that. I should be frightened of her. Formidable woman, I think. I like a homelier kind of character.'

She smiled and he smiled, too, looking at his feet. There

was a good deal of irony in his situation, he fancied there might be some in Celia's, too, and if he had looked up, he might have wondered what May was finding in hers. As she said herself, she could get to the bottom of things when she was given time and though she had not gone as far as that, she was peering, now, more speculative than puzzled, below the surface.

CHAPTER XXXIV

THE city of Radstowe stretches for a long way beyond its busiest quarter. As far as the lower, eastern end of the Easterly ridge, the suburbs straggle upwards and drop for a little way beyond it and, sweeping back, citywards, in a wide, irregular semicircle, the curve embraces other humble suburbs, the Downs and the growing district behind them and Upper Radstowe. The river makes a somewhat erratic diameter to this half-circle. Beyond it, on the high ground sloping upwards from the bridge level, scattered houses soon give way to the country and from the docks a dense growth of buildings, factories and shops and shabby rows of houses, spreads westward and almost unnoticed from a distance. Seen from the heights of Upper Radstowe and in comparison with the coloured roofs, the spires and chimneys, the sudden patches of green on the hither side of the water, up hill and down dale, this low lying part of the city looks like the dark, as yet unfruitful soil in the vast garden. It could almost be forgotten by those who did not live there or frequent it on business or good works, and for such people as the Fellows, the Greys and the Careys, the big city became a very small one. There were the Downs, there was Upper Radstowe with Nunnery Road flanking it on one side as the river did on the other, and it was to merge itself into Nunnery Road that The Slope lifted itself over its steep edge. Hereabouts were the chief shops, and, in the space of a week, May and Julia, taking their daily walk, would meet most of their acquaintances at some point of these thoroughfares. With this concentration of a certain class of society in one district, the city had some of the qualities of a country town; its inhabitants were interested in and knew a great deal about each other's concerns, and John, in direct spiritual descent from the village shopkeeper who keeps his eye on the street and steps on to the pavement for a neighbourly chat, in physical and mental descent from men who had to know other people's business, was fortunately placed for the satisfaction of his curiosity. His shop was just beyond The Slope and the branch road which took the hill in a more leisurely fashion and the tramcars with it: thus even the diverted traffic passed under his eye for he had taken care to have his office overlooking the street.

He was a busy man and a hard worker, but his occupations did not call for prolonged concentration. A stroll to the window made a pleasant interlude, and, though he saw many people, aliens and outliers, he did not know, there were not many occasions when he did not see a friend or a customer. The passengers on the top of the tramcars were almost within reach of his hand and the rattling and clanging sounds did not trouble his ears. At a certain hour of the morning he was accustomed to seeing May and Julia on the other side of the street, but Julia never looked up to give him a passing greeting and he would look down at her with a queer grin. She was a snob and he loved her. It was not in his character to wonder whether she loved him. She was his wife and he took her affection for granted. She was his wife and she had to do what she was told. She had, for instance, to follow him to the chapel he disliked just as much as she did, and while he had any authority over his children they should go to the chapel, too, just as Robert should come to the shop, whether he liked it or not.

He was standing at the window, thinking about Robert's future, whether to give him another year at school where he seemed to be doing little good, or to start his training as heir to this establishment; he was watching the passage of the traffic through the shade cast by the tall buildings on each side of the street and following it as it emerged into the sunshine beyond, and his thoughts, which had no connection

254

with Robert's possible inclinations and therefore ran smoothly on their own lines, did not interfere with his interest in what went on outside. Thus it was that he recognized Stephen's car with its roof open and Stephen and Susan plainly to be seen, and his first feeling was one of envy. He thought there could hardly be a more charmingly symbolic sight than this of a pretty daughter at her father's service and the father completely trustful of her skill, and though, in a few years time, Sybil would be able to do this for John, he knew very well there would be a difference. He would not be able to lean back and let the girl use her own judgment; he would be driving for her though his hands were not on the wheel, and he turned back to his desk with a shrug of his shoulders for Stephen's paternal admiration.

Spoilt. All three of them. Always have been, he thought, but at least part of his irritation had another cause. Here was Stephen proving all his prophecies at fault, for no one acting according to John's standards of decency, and Stephen certainly did, would allow his young daughter to carry him home after a little escapade. No, he would not return like that, with his bag on the back seat. Therefore, John argued, there had been no escapade and he was wrong and that would be very bad for Julia. Alongside his deep affection for Stephen, John had an unexpressed desire to find him less perfect than he seemed and this, apparently, was not to be fulfilled. He would have been ashamed to acknowledge such a sentiment, but it was there. He had been truly thankful to find no signs of disorder in Stephen's professional affairs, but the kind of lapse which he deplored in anyone and could forgive in a man, while in a woman it roused all his most savage instincts, would have lowered Stephen's level to his own. He saw it cancelling out his impatience with his wife's foolishness and the discomfort of Robert's sulky face. Stephen never quarrelled and his son would not have had a face like that. No doubt, in Robert's case, it was Julia's fault, but Stephen would have known how to counteract it. All through their lives, he had been ahead of John, not in a worldly sense, for John would not admit that a profession was essentially better than a trade, but he had always been a little higher in the school, he had been given more responsible positions, he was one of those people against whom no one had anything to say. His word was his bond, his counsel was honest, he strove for peace when litigation would have paid him better, and John was proud of him and had a childish, old womanish desire to catch him tripping and keep his secret.

I shan't tell Julia, he thought solemnly, for he lived in the delusion of her reliance on his judgment and chose to forget his inability to hold his tongue.

As it happened, she gave him other matters to consider. Her mental processes did not interest him, but he could not helping noticing symptoms of disturbance. This hardly troubled him. There had never yet been a difference of opinion which developed into action and he was in ignorance, for Julia could hold her tongue when she chose, of a new power of resistance bestowed upon her by Celia's gentle raillery and May's downright speech. Praise would have left her more or less contented in her unfulfilled intentions; criticism made her urgent to prove her worth, and Robert who shared with Sybil the privilege of dining with their parents, had cause, although he did not know it, to feel bitterly towards the aunts whose children he often envied. Aunt May was a fool but she did not ask questions that anyone need answer; Aunt Celia left people alone and being left alone by his relatives was Robert's idea of happiness to-night. He could hardly swallow his food. When he looked up from his plate he saw the mournful courage in his mother's eyes and that glance, assuring him of her support, telling him they must be brave together, produced in him a longing for some immediate catastrophe, the house on fire or his own death, anything rather than a scene with his father. He knew he would have to go into the drapery business and he preferred to go quietly. He did not wish to be driven into it with anger and followed there by this father's knowledge of his secret, frustrated and no doubt absurd desires. Why, oh why, had he revealed them to his mother, breaking the rule he had made for himself when he first went to school, to be silent at home about everything except trivialities? The school was the kingdom in which he was a subject. Within it he might occasionally rebel against its laws and sometimes know injustice, but these were internal matters, not to be mentioned in an outer world which would not understand them and had no real importance for him, while his enthusiasms, which his father must have had, were dangerous offerings to a mother who would spoil them with constant reference and change them into sentiments at which he shuddered. But to everyone there comes a weak moment when trouble or happiness dissipates distrust and finds expression and, for Robert, this moment had synchronized with Julia's need of self-assertion, of proving herself valuable to her son and, for his sake, capable of outfacing John.

In Robert's mind, that evening, there had been a picture of the Close, the peace of it and the beauty, with white flannelled figures moving on the grass and, for almost the only sound, the soul-satisfying one of bat and ball in vigorous impact. People came and went among the school buildings on which the creeper still had its early brightness and somewhere, out of sight, there was authority, in supreme control of this community with its rigid customs and elastic rules. Outside the railings and watching the game were all the people who did not matter; errand boys balancing themselves on bicycles, critical old gentlemen, young girls and children, nursemaids with perambulators, yet he realized that, in a way, they did matter, for were they not paying a kind of tribute to a state they recognized and envied? And, as the

shadows began to lengthen, there fell on him the shadow of
his future, of his helplessness against fate and of his folly in
not having applied himself more ardently to his work. As
anything approaching a scholar, he might have enlisted help
from the school authorities against the parental plans; he
could have gone to the university and prolonged this
existence which was the only one he wanted. Young, middle-
aged and elderly, this was the life for him and, as he wheeled
his bicycle home, walking so that he could think more
easily, he wondered whether even yet, if he worked with
desperation, there was any hope for another year at Upper
Radstowe, three years at the university and then, for the rest
of his life, a post, perhaps, in a preparatory school. He
thought he could get enough learning for that and he believed he had the other necessary qualities. And there were
still Christopher and Paul for the shop. Why should he be
tied to it because he had the misfortune to be born first?
After all, he thought, we're not exactly a royal family.

He could have wept as he wheeled the bicycle down the
gravelled drive and, to his horror and Julia's joy, he did
weep when she questioned him; moreover, he foresaw those
bedside talks he had always dreaded, yet he appreciated her
courage all the more because he had seen her enthusiasm
checked when he told her he had no leanings towards the
Church. For a happy moment she had pictured him in
gaiters and a mortar board was a poor exchange for them,
but what he did not know was that her picture of herself
became even more heroic; she was prepared to fight his
battle though the winning of it would have no outward
glory for herself.

'You all look very glum,' John said cheerfully.

'I think the weather's very tiring,' Julia said.

'Nonsense! It's just right. It's not hot enough to make
people lazy but it's bright enough to make last year's clothes
look shabby. It's the kind of weather we want and we've

been very busy.' He turned to Robert. 'I meant to have a look at the match, but I couldn't get away. What happened?'

But, before Robert could answer, Julia seized her opportunity. 'Next year,' she said brightly, 'I expect Robert will be captain. You'd like that, John, wouldn't you?'

'Any chance?' John asked quickly. He had given provisional notice of Robert's leaving, but he was ready to adapt his plans to the possibility of such distinction, even though it was Julia who suggested it.

Robert, however, honestly shook his head. Julia was annoyed with him. He could have been more hopeful than that without actually telling a lie but, after a moment's dismay, she rallied. She laughed gaily. 'And you know what that means, from Robert. He always runs himself down.'

Robert frowned heavily and John asked with some eagerness, 'Is there any chance at all?'

'No,' Robert said, glaring at his plate. 'Not unless there's a plague and I'm the only survivor.'

He had a reasonable regard for truth; he would have lied for the honour of the school; he told the truth now, in the same cause, but if the truth had been what he wished it was, he would have lied and lost his chances, rather than let his mother boast of his prowess to the mothers of his friends. He did not consider the possibility of her boasting without cause.

'Oh Robert!' she cried. 'How stupid of you!'

'Stupid?' said John. 'What do you mean? Isn't he telling the truth? Don't you want him to tell the truth?'

'Yes, of course I do, but I want him to have another year at school,' Julia said piteously.

'Well, you've gone the wrong way about it and he won't get it,' said John.

CHAPTER XXXV

He had lived with her for eighteen years; he expected her to be to-day exactly what she had been when he married her, what she was ten years ago, what she was only yesterday, and this simple trust was the measure of his own simplicity or of his impenetrability to experience. But, during the long argument in which she tried to involve him after dinner, when Robert and Sybil, warned of a storm, had found comparative shelter behind their homework, it occurred to him that some of the qualities she was displaying, persistence and pride and resentment, could not have sprung into existence at this very moment. Indeed, her own words referred them to an earlier date, and though he did not believe her criticism was fair and knew he was not bad tempered or selfish or tyrannous, he had to realize that such was the impression he had given and that her cruel misunderstanding of his character went very deep. He also saw himself fatuous in his assumption that everything was as he wished it to be.

'And you're not even interested in Rachel's teeth!' Julia cried.

He did not smile. He was unaware of anti-climax for her eyes flashed and the tears were dry which, hitherto, had seemed to water their quarrels for a richer harvest of affection and caresses. Her small figure was taut, her nostrils fluttered, but there was no pathetic play of the eyelashes. He did not like her in this guise, and, as though the sight of someone in a temper taught him the dignity and power of controlling his own, he hardly spoke; after a time, in instinctive defence of much that he had cherished, he did not listen.

'But Robert,' Julia said grandly, finishing a long speech, 'knows now that he has a mother who will fight for him.'

'Why didn't he know before?' John asked with mild shrewdness. 'That would have saved a lot of trouble.'

'To the last breath!' she added.

'Oh nonsense! You can't go on fighting as long as all that.' He went towards the door and, as she made to follow him, he said quietly, 'No, stay where you are.'

Then the tears did come because suddenly she felt helpless and she called after him, 'How horrid to me you all are! All your family! You and May and Celia. And Hester would be, too, I suppose, only we never see her. And I know why! I know why! It's because she won't put up with your bullying.'

He absorbed that statement without repentance as he went upstairs. He was obeying his father's wishes in regard to Hester; he disapproved more strongly than ever of independence in a woman and robbing Julia of any need for it might have been among his motives as he went to find his son.

When he opened the door of the little room they called the study, he found Robert and Sybil bending over their books in unnatural earnestness. It was an attitude he had often assumed himself in somewhat similar circumstances, he knew they had been discussing domestic matters and his smile must have been sardonic for he saw alarm in both raised faces.

'Is this true what your mother tells me?' he asked gravely. 'Then if it's true, why haven't you said anything about it?'

'I didn't see the use,' Robert muttered.

'And you'd be a queer kind of schoolmaster, wouldn't you?'

'Yes, I expect so. It doesn't matter.'

'And, it seems to me, you'll be a bear whatever else you are. In my day they tried to give us manners. But perhaps they've tried with you and failed.'

Sybil's lips parted, but she did not speak until John

addressed her, not unkindly. 'Well, what have you to say about it?'

'He's not a bear unless he's baited,' she said, looking at her father steadily because she was frightened, but a daughter could say what was not permitted in a son and John lifted his eyebrows comically.

'And who's baiting him? Me? I wish you could have heard the way my father used to talk to your aunts and me.'

'Oh,' said Sybil, growing a little bolder, judging her father's mood much more accurately than poor Robert could, 'that kind of thing is quite out of date. It doesn't work any longer.'

'Oh, you think it doesn't work. But what would you think if I put you into the shop, too?' Wisely, he did not wait for an answer. He left his last word ringing hopelessly in Robert's ears and stood for a minute or two on the wide landing, at a good distance from the study door, lest he should accidentally play the eavesdropper. He had a queer feeling, quite new to him, of unfamiliarity with his own home and isolation in it.

It was a solid house. The heavy bedroom doors were of panelled walnut, the broad staircase was handsomely balustraded with carved wood. A blue and red Turkey carpet had resisted and would continue to resist for a long time, the constant passage of many feet. It was rather a dark landing and the lights were on, though, outside, darkness had not fallen yet, and these lights were dimmed by parchment lanterns, repeating at their edges, the colours in the carpet. The general effect was approved by Julia and John alike, as comfortable and richly modest, but to-night he was oppressed by it. The younger children were asleep, the voices of Robert and Sybil were silent or pitched very low, no sounds penetrated the green baize door separating the kitchen premises from the rest of the house. He hardly knew what to do or where to go. He reflected, like many another member of a family, that in none of these rooms, behind none of these doors, could he find a place which was all his own. It was the first time he had wanted one. It was the first time he had been aware of more than temporary hostile criticism in his home and though it was Julia who had enlightened him and offered most of it, he was much more concerned with, much more interested in, his elder children. There was a sense in which quarrelling with a wife, accusing and being accused, was of very little importance. Ideally, the relationship implied sympathy; practically and by its very nature, it allowed, as no other did, of fierce antipathy and verbal cruelty, as though one form of passion caused and let loose the others and then, after a time, submerged them. They would rise again and meanwhile they were not forgotten, neither were they much resented: they were accepted as part of the strange intimacy which, breaking down reserves, had to submit to consequent invasions.

This invasion had been more startling than any other. She had tried to show him how he appeared to her and, in doing so, she had revealed herself, but that, eventually, between him and her would, he believed, make little difference. For the moment, however, he did not desire her company and he leaned over the banisters and saw the drawing-room door ajar and knew she was listening for sounds of fury, holding herself in readiness to rescue. She must be feeling some disappointment, he thought, and, with more perspicacity than he was aware of, he told himself that whatever happened she would make herself the gainer: she would be a martyr or a miracle worker and she would adapt herself to either part and there was no denying that it was she who had enabled John to see Robert, sulkily hopeless, and Sybil, with candid, judging eyes, as two separate human beings with whom, to his surprise, he found himself wishing to stand well.

He felt very lonely on that landing, the solid doors all shut and Julia barring his escape below. He would have felt guilty, like an intruder, if anyone had found him there, standing on the carpet he had bought, within a few yards of the children of his body, in the house where his parents had lived and where he had spent part of his own youth, and he turned and went quickly into the bedroom he shared with Julia. It was hardly recognizable as the one his father had shared with his mother. In their day it had been definitely parental, solemn, rather dark, sacred to authority and secret conclaves on a domestic policy which almost invariably and, no doubt, with the best intentions, ran contrary to the inclinations of the children. The sober wall-paper, the curly walnut furniture, the great washing-stand with its two basins and two ewers, had disappeared and it was long since John had remembered that this room was once the scene of family law-making into which he had not lightly ventured, long since the house had been anything but his very own and, in that sense of possession, he had lost his recollection of himself as a young man moving among the rooms and on the stairs, or of his sisters as young women with masses of hair to which their hats were precariously attached with ornamental pins like skewers, and frilled beribboned petticoats under their modest skirts. And he remembered how they had all had a faint, unaccountable feeling of guilt in their pleasures and the conviction that these pleasures might be denied them at any moment, out of a capricious, disciplinary impulse. Yet they had been kindly parents and, for their period, they had been indulgent, but perhaps there had been times when they remembered their own stricter youth and wanted their children to have a taste of it, or felt some primitive unsuspected need to withhold what they had the power to give. It was the revenge which one generation was inclined to take on the next one, for its own sufferings, but John had to own that he had suffered very little and, in regard to Robert, his mind was already made up. It had been made up before he left the drawing-room but only now, as he looked out of the window and rattled the keys and money in his pockets, he faced his disappointment and humiliation.

He knew that, perhaps mistakenly, the best of himself went into the business and the people who served him there. There was not an errand boy in the establishment who avoided his eye as Robert did, not a young lady behind the counter who stared at him with Sybil's summoned courage. And yet, he had never been unkind at home; he had been quick-tempered, no doubt, but he was fond of his children and expected them to be fond of him. Now he was realizing that the affection of the dependent young does not necessarily accompany the states of youth and dependence, that love must be paid for. It cost some people very little, people with charm, people with beauty, but ordinary people like himself must work or sacrifice or spend to get it.

He started as the door was opened, and the pert housemaid entered to turn down the bedclothes for the night. What would she think of him standing there? Julia had no judgment in her choice of servants, this minx was quite capable of believing he was waiting for a sight of her and he hurried from the room.

It was just as he had been telling himself. There was not a place in the house he could call his own, but he could not stand on the landing for ever and he made towards the stairs. At that moment Sybil came out of the study and he stopped.

'Hullo,' he said, as though he had not seen her for a long time.

'Hullo,' she answered politely but with reserve and he was vexed at his sense of discomfort, almost of shyness. Last night he would have told her to be off to bed and given her a careless kiss: to-night he wondered what she was thinking, not only of him but of things in general. This was a nuisance. He could not spend his time puzzling about his children. Julia did more than enough of that. It was foolish because they would only let you know what they chose, but at least he knew that this was not the kind of daughter his sisters had been or seemed to be, not the kind he had always believed he wanted, with docility as her chief characteristic. In the carriage of her head, in her frank gaze, she betrayed her calm belief in her right to criticize, to form her own judgments and act on them when her time came. She was sixteen, a shapely bud, with all its petals tightly held together and no force except Nature's would loosen them to the fulfilment of their beauty. Without that warmth and urgency, she would be at fifty what she was now, though her colour might be a little faded or tarnished, a fine, rather rigid, virginal type of independence and candour, a woman who would want to set the world right and who would do something towards that end. But John did not look so far into her future. What he saw was a girl who might be a companion to him if he took a little pains and, to her evident surprise, he gave a quick, sly smile.

Her surprise had indignation in it, for here was authority laughing while her poor brother glowered at the books which mocked him with the reminder that soon the books of his duty would be the ledgers of the shop, and she could not feel friendly towards her father. Something of this John divined. Downstairs, Julia hovered distrustfully, here, his daughter eyed him sternly and while he rather enjoyed the thought of Julia's distrust, he would have liked a kinder glance from Sybil, but he still smiled as, with his hands in his pockets and looking now at his feet, he shook his head.

'Very awkward,' he said.

'And it will get worse!' Sybil exclaimed. 'He'll be such a bad draper and you'll be so vexed!'

'Ah!' He looked up. 'But I didn't happen to be thinking

of Robert. That's all settled,' and as he said the words, he told himself that buying and selling was certainly in his blood. He was bartering his family pride and his stubbornness and his power for the possible approval of this cool young person and, less eagerly, of the loutish lad behind the door. He might be making a bad bargain for himself and eventually for the children, but he was at the mercy of a mood composed of resentment, a gaily malicious spite, a threat of loneliness, a genuine kindness and a desire to confound his judges.

'I was thinking about you,' he said. 'Were you going to bed?'

'Yes, when I'd said good night to mother.'

'You ought to have some fresh air first. In the garden. Come on!'

He took her arm and hurried her down the stairs and past the open door of the drawing-room and talked cheerfully as he went. She hung back a little but his arm was strongly fixed in hers and he ran her out of the house and on to the lawn. There the pace slackened, but still he held her as they walked to and fro and he hoped they presented a pretty sight to anyone at the drawing-room windows.

'You'll sleep all the better for this,' he said.

'I always sleep well.'

'So do I. I'm a very uninteresting fellow. I never lose my appetite or my night's rest and I shall sleep well even to-night, even with a guilty conscience. Yes,' he said, and he dropped her arm for he knew now that she would not run away, 'I know I'm not treating Robert well. I'm dooming him to living on a pittance and trying to teach little boys the things he could never learn himself.'

'Oh!' After an astonished pause, Sybil flung her arms round his neck. The scene could not have gone better if it had been rehearsed. 'Oh,' she said, with her mouth against his ear, 'how lovely of you!'

267

'I don't know about that,' he muttered, 'but you can go and tell him. But no one else, mind!'

'There's nobody else to tell,' Sybil replied happily.

Had she forgotten her mother or did she still believe that one parent was always privy to the thoughts and actions of the other? He watched her as she ran back to the house, he answered the wave of her hand and he said to himself, a trifle grimly, 'But this sort of thing will want a lot of keeping up.'

CHAPTER XXXVI

BEFORE ten minutes had passed and when no grateful Robert had appeared to offer thanks, John doubted his power to sustain his benevolent attitude. He did not remember that the young do not know how to thank with grace and hesitate to do it clumsily: he did not know that there is nothing more embarrassing than the sudden granting of a desire despaired of, nothing which so immediately, though temporarily, loses all its value, for he had never ardently wanted anything he could not get for himself. But he had never made anyone so costly a gift as this one to his son and he expected from Robert something equivalent to Sybil's demonstration.

'I wish they were all girls,' he thought.

A son to his own mind, with his own interests and ambitions, would have been a great possession. He did not imagine much or often, but he had certainly looked forward to the time when he and Robert would set off for the shop together, he had pictured their work and worries and successes shared and he believed he would actually find a pleasure in occasionally preferring the younger man's judgment to his own, for he would be a shrewd man who was shrewder than his father. That was all gone and he felt cheated, but he knew he had cheated Julia by giving her what she wanted and, soothed by this thought, he filled his pipe and lighted it and strolled to the bottom of the garden. It was a time of day he liked, in warm summer weather, when the sky was still pale though the earth and the trees and plants were darkening. The sky, at this hour, was like a kind old nurse who allowed the children a light to go to bed by and gave them plenty of time before they need settle themselves for sleep but, at what she judged to be the proper moment, she would carry the candle away, going very slowly, as though, when she left the nursery, she had a long corridor to follow. There was no fuss, no harassing; it was an orderly, time-honoured procedure against which there was no appeal. And John found it very peaceful among the vegetables. In spite of his tobacco, damp, green smells reached his nostrils and they came from his own possessions. And, from this point of the garden if he exercised a little care, he need see nothing which did not belong to him, not because his domain was vast, but because it was screened by a fine growth of trees. Yet he was not isolated; isolation did not suit him; he could hear the passing of a car, now and then, in the road beyond his palings, footsteps, too, and voices, but the trees gave him a privacy which, in his opinion, was worth all the flowers he would not have been able to distinguish from each other. He recognized the peas by their sticks and knew the edible from the ornamental kinds because they occupied different places in the garden, but they were all one in the important quality of being his. It was Julia's most important quality, too, and she was bound to him for ever. He need trouble the less about her. Such was his simple view of the situation. But, he began to see, the children were different. They could only truly belong to him if he was willing to let them go.

Queer, he thought, but he knew it was true and he marched quickly up the garden to the house. He would not wait for Robert's thanks. He would go and make them easy for him or pretend he did not want them, and it occurred to him, as he went up the stairs, that dealing, as a matter of course, in this sort of way with his customers, he rarely failed to be on good terms with them.

The Turkey carpet was thick, the study door was open and he was arrested on the topmost step by the sound of Julia's voice, by a special note in it, a little like the one she had used earlier in the evening with him, but strained of its anger, its spitefulness, to an exalted patience.

'It's a campaign,' she was saying, 'not just a single battle. I've won that for you, but a single battle doesn't settle much. Your difficulties are beginning. It's not only the fighting that counts. It's the endurance of all sorts of hardships.'

'I can't see any hardship in doing what you like.' This was Sybil's voice, cool and slightly scornful, the voice of the rising generation, and John knew that Julia would now be smiling with tender pity for her ignorance. He made no scruple of waiting for her next words. He had always assumed that, as he had no words for his children she could not hear, so there could be no question of overhearing what was not meant for him. Now, realizing this mistake, he was held where he was by a kind of fear.

'Not hard,' Julia said, 'when other people want it for you, too, but very difficult when it hasn't been given willingly. Robert will have to struggle against the feeling that he is doing wrong. I'm afraid he must be prepared for ridicule. He will have to be very brave and cheerful and patient. If he can't be all that, he must do as his father really wishes.'

'And not be brave and cheerful and patient?' Sybil inquired. 'I don't believe he need be anything but ordinary. I'm sure, in his heart, father wants him to be happy. Just be ordinary, Robert.'

'That's what's the matter with me. I can't be anything else.'

'And go and tell him how glad you are. You ought to do that.'

'I'm going, I'm going, but I don't know what to say.'

'It will be easy. I kissed him, but I suppose you can't do that. Just grin and mutter something. He'll understand. He was nice about it. Not cross a bit, and he won't be mean and make you miserable.'

'Ah, that's right. I'm glad you feel like that,' Julia said thankfully.

'Then why are you trying to make Robert believe he's going to be horrid?'

'Darling!' Julia exclaimed reproachfully, and John turned and went very quietly down the stairs. The fact that Julia was right and Sybil wrong, that he probably would be mean and make the boy miserable, in spite of that moment of revelation in the garden, only made her treachery worse. He did not understand it. He was too much astonished to be enraged, but he was really wounded for the first time in his life and he did not know what to do with the sharp pain in his chest, the tight feeling round his head. He had an instinctive desire to leave the place where he had been injured, and, obeying it, he let himself out of the front door and marched up the drive, and in front of him, as though it were carried like a banner, there went the picture he had not seen of those three in the study. It was quite clear to him. It might be wrong in detail but, essentially, he knew it was correct. He saw Julia with an arm round Robert's unwilling shoulders and Robert wishing he could jerk it off. He saw Sybil with her fair head held up, the corners of her mouth turned down and Julia was not pretty any longer. Her face was blurred with the confusion she had made in his mind. She was a fool. He had always thought she was a fool and often said so and he had not cared. Her affectation of wisdom, combined so oddly with her childish beauty had been an irritation and a delight. He liked to mock it and he wanted no rivalry with his own hard common sense. She was a relaxation, a plaything, an opportunity for tyranny or kindness. Silly and sweet, she was, but not malicious, never malicious. Her anger, though he had been influenced by some truth in what she said, had seemed like the simulated anger of a puppet, but it came to him now that it had been real, that it had been stored for a long time, that Robert's affairs were the immediate, not the true cause of it. What was the cause then? he asked, bewildered.

The picture had vanished and the Downs lay stretched before him. The double row of elms looked black and solid, sure of themselves, their place in the world and what they had to do in it. Far away, he saw their point of convergence and he knew they did not meet, yet he was glad they seemed to do so. In a vague way, without thinking, he felt reassured by this semblance of a design, but perhaps it was only the quietness of the night and the sense of space that calmed him. He could see no moving figures on the grass; the surrounding roads shone so whitely that there was hardly need of the lamps edging the pathways. On these there were a few stray walkers and he could hear their footsteps; he could hear, too, the sound of tramcars, out of sight, as they laboured to the top of Nunnery Road. On his left, half a mile away, he both saw and heard them; on his right, by the railings of the cliff wall, motionless figures were standing and the solitary ones seemed symbolic, even to John's mind, and larger than life size, as they looked over the gulf and towards the sea.

But why was Julia angry? he asked again, stepping on to the dark grass. Her rage had broken on him suddenly, like a big wave appearing out of a gentle sea. He could understand that. He did not want to find a cause for that. He had his own violent uprisings and never troubled to trace them to their origins. They were gone in a moment and he forgot them and expected his victims to forget them, too, but Julia's gentle words in the study were like the backwash his own waves never had, because they wasted their own force. Julia's backwash of shallow water flattened itself viciously on the shore and dragged things from it, not only common pebbles but little treasures dropped there, as though it had a thousand eager claws, and yet its voice was soothing. 'I don't understand it, I don't understand it,' he

s
273

said aloud, as he walked down the avenue of elms, then, seeing that satisfying point of convergence gradually disappearing to make a doorway for the sky where some light still stayed, he turned back, to see another point at the other end and this, too, widened, but now the doorway was almost blocked by a big house standing back from the Downs. The trees were playing tricks with him, Julia was playing tricks with him. Why should she? Why should she try to set the children against him, telling them the worst truths about him, instead of helping him to make them false? That was the action of a woman who hated him and of course she loved him. Then why? he questioned piteously. He could explain why the trees teased him: it was because he chose to deceive himself, to see them as they were not, and, stopping as he stumbled over a protruding root, he found that he had stumbled, too, on an idea and aloud, he said solemnly, in a low voice, 'Perhaps I've never really seen her. Perhaps I've never looked,' and then he added, 'And I don't want to. I don't want to see her again.'

But he knew he could not escape that discomfort. He was the prisoner of his circumstances and convictions and the conventions of his world. He was much too practical to dally with the possibility of sacrificing his position and his obligations to a disappointment, a disillusion, which would soon lose its poignancy. That sort of thing, he thought, was what middle-aged men did in books. It was what he had half-suspected Stephen of doing. They came to the limit of their endurance or they had a sudden sense of futility and they walked off, leaving their possessions behind them. It would take much more than malice and deception in Julia to persuade John to such a parting and the neglect of his undertakings. He had every intention of sleeping in his comfortable bed to-night and going to the shop to-morrow, though in one he would have Julia for a close neighbour and in the other no hope of Robert's company. He would just go on as usual, like other humdrum men with a sense of duty and already he was suffering a little less.

She's done herself more harm than she's done me, he decided, making for the cliff wall and wondering if it was too late to call on Stephen. It was ten o'clock and as dark as it was going to be. Where the sky seemed to overhang the distant channel, there was a bar of light and the chief darkness was in the woods on the other side of the gorge. It was low tide in the river and the lamps on either edge of it, looking very thin and small, two hundred feet below, seemed humbly to cast their reflections on the mud, protesting that this was the utmost they could do, and John, glancing down, regretted, as a good citizen should, all this mud which so seriously affected the size of ships capable of docking in the port of Radstowe. Slowly he followed the curve of the railings. A pair of lovers, close clasped, did not stir as he passed; a man, gazing seaward, his head lifted, gave John a quickly ignored impression of distress; a woman, at the point where the railings ceased with the sheerness of the drop, made a movement towards him as he approached, then seated herself, facing him, on the low stone wall.

He distrusted any movement of a lonely feminine figure at night and he turned on his heel sharply, but a voice called him by his name, Celia's voice, unexpectedly pleasant to his ears in its familiarity and warmth.

'It's only me,' she said. 'I'm afraid I frightened you.'

'Pooh!' he said, 'what should I be frightened of except finding you alone here at this time of night?'

'I'm safe enough,' she said. 'A more roving eye than yours, John, would have seen at once, by the shape of me, that no one else was in danger, either,' and he, off his usual guard of primness in such matters, said tolerantly, 'Oh, there's no accounting for tastes.' Then, as she laughed, he remembered to be an elder brother.

'But what are you doing? Where's Gerald?'

'What are you doing yourself? Where's Julia?'

He dismissed this retort very simply. 'Don't be silly,' he said. 'I suppose you've been to the Careys'.'

'If I had, I shouldn't have been allowed to go home by myself. So few people understand the pleasure of being alone. I'm just having an evening out because there's nobody at home. And Mrs. Carey's away. I'm sure you wouldn't approve of my dining with her husband in her absence. Neither would Julia. Ask her!'

'No need. Of course she wouldn't. And I don't much approve of your visiting them at all. You shouldn't run after people better off than yourself. It looks bad and so would Mrs. Carey if she was younger. All that paint! As it is, she's just a figure of fun. And you say she's away? Why, I saw her myself this very afternoon from my office window.'

'Did you? Are you sure?'

'Perfectly. You can't mistake her.'

'No,' Celia said, and she looked towards Pauline's house, only a long stone's throw away and a little downward. 'In her car?'

'I've never seen her out of it.'

Celia lifted a hand and swung it back and forth. 'Which way was she going? This or that?'

'Towards The Slope. You're very curious. It's quite plain,' he said disapprovingly, 'that it's you who do all the running.'

'I never run. I'm much too lazy,' Celia said, as she stood up. 'But let's walk to the other corner, I can manage that, and then I'll go home.'

'I shall have to take you.'

'Oh, nonsense!' Celia said. She could see the chimneys of Pauline's house against the brightness in the sky. A light from a window might have found its way through the trees and shrubs, but she could see none and for reasons which

276

seemed to her absurd but were nevertheless powerful to stay her, she could not go and rouse the household and have her fears quieted or confirmed.

'I'll go back now,' she said, 'and you'd better go home, too. Julia will be anxious.'

'I daresay,' he replied grimly, 'but I thought I'd pop in and see Stephen for a minute.'

'So he's back, too, is he? What a lot of disappointments for Julia!'

She expected a question or a protest, but he was silent. What she did not expect was that he would take her arm and hold it until he left her on the Terrace, and kiss her affectionately at parting. He was doing all the unlikely things and leaving the likely ones undone.

'They must have had a quarrel,' she thought, as she went, upstairs, hoping that Catherine had not arrived before her and hurrying up the last flight when she saw a light through the fanlight above the door.

'I don't like you to be here alone,' she exclaimed. 'I made sure you wouldn't be back before ten o'clock.'

'I wasn't. It's a quarter to eleven.' The bland face of the kitchen clock confirmed this statement, and Catherine, munching a well-buttered crust, said indulgently, 'You haven't much sense of time, have you? But it didn't matter. I looked under all the beds and in the cupboards, because I'd always rather know the worst at once, but it wasn't there. Of course, I made up that Jimmy had been hurt and you and father were at the hospital, and things like that, you know, variations on that theme, but it didn't spoil my appetite. I was frightfully hungry. The Sanders's meals are much worse than ours.'

'You restore my self-confidence.'

'Heaps of silver dishes, though.'

'Ah, there I can't compete.'

'A silver tureen . . . and the parlourmaid ladling the soup out so grandly, as though there were turtles in it, and all I found was a very thin slice of carrot and one pea and absolutely no flavour. Then we waited for a long time and Mrs. Sanders talked quickly so that we wouldn't notice the pause, till another silver dish came in with five fish-cakes on it, tiny, about the size of pennies. Five, for four people!

Of course, I couldn't take the last one when I had the chance. I thought Mr. Sanders might want it. But he shook his head at it and so did Mrs. and so did Mary, and down it went to the basement. But I still hoped for the best. I thought there might be a chicken to make up, but not at all. Four extremely skinny cutlets, leaning against a small mound of potato, and after that, rhubarb. Rhubarb! Without blanc mange or anything sturdy like that to bolster it up. Just rhubarb, washing about like seaweed in a pool. I don't know how the Sanders live! I like my inside to tell me when I've had enough to eat, but perhaps intellectual people don't need so much. You know, they talk to each other across the table about serious subjects, asking each other's opinions and then listening attentively to the answers, as though they'd never met before. That's not what I call family life. And I was so cross and so hungry that I almost didn't care about Grandmamma eating gingerbread out of a paper bag. So you see, I was brought pretty low.'

'And you've nearly skinned that loaf. Well, I took a lot of trouble about bone-building foods when you were a baby and your teeth are my reward. What we lose on the loaves we gain on the dentist. Go to bed. We'll ask Mary Sanders back one day and have an enormous lump of boiled beef, with dumplings, and a roly-poly pudding.'

'Yes, let's. Good night, pet. Where's Jimmy? Where's father?'

'I don't know to both those questions.'

'What a good thing. It's lovely that nobody need tell. I'm sure Mr. Sanders wouldn't go a yard without explaining, and he'd probably take his umbrella.'

'I'm glad you're satisfied on the whole,' Celia said meekly.

'It's very gratifying. But what can be the matter with you? It's not at all the proper thing for a young person to approve of her home.'

'I don't approve of it much, when you're not in it.'

'It doesn't often happen.'

'No. What have you been doing?'

'I went for a walk.'

'How exciting!'

'And I met your Uncle John.'

'On purpose? Did he scold you?'

'No. No, I shouldn't call it scolding. A little advice, you know. As a matter of fact, he was rather sweet and I enjoyed being with him very much. He hardly spoke all the way from the cliff wall until he left me here.'

Catherine laughed, as she was meant to do, then she became grave.

'If you can enjoy that, what a dull life you must have.'

'Dull?'

'Well, isn't it? Just looking after the house. The same old thing day after day.'

'All the days are different,' Celia said, clearing away the crumbs Catherine had left on the table. 'And there's a different dream every night. I promise you I'm not dull and I'm very happy.'

It was true, though it might have been truer to say that she was not unhappy. She was anxious about Richard and uneasy to hear of Pauline's presence in Radstowe. Whether it was a good or a bad sign in regard to Richard's illness, it was strange that she had not spared a few minutes to give the latest news, but Celia's happiness rested on her knowledge that, whatever happened, she had the best she would ever have of him inviolably safe. Then she remembered Meredith and saw how stupid she had been. Yet if Pauline could leave Richard for Meredith, why had she ever let Meredith go? And remembering that boy as she had last seen him, Celia said seriously, 'I have a great deal to make me happy.'

'That's all right, then,' Catherine said, with one of her hearty kisses, 'but it can't need very much to please you.'

Fortunately, she did not understand how big a thing in Celia's life she was herself. She was the reward of virtue, if ever there was one, of physical virtue though of mental frailty. She had, as it were, three parents, two of the flesh and one of the heart, and the result was a daughter who was more than any woman had the right to hope for. Celia allowed herself, this evening, to be a little doting and she decided that without Jimmy, without Richard, even in a slum instead of in this fair city, she would have no cause for complaint so long as she had Catherine. No doubt she seemed ordinary enough to other people; to Celia she was like a constant spring-time, with the warmth of its sunshine, the freshness of its winds and the clean smells they carried. She was rough sometimes, frank always, never stupid. She might be witty when she was old enough to choose her words and targets and already she was pretty and did not know it.

But she'll marry the first reasonably possible man who wants her, Celia thought, because she won't value herself enough or think it's worth while to say no. How can one save her from that? But she'll make a job of it, she'll make a job of it. Better than I've done. She's loyal all through. I don't know where she got it from. It can't have been from me.

She foresaw that the cause of present happiness might be the one of future sorrow. She could not bear to have Catherine wasted; yet, actually, she knew no one could waste her but herself. She let it go at that, and gladly, because she dreaded problems and it was foolish to look ahead for them. Already she was faced with one which must be solved — the necessity of enabling Catherine to earn her living. The problem was one more of choice than of means, but week by week and month by month she shelved it, telling herself that she disliked discussion, the reading of prospectuses, and, most of all, the making of a decision.

But I shall have to talk to Gerald, she thought, as she

prepared for bed and looked about her with permanent distaste for her surroundings. How many days were there in the year? She had to think for a minute before she found the answer. There were three hundred and sixty-five, except when something funny happened in leap year. And there were just as many nights and she had not spent a single one of them outside that bed for years and years, except on the rare occasions of family holidays when she had slept in a worse bed with the same companion. For just as long, she had not eaten a breakfast she had not prepared herself, or missed taking in the milk, washing the dishes and plying a duster and because, in truth, she was not dull in following this routine, she feared there must be something definitely lacking in her though she was not aware of it herself. But then, she thought, folding her clothes neatly on her own particular chair, leaving the other vacant for Gerald's garments and thinking how very sordid the aspect of this room would be to the eyes of people whose maids and men whisked away their underclothes and produced clean ones the next morning, but then, she thought, it was just as monotonous to eat, each morning, a breakfast someone else had cooked and not to do the dusting and wash the dishes. Her's seemed a very narrow world, but these simple tasks gave her mind space to roam in, far more space than was possible to a woman who was doing important public business. That sounded very well, she decided. It sounded meditative and wise and she was neither. She was simply making excuses for the laziness which would not learn why leap year had to be, or which of the heavenly bodies chased the others, for the nature which feared excitement and change and strong emotions.

'I believe I drugged myself twenty years ago,' she said, 'and I've never broken the habit. It produces inertia and I'm sure that's what I've got.'

Nevertheless, she was lively enough to listen anxiously for

the steps of her menfolk on the stairs, to feel relief when she heard them and later to be irritated into sleeplessness by Gerald's gently puffing snores. She blamed the snores, though they were not altogether responsible. She had pretended to be asleep while he undressed, and she heard him breathing rather heavily in his care not to wake her, but once she had half-opened her eyes because the breathing and the creaking stopped, though the light was still shining on her face, and she had seen him standing in his vest and trousers, a middle-aged figure no more attractive than her own, but his attitude, the lift of his head, the way he held his arms, was like that of a runner about to leap forward in a race. Honour among thieves, she thought, shutting her eyes again. She had no right to watch him, she was vexed by the memory of that unlikely look of eagerness and purpose, ashamed that she should be happiest when he was uninteresting, commonplace, set contentedly in his rut even though, or because, she did not like the rut he had chosen. Then she could feel that she had done as much duty by him as he could appreciate or should expect, but she knew, and to-night her certainty was confirmed, that sometimes, when he was out of her sight or thought himself unobserved by her, he was another person, for better or for worse, for worse, probably, when he was with the builders of his little houses and readily adapted himself to their ways and speech, for better now, when he believed she was asleep. It was a strange thing to say of that stoutish man, in a drab vest and with his braces hanging down, but he looked like a man on a hill, with the wind blowing and a goal before him.

When he began to snore she distrusted that swift impression. It was highly incompatible with the noise he made. A more shattering sound, a fierce trumpeting, would have been more fitting than this gentle puffing, but it was a shame that any but loving ears should hear it and on this kindlier thought she fell asleep.

When she woke, she could not tell how long afterwards, it was to a heavy silence. Perhaps the silence had waked her. It was heavy, but it had the quality of a thick mist which may stir at any moment and allow a glimpse of beauty or danger before it settles down again, and the silence was broken, the mist stirred, when Gerald began to speak. In its peculiar clarity and high-pitched tone, she recognized the voice of a sleeper and almost at once she touched him and with pathetic docility the talking stopped. He did not wake. He need never know what he had told her, so little in actual words that she could discount it altogether, so much in possibility and even likelihood, it fitted so well with the hints John had given her and she had tried to forget, that she could not prevent her mind from speculating or her heart from feeling anger and distress.

Holding to her edge of the bed, she stealthily put another inch between her body and his and even the thought that she, too, might at some time have made revelations in her sleep, did not lessen the necessity to avoid him.

CHAPTER XXXVIII

'You were very late last night, Jimmy,' she said.

'Not last night,' he corrected her amiably. 'It was this morning. Did I wake you?'

'I wasn't asleep. I hardly had any sleep last night,' she said. Then, disliking this slight note of complaint, she added, 'But people always think they sleep much worse than they do.'

'I'll get my own breakfast to-morrow and you can have an extra hour. I'll get it every morning, if you like.'

'I shouldn't like it at all. I want you to have a few extra hours yourself. You're burning the candle at both ends, as my mother used to say, though we had very little chance of doing it.'

'I don't suppose you had a handy cousin, had you, to give you a taste of night life in Radstowe?'

'Is there such a thing?'

'If you know where to find it.'

'Fit for Susan?'

'Yes. She liked it.'

'That's a very poor answer.'

'Well, she wouldn't have liked it if it wasn't fit for her, would she?'

'I suppose you think not.'

Jimmy looked at her gravely. 'Yes, you're right. I'm sure you had very little sleep. I don't believe you slept at all.'

'I'm sorry, Jimmy. Go on. Did you dance?'

'Dance? No. But we walked for miles.'

'In the country?'

'Down by the docks. Backwards and forwards. Over the bridges. Across the water in all the ferries and then I got a boat and rowed down the river in my waistcoat and shirt sleeves. Pity I wasn't wearing a bowler hat! I was pulling against the tide and that took time, but I came back with it easily enough.'

'That was a novel kind of excursion.'

'Yes,' said Jimmy dryly, 'that was rather the idea. And now I shan't go near her for at least a week.'

'And will that be a long time?'

'I think it will be about right.'

'You've worked it all out,' she said, a little sadly.

'No, I'm trying experiments as I go along.'

'But you can't spend your life doing that.'

'Why should I?'

'If it's necessary now,' she said slowly, 'to be a little different, to rouse curiosity, it will be necessary afterwards. I mean for happiness. The state of marriage doesn't dissolve difficulties that were there before. It increases them. At least it does for women.'

'I thought you liked her.'

'I like you better. Yes, it must have been very romantic, even with you in your shirt sleeves, to go down the river at night, especially if her family didn't know where she was.'

'Prudence knew. But you needn't try to spoil it.'

'Oh,' she said from her heart, 'I'm not trying to do that. Keep what you can. There's never much of it. I'm only trying to spare you pain. It's a foolish occupation and I always meant to avoid it.'

'I don't intend to be hurt.'

'None of us does, my dear. But you mustn't tell me these things so early in the morning. You'll agree that I'm not genial and I haven't had time to gather my wits together.'

'What do you want your wits for?' he asked slyly. 'To manage me tactfully?' He made a grimace, less sentimental than a sigh but doing duty for it. 'I rather wish you could.'

She followed him down the stairs and then stood on the Terrace in the cool emptiness of the morning. The sky over

286

Easterly was pale but, above Celia's head it was already blue and the birds among the trees across the road had been singing for a long time. They had waked in a better temper than she had and they meant everyone to know it, but there were not many people to hear them. As she looked along the broad sweep of the pavement, she could see a maidservant beating a mat against the railings and another kneeling to scrub a doorstep, but habits had changed since her mother's servants had risen at six o'clock and now, at a little after seven, she had the place almost to herself. A milkcart was in the road below, a charming vehicle, low hung and backless to make ascent and descent easy for the driver who drove standing. It had a jaunty appearance with the reins lifted over an iron bar to avoid the shining cans: it was rather like an ancient chariot, but its uses were for peace and a common necessity for the morning milk had preserved this relic of the past. No motor car could have followed of itself the movements of the agile milkman, as this pony did. He moved very slowly past the area doors that gave on to the street, the areas of those houses still inhabited by a single family. He stopped where a flight of steps gave access to the Terrace, while the milkman deposited his cans and bottles for the dwellers in the flats and Celia had not a doubt that the pony knew how many pints each household took, knew the price of the milk and did addition sums in his head. The clattering of the cans, the jingle of the harness, the wise pony, the cheerful briskness of the man, all this she could have seen and heard in her youth and she felt tender for her youth which was far enough behind her to seem excellent in many of its aspects. And so it had been. There had been rigour in it and a certain narrowness — there would have been serious trouble if she had wandered about the city in the middle of the night, even though she had been accompanied by a stalwart cousin — there had been too little elasticity about what could or could not be done and thought and said, but there had been a great simplicity, a frugality of material desires and satisfactions not dependent upon incomes. It depended on the point of view, on a fear of self-indulgence or indulging others to their hurt, a view lacking generosity and courage but productive of a kind of hardihood, as was the comparative disregard of the feelings of the children. Their sensibility was hardly acknowledged. It was hit or miss with words and actions and effects were only noticeable when they happened to annoy authority, while she, with her one son and one daughter, was sensitive to every expression or tone of voice, and that could not be good for them. She did her best to conceal this weakness; this morning it had got the better of her.

'But she'll never marry Jimmy,' she said. 'I wish to goodness she'd marry someone else and do it quickly, and then, he's so scrupulous, he'd never look at her again, he'd manage not to think of her.' It seemed as though it were she and Gerald, with their sterner upbringing, whose thoughts strayed and whose eyes took their pleasure, and she decided that the best of Jimmy's generation must be the best there had ever been. With far more liberty of action and less force of public opinion, it was readier than hers to follow virtue for its own sake. She wondered if he would despise her, if he knew her, but she did not think he would. These young people were not censorious; they had dropped so much that was not necessary; they travelled very light. And she could not go with them. She could start them on their journey and then she could only watch them and welcome them back if they came.

She saw the postman coming along the Terrace and knew it was time to coax or scold Catherine out of her bed and into her bath before Gerald wanted his, but she waited for the letters and took all there were for the house, promising to drop them through the appropriate doors as she went upstairs. She saw that there was one for her, from Hester, with a London postmark, and she read it as she stood on the landing under the skylight. She read it several times before she put it in her overall pocket and went about her business, stirring the porridge, toasting the bread, frying the bacon, making Jimmy's bed while Catherine had her breakfast, keeping an eye on the clock lest she should be late for school and an ear on Gerald's movements, lest his food should be overcooked or underdone. This was her busiest hour and it was her boast and the only domestic achievement on which she prided herself, that no one had ever been late for school or business through her fault.

But Gerald had no definite time for his departure, an inconvenience under which she endeavoured to be patient, and this morning he had not finished dressing before Catherine was running at a great pace down the stairs.

'She'll break her neck, one of these days,' he said, with a chuckle, and complacently pulled and patted his coat into place.

In his least shabby suit he looked fresh after his bath and cheerful after the night's rest which had ruined her own and she felt, or rather there suddenly flowered in her, a long suppressed rage at the necessity of serving him in his bed and at his board. It flowered because he took it all for granted, though he talked to another woman in his sleep, because he looked pleased with life this morning when Hester's letter had set her own nerves on edge, because he dared to talk jokingly of disaster to Catherine and she felt an uncontrollable desire to hurt him and wipe the cheerfulness from his face.

'Ah well,' she said, speaking with false calm, 'if Catherine's hurt, the staircase will only be taking its revenge. You've spoilt a lovely thing. It might be glad to spoil another. But I've tried to appease it. I always apologize,' she spoke more vehemently, 'I always apologize as I go up and down.'

'I don't see why you should. You're not in the least responsible for anything I do. At first you wouldn't be and now you can't be. And that must be a comfort to you.'

'Yes,' she agreed, hitting back swiftly, 'but I can't help seeing it.'

'No, and I see it too,' he said. 'I'd rather someone else had done it, but then the someone else would have had the profit. It's not so simple,' he said a little wearily and looked vaguely for his breakfast.

She brought it to him. 'At least that's always ready.'

'Yes. Thank you.'

'And do you realize,' she said, deliberately choosing the wrong moment, 'that we have to do something about Catherine's future, unless the problem's solved in the way you suggest so pleasantly, and I shall want the money we've been keeping for her.'

'Not for a year or so, will you?'

'Perhaps not, but I'd like to have it, in the savings bank or somewhere.'

'I don't see the sense in that.'

'I'd like to have it,' she repeated stubbornly.

'But why? Why now?'

'In case I want it.'

'What for?'

'For Catherine.'

'But,' he said, puzzled and uneasy, 'isn't it just as safe with me? Aren't her interests mine?'

'I don't know,' Celia said quietly. 'You may have others that are more important.'

He pushed away his plate and stood up. 'Have you?' he demanded, and when she shook her head, he said, looking at her steadily and not with friendliness, 'I believe you think I haven't got the money. What d'you think I've done with it?'

'I don't think anything. I just want it. I don't know anything, either. I don't know what you earn, or what you owe or how much people owe you. You've never told me.'

'You've never asked.'

290

'Why should I? You give me as much as you can afford, I suppose. Perhaps more.'

'Or perhaps less?'

'No, not that. And I'm more afraid of getting too much than of too little. And I do my best with it.' She paused. She felt some praise was due to her for innumerable small self-denials, but she did not get it, and, for a moment, she forgot his presence. 'But not cotton handkerchiefs,' she said. 'I never went as far as that. The children, had them when they were little and I always felt ashamed, but then, they lost so many. A dirty cotton handkerchief is one of the nastiest things there is, except a clean one,' she smiled, 'spread on the knee to catch the crumbs.' But Gerald seemed to miss this allusion to his mother.

Very slowly, he looked round the room as though he wanted to find something he could recognize. 'I can't make you out,' he said in bitterness and bewilderment. 'I can't make you out. Haven't you any feelings, that you are so careless about mine? Or are you stupid? Perhaps that's been it — all the time. You say the cruellest things you can and then begin babbling about handkerchiefs. That's important. Much more important than anything I'm trying to say. But then, you despise me. You've despised everything I've ever done, and I've known you did, though I've tried very hard to pretend you didn't, poor fool! But I suppose no one could live at all if he couldn't deceive himself a little. The reason you've never asked me about my earnings isn't that you trust me, you've shown you don't do that, but because you think they're the fruits of — of sin, and you try to forget them.' He added dryly, 'But not always. Sometimes you like remembering them.'

Instead of further lowering her eyelids at this true charge, she lifted them and looked at him fairly, in the sort of self-defence she would have used if a stranger had gazed at her naked body. There was no dignity in trying to retreat or

291

hide. She put the burden of retreat on him, but he was in no mood to accept it. Thoughts long kept in check were now unleashed, and he said scornfully, 'You've never considered, you couldn't imagine, that I might see them like that, too. But what would you and Catherine do if there were no fruits at all? It isn't you who've had to force the crop. I know I'm not particularly talented. I'm not like your friend Carey, but I might have done better work if you'd ever tried to help me. You haven't. You've just been tactfully and damningly silent or said how neatly the plans were drawn! And as a matter of fact, though this won't please you, our tastes are very much alike. That house of yours . . .'

'My house?'

'The one you cut out of a newspaper, months ago. It was lying on your desk for ages, on purpose, perhaps, but that wasn't necessary. It's just the one I wish I could have designed myself. Mind you, I'm not asking for help now. I don't want it, it's too late. And you shall have your money as soon as possible.'

'No,' she said. 'No . . .' but he had gone and almost at once she heard the banging of the hall door.

CHAPTER XXXIX

THE first thing she did was to find the picture of her house and tear it into little pieces. It had lost its value for her. When she first found it she had left it on her desk only because it was a real effort to her to put anything away and Gerald was quite mistaken in thinking she wanted him to see it; he was much at fault in fancying she would choose this method of instruction, and he was inconsistent, for if he could believe her capable of this tiresomely delicate hint, how could he believe in her complete disregard for all his doings?

'But now,' she thought, 'he wants to believe it.'

Did she not know, from experience, that desire to disclaim an outworn allegiance? But she had not suspected it in him and she realized that there were limits to the power of her womanhood, of all the physical attributes he had loved in their young days, the rich indolence of her movements, the low voice, the drowsy eyes. She knew he might learn to hate them, she was not sure he had not begun already. His quick response to any kindness had always touched her to a sense of guilt, but because it assured her of an affection still strong and eager, it had made her capricious and ungenerous with her gifts. She could see all this; she had a humiliating sense of failure, a strange sense of insecurity. This was in no way connected with material things, though it was perhaps comparable to Gerald's feelings in transferring her capital from his account to hers. She had lost her reserve, her guarantee of worth, her resource against a rainy day and, thinking thus, it occurred to her that Gerald's position was exactly the reverse. He had been enduring his rainy season all these years, drawing on her for the little she could spare him, and now the sun was shining and he had no need of her, he could afford, now, to relax his hold of his poor support. He must, however, have found someone to take her place, or why had he looked like that last night? Who was this Maudie — and what a perfect name for her — whom he apostrophized in his sleep? And what did it all matter? As she had once priggishly reminded Gerald, there were worse things happening, all over the world, and if she had not waked, hot and flaccid, after a wretched night, if she had not been troubled about Jimmy and Susan, if Hester had not written an annoying, rather silly letter, and Gerald had looked tired instead of pleased and hearty, she would not have lost her careful rhythm, there would have been no storm in a teacup.

'In a teacup,' she repeated. 'I live in a teacup and forget it isn't the whole world.'

Then she heard Miss Riggs in the hall and remembered the breakfast things left untidily on the kitchen table, Gerald's half-empty cup, his broken toast, the congealed bacon on his plate. It was too late to conceal these evidences of disturbance and she found Miss Riggs looking at them calculatingly as she removed her hat.

'We're very late this morning,' Celia said cheerfully.

Miss Riggs said nothing, and Celia began gathering up the plates and sweeping the fragments into the sink basket.

'That bit of bacon,' said Miss Riggs sternly, 'would have made a nice flavour for the soup.'

'I'd much rather it didn't.'

'And you'd better let me do the washing up.'

'I don't trust you,' Celia said. 'You're quite capable of picking the bacon out of the sink basket.'

'And there'd be no harm either, after I'd held it under the tap.'

'And you wouldn't tell me and that would be deceit. You're so sure of your own virtue, you think you can take risks with it. No, I'll look after all this. You can go and make my bed.'

Miss Riggs jerked her chin up and clicked her tongue against her teeth.

'I know, I know,' Celia said. 'It's the high point in slovenliness. I dislike it as much as you do, but one has to forget sometimes. One isn't a machine.'

'It'll have had a good airing, anyhow.'

'Yes, that's a comfort.'

Miss Riggs turned when she reached the door. 'But do, pray, keep a look out for the mustard on the plates.'

'I always scrape it off with my thumb-nail.'

'Yes. When you notice it. You'll never find it on any of the plates I've washed.'

'Oh, you're perfect,' Celia said. 'I've known that for years.'

Left alone with the dishes, Celia found herself repeating words she had read often, long ago, and not consciously remembered for years.

'Birds in the high hall garden,' she said. 'Birds in the high hall garden.' Where did they come from, those words? They made a most unsuitable accompaniment to her present task. 'High hall garden.' She knew better than to search for the next line. It would come if she pretended to be content with what she had. It was a good thing Miss Riggs had not heard that last remark. She would have made a lesson out of it. She was full of lessons, but she did not, as it were, bring them up. They just slipped easily over her brim, like water over the edge of a bowl.

'Birds — ' Celia said again and, suddenly, 'Birds in the high hall garden, when twilight was falling, Maud, Maud, Maud, Maud, they were crying and calling.'

Tennyson's Maud, of course. She had not read it since she was a girl but Maudie had brought it back unbidden. How strangely the mind worked. She had heard a name in the night and the indefatigable secretary who had charge of her memory had been silently busy with the files and the card indexes and, determined to find some sort of connection, had at last produced it.

She stepped back from the sink and leaned against the table, the little mop still in her hand and water dripping from it unheeded, while more of those words came back to her. Maud in the high hall garden, in gloss of satin and glimmer of pearls. Shine out little head sunning over with curls. Queen rose of the rosebud garden of girls. Pretty, but a little facile, she thought now. The black bat night was better, and the passion flower at the gate; the flute, violin, bassoon. She was very old-fashioned, she supposed, but she thought these were lovely words. They came back to her and with them came her youth when it seemed that for her, too, there must be a lover waiting in the scented darkness of a garden, when she could think happily of passionate grief and of love frustrated. Lovely words, she thought again; the words Maudie had brought back. Was Maudie lovely too? She did not believe it. She could not help seeing her as the typical barmaid of her girlhood, when barmaids were the dread, the ultimate horror of parents like her own, when they had bosoms and yellow, high-piled hair, a gift for improper repartee and a good-humoured rapaciousness. It was that, that idea of Maudie, although she had not thought it out, which had inspired her to ask for Catherine's money. If Gerald had called on Mary or on Ellen, she would not have trembled for her nest egg, but Maudie seemed to have her shining, pointed finger-nails already on it.

And I could be funnily improper too, if I liked, she thought unexpectedly, almost defiantly. Then she shook her head. But not with Gerald. She feared his response to that kind of humour, the piquancy whereof lay in restraint, and yet to him she must seem all restraint without the piquancy. Slowly and thoughtfully, she set the dirty water swirling in the bowl. It was true she had been of little use to him and if it was true that she had prevented him from doing better work, then she had sinned grievously, but these might-have-beens were so easy to produce and to believe in, they were so consoling to mediocrity. She might have been a perfect wife to another man, but would she? When two personalities tried to fuse they seemed to separate, to discover antagonisms, in the very effort.

'Miss Riggs,' she said, for Miss Riggs was getting the carpet sweeper from the cupboard, 'is Jo a good carpenter?'

'I reckon he must be.'

'Why? Just because he's your young man?'

This sally neither amused nor angered Miss Riggs. 'Because he's never out of work,' she said.

'Perhaps he always has to do it twice, or is that only plumbers? Oh, I'm sorry, Miss Riggs, dear. I forgot that Fred was one.'

Miss Riggs spread a newspaper on the floor to receive the accumulated fluff and grit from the carpet sweeper and she gave Celia a glance of reproach which had nothing to do with Fred or Jo, before she inquired, 'Are you trying to put me off him?'

'No, I'm just interested. Yes, I've seen the dust. Heaps of it, but I never do what I know someone else will do for me.' She raised her eyebrows. 'A mistake, perhaps. I was wondering, when you see Jo in the evening, and I suppose you see him every evening, does he tell you what he's been doing all the day?'

'He was never one to talk much.'

'Do you try to find out? Would he like you to try? Would he be hurt if you didn't?'

'Hurt? What would he be hurt for?'

'I just wanted to know,' Celia said meekly.

'There's only the one way of putting up a shelf and that's the right way and that's the way Jo'd do it.'

'You're sure of that?'

'Yes, but you can't talk a lot about it, can you?'

'I suppose not.'

'Any more than I could talk about the way I scrub this floor.'

'But suppose he was a cabinet maker,' Celia said persuasively, 'designing his own work, inlaying it with ebony and satinwood?'

'He'd just have to stop being,' Miss Riggs said. 'There's no call for that kind of thing nowadays. It's a pity,' she said, holding the shaft of the carpet sweeper with both hands and resting her cheek against them, 'but, the way I see it, a man's first job is to earn his living. And a woman's too,' she said, remembering her duties. 'We'll never catch up with the day at this rate.'

'Oh,' said Celia, 'must everything be sacrificed to speed? The cabinet makers, all the lovely leisurely things? The art of conversation went long ago, but why shouldn't we talk when we want to? We shall soon lose the use of our legs, except for stamping on pedals, and then words themselves will go because they won't be heard above the roaring of machinery.' She spoke with unusual animation and with some of the speed she disdained. 'Just gibbering, grimacing apes, that's what we shall be, hurling bombs at each other instead of coco-nuts. The other apes will be highly civilized in comparison. Perhaps they are already.'

'Don't you worry,' said Miss Riggs. 'There'll be plenty of talk as long as there's all these silly women about, saying everything three times to make themselves believe it matters.'

'You overrate their motives,' Celia said in her ordinary tolerant tone. 'They don't start with any doubts. They just start and for the same lack of reason, they go on. But perhaps there is a reason, hidden away somewhere. A psychologist might find it.'

Unfamiliar with this word, Miss Riggs marched off with the carpet sweeper and, through a natural association of ideas Celia found herself thinking about May and thinking about her with the kind of homely tenderness she had felt last night for John. It was extraordinary, she thought, this tie of blood and a shared childhood. The knot remained fast in spite of disagreements and essential differences. It hardly felt a strain which would break it in any other relationship, and putting her hand into the pocket of her overall, she took out Hester's letter and tore it up as she had torn up the picture of her house.

CHAPTER XL

'I DON'T see why I should have to climb up all these stairs to see an unprofitable client,' Stephen said, a few days later.

'Client? Has somebody left me a fortune? But in that case I shouldn't be unprofitable, should I? And upon my word, I don't believe I should know what to do with it. Yes I should though.'

She would settle an income on Gerald, relieve him from financial care and give him the opportunity to design any house he chose and then, she thought, as she rocked herself in her little chair, they would see what he could do. An income was probably the cruellest gift she could make him.

'What's the business?' she inquired.

'Mostly an excuse for seeing you.'

'Yes, I thought you'd be coming soon. That's why I put on my best frock.'

'Did you? Is it?'

He moved about the room, looking at one thing and the other, but he did not look at her; he did not so much as glance at the best frock which was a humble enough affair and a knowing eye might have discerned, under its general blueness, a suggestion of the pattern the silk had shown in its first state of a different colour. This negligence did not disturb the good conceit of herself that Stephen always gave her. No one made her feel more feminine, so little touched by time. If he did not look at her, he was conscious of her, not so much, she believed, of this separate woman Celia, as of some one roughly representative of woman, to whom he could mentally refer the others and even speak of them. She hoped he did not think of her as a safe, sympathizing soul. She wanted him to think of her as a materialization of all those qualities that tantalized, charmed, escaped, or comforted, but since he was rather a mysterious person, she was quite aware how mistaken she might be about him and about herself. However, this was the impression she had and it was the impression that mattered. It did no one any harm and she made the most of it. She rocked the chair; otherwise she was motionless; otherwise she might have been asleep.

'Gerald asked me to see you,' he said suddenly.

'How disappointing.'

'I told you it was a good excuse.'

'I don't see why you need one.'

'Well, a busy lawyer generally gets his clients to come to him, unless they're bedridden and I can't really afford the time I intend to spend here, but when else can I be sure of finding you alone?' He sank on to the sofa, rested his head on the cushions and stretched his long legs in front of him. They almost reached Celia's chair. 'Silly, of course, to want an excuse, but I can never enjoy myself in working hours without feeling guilty. D'you think our children feel like that?'

'Yours haven't any working hours,' Celia said suavely, but he would not be provoked into saying how much happier they would be and how much freer, if they had.

He chose, instead, to provoke her. 'About this money,' he said. 'Why don't you leave it where it is?'

'I don't know where it is.'

'But I do and it's quite well invested.'

'Then let it stay there,' Celia said slowly.

'It's in Gerald's name.'

'Well, I don't mind.'

'He seemed to think you did.'

'Yes I did, but now I don't and I told him not to bother about it. In any case, couldn't he have managed it without your help?'

'Easily, but I'm glad he came. Did you know he's been saving the interest?'

301

'Has he? Well, there can't be very much of it.'

'You ought to be thankful. There it is, for any emergency. He's been a good husband of your money.'

'But what's money for,' Celia cried, 'except to spend? And to think,' she said indignantly, 'to think how often I've gone miles out of my way and wasted shoe leather to avoid the butcher!'

'Do you owe him much?'

'Not a penny at present, but sometimes I've had to keep him waiting for a week.'

Stephen laughed, almost silently, with his head thrown back and his lean throat exposed. 'My good dear, don't you realize that there are dozens of people, with plenty of money, too, who insist on the best joints and keep him waiting for months?'

'Yes, I know, but it doesn't make me feel any better. I can't help believing he's anxious all the time, under his straw hat. He wears it all the year round you know. It seems such a strange thing to do. How much does the interest come to in a year? About fifteen pounds? Oh, if I'd known we had that to spare, I'd never have been so meek with him when he gave me too much fat.'

'It's as well you didn't know. You're just so much better off. Gerald's been a good husband of your money,' Stephen said again.

'And why shouldn't he be?'

'Why not indeed?'

'But you seem surprised.'

'Well, yes, a little, but not so much as you are. Anyhow, he's asked me to take over the job and I don't want to do it.'

'Two or three days ago you wouldn't have had the chance. Some trustful members of your family were afraid you'd made away with much more than my few hundreds. Did you think of that?'

'Yes, I thought of it.'

'But May didn't.'

'No, she wouldn't. But about this money.'

'I'd rather talk about you because I don't really quite understand why so many people, not your relatives, believe in you as they do. You haven't the kind of noble face which is the ultimate ruin of spinsters and old ladies, especially spinsters.'

'You've got to look after your money yourself, or let me, because Gerald won't.'

'Then you must.'

'Unless you tried to persuade him . . .'

'I have tried.'

'All right. I don't think you'd better sell out. The shares must be transferred to you and if you want the interest for the butcher, I'll let you have it as it comes in. Then that's settled, but it's a pity.'

'So many things are a pity. Haven't you any of your own without fussing about mine? With all your experience, you ought to know better than to try to help other people.'

'It's a professional habit. And Gerald's very decent, very decent.'

'You're rather late in making that discovery, aren't you?'

'Yes,' Stephen said frankly, 'I like him better now than I ever did before.'

Celia's smile, directed towards the hands folded on her lap, had a wifely sweetness, a superior knowledge and faith. It was almost worthy of Julia, but the effect was unpremeditated. She was picturing Gerald in Stephen's office, unconsciously and quietly a little dramatic, a simple, honest man who had been wronged but remained as loyal as possible in the circumstances, revealing a great deal in the very carefulness of his statements, portraying himself in an aspect to which another man must immediately respond. And because he had proved his honesty in this matter and the falseness of her feelings, too vague to be called suspicion

303

but, in his mind definitely and irremediably wounding, she was quietly and bitterly angry with him. He had put himself right with Stephen, as a representative of the family, at her cost, while she would have suffered many things rather than betray the least dissatisfaction with him. She forgot that this was less loyalty than pride and that he had his pride too. With her relatives he had always been conscious of their view of him as a worldly failure and also, perhaps as a man not quite up to their modest standards of manners and behaviour. In a fairer moment, she would have seen how much more important to him was his personal honour, possibly breathed upon by others as well as by herself, than any show of perfect union in the home. And deep in her heart, in spite of the intactness of her money, apart from any question of money, she remained distrustful of him, of something in his essence, as though his little houses were the expression of his meretriciousness and could not have been designed by an honest mind. And she had felt like this long before Maudie had taken definite shape in her mind. She had always believed there were minor Maudies with whom he had his little jokes; he had the look of a man who knew exactly what to say to them and she wished she had never seen him middle-aged and a little coarsened, never seen him out of the uniform with which he wore his young air of dedication, when he was timid of Maudies and indifferent to them. Yet she had seen that air again the other night, or something like it, and she regretted having seen that, too, for it put her somehow in the wrong; it also seemed to put him in a world, a good one, where she had no place. She had her own private world of the mind and she had never grudged him his, until she discovered that he really had one.

She lifted her head, and referring to Stephen's last words, she said, 'You've never taken the trouble to know him and can't you see that this sudden enthusiasm is a kind of insult?

It's the expression of your surprise at finding him as honourable as you are yourself.'

He gave her his queer oblique glance. She knew he was seeing through her, though he hardly looked at her. 'Don't give yourself away,' he suggested gently. 'What makes you think I should be surprised? You're a little, yes, just a little clumsier than usual. You are much better in defence than in attack but, with me, I don't see why you should bother about one or the other, except by way of practice. I think we understand each other pretty well.'

'All right,' she said. 'Put the foils away. Take off the masks or whatever those meat safes are called. You've done your duty as the family friend. Now you can start on what you came for.'

'Are you going to play fair?' he asked.

'Oh, this is your game, not mine. Have you had a letter from Hester?'

'Yes.'

'So have I. A day or two ago. And it wasn't a bit like her.'

'Wasn't it? But then,' Stephen inquired, 'what is she like?'

'Well, she isn't facetious.'

'Certainly not.'

'And her letter was. I didn't count the exclamation marks, but there must have been dozens. Very merry. Were you merry when you came home the other night?'

He did not answer that question. He said, with a little hesitation, 'May I see the letter?'

'No. I tore it up. It wasn't a letter I wanted to keep.'

'As bad as all that?' He moved uneasily, then rose and seemed to find some interest in the book-shelves.

'Well no, I don't suppose you would have thought so,' she said and she slipped into his place on the sofa. Sitting there, she had her back to the light and she felt safer, though it was not likely that Stephen would discover how much less that letter had troubled her for Hester than for herself, and if he

305

discovered it, he would not understand how these strangers to her secret, first Susan and then Hester, managed to spoil the vision she had cherished for so many years. It was she who had sent Susan to Paris and Susan had brought back a hat and the statement that Richard was a nice little man: it was she who had suggested Hester as an aid to Pauline in her ministrations, and Hester's letter, meant to be amusing, had made him a different person from the one she knew; it had shown her a man whose mantelpiece was thick with invitation cards, who seemed to have innumerable women friends calling to make inquiries and to leave flowers and fruit. All these invitations, all these flowers, seemed to turn him into a spoilt middle-aged bachelor, the sort of man whom women would naturally, and could safely, pet. She had not pictured him at parties, welcomed as a useful odd man at dinner tables, and she was jealous for her own view of him. For her he was rather solitary, genial enough when approached and always of a ready humour, but living, as she did, largely in the past. And, she had to own, that was where she wanted him to live.

Stephen was standing by the fireplace and looking at the ornaments on the mantelshelf.

'You see,' he said, addressing them, not Celia, 'I think I've been in love with her since she was about fourteen. I didn't know it then, of course. Why, why, why,' he demanded, and he picked up a little china figure and set it down again sharply, 'Why are we not allowed to know the important things until it's too late? It looks like malice. It's so senseless. Nobody wants to get into these tangles, they don't do it on purpose, and the punishment doesn't fit the crime. Crime!' He mocked his own word. 'That's a queer name for the best feelings one's ever had. I don't think I knew,' he said more quietly, 'until after your father died and she said she was going away. Well, then we had our few hours, good ones, very satisfying for the moment, but a sparse diet for a term of years. Sparse,' he repeated, and he turned to Celia as though he blamed her.

'Yes,' she said, and there was a thin, tired quality in her voice, 'yes, it's very sparse. But you've seen her sometimes, haven't you?'

'About once a year, when I'm in London.'

Celia nodded. 'Once a year.'

'Oftener than that, perhaps.'

'Oh, oftener!' She seemed to think this was not fair.

'But mind you,' he was determined to make the worst of his poor diet, 'It's only for an hour or two. At the very best, how many hours in the year?'

There was a pause before she answered. 'Six or seven, perhaps. In a lucky year there might be a few more.' And, as she spoke, she wondered why all the years had not been lucky and she felt a sudden anger for the excessiveness of Richard's restraint, while Gerald could spend his evenings as he chose, and against her will, she renewed her first doubt of the genuineness of the message Pauline had transmitted. Had it, at best, been inspired by her, in that softened moment when she believed Richard would recover?

'Six or seven,' Stephen was saying, 'I came to the conclusion it wasn't enough. Why should I waste happiness that couldn't possibly hurt anyone else? Why shouldn't Hester have some? But there were all the usual scruples and then, quite suddenly, there weren't any scruples at all.' He was silent for a moment before he asked, 'Do you remember how I told you to find the monkey in the puzzle? Well, Hester — it doesn't sound polite — but Hester was my monkey.'

'Yes. I knew. For one thing, it was odd that you should go away mysteriously at the very time when Hester wasn't to be found, when Pauline Carey wanted her, and now she's there and you are here.'

'Awkward,' he said, turning his back on her again but watching her through the mirror.

'I don't think so. I think I'm the only person who knows all the facts.'

'But you don't know all of them. I didn't ask Hester to meet me. I'm rather ashamed of that. Caution must be in my blood and it doesn't dissolve even under considerable heat. But I hope it was partly because I didn't want to ask her to do anything she would hate to refuse. I just told her where I was going, a place she'd told me of herself. And she was there. I knew she would be.' He paused and shrugged his shoulders, then lowered himself carefully into Celia's rocking-chair. The seat accommodated very little of him; part of his body and his legs made a shallow arch ending at his feet and he steadied himself with his hands on the carpet.

'And what do you think we did?' he asked. 'We walked up and down on a patch of grass in front of the house for about half an hour and then I marched five miles to the next inn. What d'you think of that?'

For a little while, Celia did not speak. She sat forward, holding her face in her hands and the picture of Stephen and Hester, pacing up and down in front of the guardian inn, was overlaid without being hidden by another, older picture with younger figures in it. And in this one the man limped painfully on his new leg. It was easier for the others, she thought, walking briskly, being sensible, with all their experience behind them. In neither of them was there physical suffering and loss, the bearing and the seeing of it, to weaken resolution. And they were not young. But, she was not sure; perhaps that made it harder. In youth there was so much hope.

'What do you think of that?' Stephen asked again.

'Well,' she said with a slight acidity, 'you seem very proud of it, but I think you did what was going to give you most happiness in the end. I'm sorry not to be more congratulatory, but that's what I think you did.'

Rather to her surprise, he said, 'I'm sure of it. I don't want congratulations. I don't feel particularly proud, but I'm puzzled about motives.'

'And you'll remain puzzled. Motives are the joker in the pack of cards — highly adaptable.'

'I'm not sure it wasn't a kind of cowardice, but whatever it was, we were agreed. As soon as we met we each knew what the other wanted and it was the same thing. The other thing just, somehow, didn't do. She went back to London by the first train the next morning and I had a day by myself, in the heather, in the sun, beside a stream.'

'Feeling better than you'd ever done before,' Celia said slowly. 'Profoundly at peace and yet elated.'

'Exactly.'

'But I wonder,' she said, 'I wonder how you would have

felt if it had been a very wet day and you'd had to stay in the inn parlour. Or do you think you would have gone striding into the storm and battled with the elements? — Again,' she added.

'There hadn't been a battle. I tell you it just happened, as easily as taking off a coat.'

'Ah yes, the chill comes later.'

'I don't know about that,' he said. 'It isn't an ordinary case.'

'My poor dear, have you ever heard of an ordinary one? There are always special circumstances or they wouldn't happen.' Nevertheless, she thought that only her own was completely beautiful and free of some touch of sordidness or stupidity.

'But these were very special,' he said, and with a shade of embarrassment, he added, 'There's a queer family likeness in all you girls. You seem to complement each other. That made the love more natural and the treachery much worse. Impossible. Anyhow, I've got back to my moorings and I'm glad to be there. I don't like and I'm not equal to these cutting out expeditions. I'm glad to be there,' he repeated, 'and not,' he said emphatically, squinting at her rather more than usual, 'not just because I prefer to be respectable and technically innocent, but because I really like them.'

'I'm very glad,' Celia said, and she thought May must have been inspired to a perfection of tact when he returned, and then, remembering her dignity in this very room, her stricken but loyal silence, her unlikely gift for producing beauty and serenity, she said softly, 'Have you ever looked for the monkey in May's puzzle?'

'Yes,' he said, 'I'm on the track. Rather a solemn ape, rather a superior animal.'

'H'm,' said Celia. 'That had occurred to me, too. If you can't persuade your mate to share the upper branches you prefer, you really must descend occasionally.'

'Do you do that yourself?' Stephen retorted.

'I've no need to,' Celia replied.

'Neither have I. It's not a question of higher or lower. It's only a different kind of tree.' He sighed. 'And it takes more than half a lifetime to learn that simple fact.'

'Arboriculture,' Celia said. 'The best hobby for the middle-aged.'

'Yes. I don't know why I'm sitting in this extraordinarily uncomfortable chair.' He struggled to his feet and then stood over her, frowning as he looked down. 'D'you know what troubles me most?'

'Still troubled? I thought you were all peace and plenty, so to speak.'

'You're a little bit tart, aren't you? What troubles me is that all these years I've had Hester on a sort of string. She could have broken it, I suppose, if she'd seen anything she wanted badly enough, but she didn't look. She was tethered by a sense of honour to me — what some people would call dishonour, and she might have wandered so far and had so much. And now she's forty. I have a home and I have children, but what's she got?'

'I don't think she's done so badly. She gets quite a lot of fun.'

'That's the stupidest and shallowest remark I've ever heard you make. What's the matter with you? What's Hester going to do when she's fifty, when she's sixty? Why didn't I think of that at the beginning? But then, one doesn't mean to have a beginning. We were in the middle of things before we knew we'd started. And what's living for if we have to be so careful? But I might have seen, afterwards, if I'd thought less about myself. Yes, it was peace when I was lying beside that stream. Still thinking of myself, you see. But I can never give back the years I've taken and I don't believe it was peace for her when she went back to London alone. Oh, not at losing me. All the things she's missed. Facetious, did you say?' he demanded angrily.

311

'Rather jaunty. Keeping up her spirits, I suppose.'

He turned away. 'This', he said miserably, 'is what makes the rest seem not worth bothering about. And yet I have to bother about it. What's that rot about making stepping-stones of our dead selves? Very unstable stepping-stones, I should say. Your nerves have gone already. You think you're bound to slip. I wish to Heaven', he said, 'she'd marry that man she's helping to look after. If he's good enough.'

'You've set such a high standard.'

'Oh, don't be snappy. He's all right, isn't he? Has he any sense? Sense enough to try a chance like that?'

Celia unclasped the hands she had been holding together. 'I don't know that I should altogether trust his taste,' she managed to say dryly. 'But that would be a comfortable solution for you, wouldn't it?'

'And a jolly good one for him, if he wants one.' He straightened his shoulders and drew a deep breath. 'I must go back. I must just go on. That's what it comes to at our age. We just go on. And, after all, it's not such a bad thing to do.' He became aware, then, of something unusual in her habitual stillness, and he said quickly, 'Are you cross? I don't wonder, but kiss and be friends. There aren't too many friends about.' He stooped and kissed her on the forehead. 'You're very much alike, you and Hester.'

'She's younger,' Celia said with what seemed like anger or disdain.

'Five, six years? That's nothing, but it's true she looks younger than her age.'

'Because she's slim,' Celia said in the same tone.

'But you are very nice as you are. It suits you to be plump.'

'Dreadful word,' Celia murmured.

'It suits your . . . your placidity.'

'Oh yes, I'm very placid. And Susan's slim and I've been told that she's like me, too.'

'Well, yes, I think I see what you mean.'

'I don't mean anything,' she said sharply. 'I don't believe it's true, about her or about Hester.'

'Have it your own way,' Stephen said patiently.

'That's so likely, isn't it?'

He shook his head ruefully. 'I can't say the right thing to-day. I won't try any more. Good-bye.'

She waited until he reached the door and then stopped him with his name, and when he turned he saw her mouth curled upwards in amusement and he found this a pleasant change from its former droop of irony.

'Why did you come to tell me all this?'

'There's no confessional in the church I'm supposed to belong to.'

'Strange,' she said, 'I've never wanted one. But you know, if you had to confess, John was the proper person to go to. It would have been interesting to watch the effect on him. The friend of his boyhood, his sister's husband . . .'

'Ah don't,' he begged, 'you're making it sound sordid and it wasn't. Are you trying to make me face the facts? I've done that already. They don't look pretty, but who can see them as they really are? Poor old John couldn't. No, he'd be like the learned judge in court, the righteously indignant barrister, stirring up mud that was never there. But John's a bit chastened himself, you know.'

'No, indeed I don't. What's happened?'

'The heir to the throne has rejected his inheritance. Robert isn't going into the business.'

'Not going into the business? How on earth has he managed that? Has he rebelled? Is he being tortured?'

'No, it's all quite amicable, I believe, but there's no doubt it's a blow to John.'

'And he needed a blow. Ah, I wonder if he'd had it, a few nights ago, when I met him on the Downs.'

'The night when I came home.'

313

'Yes.' It was also the night, as she remembered, when Jimmy had taken Susan down the river. 'He was very sweet, people often are when they're unhappy, and I liked him. What does Julia say about it?'

'That', said Stephen significantly, 'is what we don't know. There seems to have been a little disagreement between her and May.'

'Yes, it happened here and I must say I longed to wring Julia's neck. Hasn't May seen her since?'

'Not since Julia called to tell her you had run off with Reginald Carey.'

'The woman's crazy,' Celia said, 'or thinks everybody else is.' And yet, she reflected, poor silly Julia was not so far wrong as she appeared. That was the worst of it. Stephen had been mentally unfaithful for years and narrowly escaped being unfaithful physically. Celia had been mentally unfaithful for more years still and no power outside herself or Richard could have changed her feelings. Was Stephen to blame? Was she? For him and for Hester and for her there had been and there remained a fine beauty in their emotions; the judges and the barristers and the Johns of the world made them mean and ugly.

'There's nothing either good or bad but thinking makes it so,' she said, and Stephen who could not follow all her thoughts, though he could often read them, said with amusement, 'You're not endowing Julia with the capacity for thought, are you?'

'A kind of cunning,' Celia said crisply. 'And what an excursion it was, too, with poor Reginald! I had to go, but I wish I hadn't had to. D'you know,' she said seriously, 'I think everybody's a bit crazy. You needn't look at me like that. I know as well as you do that the remark has been made before, but it's new every time some one discovers it for himself.'

She had the recollection of Reginald perched in his car,

driving it with a care assorting so ill with his unguarded words; she heard Pauline's distant voice over the telephone and had a vision of her racing across the country to see Meredith whom she had exiled, without a moment to give her friend and perhaps none for Reginald, and since then there had been no message from her, not so much as a postcard with a word of reassurance or of thanks. And meanwhile, Hester and Stephen were making their two long journeys, meeting and immediately parting. At that moment, they all seemed to her like puppets jerked hither and thither by the hand that held the string.

'Except Miss Riggs,' she said. 'And Catherine.'

'And what about my girls?' Stephen asked with mock indignation. 'You can't bag all the sanity for your own.'

'I suppose not,' Celia said, and, after a minute's hesitation, she asked, 'Did you know that she and Jimmy were prowling about the city till all hours of the morning, the other night?'

'Were they? Well, she's all right with him.'

'But is he all right with her?'

'What on earth do you mean?'

'He thinks he's in love with her,' Celia said, and hated herself for speaking slightingly, like an elder person, of young love. It was a disease from which most people could recover, but one in which something always died, and she said sadly and in shame, 'I mean I'm afraid he's in love with her. And I'm afraid because I don't think she cares for him. Your real troubles haven't begun, Stephen. Mine are just beginning. You won't have time to grieve about Hester when one of your children is unhappy,' and changing her mournful note to one of impatience, she cried, 'It's so tiresome of him to choose a cousin and make me seem so unenthusiastic. I can't be properly kind about it.'

'But you like Susan, don't you? I thought you were so fond of her.'

'I think she's charming,' Celia said quickly. 'Too

charming, in this case. After all, Hester isn't so badly off. She only has herself to bother about while we have the children to see through all their troubles, and then, if we live long enough, we shall see them having the same worries with the next generation. There's no end to it.'

'I've never seen you like this before,' he said.

'You'll probably never see me like it again.' She laughed. 'It's odd to think that John is miserable because he's making his son happy. It's borne in on me that I shall have to go and call on Julia. What can she be doing with herself without May? What's May doing without her?'

'She seems to be managing very well, thank you,' Stephen said with a slight stiffness. Then, in a friendlier tone, he added, 'I believe Julia was a kind of pleasant irritant, but May has had an overdose and I don't think she'll want any more of it.'

'Yes, there's something in that,' Celia said, but she knew it was not everything. She had always believed in the sane core hidden away in May and it seemed as though she herself might have discovered it, but Celia felt her respect for Stephen a little lessened, not for what he had done or left undone but because he had felt the need to tell her all about it.

CHAPTER XLII

'SHE'S sitting on the seat again,' Catherine said one afternoon, a few days later.

'Who? The cat's mother?' Celia asked, without looking up from the letter she was reading.

'What a dreadful expression!'

'Yes, dreadful, dreadful,' Celia agreed with pacifying quickness.

'And you make such a fuss when I use a little harmless slang. I suppose you realize that I do it all the time at school.'

'Couldn't you make yourself understood if you didn't?'

'I'd be misunderstood. I'd seem priggish. But the cat's mother! That's worse than slang. It's common.'

'Yes.' Celia put down her letter. 'It must be a legacy from a nursemaid. You never had a nurse. We had lots of them. They were always coming and going — young minxes. But they and their friends did give colour and variety to life. Your walks abroad must have been very dull compared with ours. You just had Jimmy and me. We had all our nurse's acquaintances and their conversations, most interesting, well worth the occasional slaps.'

'You don't mean to say you were slapped!'

'Not often, not badly. Just a smart rap now and then because we were dawdling or hanging on to the perambulator or the nurse was tired. We knew there was no malice behind it. The slaps were part of the general mystery. I must have deprived you of a lot of mystery by taking you for those weary walks myself.'

'Better,' said Catherine, 'than letting me be slapped.'

'I'm not so sure. I don't know what I should have done to anyone who hurt you, but I think I might have run the risk if I could have afforded to have a nurse. I liked you very much, Catherine, but I did hate your little tapes and buttons and pushing your fingers into your gloves and doing up your gaiters. I used to try to make myself believe it wasn't a day for gaiters and then make you wear them far longer than you need, in case I was being selfish.'

'Did you?' Catherine said with amusement. 'I suppose you're not naturally maternal. Some people aren't, but I don't think I'd mind looking after babies myself. How would it be for me to be a nurse, a properly trained one? Still, there's no hurry and we've left the cat's mother on the seat. But father isn't in the least like a cat. More like a dog, but I don't quite know what kind. A patient dog who doesn't really expect anyone will take him for a walk.'

'Oh Catherine, he's not like that.'

'Getting more like it. Just age, perhaps. I think I'll try making a bit more fuss of him, but I don't get much chance, do I? He comes in and he goes out and there's my home-work. But I can't please him by pretending I love my grandmamma.'

'Did you speak to her?'

'Yes, I asked her to come to tea. It was the first time I'd seen her since she curried all that meat.'

Celia glanced at the window where the curtains were flapping in a strong breeze. 'She ought not to be sitting there. The sun always goes off The Terrace at this time of day and the wind's rather cold. I'll go and speak to her.'

'Now, that's just like making me wear my gaiters when I needn't. Overdoing it. I was charming to her and that's enough. And what d'you think she said? She said, "How's your brother?" pretending she didn't know his name.'

'He does nothing to remind her of it.'

'Men always have the best of things.'

'And I'm sure she's miserable. I'll go and see what I can do.'

She put away her letter. This one did not need tearing up. It told her that the patient had made a good and quick recovery and Hester was not needed any more. 'Not,' she wrote, 'that I was ever really needed, except when Mrs. Carey had to go away for a whole day, but I've done a few odd jobs, shopping and writing letters and I hoped I'd be some comfort to her, someone to talk to. But she doesn't talk when she is worried. She gets grim. She isn't worried now, but she's even grimmer. I don't like her and she doesn't like me and I didn't want to be paid. I was glad to do what I could for a friend of yours, but she made it clear I wasn't a friend of hers and I had to take the money, and too much of it. I hate that and, in this case, it was so illogical. But I like Mr. Milligan. He'll soon be well enough to go away and then he'll go home with her. And, in case my other letter worried you a little – I know it was too gay – I'm feeling better. I've accepted my middle-age and I don't resent it, and I'm on the tip, I believe, of getting a good job. It's rather good-workish, but I've come to the time of life when brushing other people's dogs and taking them for walks doesn't seem enough.'

It was a letter to make her a little sad for Hester, troubled about Pauline, but glad for herself and as she stepped on to The Terrace, she honestly wanted to be kind to the old woman who wanted to be miserable, but the desire noticeably lessened at the sight of her sitting on the seat like a figure cast in iron and with difficulty put into her clothes, the feet in the boots with the knowing buttons; one cotton-gloved hand clasping a tall umbrella and trying to drive the point of it into the pavement; a black silk mantle over the shoulders; on the head a little bonnet with pink roses in it and suddenly Celia realized one of the reasons why Mrs. Marston's appearance was so unpleasant. Her dark hair had no grey or white in it and in its resistance to time it was as rigid and stubborn as the rest of her.

'And so ugly,' Celia thought, as she smiled gently at the woman whose formidability really lay in Celia's strong dislike of her.

'No,' said Mrs. Marston. 'No thank you. I'm just sitting here, waiting for Mrs. Fellows.'

'Do you mean Julia?'

'Well, that's not what I call her, but that's the one. She said she'd like to come to tea and so she's coming.'

'But you may miss her here. She may be at your house now.'

'Oh no,' said Mrs. Marston, 'that girl of mine can't open the front door, or won't, more likely, the way I've tried to teach her, and I wasn't going to have any of that, so I said I'd meet her here.'

'But it's so cold for you. Couldn't you have opened the door yourself?'

'It's not what I've been used to with my callers. I'd rather let her in from the outside. I told her I always took a walk in the afternoon and she could pick me up.'

'Good idea!' Celia said brightly while she thought this old woman was almost as much the slave of her taboos as any savage was of his, though she doubted whether Mrs. Marston's callers in the Midlands were of a kind to be received with ceremony and whether it was not Julia's standards to which she was trying to conform.

From beneath the ribbons tying her bonnet and those fastening her mantle, Mrs. Marston produced an old flat watch attached to a gold chain and after holding it at some distance from her long sighted eyes, she returned it to its nest without a word, and continued to gaze at the landscape.

'Let's walk to the end of The Terrace,' Celia said. 'If she doesn't catch us up, we shall meet her when we turn back.'

'You haven't a hat or coat on.'

'But I'm quite warm.'

320

'I don't see why you should be any warmer than I am,' said Mrs. Marston. Nevertheless, she rose reluctantly and, clutching her umbrella, she walked at Celia's side in the shadow of the tall houses. Beyond the reach of that shadow, there was colour brightened by the patchy sunlight and Celia, looking over Mrs. Marston's bonnet, could see trees and roofs and chimney-pots slipping down the slope to the river which was out of sight. Beyond the unseen water, the serene, unchanging fields, carrying their heavy elms, rose to the level ridge of Easterly and the church tower, in one of its optimistic moods, directed the observer towards heaven.

Mrs. Marston looked neither to right nor left, but when Celia greeted someone she knew, Mrs. Marston walked on for a discreet yard or two and then asked sharply, 'Who was that? You've got a lot of friends, it seems.'

'Not friends, not many of them. Neighbours, you know.'

'I don't call it a neighbourly place myself.'

'Don't you? Well, it may only be that I've lived here all my life and I've picked up a lot of acquaintances as I went along.'

'And you keep them to yourself.'

'I don't bother about them and they don't bother about me.'

'Until the other day, I'd never met your sister-in-law.'

'Hadn't you? But you had a nice long time with her all to yourself.'

'And I haven't seen you since.'

'The days go by so quickly,' Celia said.

'Not that I believed half she said,' Mrs. Marston remarked unexpectedly. 'There's reason in all things and, as far as I could see, you'd nothing with you but your purse.'

'And even that wasn't necessary.'

'Not when you're out with a gentleman,' Mrs. Marston said, and across Celia's amusement there went a flash of rage

321

that this was the children's grandmother, a flash of pity for Gerald who had her for his mother. 'Had she said less, I'd have believed more. I don't mind telling you that. Not that she says so very much, though.'

'Oh, I know what she doesn't say and what a lot of fun she gets out of it.'

'But,' said Mrs. Marston repressing a ghost of a smile, 'I don't have so many visitors that I can afford to miss some company,' she said. 'We'd better be turning back.'

They turned and at once descried Julia's figure in the near distance standing beside the railings, her hands on the top bar, and again Celia had the enlightening experience of seeing someone who was unaware that familiar eyes were watching and while Mrs. Marston grunted disapproval of the carelessness, or envy of the wealth implied in Julia's white-gloved grasp of the dirty railings, Celia had a feeling that her hands had dropped there heavily, that, though she looked down, she found nothing of interest in the road below, that for once she had forgotten to be the Julia Fellows she presented to the world. Thus she had once seen Pauline Carey as she drove across the bridge, she had seen Gerald in his vest and trousers and here was Julia, insulated by something akin, in its effects, to Pauline's grief and Gerald's exhilaration. She had turned her eyes from Pauline, she had shut them against that vision of Gerald and now, in chivalry, she called to Julia while she was still some way off and at once, it was like a trick, Julia returned, fluttering and smiling, to Upper Radstowe and The Terrace, to her sister-in-law and Mrs. Marston whose age demanded a softening of the voice and a playfully cajoling manner.

With Celia she was grave. 'So you are at home again,' she said, and Celia, with a wide smile, begged her not to be an idiot. But she added, as she walked backwards towards her own door, 'Come in and see me on your way home.'

Mrs. Marston's face accomplished the astonishing feat of

becoming a little stiffer. Not to her were such friendly invitations issued, and Celia said to herself regretfully, 'How very difficult life is! But how interesting, too,' and she wished she could be present and invisible at the tea-party in that little parlour where the furniture shone without warmth and even the edges of the crochet doylies under the cakes looked as cold and dangerous as jagged ice.

'Did you think she'd eaten me?' she asked Catherine.

'I was getting a bit anxious. She's rather like the wolf in Red Riding Hood.'

'Poor thing,' Celia said indulgently. 'Wouldn't it be a nuisance, wouldn't it be upsetting, if I ever found I liked her?'

CHAPTER XLIII

FROM Julia's point of view the tea-party was not successful and she was puzzled. It would have been false modesty to pretend she had not been a pleasant guest and Mrs. Marston, in her own way, had been a hospitable hostess, but it was definitely in her own way and not in Julia's. Julia was urged to do what Mrs. Marston described as making a good tea and, realizing that any delicacy of appetite would be considered disparagement of the fare, Julia was obliging in this matter. And she liked pleasing people. She sometimes thought this liking almost approached a fault involving, as it did, some neglect of her duty towards herself, but she had never tried to cure it. She laughed at her weakness, she shook her head at it, knowing a struggle was useless and her heart would always get the better of her head. She was ready to make a pet of Mrs. Marston. Being petted was the right of an old lady and she seemed to get very little of it, but to-day, she was not responsive to little flatteries and attentions and a deep depression fell on Julia in that chilly parlour. She did not know that Celia's invitation involved the receiver as well as the giver of it, or that Mrs. Marston's sturdy middle-class pride resented a hint of patronage from comparative youth to age, from wealth to comparative poverty, from retail trade to the professions. She did not guess that Mrs. Marston used some self-control in refraining as hostess, from any disparaging reference to the shop, but she took her departure as soon as she could and without any encouragement to stay.

She did not go at once to Celia's flat. She turned up the street of which Mrs. Marston's was the corner house and walking without a definite goal, she found herself in sight of the river with the bridge on her right hand. But she could not see anything very clearly. The sun was overclouded and the wind had sharpened; it was almost sharp enough to have brought the tears to Julia's eyes; she had the wind ready for an excuse if anyone she knew should stop and speak to her and in the supreme need of keeping up appearances, she would not allow more than one fill of tears to overflow. To manage this, she had to restrain her thoughts, her bewilderment at Mrs. Marston's obvious lack of pleasure in her company, her woeful consciousness of May's desertion, her fear of John, who had not kissed her once since she had rescued Robert from the shop, her grief because Robert did not thank her effusively and every day for saving him.

She stared with dimmed eyes at the garden in front of her, a few yards of grass and shrubs and then a gradual descent, threaded by a winding path; she raised her head to look at the cliff across the river, slowly sloping to the level of the ground stemming the waterways; she turned it to look at the bridge, the vehicles crossing it at a walking pace, the figures by the railings, looking down, and it all seemed strange and alien and she had no place in it, and she thought, with a rare nostalgia, of her old home, that house smelling of generations of healthy men and women, wholesome food, beeswax, flowers and fruit, stables and cow byres, and she thought of the square hall, the front door always open on it, its air of welcome, the matting on the floor, a litter of boots and riding crops and sticks in one dark corner, the row of brass candlesticks on the table at the foot of the shallow stairs. All round the house was the wide flat country and, not very far away, a wide flat sea and, picturing that sea, she had a feeling of being trapped here, at the head of this gorge. The open sea was so far off; the sullen river made its way between the cliffs and when it freed itself from them it continued through the country for twisting miles and at last found its exit in water that was land-locked still.

I'd like to go home, she thought, but even she could not

deceive herself into believing it was her own home now. Her stepmother reigned there as regent for her son, it was better to remember it as it used to be and, at that decision, the tears brimmed over. But Julia blew her nose, she summoned her resources, she was unhappy but she was brave and she retraced her steps, tripping where she had walked, ready to wave a hand at Mrs. Marston if she was lurking behind the flower-pots in her window. Unhappy and lonely herself, she had tried to cheer another who was afflicted in the same way and though she knew she had not succeeded, she was not daunted. She could not believe in the complete failure of good intentions and she had plenty more of them to carry with her up Celia's stairs.

The front door was ajar and when she had beaten a light tattoo on it, she put her head round and asked gaily whether she might come in. She felt both vexed and foolish when no one answered and she found she was addressing an empty passage and doors that were all shut. But if no one answered, no one could have heard and she repaired her little mistake by stepping outside again to ring the bell. At that, one of the doors was opened, and Catherine appeared.

'Hullo, Aunt Julia. Was there gingerbread and seed cake for tea?'

'Oh,' Julia began, pitching her voice on the high note suitable for telling children of delights, 'there were all sorts of cakes, darling. It was a lovely tea. Now let me see.' Raising her hands, she prepared to count on her fingers the varieties Mrs. Marston had offered her, but Catherine said, politely, 'Please don't bother. I'm not supposed to come out of this room just now and I only wanted to know about gingerbread and seed cake. I wanted to know whether she, grandmamma, knows there are any other kinds, that's all. Mother's in the sitting-room.'

Julia advanced to the sitting-room and, standing on the

threshold and holding the door from her at arm's length, she said gravely, 'Is Catherine being punished?'

'Punished?' said Celia. 'Punished? How old do you think she is? Come and sit down. She's doing her homework and she has to stay there till it's finished.'

'Has to?' Julia repeated. 'I don't like the sound of that. Do you think she can do her best, dear, under a feeling of compulsion? I don't make any rules for Sybil. She would rebel against them at once.'

'Awkward,' said Celia. 'Then I suppose you tell her to do exactly the opposite to what you want.'

'I don't think that would be honest. I say nothing and simply trust her.'

'And how does that suit the people at school? Are they satisfied?'

'I don't think they understand her.'

'Strange, isn't it,' Celia said with sympathy, 'that these experts who've spent all their lives at the job, never know how to manage the material they're handling.'

'They are not mothers.'

'As far as we know,' said Celia.

Julia could not spare this jest more than half a shake of the head, enough to acknowledge a pleasantry and show she was not shocked, but not enough to make a serious diversion from her favourite subject.

'They can't,' she said sadly, 'have even an ordinary love for all these hundreds of children and love is so important.' She raised her brows at her own moderation. 'The one importance.'

'So some people seem to think, or want to think. They like to feel they're necessary. I'm not so sure about the children. I believe they want to be treated kindly and left alone.'

'Just what I say. Let them develop in their own way. That's what I want for Sybil and I've tried to make it clear to the headmistress. I've been very insistent about it. But she seems so hidebound. They get into such a rut. But I am not going to have Sybil made into a scholar.'

'Is there any danger?' Celia asked. Then she laughed. 'Do you know you're talking nonsense, Julia, or can't you help it? I think that must be it. You never do anything else, not when you're with me. Now, don't begin to cry! Don't begin to cry! You make me feel such a brute and I'm only saying it for your good, it hurts me more than it hurts you, and all the other remarks of that kind. Be angry if you like, but don't cry. Why should you?'

'Because,' said Julia, her mouth drooping, her pose the most natural Celia had ever seen her take, 'because I want to. Because I should enjoy it. Because I've been wanting to cry for days.' She found her handkerchief. 'For years!' she exclaimed from behind its flimsy folds.

'No, not for years,' Celia said. 'That sounds well, but I don't think it's true. Now tell me, have you really been wanting to cry for years?'

'Not . . . not the whole time,' Julia sobbed.

'Of course not. Nobody could. And if you do it in my house, you're bound, out of politeness, you know, to tell me exactly why. Exactly, mind,' and she added, 'if you can.'

There was a sudden splattering of hard raindrops on the window, the room darkened a little and Julia shivered.

'I'm cold,' she said, and Celia reached for a match-box and lit the fire.

'One of the pleasures of life, a fire on a cold summer evening. It will soon burn up. Come nearer. You'll be able to dry your handkerchief. Why did you wear this frock? It's much too thin.'

'I thought it was pretty. I don't keep my best clothes for people who have plenty of their own. I'm sure it's a mistake to dress down to people. It doesn't make them envious to see nice things, it cheers them up.'

'Did yours do that for Mrs. Marston?'

'In any case,' Julia said evasively, 'don't you think it's a duty to look as nice as one can?'

'No, I think it's a pleasure.'

'And duty's a pleasure, isn't it?'

'Oh, oh, oh,' Celia groaned, 'try to remember I'm a middle-aged woman and whatever other duties and pleasures you may have, you needn't improve the occasion for me. Can't you see that it's not only frightfully boring but an infuriating kind of impudence? Who are you, pray, to be putting everybody right?'

Julia, who had been kneeling in front of the fire and holding out her handkerchief towards the feeble flames, now found another use for it as she sank back on her heels, but this subsidence only lasted for a minute. She raised herself and crumpling her handkerchief into a ball, she threw it pettishly on to the fire.

'It's so wet, it will put the fire out,' Celia said, and with the tongs she moved the small, blackened object to the hearth. 'Have you another in your handbag?'

'You're hateful,' Julia said, 'and I hate you. I hate you all. You've never been kind to me, not one of you. Even your mother wasn't kind. I pretended not to notice . . .'

'Yes, you always pretend.'

'But in my heart, I knew she didn't like me.'

'And there you're wrong. She was rather fond of you.'

'She never let me suspect it!'

'No, she was not demonstrative, but John was happy with you and she was grateful and then, she got a lot of amusement out of you and that's so endearing, you know. You weren't quite such a fraud then, Julia, not such an arrant little fraud. Have you another handkerchief, or shall I get you one? You'd give your best friend away if you could make yourself interesting and noble in the process, and never know you'd done it. Look at May!'

'I haven't seen May for days!' Julia cried.

329

'No, and I don't think you'll see her for some time. I believe you'd even give John away for the sake of looking brave and pathetic. And it's a mistake from your own point of view. Children are very clear-sighted.'

'Children? When have I betrayed John to the children?' she demanded, but Celia fancied she detected a thoughtful gleam in her eye.

'Never, perhaps, but you know best.'

She rose and went out of the room and opened Catherine's door.

'Don't come into the sitting-room,' she said. 'Your aunt and I are having a serious conversation.'

'Then you must be doing all the talking.'

'I am. Most unusual. My tongue aches. And if you hear your father, shut him up in the dining-room.'

'He won't be here for hours. He gets later every day. Don't you think you ought to speak to him about it?'

'He knows I don't fuss much about punctuality.'

'Oh,' said Catherine, 'I wasn't thinking of that. I was thinking perhaps he was working too hard. He looks very tired sometimes.'

Celia opened a drawer in her baronial dressing-table and paused in the act of picking out her largest handkerchiefs. 'God forgive me,' she said, 'whom am I to bully that poor little creature in there?' And she thought it was she who had committed the unpardonable sin in refusing kindness where it was wanted. And thinking Gerald wanted it no longer, she told herself that the nearest, the immediate kindness, was the one that should be done, not the distant one in which she imagined she would fulfil herself, the one that never came within her reach.

But all the same, I shall go on bullying Julia, she thought. It may or may not be kindness to her, but it's certainly doing me good.

'I don't think the rain's going to stop,' she said cheerfully

330

when she returned to the sitting-room, and she spoke loudly because Julia, in an abandoned attitude, her head on the seat of a chair, was weeping uncontrolledly. 'You'll have to stay for supper. You may have to sleep on the sofa and John will think . . . I'll tell you what he'd think if he were you, Julia. I've brought some of Gerald's handkerchiefs; they're more adequate. He'd think you'd run off with someone or something, like Stephen, you know, or like me.'

'And so I would', Julia cried, 'if I had anyone to go with!'

'And leave the children?'

'He hasn't kissed me, he's hardly spoken to me, for a week!'

'How dreadful!' Celia exclaimed. 'But what,' she asked, 'have you been doing to him?'

'To him? Nothing,' Julia said, but again Celia saw the retrospective gleam in her eye. 'I was only trying to help Robert. I had to show him it wasn't going to be so very easy, even though he wasn't going to the shop. I had to make him face his difficulties.'

'And John, of course, was the difficulty and you were the guiding star. Pleasant for John!'

'Well, I may have been wrong, but I meant to do right. And there's always someone who must be sacrificed.'

'And apparently someone has been. I'm not surprised he hasn't kissed you. You ought to be smacked.'

'But how does John know that?' Julia asked ingenuously. 'He wasn't there. You don't think Robert can have told him, do you?'

'No, I think he must have been listening, on the sly,' Celia said sourly, but Julia missed the scorn in that remark and the curl of Celia's mouth, for she was remembering the banging of the front door that night and the long, silent hours before a silent John crept into her bed. This had seemed like the humility of the conquered foe, but his subsequent manner with Robert, not too genial but definitely friendly, his manner with her, neither friendly nor genial, was that of an enemy who turned defeat into triumph, while Robert, still a little suspicious of his father, was undoubtedly avoiding his mother.

'And it's I', Julia mourned, following her own thoughts, 'who've saved him from that awful shop! But John's getting all the credit and Robert has never thanked me!'

'I'm glad you've saved him from the shop. I should think young Christopher will do much better there. But you don't know much about children, do you, poor Julia? You're much too busy thinking about yourself. That's a common fault, but some of us hide it better than you do.'

'I live, I've always lived for the children!' Julia cried.

'Then don't do it any more,' Celia said gently. 'Let them live for themselves. You know, they're rather like your hats and your bits of jewellery. They decorate you. For you they're like those necklaces one sees in the shop windows. Convertible into two bracelets and a brooch. But what are you going to do when they're too old to be treated like that, when they've seen through you, if they haven't done it already, when there isn't a child left in the house? But I suppose you'll manage somehow. You'll always be able to dramatize yourself, but it won't be nearly so much fun when you're really unhappy, really lonely, when there's no one to listen. John's much the best investment you can make for your future. Dull but safe.'

'He doesn't understand me,' Julia sobbed.

'No, that's where you're so lucky,' Celia said.

CHAPTER XLIV

WITH this parting shot she made what was actually a retreat for on Julia's tear-stained face she had seen an alarming expression of spitefulness. The poor little worm had turned and all Celia's instincts warned her that pertinent retorts would be made, that John, with an excess of marital devotion had imparted his suspicions about Gerald to his wife.

'How murky it all is,' Celia sighed.

She could face her own failure in privacy, for she owned to failure; she might even have endured hearing of it from Julia, as wholesome humiliation, if she had not suspected Gerald's faithlessness of a vulgarity altogether absent from her own. She would not listen to any mention of it. Was this loyalty to him, she wondered, or only to herself, to the young self whose choice had been mistaken, to the old self whose pride was hurt? She did not know. There seemed to be no clearness or simplicity in any human emotion, and life, which ought to have been noble, was cluttered with mistakes, words, looks, there was no retrieving. But, she thought, they might with patience, with care and courage, be overlaid by something better. But had she, did she want to exercise the patience and care and courage? Again, she did not know and her musings were interrupted by an imperative ring and knock.

She opened the door to a telegraph boy who stepped back and leaned against the rail of the banisters and watched her with bright, callous eyes above his gleaming mackintosh cape.

There was no answer. 'But wait a minute,' she said. 'It's a long way up these stairs.'

She did not know where she had put her purse, but she knew where to find Julia's handbag.

'Lend me threepence, there's a dear,' she said to the disconsolate little heap on the hearth.

'Take anything you like! Take anything you like! You've taken so much already.'

'And what exactly have I taken as well as these three pennies?' she asked, shaking them in her palm. 'Think it out. I shall expect the answer in about half an hour. It's still pouring with rain. It's coming down on the skylight like bullets.'

'I don't care if it never stops.'

'You'll miss the children's hour.'

'But that won't matter to the children.'

'Not a bit,' Celia agreed pleasantly.

As she shut the door on the boy, Catherine came out of her bedroom.

'What was that?' she asked.

'Just a message from your father to say he can't get back for supper.'

'Oh, can't he? Is the serious talk over?'

'Yes, but don't go in there yet. And when you do, you'd better stamp about in the passage first.'

'She's not crying, is she?'

'No. Thinking. Have you finished your work?'

'Not quite.'

'Then go back until you have. I do hate people who pop out like rabbits when they hear a bell.'

'But rabbits would pop in,' Catherine said gently.

After the manner of Miss Riggs, Celia ignored this remark. 'It reminds me', she said, 'of our dentist's children when we were young. We were miserable enough already, in all conscience, and as soon as we entered the house dozens of young dentists appeared to look at us, peeping over the banisters, round doors, the image of their father, too, taking a fiendish interest in his victims. I'm sure they hoped we were going to yell.'

'And did you?'

'Of course not,' Celia said grandly. 'But then,' she admitted, 'we all had remarkably good teeth. No, those little gnomes didn't get much fun out of us. They would have put anybody on his mettle. Perhaps that's what they were for. I see some of them now, occasionally, and they still seem like gnomes, even when they're wheeling perambulators, or wearing bowler hats and reading newspapers in tramcars. Why are you smiling in that superior way?'

'I was wondering when you'd remember that I ought to be doing my work.'

'Are you so bored?'

'No,' Catherine said emphatically. She lounged against the door frame. Her hair was rumpled, she would probably forget to comb it before supper; her eyes were as eager as those of a child who listens to a story, but her smile was not a child's; the amusement in it was not for the story, it was for the person who told it. 'I love listening to you,' she said kindly, 'especially when you're breaking your own rules.'

Celia gave her a light tap on the cheek. 'You'll soon be beyond my jurisdiction,' she said.

There was no doubt about it. She was growing up. It was evident in the curve of her small breasts as she lifted her arms above her head and eased herself in a long stretch; it was still more evident in the words to which that stretch was an apparently careless preliminary.

'What's father doing, do you know?' she asked.

'No. People are so queer with telegrams. They'll leave their friends in horrible suspense for the sake of getting their message into the right number of words for sixpence.'

'Are you in suspense?'

'Not in the least. It's rather lucky, as it happens, because your aunt can have his share of supper.'

'She won't eat it all, though. I expect she thinks it's interesting to have a poor appetite.'

'And there won't be anything to stimulate it,' Celia said.

She looked again at Gerald's telegram before she threw it away. He had not taken his full sixpenny worth. For that price, he might have said he would not be home till late or could not be back for supper, instead of his slightly pompous, rather unnatural, 'Dining out'. Was it with Maudie? Surely one did not dine with Maudie? But how hateful I am, she thought with disgust. I'm as bad as Julia. She opened the larder door and looked vaguely at its contents. 'Ugly, ugly,' she said. I used not to be like this. I'm sure I used to be a nicer person. I wish I could go away, by myself, and sit beside running water. Like Stephen! she thought with irony, and she wondered whether she and he and all her generation had not come to the meeting-place of two roads, and on one they would grow warm and mellow, dry and wizened on the other. Stephen had chosen his road, but no one could tell yet which one it was. Possibly the much recommended strait one was too narrow, too much overhung by prohibitions and restrictions for the sun to reach those who walked there; or it might be a tiny sheep track on a bare hill-side and perhaps the important thing was not the road one took but the way one walked on it.

But the more I moralize — it's always a bad sign — the worse I get, she thought, and she busied herself among the pots and pans.

'Who,' said Jimmy, appearing in the doorway, 'is the person lying in a heap on the hearthrug?'

'Still in a heap? How ridiculous! It's your Aunt Julia. Did you speak to her?'

'Not much! I thought it must be someone you'd brought in from the street. There was a found drowned sort of look about her, so I hopped it. What's for supper?'

'Bits and pieces. You're very early.'

'Yes, it's my night out.'

'I warn you, you may have to take Julia home.'

336

'And I don't mind, so long as the family emporium pays for the cab. I'll go and smarten myself up for her.'

'Yes. But Jimmy . . . how do you think you would all manage if I went away for a little while?'

'Muddle along, I expect. But you could farm out Catherine with the grandmother, she'd like that, or couldn't she go to Aunt May's? And the old man and I could look after ourselves. Where d'you want to go?'

'Oh, I don't know. There must be some lovely places with streams I could get into or go to sleep by.' And there was that interest on her money, carefully saved by Gerald, but she could not think of it without feeling it was tainted by her own suspicions and must not be used on any pleasure for herself.

'It would do you good,' Jimmy said encouragingly.

'I expect so, but do I seem as if I want some good done to me?'

'Not a bit.'

'That's all right then. I don't suppose I shall go.'

'The worst of this house,' said Catherine, appearing in her turn, 'is that when I want to wash, Jimmy's always in the bath.'

'Tell him to hurry. Or wash in the sink. And just watch this pot for a minute.'

She found Julia fast asleep, and she doubted whether John's anger would survive the sight of her now. With a mouth that drooped and pouted at the same time and the smooth eyelids with the long, dark lashes, in the laxness of her small body, she looked younger and much less sophisticated than Sybil. The firelight played on her blue dress and a high-heeled shoe; her broad hat with its blue ribbons had been thrown aside and on the fender she had arranged Gerald's handkerchiefs to dry. They were in danger of being scorched and Celia reached over her to remove them and she found something orderly and yet childish, something simple and sensible and undramatic in Julia's having put them there when she knew she could cry no longer. Celia felt quite tender towards her. It seemed a shame to wake her and she went out quietly, to return with the shawl which had enclosed Jimmy and Catherine when they were babies. Very gently she spread this over Julia, not without some suspicion of so profound a slumber, and finding Catherine, she said, 'Don't stamp and don't go in. Julia's asleep.'

'Asleep! What's the matter with her?'

'Exhaustion. Too much sensibility.'

'Oh dear!' Catherine said. She seemed to look, for a moment, into the dark mysterious places of a life which should have been uneventful and unemotional, because it was so much older than her own, and Celia hastened to say comfortingly, 'Too little sense'.

'Well,' said Catherine with relief, 'she doesn't really belong to us. That makes all the difference. Like people who slap their lips when they're eating. It's rather interesting when they're strangers, but if any of the family did it I should scream. Even Grandmamma doesn't.'

'You've got your grandmother on the brain. You'd better get rid of her.'

'I don't want to. I find it most satisfying to have a really good hate.'

'Yes, but I can never keep it up. Besides, it simply means that one lacks imagination.'

'Then you really are beginning to like her a little! And we've always been such friends about her!'

'I don't like her yet, but if I were a little and she were altogether different, I think we might get on very well together.'

Catherine stifled her own laughter. An atmosphere of stealth stole over the little flat. There was no controlling the gurgling of the bath water as it ran out, but, in the dining-room, china and cutlery were handled tenderly, voices were lowered and ears turned apprehensively towards the passage.

'This isn't love,' Catherine explained unnecessarily. 'This is self-defence. I do like to be able to concentrate on my food.'

'And it isn't natural, is it', Jimmy asked, 'to have an aunt on the carpet like that? Anyhow, I don't intend to wait until she's had her sleep out. Don't you think it's time we began to make a row?'

It was made for them by another ringing of the bell, another imperative knocking on the door, and Celia opened it, without surprise, to John.

'I can't find Julia,' he said. He was agitated, a little out of breath. He was hatless and his hair was wet. 'She's not at May's and if she's not here I don't know where to look for her.'

'But she is here.'

'Then why the deuce aren't you on the telephone? I never heard of anything so idiotic in these days. It's positively uncivilized. And even if you haven't one, isn't there one in the street?'

'Yes, but there's the rain, too. Come in and don't make such a noise.'

'Noise! Who wouldn't make a noise at being brought out on a night like this when the post office is just round the corner?'

'You have a car, haven't you?'

'Yes, I've got a car, but I can't drive it on to The Terrace, can I? I'm half-soaked with just running these few yards.'

'And of course the rain wouldn't have soaked any of us! Come . . .' She hesitated. She had no intention of letting him see Julia in her pathetic attitude. There were probably some fresh tears trickling down her cheeks by now. 'Come into the dining-room.'

'You don't mean to tell me she's actually been having dinner with you while I've been rampaging all over the country.'

'No, no, and don't exaggerate. I know it's only because you've been so anxious, but you needn't shout. Did you think she'd gone over the Sea Cliff? She'll never do anything like that.'

Jimmy and Catherine had disappeared at the first burst of the storm and John and Celia were alone among the broken meats.

'But you imagined things like that, didn't you? One always does. And you forgave her all her sins. And I expect you wondered how much you would have to reveal at the inquest. Yes, you would have to say, we had had a little quarrel. Didn't you think of that?'

'Oh, don't be a fool,' John said.

'So bad for business, too.'

'I never thought about the business. Tell her I'm here and let's go home.'

'In a few minutes. Listen. I want you to make her tell you everything I've told her. Will you do that? But no, it's no use.' She took the precaution of moving to the other side of the table before she added, 'She's such a little liar.'

There was not a sound from John, not a movement. She looked up and saw him staring straight in front of him. He seemed strangely deflated. Miserably he accepted a statement she would have upheld vigorously under his reproaches; under his silence she was constrained to modify it.

'But she doesn't know she is.'

'And she never used to be,' he said tonelessly.

'You might as well say someone with cancer never used to have it. What she always did was to dress herself up as someone else. Now she's beginning to dress up other people and it's dangerous. She'll get you into trouble one day.'

He grunted. 'I'm in trouble already, right enough. She's dressed me up in a very pretty costume, I can tell you.'

'Ah,' said Celia dryly, 'one notices it when it happens

340

to oneself. Not that it's happened to me — or only partially. She has given me — what shall I say? — a hat of the wrong period for the dress.'

Characteristically, John took no notice of Celia's possible wrongs.

'I don't understand it,' he muttered. 'I never shall. Oh, what's the good of talking? I suppose I've just got to go on.'

Those were Stephen's words and now Celia said quietly, 'Yes, that's what we all do,' but she knew John's case was both better and worse than hers or Stephen's. John still had a romantic love for his wife and, strongly aware of it himself, he could not imagine its having less meaning for her than it had for him; in his view, its permanency and ardour were lavish compensation for any faulty treatment of her. It was his treasure and it ought to have been hers. He felt, in a dim way, that his temper, his impatience, his mockery, were only the straw and the sacking in which he wrapped it for safety. For her, the only thing inside the unsightly wrappings was a false image of himself, and this she had shown his children. Yet, in the rooted honesty of his nature, he suspected that if she had not displayed it, it might have been the true one.

This was too difficult for him who was essentially simple, and he looked mournfully at Celia, asking for the help he would have believed, at another moment, she was incapable of giving.

She was sorry for him, with his self-assurance gone, and she said gently, 'You've spoilt her, John.'

'I know. That's where I've made my big mistake. I can't remember anything she's wanted that I haven't given her.'

'Yes, that must have been very nice for you.'

'For me?'

'Well, wasn't it? What I mean is that you've spoilt her character. You haven't let her have one. She's had to make one up. You've treated her like a badly treated baby,

341

teasing and scolding and petting, and she's had to see herself as all sorts of things she isn't, that everybody knows she isn't. She's just as unhappy as you are. I should think she's been unhappy for much longer. Can't you give her fewer kisses and more respect? She's in the sitting-room. Take her home. I'm weary of her. Don't bully her. Don't comfort her. It's most unfortunate for both of you that she can cry without looking hideous. Don't give her any comforting for a long time, but don't forget she needs it.'

Quite meekly, looking slightly stunned, he went out of the room and almost immediately it became necessary to wrap Julia in a mackintosh which was much too big for her, to kiss her sulky face and shut the door on her and John. Celia had not the heart to watch their sad descent of the stairs. Instead, she warmed up the chilled pudding, thinking how well she could manage her own affairs if they were someone else's.

CHAPTER XLV

IT rained the next day and the next and Celia needed her mackintosh, but remembering the circumstances in which it had been borrowed, she realized the unlikelihood of seeing it again, and then the weather cleared into a saintliness of blue and gold and it seemed blasphemous to think of mackintoshes and umbrellas, to doubt the lasting quality of this miracle of serenity and warmth, and in the confinement of the little flat, with its low ceilings and high set windows, her thoughts turned again to streams and hills.

'Pity you haven't a nice little bit of garden,' said Miss Riggs.

'There's nothing I should like less,' Celia said. 'The only garden that's any use to me is a big one, complete with gardeners.'

'Ah, you want too much,' said Miss Riggs. 'I'd be content with a little bit of green and somewhere to hang the washing.'

'And then there'd be no excuse for sending most of it to the laundry. But I suppose pushing the mowing machine up and down would be good for the figure.'

'It would be a nice job for Mr. Jimmy of an evening.'

'How do you know that? You're one of those irritating people who always pretend people will enjoy doing the things that should be done. It's one of your blind spots.'

'Well, I enjoy doing them myself.'

'I know, but then you're so good,' Celia said with the tender malice Miss Riggs inspired in her. 'Now, just listen. Have you ever done anything you shouldn't, or left undone anything you should?'

Miss Riggs gave these questions her serious attention. 'I've put by a little something,' she said at last.

'Thrift? I don't know how you've managed it, but thrift's a virtue.'

'I'm not so sure. I'd better have spent it on someone else. The Bible says take no thought for the morrow.'

'And it also praises the lilies because they don't toil or spin, and when I try to be a lily, you preach at me.'

'I can't think what you've done with my clean dusters,' said Miss Riggs. 'And anyway, the Bible's right about to-morrow, for here's Jo come along with a tidy little business and I needn't have bothered.'

'I almost wish,' Celia said, 'the Lord had chosen to take Jo himself, instead of his late wife. The present arrangement is lovely for him, but what about me? With that tidy little business, he'll be much too grand to let you come out to work. You're going to be planed down and dovetailed in and nailed up to your carpenter.'

'Not me! How's he to know what I'm doing when he's not at home? I'll be helping you and doing him no harm.'

'And taking the bread out of another woman's mouth.'

'I can hear somebody on the stairs,' said Miss Riggs.

'When is there anybody off them?' Celia inquired.

Her whole life, she thought, in a moment of impatience, was spent in opening and shutting that door, in hearing other people opening and shutting it, in watching people go down the stairs and hearing them come up, and lately, the atmosphere of the home she had made had been invaded by emotions from outside, and they would not go. They hung about her sitting-room and disturbed the dreams she had housed there, threatening their beauty and their truth. For this disturbance she liked to blame Stephen and John and Julia, with their troubles and disillusions and the doggedness of middle-age taking the place of youth's high courage, but she knew she made some of it herself through her unkindness to Gerald, her anger that he found comfort elsewhere; through Jimmy whose love she did not approve;

344

through such a pettiness as remembering Richard's many invitations to parties and his attentive women friends; through Pauline's continued silence and the lack of any news. She could not understand that silence, but it was not for her to break it. In all these years, it had been Pauline who, half-scornfully, offered her tiny crumbs of information; it was never Celia who asked for them. She would not ask now, but she was uneasy. She realized that Pauline in caprice, in impatience with this ethereal sort of attachment, was capable of suddenly deciding to ignore it. And Richard had always been as outwardly passive as Celia herself, that was the rule they had made and kept, but now, even as she opened the door once more and braced herself to see him, miraculously restored to health enough for the long ascent and leaning on his stick, she thought he need no longer keep the rule so strictly; they were safe enough: they were used by this time, to separation and through her mind there ran the faithless thought that they might not know what to do with each other now if they could be together. Nevertheless, at this moment she was young again, ardent, claiming admiration. It was still her right to be necessary — a hampering condition with Gerald while it endured: to be desirable — a distress, until it ceased to be a quality he found in her.

But, to her absurd disappointment and resentment, there was only Susan on the landing. Her head was bare, her hands loosely gloved; her face was lightly decorated with the colours suitable for a summer morning; this was the familiar, pretty Susan, but Celia's keen, sleepy eyes saw agitation in the special brightness of her manner.

'It's a lovely day,' Susan said, 'and the car's in the road. Will you come into the country?'

'How do you manage to keep your hair so smooth?' Celia asked. 'It must be a different kind from what we grew. But everything's different. When I was at school — Catherine says I must be getting old because I'm always talking about

345

the past — the girls who frizzed their hair were a kind of blacklegs. And as a matter of fact, they nearly always were the silly ones.'

'You didn't need to frizz yours.'

'No, I had no chance to testify that we were as God made us, that straight hair had to be straight and plain girls plain. There aren't any plain girls now and Queen Elizabeth, if she came back, wouldn't need to provide any dowry for the poor souls. Funny that she should do that when she dodged marriage so nimbly herself. But I suppose she thought it was the proper state for lesser women. Quite right. I wish I could persuade Miss Riggs to emulate her.'

'But why shouldn't Miss Riggs have a home of her own?'

'She has, and it's very nice, though it's only one room, with a photograph of Fred on the chest of drawers and all his virtues intact. I'm sure she's only marrying Jo to oblige him, but as she's a very unusual person, he won't find out. You have to be very unusual,' she said with careless emphasis, 'if you're not to be found out as a person obliging under pressure, out of a kind heart. And I don't suppose he'll mind having Fred to watch him all the time. But I expect Fred will be put, tactfully, in the parlour.'

'But,' said Susan, clasping her hands and then unclasping them, 'you might be fond as well as obliging, mightn't you? And everybody doesn't get married with a Fred behind them.'

'No, he's often in front of these obliging people.'

'And then it can't be helped.'

'But it has to be paid for in one way or another.'

'But that's not fair!' Susan cried.

'And you are a tradesman's granddaughter! Haven't you learnt yet that you can't get anything for nothing? Why, it wouldn't be worth having!'

'But if you never meant to buy it . . .' Susan suggested.

'I buy so much that I don't want,' Celia sighed. 'At the

346

door, you know. I can't get away from that door. Things like kettle-holders from terrible old women with their heels out of their shoes. I have dozens of them. Kettle-holders, I mean. And I wonder if that's one now,' she said, for there was another knock, 'but if it is, Miss Riggs will deal with it.'

Miss Riggs, however, found herself inadequate to deal with Mrs. Marston's little servant who arrived with her large cap set on her head more crookedly than usual and in the indignity of her striped flannel apron.

'It's the mistress,' she said, in a state of pleasurable agitation. 'I had to come and fetch you, Mum. She's carrying on so funny.'

'Funny?' said Celia.

'Yes, Mum. She's neither in her bed nor out of it and she's got her bonnet on and I can't take it off her.'

'I'm not surprised that she didn't allow that.'

'Ah, but she's not right in her head, Mum, the way she's talking and I'll have to get back or she'll be out on the pavement in her nightgown. I didn't ought to've left her, but what was I to do, being single-handed? So I just run along The Terrace . . .'

'Quite right. Run back and I'll come as quickly as I can.'

'Come in the car,' Susan said. 'It will save a minute or two if I take you by the road and then I'll be there in case you want me. But we shan't have our drive into the country.'

Celia gave her a momentary glance with widely-opened eyes. 'Never mind,' she said as she put a thermometer into her bag, 'I don't suppose we should really have gone much farther if we'd gone a hundred miles. Do you?'

'No,' Susan said, and under her rouge and powder she looked a little white and strained. She held the door open for her aunt and then followed her on to the landing. 'I know what you mean,' she said with dignity, 'and you may be right, but I thought you might let me talk about it. I don't know what I ought to do.'

'You've told me yourself,' Celia said, starting down the stairs. 'If there's an ought in the matter, there's nothing else.'

'But it's not so simple as all that.'

These words, uttered quietly and not intended, perhaps, for Celia's ears, seemed to gather volume in the spaciousness of the stone staircase overhung by the glass dome, and Celia heard in them not only the truth she knew already and had chosen to deny, but the bewilderment and the essential loneliness of the young, and she paused on the next landing and waited for Susan to come level with her.

'I wonder what Mrs. Marston would have said if I had consulted her about marrying Gerald!'

'She would have been like you,' Susan said without an answering smile. 'She would have washed her hands of it, but you wouldn't have asked her. You haven't loved her all your life and known she would be honest with you — and kind.'

'It's difficult to be both.'

'Not for you, Aunt Celia.'

'You don't know me, child,' Celia said a trifle sharply. 'And this isn't the moment, with Mrs. Marston wearing her bonnet over her nightgown. This isn't the moment.'

'No.' Susan lifted her head and hurried down the stairs. She had started the engine of the car before Celia reached the road; she was alert and helpful, promising to wait outside the house, to telephone to the doctor, to fetch and carry; she was ready, if necessary, she asserted, to help with the removal of the bonnet, but it was with a sense of loss that Celia entered the narrow little hall. Those moments, those opportunities for help or kindness, one did not recover them, she thought, peeping into the front room, then into the back one, both in perfect order and both untenanted. It was strange to look at Mrs. Marston's belongings without the consciousness of her readiness to detect criticism and her fierce belief in the value of her possessions, mingled with resentment for the owners of better ones. It was stranger still to see her, for the first time, in her bed, with the little maid sitting on a hard chair at a respectful distance. The bonnet was perched on one of the brass posts at the foot of the bed; Mrs. Marston's dark head rested on a spotless pillow in a cotton case; her face, always red in patches, was of a yellowish hue elsewhere.

'She don't seem to breathe easy,' said the little servant.

'What is your name?' To Celia she was only known as the girl or as that girl in moments of special irritation. 'Then, Sophy, go and tell my niece, outside in the car, I want a doctor.'

Less anxious now, relieved of responsibility, Sophy was prepared to enjoy this admirable break in her routine. 'I had a job getting her there,' she said, her hands on her hips as she looked patronizingly at the figure in the bed, at the tyrant who was helpless, at the eyes, so quick to see a speck of dust or a smear on a piece of furniture, shut now, under a frown of pain. 'Coaxing wasn't any good. I had to speak very sharp.'

That was what she would tell the tradesmen who came to the door, her acquaintances among the neighbours, her mother, when she went home on her night out. It was the crowning achievement of her short life. At the back of her mind there might be a hope that Mrs. Marston would not remember the extraordinary liberties she had taken, but, in the meantime, there was excitement, importance and a general feeling of holiday.

'And now you can run sharp,' Celia said.

She approached the double bed and, raising the stiff body with some difficulty, she slipped under it the other pillow which lay untouched and reminiscent of the late Mr. Marston's rightful place.

Mrs. Marston opened her eyes. 'Go away,' she said distinctly.

CHAPTER XLVI

CELIA did not go to one of those places where there were hills and streams but, owing to Mrs. Marston's insistence on sitting on The Terrace in a cold wind and to a quarrel with the greengrocer which, according to the little servant's testimony, had involved several excursions in the heavy rain, she had her change of air and scene. Mrs. Marston had told her to go away, but the doctor and her own sense bade her stay and much as she disliked some of the offices she had to perform, she shared the little servant's feeling of holiday.

In addition to the tiny room occupied by Sophy and her tin trunk, there was a gaunt apartment behind Mrs. Marston's front bedroom. It contained a very large flat bed and what was known as a suite of furniture in bright yellow wood. Vigorously polished once a week for many years, it gave an effect of sunlight, but it was sunlight on a cold desert of linoleum, with one oasis in the form of a rug beside the bed. It was well-made furniture. The drawers ran sweetly and they and the shelves in the wardrobe were lined with white paper without a crease. They were all empty. Mrs. Marston did not, like weaker spirits, keep her unseasonable garments in the spare bedroom. It was always ready for those visitors who were not wanted and never came. On the narrow mantelshelf, two large shells flanked an ornamental clock that did not go and had probably never gone with much determination. A picture of a woman clinging to a cross fixed on a rock in the midst of a stormy sea, hung above the washing-stand. There was no other attempt at decoration except for the gleaming white covers on dressing-table and chest of drawers.

'We wash them every so often and put them back,' Sophy said. 'Clean, isn't it?' she asked, looking round proudly.

A few hours later, Susan carried Celia's bag and a bunch of flowers into this room.

'You must have something to cheer you up,' she said.

'But I don't need cheering. I feel as if I'm in rather uncomfortable seaside lodgings and I like it. And Susan,' she said gently. 'I wasn't kind, but perhaps I gave you all the help I could.'

'Yes', Susan said. 'And don't worry about the family. Miss Riggs and I are going to look after them.'

'The view from this window isn't very good,' Celia said, looking at someone else's patch of back garden and a tin bath hanging on the house wall, for in this corner of Upper Radstowe streets that were almost slums elbowed the past grandeur of The Terrace. 'But then, I'm used to having none at all and if I put my head out and crick my neck, I can see Easterly church tower. No, no, I shan't worry about the family. The children are lucky not to have been orphans for years.'

Mrs. Marston's bedroom seemed like a village set among palm trees compared with Celia's desert. It had a carpet, a little table, an old tea caddy and various knick-knacks on the chest of drawers, some empty cut glass bottles on the dressing-table. There were framed photographs on the walls and Celia thought it wiser not to look at them. A closer acquaintance with the faces of Gerald's aunts and cousins and the benignity of Mrs. Marston's favourite minister might make her a less tender nurse to the patient who lay quite still, propped on her pillows, as though exhausted. The high temperature, in which perhaps the disagreement with the greengrocer had been exaggerated into an unfinished feud, was going down satisfactorily before Gerald knew that she was ill. She had a magnificent constitution, the doctor said.

'Iron,' said Celia.

He politely accepted this emendation. An iron constitution, but Mrs. Marston was not young. There was some bronchitis; there was always the danger of pulmonary complications; she would need care and Celia longed to ask why she should have it. As far as she knew, there was no one who would much regret the passing of this old woman and, behind her physical determination to live, the refusal of the machine to stop working before every ounce of energy was used up, there might well be a mental desire to let go her grasp of the material things which seemed to be the only ones she had, to renounce her ceaseless anxiety to have the furniture polished and the pots scoured, to find tasks for the little servant all day long and make sure the tradespeople did not overcharge her by a farthing.

'Who was that came in just now?' she asked wheezily.

'That was Catherine.'

'She's very heavy on her feet. What did she come for?'

'To ask about you and to say good night to me. I'm going to sleep here in case you want me.'

Mrs. Marston raised herself a little. 'Then I'll have to get up and see about the sheets. I don't trust that girl's airing.'

'For a few days, you must trust me.'

'But what if they're the wrong sheets? You're not using a top one at the bottom, are you?'

'Certainly not. I shouldn't be able to sleep,' Celia said gravely.

Mrs. Marston turned down the corners of her mouth, her frown deepened. She lifted her hands for an inch or two and dropped them. 'Ah, you're very funny, aren't you?' she said wearily.

It must have been a long time since that little house had received so many visitors. Susan and Catherine had come and gone, then Jimmy came, on tiptoe, anxious not to be heard by the invalid whose possible wish to see her grandson would have to be obeyed. Whispering, he interviewed his mother in the pale parlour at the back, made a prowling inspection of the ornaments, shrugged his shoulders at the pictures, shrugged them at the whole situation and then went off and Celia heard his footsteps growing loud and purposeful on the pavement.

When Gerald came, his mother was asleep. He looked in at her, then returned to Celia in the little parlour. There, an electric light in a glass globe shone cruelly on the flowered carpet, the stiff chairs, the cabinet of black wood with velvet-lined shelves on which Mrs. Marston's most valued pieces of china and glass were disposed. The room had french windows opening ironically on a tiny gravel path and a square of shabby turf, and Celia stood beside them, having for her background the thick lace curtains arranged as a screen against the neighbours' windows.

'She's not very bad, is she?' Gerald asked.

'No, I don't think so.'

Two of her slow, lazy steps took her into the middle of the room and she felt absurdly shy of Gerald on this ground which was completely alien to her but not to him, and she was also a little embarrassed, for his sake, by the neat barrenness of the room, its lack of grace or any evidence of a gracious personality.

'Then why shouldn't I sleep here instead of you?'

'I might be needed.' She was not going to be deprived of her holiday in the seaside lodgings. 'I feel . . .' she looked round for a comfortable chair, shook her head and remained on her feet. 'I feel rather important, everybody coming in to see me. Rather grand, being left in charge of someone else's house. Flowers in my bedroom.'

'Flowers?'

'From Susan.'

'Susan's a nice girl. She's seeing to our supper. It's going to be very late but they're having a grand time over it in the kitchen.'

That was why there had been so much hope in Jimmy's footsteps, and Celia said quickly, 'I'm sure Miss Riggs left everything ready. It's quite unnecessary for Susan to help.'

'But not unnecessary,' Gerald said, 'to have some fun. Potatoes, for instance, seem to be very amusing when you're not used to them in their raw state.'

'Oh well,' Celia said, 'we all seem to be enjoying ourselves in our own ways. It's quite an excitement for Sophy and she's going to bring me some tea in the morning.'

'You're not going to sit up, are you?'

'No, I shall go to bed and leave the doors open. The bed looks unyielding . . .'

'But at least you'll have it all to yourself.'

'Acres of it,' she said lightly.

He went out of the room and she thought he had gone without saying good night, but in a few minutes he came back.

'I've stoked up the kitchen fire. It ought to last till the morning and I'll come in directly after breakfast. Good night.'

She went with him to the door and, standing outside it, she heard, in the growing darkness, the first real sounds of summer: slow, soft footsteps of people on The Terrace who were not, like Jimmy, in a hurry; voices tempered to the warm air and fitted to the mood of lovers clasped in the shadows; and the noises down by the docks had a gaiety, as though the work done there was in the nature of a festival.

'Somehow,' Gerald said awkwardly, 'I don't like leaving you here. You're not afraid, are you?'

She had a feeling that he hoped she was, that the sight of her in new surroundings and the sweetness of the summer night had melted some of his cold anger and made her fresh to him and desirable again and she wished she could say she was afraid and take him with her into the desert and make it blossom like a rose. Even in the sour neighbourhood of

Mrs. Marston, it might have blossomed with exotic incongruity, and she rebelled against the thriftlessness of denying it; she mourned her hard inability to say a word or make a gesture to meet those he had waiting for her.

'Of course, I'm not afraid,' she said sensibly.

His own tone changed at once. 'I thought it might feel rather gruesome, being left alone with someone who is ill. That's all.'

His footsteps were not like Jimmy's nor like those of the idlers on The Terrace; they were quick and light, as though he did not want to hear them, as though, by subduing them, he could forget whence he came. He walked as she would have walked in his case, almost gaily, in the way a child hurries from a scene which must not be remembered, which, by the exercise of great care, has never happened.

She turned into the house. After all, she thought, it was easier for him to be magnanimous. In him, physical desire could swamp the memory of his grievances. She had no grievances — unless the lack of any made one — but her mind and her imagination had to be fired before she could feel more than the kindness of long, if not very close, companionship, and because she had once seen him looking as though he were fired in that way, too, and not by her, she resented his readiness to take her on lower terms, merely because she was there, because she was his wife and it was a night for love.

She went upstairs and saw the door of the desert open and heard a pleasant sound of crackling wood. Sophy was kneeling in front of the grate and feeding a newly lighted fire.

'But I don't need that,' Celia protested in a whisper.

''E said I was to light it,' Sophy whispered back. ''E said it would be chilly come the early morning and you pottering about. And so it will be. And plenty of coal I was to bring up, to last you well. But I don't know how this

355

chimney's going to draw. It can't ever have done it before in its life.'

'This is really heaping coals,' Celia sighed.

'Oo, there's plenty in the cellar,' Sophy said in a carefree manner, and, spreading her fingers across her mouth and supporting her chin with her thumb, she added warningly, 'And now all we've got to do is to take care she don't find out. I wouldn't use the tongs, Mum, if I was to be you. I'd pick the coal out with my fingers.'

'And have a face like yours?' Celia inquired, turning Sophy to the glass. 'Mind you wash it before you go to bed.'

Sophy giggled and guiltily caught her lip. If she said her prayers that night and made any petition for her mistress, it must have been that God would see fit to keep her in bed for a long time. She liked the younger Mrs. Marston. In Sophy's view she was a real lady, one of those who could be funny with a girl and still keep her in her place. 'I'd work my fingers to the bone for her,' she told her pillow, and, as it happened, little Sophy had to work very hard. She did it with ardour and selflessness, taking her part in the campaign which was waged upstairs, which Celia fought, as a point of honour, in her real indifference to the issue.

Gerald's thought and Sophy's lavishness with someone else's coal were to blame for the serious development of Mrs. Marston's illness. The chimney drew very well and Celia, meaning to doze in snatches between her visits to the sickroom, fell into a deep sleep induced by the unwonted warmth. She woke, uncomfortably hot, at the clutch of a hard hand, and saw Mrs. Marston standing over her, her feet bare, a shawl slipping from her shoulders, her state one of indignation at wicked extravagance and neglect.

This little excursion need not have done her very much harm, but the indignation was exhausting and, in an attempt to express it adequately, she refused to return to bed. What was the use of doing that, she asked, when she might call and cough for hours unheeded? She was better up and looking after herself.

'Much, much,' Celia hastened to say, but Mrs. Marston saw through that little ruse.

No doubt she was somewhat light-headed, but she knew what she was doing when she insisted on inspecting her larder and all her cupboards, arguing that people who could take her coal would take other things as well, so up and down the stairs she and Celia went, and in and out of the rooms; they sat on spindly chairs in the parlour, on slippery leather ones in the dining-room and when Celia conscientiously and hopelessly tried to throw another wrap round her mother-in-law's shoulders it was immediately thrown off.

'You'll be ill, you'll be seriously ill,' she said at last, 'and that will cost you a lot of money.'

'And I can well afford it,' Mrs. Marston said, jerking her head up and keeping it at the haughty angle of the slightly drunken. 'And you needn't follow me about. I'm not a lunatic.'

But this, after the distasteful task of forcing Mrs. Marston's feet into her bed socks was all Celia could do to make amends for the betrayal of her trust and, just before six o'clock, when Sophy stole downstairs, she found the two Mrs. Marstons in the kitchen and the elder was asleep with her head against a pile of pillows Celia had wedged between the table and her chair.

'Can we carry her up between us?' she asked wearily.

'No,' Sophy said at once, 'but there's a friend of mine's father lives three doors up the street and I reckon 'e could.'

WHAT impressed Celia was the genuineness and simplicity of Gerald's feelings in connection with his mother's illness. She did not see how he could suffer much sense of loss if Mrs. Marston died, but she was sure he had no thoughts he would have been ashamed to confess, none unworthy of the most devoted son, no slightest sneaking calculation of the immaterial benefits, and she knew he expected no others, that might be derived from the removal of the cause of unacknowledged friction, and it seemed to her that men, as a whole, had a wider humanity than women as well as a stronger sense of decency. Possibly that sense was a controlling factor in their emotions, but it could not altogether change them. Gerald was very anxious; he was distressed to the point of blaming Celia sharply, first for falling asleep in the heat his thoughtfulness had engendered, and then for not getting an amazingly strong and determined woman into her bed and keeping her there against her will.

'But where were the ropes?' Celia asked. 'They are not things the average person keeps in the house. And who was to hold your mother down while I tied the things that weren't there round her?'

'Must you be flippant, even now?' he asked.

With her hands loosely clasped in front of her, her eyes downcast, she said meekly, 'I was just trying to work it out.'

Her lips twitched, she suppressed a nervous desire to laugh uproariously when she remembered the absurdity of the perambulations of the night and she decided that even given the strength and the ropes, Mrs. Marston's life was not worth the brutal struggle she could envisage.

Her life seemed worth very little during the days that

followed. The case was now beyond Celia's unskilful ministrations, the seaside lodgings were given over to the nurses and after the night when Mrs. Marston discovered that she was alone in the house with hirelings, Celia made a bedroom for herself in the parlour. She liked pushing the furniture about to make room for her camp-bed and huddling all the ornaments into the cabinet among the treasures; she felt a personal enmity for ugly things and when Mrs. Marston was their owner she took a special pleasure in letting them know what she thought of them. Her heart was not softened towards the old woman upstairs, simply because she was ill; that would have been unreasonable: it did not yield under the pressure of Mrs. Marston's constant desire for her company; she suspected that as a determination to make her do what she least liked, but she did it with every appearance of willingness in what time she could spare from all the duties falling on her in the little overcrowded household and a certain amount of attention to her own affairs. There were not many of these. Catherine had gone to stay with May; Miss Riggs saw to the men's morning and evening meals and Celia did not deceive herself or anybody else about her enjoyment of the situation. She was more fully occupied and more fatigued than she had been for many years; every hour there were things to be done which could not be left till to-morrow, but they were new things and she was dealing with new people. She took a childish pleasure in her bedroom with the french windows opening on to the patch of grass and sometimes, on these warm nights, she left the camp-bed which was not very comfortable, to stand beside the windows and listen to the sounds down by the docks or hear a steamer hooting on the river, and sometimes she would creep upstairs to share one of the many cups of tea the night nurse brewed.

The night nurse did not like that hooting. She said it gave her the shudders.

359

'Does it? I think it's a lovely sound,' Celia said, and then she caught her breath so suddenly that the nurse looked at her with a professional eye and wondered if here was another patient.

'What is it?' she said. 'A pain?'

'No,' Celia said slowly. 'Not exactly.'

'Well, you'd better go back to bed and I'll bring you a hot bottle. We can't have you getting a chill too.'

There was pain and there was chill in the little gasp of surprise Celia had given. She had been hearing that sound with its memories of her youth when she heard it from Pauline's garden, when its voice of doom for unnumbered men and women had been one of triumph, of deep content, for her, but not once had she wondered whether Richard could be listening to it too. By this time, surely, he must be staying with Pauline and she had forgotten to imagine him there. She had been too busy, she excused herself, clasping the hot-water bottle to her disloyal heart, but, if he were there, she thought, shifting the disloyalty to him, why had he made no sign? Then, with a great effort of will, she forced herself to sleep before she could answer her own question or blame herself anew.

And the next day brought its duties, its visits from Catherine and Jimmy and Gerald who, seen from this angle, all looked a little changed; she cooked and made beds and dusted; she listened with unfeigned interest to the private affairs of the day nurse who was young and incapable of deciding which of her admirers she liked best, and she had her little jokes with Sophy. Miss Riggs arrived to make her daily report and, if possible, to find something to do and, in the afternoon, Susan brought her mother in the car.

May entered the house alone, and as Celia asked brightly, 'Where's Julia? Haven't you brought her, too?' she felt the pathos of all these incursions into the house few people had entered hitherto, of the ease with which unhallowed hands misplaced Mrs. Marston's sacred and rigidly arranged possessions and the helplessness of the old woman herself.

'Julia?' said May.

She seemed much too big for the little dining-room; her ox-like gaze fell mildly at the pleated paper in the grate and the crochet head rests on the slippery arm-chairs.

'Awful, isn't it?' Celia said.

'Isn't she going to get better?'

'I meant the room.'

'Oh, the room.' May was not in the least disturbed by other people's lack of taste. She looked again, taking it all in, accepting it as the proper setting for its owner and indeed Mrs. Marston's appearance would have suffered severely in May's house.

'Polar regions,' Celia said, 'even on a day like this and you can get a perfect toboggan slide on these chairs. Thank you, for taking care of Catherine. She's having a very happy time and very good things to eat. Salmon, the day before yesterday, I hear, and chicken is quite an ordinary occurrence.'

'Nobody wants to eat much meat in this weather.'

'Lucky for the poor, isn't it?' Celia said.

She was not referring to herself but to people who knew what it was to be hungry and to have no means of satisfaction. She was not as poor as all that, but it did occur to her that May, with an excellent cook and plenty of money, might have used both towards filling a hamper with good things, beyond the time or skill of Sophy or herself to produce. A little anxiety for the morrow no doubt quickened the imagination; no anxiety or too much might deaden it altogether.

'Eggs in aspic,' she said thoughtfully. 'A Russian salad, a cold chicken, or even two of them, nicely glazed.'

'Yes, that's the kind of thing,' May agreed.

Handsome and serene, sitting on one of the toboggan slides with all time, her own and Celia's, at her disposal, she had singularly little to say. She had been silent that day, which seemed very long ago, when she walked with dignity out of Celia's flat, and perhaps she had been silent ever since. Was this a permanent stupor, or had she some abiding cause for content? In either case, Celia felt a desire to rouse her.

'What about Julia?' she asked again. 'What have you done with her?'

'Nothing. Just ignored her. Silly little thing,' May said calmly.

'But you can't, can you, suddenly maroon her like that?'

'Maroon?' May took a little time before she said, 'Oh, I see what you mean.' And putting her hands together and dropping them on her knee in sign that the whole matter was satisfactorily settled and her conscience was clear, she said, to Celia's great surprise, 'She has a perfectly comfortable island. Everything she could possibly want. What are you laughing at? It's quite true.'

'And can't the truth be funny? It's often the funniest thing there is. But I agree. Her island has all the amenities. Faultless children, an adoring husband.'

'Well,' said May slowly, 'I rather wonder about that. After all, John is a very sensible man.'

'Yes. It would be interesting to know exactly what the men we married think of us, but which of us would dare to ask?'

'It would be very foolish,' May said.

She rose and went to the window. On the left, at a little distance from the house, the car was drawn up at the side of the street. In front, The Terrace could be seen until the cliff-like row of houses, casting its broad shadow, curved towards the road, leaving at first a narrow strip of pavement and then none at all in view. Susan sat at the wheel of the car and used it as a book-rest. She did not move except to turn a page and the sunlight fell on her pale frock and her wide hat.

'Foolish?' Celia said.

'When you know already,' May replied.

'But if you don't know?'

'Better not,' May said.

Celia joined her at the window. It was a narrow one and the space above the plant pots was filled by the two women, mature, comely, broad-shouldered and tall; they stood almost touching and never in their lives had they seemed so near each other in comprehension. Celia was the younger by only a few years, but now while she felt wiser than May and quite as experienced, she also felt almost girlish in the consciousness of her own resiliency in comparison with this sister who suddenly seemed heavy with years, with going on in the way she had chosen or slipped into by carelessness or chance.

'How still she sits,' she said, looking at Susan absorbed in her book.

'Yes, I could never do that. She's more like you.'

Belying her reputation, Celia made an impatient movement. May did not notice it. She said thoughtfully, 'Catherine talks a lot about you.'

'How stupid of her! Accept my apologies.'

May sighed quite frankly. 'I don't know how you manage it.'

'What, exactly?'

'Making her think you are pretty nearly perfect.'

'It does sound rather a feat, but it's news to me. I can assure you she finds fault very often.'

'Yes, that's just it,' May said sadly. 'Jimmy, too, I dare say, and Gerald.'

'Oh yes, Gerald certainly,' Celia said cheerfully, but, as she spoke, she realized how seldom he had done it.

'Well,' said May, turning to look at Celia with something like grief in her eyes, dark, with a bluish film over them, 'my girls, even Priscilla, never find fault with me at all.'

This was a confession, not a boast. It could not be received with flippancy, consolation could not be offered. It simply had to be heard.

'Neither does Stephen,' May added. 'I suppose they know it would be a waste of time.'

'Are you sure you're talking sense?' Celia inquired gently.

'Yes, it's a change, isn't it?' May said. There were tears in her eyes now. 'It's my own fault. They just put up with me. That's all they do. They just put up with me. I don't know why I've been so long in finding out.' She sniffed violently, then controlled herself. 'They're so polite!' she exclaimed with intense annoyance. 'I don't believe Catherine's polite to you.'

'She's never rude.'

'Oh, that's quite different.'

'And she laughs at me a great deal.' She was almost ready to be disloyal to Catherine for the sake of cheering this large disconsolate person who looked at her now with a sort of scorn.

'You're trying to be kind but you're only making it worse. My children don't laugh at me. If they started, they'd never stop and it wouldn't be a nice sound to hear. It wouldn't be like Catherine's laughter. You must know that yourself. You know they think I'm a fool.'

'But you're not.'

'Then,' said May piteously, 'why do I seem like one?'

'Yes. Why?' Celia asked.

It was time to get the nurse's tea and Sophy had gone out to do some shopping, but the nurse would have to go thirsty for a little while. At that moment a cry of distress from the room overhead would hardly have taken Celia from May's side and, instinctively, she made herself go limp, lest May should stiffen under the eagerness of her curiosity. What she wanted to know was whether her sister had found the monkey in her own puzzle, whether she knew she had hidden it herself, years ago, under a flood of talk, under Julia's companionship and a deliberate stupidity, and blinded herself with the queer film over her eyes.

'I'm not clever,' May said gratuitously. 'I never was, at school. Lazy, I suppose. But you weren't clever either.'

'Won't you let me have been lazy too?' Celia asked, but May did not look for the point of that remark.

'I don't think you're clever now, are you?' she went on ingenuously.

'Ask Julia.'

'Oh, Julia — ! But you seem,' she said slowly, 'to know how to live.'

'No, no!' Celia cried. 'I haven't even begun to learn.'

'To make people happy, then.'

'That, least of all,' Celia said.

'The way they all talk about you —'

'All?'

'Catherine and Jimmy and Gerald.'

'But when do you see Gerald?'

'He comes sometimes, in the evenings, nowadays.'

'Ah, yes,' Celia said. She remembered the bond of her distrust existing now between him and Stephen, the mutual recognition of two generous souls, and the droop of her eyelids had an ironic slant.

'But he doesn't stay long. He's working very hard, he tells me.'

Celia stepped sideways and leaned against the wall bordering the window. From that position she had a view of her sister's profile, the chin just threatening to become fleshy, the shapely nose and the clear skin.

'Of course, I was a fool to be a fool,' May said, 'and now I don't know whether I can be anything else. We don't change much at our age. And I suppose,' she smiled awkwardly, 'I'm a fool to talk to you like this. What I really came to tell you is that Stephen and I are going away for a little while, and will you trust Catherine to the girls?'

'Why, of course. Where are you going?'

'I don't know yet. Somewhere new,' May said with a certain crispness.

'One wants something new occasionally. I'm getting it here. Shall I ask Susan to come in and have tea? She's very patient out there.'

'She wants to finish that book. It's Mrs. Carey's and she's taking it back after she's seen me home. She's been there several times lately. It seems to me that Mrs. Carey is the kind of woman who picks people up when she wants them and then drops them. I suppose Susan helps to entertain that brother. But we mustn't stay.'

Celia held out her cheek to be kissed. 'They'll be able to have tea in the garden,' she said, staring at one of the four pictures representing the seasons. 'But the tide's out.'

The nurse, coming downstairs a few minutes later, in search of tea, found her standing in the passage with a most unusual expression on her face.

'What's up? Have you seen a ghost?' she asked in her jaunty way.

'No, no,' she said slowly. 'It seemed rather like one last night but, after all, it turns out to be flesh and blood.'

'H'm, that's what they always are, if you ask me.'

CHAPTER XLVIII

'HULLO!' Celia said an hour later. 'Have you brought my mackintosh?'

'That old thing?' said Julia. 'I didn't know you'd want it back.'

It was her first appearance on the scene of woe, and Celia, remembering their last meeting, was surprised Julia should come at all with her conventional offering of flowers. It was rather a shabby little bunch, for Julia had her small economies. It was by no means what she would have carried to one of her wealthier acquaintances.

'Will you give them to Mrs. Marston with my love?' she said.

Celia shook her head. 'I'm afraid she's not interested in flowers.'

'As bad as that?'

'A very slight headache would be bad enough for that with me. Any bodily discomfort soon overcomes my sense of beauty and Mrs. Marston never had any and she's seriously ill. A little better to-day, though.'

'What a relief for you!' Julia exclaimed, and, getting no response, she said in a dreamy manner, 'But all the same, I think even if I were dying . . .'

'No, you wouldn't. I'm sure you wouldn't want to gaze at lilies. It's a pretty thought, but dying isn't pretty. It's grotesque, very often. It's undignified; it's the last insult. But death accomplished — that's different. Then you get far more significance than you ever had in life. It's really almost something to look forward to.' She glanced at Julia who sat rather sullenly under instructions from such a quarter, and said in a different, businesslike tone, 'But about my mackintosh. I wanted it very badly when we had all that wet weather and it's the only one I've got.'

'Then, dear, why don't you get a new one?'

'I shall, at your expense, unless you send the old one back.'

'I'll give it to Sybil to-morrow to give to Catherine.'

'That's rather hard on Sybil. It will make her blush. And anyhow, Catherine's staying with May, so you must post it to me. Ninepence, I should think, and I owe you threepence, don't I?'

A tiny shrug of Julia's shoulders dismissed these sordid details. 'I haven't seen May lately. To tell you the truth,' she said in a tone of confidence, 'she was rather a bad habit. A dear old thing, but terribly limited. I couldn't go on for ever, just taking her to look at the shops, could I?'

'Why not?'

'Such a waste of time.'

'And what are you doing with your time now?'

'Oh, I can assure you it doesn't hang heavily on my hands!' She showed her little hands in their clean gloves. Some of her old playfulness had returned. She was the busy wife and mother, overdriven but indomitably gay. 'But I really must pop in and see her soon.'

'Then you'd better pop at once. She's going away for a little while, with Stephen.'

'Oh, with Stephen.'

'Naturally. You don't think she's going off with someone else, do you?'

Julia frowned. 'I know it's a joke, Celia, but I don't like it. It's so vulgar.'

There were plenty of retorts on Celia's lips, but she realized the futility of making them and she could only laugh. 'May's right,' she said. 'We don't change much at our age. Now, run along. I've dozens of things to do and I happen to know that May's at home this afternoon. You'll be sure to find her.'

'I'm afraid I haven't time,' Julia said regretfully, 'but if you see her before she goes . . . ' There was a faint shadow on her face and it might have been caused by envy. 'I shouldn't really like to have a holiday without the children,' she said slowly as she went away.

She seemed lonely; she could hardly fail to be, and perhaps she was wishing John would carry her off for another honeymoon. Was that to be the character of May's holiday with Stephen? Celia wondered. And she felt a strong distaste for the thoroughness of Stephen's good intentions; there was a sort of insensitiveness about it, but who was she to judge? For all she knew, it was May who had proposed the trip, in innocence or in shrewdness. And she thought they were all rather pathetic, these men and women of her family. They were all more or less mis-mated yet they could not and they did not wish to break their bonds. Even she could not break hers. Though the one attaching her to Gerald had worn thin, it held still, and primitively, unreasonably, she resented the idea that the one from him to her had worn thin too. Why was it? Was it only pride? If pride could be eliminated, would she really care? She did not know, but, late that night, long after he had paid his hurried visit, long after, she hoped, Catherine had fallen asleep in one of May's luxurious beds, she went on to The Terrace.

Looking behind her, she saw the dim light in Mrs. Marston's bedroom; there was nobody in the street where Susan's car had stood that afternoon and there were no lights in the houses. The street lamps, hardly noticed in the daytime, had become discreet and competent persons and those on The Terrace, following the pavement's curve, stood straight and steadfast, like beacons set up as warnings against the dangerous coast towering behind them. She heard the footsteps of someone out of sight and going away from her and she felt they must be disembodied, yet they were dramatic; she could fit emotions to them, those of a fugitive, a lover, an ordinary citizen, burdened with cares, perhaps, but going home. She was making for home herself although she hardly knew it. With her slow, easy movement, she went forward, then paused to lean against the railings. The road below was like a pale river; its whiteness could be seen as the swiftness of its flow; the real river she could not see, but there was a blaze of lights down there whence came sounds as familiar as the sirens, sounds she did not understand, as though men were juggling with sheets of iron and assaulting them with hammers. It had something to do with the ships, repairing, loading or unloading them, and she was content with that sparse knowledge but, through the satisfaction she always felt when she contemplated this part of her native city, there came a picture of Jimmy and Susan wandering down there, then of the girl's set face when her confidences had been refused, her doubts disregarded, by the friend she trusted, and Celia remembered the Susan of this afternoon, sitting in the car instead of entering the house, composed and charming, absorbed in the book she was to carry to Pauline.

Thoughts raced through Celia's head and tripped each other up. It was she who had sent Susan to Paris, it was she who was now sending her across the Downs where a man, again recovering from an illness, lay in that garden perched on the high cliff, with the gulls like spread fans above his head, or deadly missiles dropping into the gulf, for if she had encouraged Jimmy in his love and Susan in her affection, Susan would have had something else to do than the reading and returning of borrowed books and entertaining Pauline's brother. And everybody said she and Susan were alike! She heard the pitiful childishness of this cry and she was ashamed of the angry jealousy that moved, like a snake, in her breast. There was no cause for it and yet her heart misgave her, telling her there were causes in plenty. There were youth and sweetness on one side and on the other a man whose first romantic love had been frustrated, who might well be weary of a solitary life and see in Susan a reincarnation of herself, appearing in the same place, but free, without a baby crawling on the grass.

She knew she was ridiculous, standing there, a middle-aged woman, torturing herself like a love-sick girl, but in truth, under the fleshly envelope already past its prime, she was a girl. The emotions of her youth had never been properly released and now they warred with her age, her experience and the humour she could always turn upon herself. Her pain was complicated by her mind's disdain of it.

'What folly!' she exclaimed softly, looking from the reddish lights clustered round the docks to the pale ones in the sky, tolerant and wise, powerless to bestow their wisdom but assuring her, somehow, that like truth and beauty, it did exist, and she thought she was lucky to be able to see them still as they had been when she was a child, as observers who came out and watched the world when it was dark. Scientific explanations only made things more difficult, she thought, but the watching stars could not comfort her to-night. She felt very lonely and she shivered in the warm air as the first siren hooted in the river. She smiled wryly. The sound was giving her the shudders too, and to-night it did not fail to take her to Pauline's garden, to Pauline herself and the friendship Celia had believed was lasting. It seemed to be founded on some inexplicable attraction of opposites who made no foolish attempt to get closer or to merge. That was its strength. It was more like a friendship of men than of women, steady, unexacting and secure, and suddenly it had gone and Richard was with Pauline and neither of them had made a sign and she felt bewildered and betrayed.

Approaching one of the lamps, she looked at the watch on her wrist. It was twelve o'clock and except for the clamour by the docks, everything was very still. She wished she could hear some footsteps, those of Jimmy tramping home, or Gerald's, returning, as lately they had done so often, at this hour, Jimmy coming from seeing Susan or consorting with his friends, Gerald from she knew not where and, though he might come from Maudie, to-night she would not care. She wanted the companionship of a human being on whom she had undeniable claims and who had them on her, but there was no such person, no person at all, in sight. Perhaps they were both asleep, she thought, up there at the top of the cliff and she was like someone ship-wrecked on the rocks below, cold and desolate.

Rather stealthily, she began moving towards her home but the attics were a long way up and from her position beneath them she could not see whether the windows were lighted or all dark and she stepped down the nearest flight of steps to the road. Then, from its farther side, she could see the dining-room window illuminated, the only window in all the long row to show a light. It seemed to be a signal for her and she ran up the steps as though she outran the strong breakers on the coast and, with her arms outstretched, she pushed the door. It did not move. It was the outer door, shut for the night, and she had no key. She remained there with her hands against it, and she thought, I'm just like the picture over the washing-stand in the desert!

She did not consider ringing the bell that connected with the flat. Her impulse would have died while Gerald came down the stairs expectant of bad news about his mother. It had gone already. She would not have known what to say. She could not tell him she wanted the warmth of his arms and the consciousness of their binding quality, simply because to-night she was unhappy, because like the lady in the picture she must cling to the nearest succour. How could she say that and then let go of it in a calmer sea?

Stepping back a few inches, she let her fingers slide down the panel of the door before her arms dropped to her sides.

They dropped heavily, with a finality untouched by despair, and she walked back towards the dim light in Mrs. Marston's bedroom without a pause. That little outburst of emotion had done her good and fortunately no one else could know of it. She was not deceived about some of its apparent implications: her mind, at least, was not a girl's. A girl might have mistaken for true love that homing instinct towards the person who was familiar and whose kindness was stronger than the consciousness of his own hurts. The need for kindness and the giving of it were not necessarily involved in passionate love. There was just as likely to be a sort of cruelty, an antagonism set up by the determination of each lover to preserve an identity in danger. She divined this; she did not know it from experience. She had not had an opportunity for testing it, she told herself, as she shut the front door very quietly. On the face of it, her experiences had been very limited, her life narrow. She had made it narrower than it need have been, a little enclosure for her thoughts, her memories, her dreams of what things would have been if they had all been different. It was charming, cloistered, full of flowers that received intensive treatment about once a year and bloomed more richly and spread their roots, but while she stood in Mrs. Marston's hall, as narrow as her cloister and much less delightful, she surprised a suspicion of her own enclosure, she had a wretched fear that Richard himself would have been astonished and perhaps appalled to know she had that secret place, and, picturing him with his dry air of humour, the eyebrows raised above the spectacles slipping down his nose when he looked up from his reading or his knitting, she realized that such sentimental fancies were strangers to his temperament. Gerald, she thought — and what could he be doing in the dining-room so late? — Gerald would understand them better. He understood much more than she was willing to let him share.

CHAPTER XLIX

NOTHING, she thought, watching him during the days that followed, would have been more romantic, more satisfactory and more convenient than discovering in him, at last, all she had always wanted and never found, nothing more exciting, in these circumstances, than trying to persuade him that his early conception of her character was the true one. And it would have been consonant with this happy ending if Mrs. Marston had shown signs of softening, of an essentially sweet nature under the rough husk in which life had enclosed it.

None of these things happened and Celia was glad to be spared the remorse of having misunderstood Mrs. Marston, the embarrassment of affectionate reconcilia- tions. Gerald was kind, thoughtful and grateful. He treated her as though she were a friend, of long standing but of no great intimacy, who was generously devoting her- self to the care of his mother, and Mrs. Marston continued to compress her lips, to stare suspiciously from the back- ground of her heaped pillows, at anyone who approached her. She was very weak; her heart was doing double work for the lungs which were not doing their share, but no one could be in the room without knowing that her mind was busy and highly critical of everything that was done. The trained assurance of the nurses could ignore her doubts of their skill; it was harder for Celia to deal with Mrs. Marston's anxiety to dispense with their attentions, her grim surprise at Celia's unwillingness to undertake these simple tasks herself. The thought of Sophy, to whom the sickroom was forbidden as a heavy footed and likely irritant, who, doubtless, was leaving dirt in corners and saucepans un- scoured, and, under Celia's easy rule, could not be earning the enormous meals she was probably consuming, was a perpetual annoyance to Mrs. Marston. She was not the mistress in her own house; it was in the possession of people she did not trust, and her will to live, in itself an aid to recovery, became an additional danger, owing to the fret and helpless anger behind it. The nurses, addressing her endearingly as their habit is, and persistently making the best of everything, annoyed her when they meant to soothe.

'A difficult old lady,' said the doctor.

'You can't please her,' said the nurses.

'She'll be in bed for a long time yet, won't she?' Sophy asked, with a solemn shake of the head and hope in her voice.

'I hope she won't ask to see me,' Catherine said. 'I can't bear ill people and even if she dies, I shan't be able to pretend I cared for her.'

'Yes, it's uncomfortable,' said Celia. 'One likes to have the correct reactions. Well, I have admiration, though I have no affection. She has real character. She's never taken anybody else's shape or colour and she won't now and, in a way, that's an achievement.'

It was late afternoon, the usual time for Catherine's visits, and she and Celia were in the parlour, careful not to disturb the night nurse who was still asleep in the room above. The french windows were wide open and Celia sat just within them and darned the family's socks and stockings while Catherine, opposite to her, lounged against the wall. The neighbour's tin bath and a cat sitting on the boundary fence were the chief objects in view.

'Lovely weather for May and Stephen,' Celia said.

'Yes.' Catherine crossed the grass plot in two long steps and approached the cat who at once looked proudly in the other direction.

'Don't touch it!' Celia called out as Catherine, uttering soft noises, raised a hand. 'I'm sure it's mangy.'

'I don't think so. Why should it be?'

'It belongs to the tin bath and I feel it must be. Oh,' Catherine had picked it up, 'don't put your face against it. And it's such a waste of affection. It only despises you. I think you'd better go and wash.'

'It's all right.' She had dropped the cat and now she scrubbed her cheek with her handkerchief. 'They're nice clean animals, cats.' Returning to the window, she said thoughtfully, 'I like it better there, you know, when Aunt May's at home. I suppose it wouldn't be at all convenient for me to go back to the flat?'

'Aren't they kind to you?' Celia asked quickly.

'Of course they are. But there's a sort of loose feeling in the house. Just', she made a little shaking movement with her hands, 'just loose. Anybody can do pretty nearly anything she likes.'

'And that's quite a common idea of bliss.'

'I know, but it isn't a bit nice when you get it.'

'And,' said Celia, who was not an asker of questions but knew how to get them answered, 'I don't suppose they behave any differently because May's away.'

'No, and it's funny because when she's there they don't take much notice of her. Very polite and all that, but not real notice. It's the kind of feeling you get when the head mistress isn't at school. It all goes on exactly the same, but it's all a tiny bit loose.'

'I'm afraid you'll have to put up with it. It doesn't sound very serious.'

'As a matter of fact,' said Catherine, stepping across the threshold and seating herself heavily on the camp-bed, 'as a matter of fact I feel thoroughly sick.'

'My child! Too much good food. Let me see your tongue.'

'Mentally,' Catherine said rather grandly. 'And I'd like to be at home.'

'I can't have you left there all alone in the evenings.'

376

'But Father's there. He says he's working every night until twelve or one o'clock.'

Celia absorbed this piece of information without showing surprise, but she registered the fact that when she was away he stayed at home; when she was at home, he was somewhere else and she was hurt enough to say quietly, 'You can't do without May, but you can manage without me very well.'

'Pet! Don't be silly! I should have my own father and we've been getting on very nicely lately. I think it's rather a mistake to have two parents about at the same time. You can't appreciate them both, and I should think,' Catherine said wisely, 'he feels I belong to him more when you're not there. And so I do. It's quite natural.'

'Quite,' Celia said with truth, but what she wanted to say was that Gerald had no right to her at all, that she herself had tried with all her moral and mental strength to resist the conception of this child who had become so dear and, failing there, had imaginatively given her the father she should have had. 'However, I can't give Miss Riggs any more work to do and I shall be happier if you stay at May's.'

'Even though your daughter's suffering?' Catherine asked with an indignation not altogether assumed.

'I think you'd better tell me why.'

'I expect you'll be cross but I can't help it.' She flung herself back on the pillows and addressed the ceiling. 'It's that man,' she said. 'That Mr. Milligan.'

Celia gave a little gasp of laughter, the statement came at so odd a time and Catherine, justifying herself, said with mournful horror, 'He only has one leg! If I hadn't been told I'd have thought he just had a limp and I shouldn't have cared much for that, but to know, to know — I mean he must go to bed and have a bath, mustn't he? I couldn't stay in the room with him and now I shall always be terrified in case I find him there when I go back.' She sat up with a jerk. 'Why don't you say something? Too furious? I know it's cowardly. There's really no harm in him. Nice, funny little man. But anyhow, that's why I feel sick.'

Celia dropped her hands in her lap, one of them wearing a sock of Jimmy's, like a glove, and she looked at the fence to which the determined cat had returned. She was conscious of a slight vibration all over her body but she knew there was no visible sign of it. The cause of it was complicated. It seemed impossible for her to have an entirely simple emotion. There was the realization that Richard, well enough to visit other people, had not sought her out. There was a probably unscientific wonder whether her own consciousness of his injury had prenatally affected Catherine. There was scorn for this young thing on the bed who had not lived through massacres and seemed callous to loss and suffering and in her mind there was a picture of Richard limping about May's house, of all unlikely places. She knew the sound of that uneven footstep which would hardly be heard on the thick carpets and she saw Prudence and Susan tactfully getting him into the most comfortable chair. And charming they would look in the beautiful drawing-room, with their smooth heads, their reddened lips and pretty frocks. But their feet are rather big, she found herself thinking as this picture connected itself, to her discomfort and sour pleasure, with all those invitation cards in his sitting-room, all the kind ladies bringing offerings of fruit and flowers. Did they, like Susan some time ago, like Catherine now, describe him as a nice, a funny little man? For her, since she first saw him he had been the only man of real importance in the world, subtly distinguished in spite of his rather ordinary exterior, a person of most satisfying humour and infinite comprehension. Funny? Yes, when he chose. In Paris had he not succeeded in amusing Susan? Little? He was as tall as Celia herself, above the average height for a woman. And nice? This word in

378

conjunction with the others suggested a sort of harmlessness in him that was disparaging. Celia herself had always known him gentle. Even when she resisted his persuasions he had been gentle, making it as easy as he could for her, and thereafter his perfect scrupulousness, his generous lack of reproaches, had been her pride, because she believed they were his strength.

'Are you as disgusted as all that?' Catherine asked. 'I know it's very babyish.'

'Babyish?' Celia echoed, trying to pick up her cue, 'Oh yes, yes, but it's worse than that. It's so unchivalrous. But I remember, I used to feel like that about people with squints. I couldn't believe anyone with a squint was honest. It would be pleasant to think I'd conquered the feeling but, when I come to think of it, there aren't any squints nowadays. Things do improve. There's no doubt about it. Lots of children squinted furiously when I was young and most of the poorer sort had legs like Norman arches.'

'More reminiscences!' Catherine said with a chuckle.

'There's so much more behind me than there is in front,' Celia said.

'Darling! You've got to be my children's grandmother for ages. You're not sad, are you? I'll try to be more sensible if I see him again and, anyhow, he won't know. He won't take much notice of me when Prudence and Susan are about. I seem to be at the age when I'm not noticed. Too lumpy. D'you think I'll ever be like them? Really feminine? It must be an awful bother.'

'Does Mr. Milligan know who you are?' She could not resist asking that question.

'I should think so,' Catherine said carelessly, 'but Mrs. Carey seemed rather as if she had forgotten. Funny, that. She came and fetched him like the nurse at a children's party. And she's always been so nice to me, because she's your friend, I suppose.'

'Yes, and it can't have been very easy. You are about the same age as Meredith, you know.'

Catherine frowned slightly. 'D'you think she's miserable?'

'Nobody can remember to be miserable all the time.'

'You don't look very happy yourself. What are you staring at so hard?'

'Trying to see myself,' she said, for the window, pushed back against the outer wall of brick, made a kind of looking-glass.

'You're all right. Just the same as usual.'

'That's what I'm afraid of. And I've never seen myself any more clearly than I do now, in that window, through a glass darkly. Eyes overstrained, perhaps,' she added dryly, 'with looking for things that were never there.'

She had been leaning forward to peer, but now she straightened herself with an unusually quick movement and looked at Catherine who sat on the edge of the bed, her head bowed, her hair falling forward, her toes turned in and tapping the floor, a much more important person than that dim figure in the glass for whom life's pace was necessarily beginning to slow down of its own accord. She had a vivid, almost physical impression of the energy, the potentialities for joy and pain, stored in Catherine's mind and body and she felt a passionate desire not to make things easy for her, since ultimately that was no kindness, but to give her vision, the power to see and to feel the truth, the values, that lay beyond herself. That, however, was not in her gift for she did not possess it. The nearest she came to it was knowing she ought to have it and of almost being willing to resign everything for its sake. 'Almost,' she sighed, aware of her own weakness.

Catherine's feet tapped a little faster. 'D'you know what I think?' she said.

'I do not,' Celia replied gravely.

'Well, I think father's got some kind of secret, something

380

that makes him happy,' and at these words Celia became more than ever aware of her own weakness.

'What makes you think that?' she asked.

'Oh, he looks sort of younger and livelier. Rather like Christmas when we were little. Haven't you noticed it?'

'When he comes here,' Celia answered slowly, 'he's always rather anxious and distressed.'

'Yes. Funny, isn't it? But very nice of him and I suppose there's always a sort of animal instinct about parents and a sense of duty.'

'Thank you very much,' Celia said.

With a spring imperilling the camp-bed, Catherine enveloped her mother in a rough embrace. 'You've never been a parent in that way,' she said. 'Even Father hasn't. He was rather — nothing in particular, but I'm beginning to see him as much more of a person.'

IT soon became apparent that Mrs. Marston was not going to get well. She sank lower into her pillows, her eyes grew weary of keeping watch. She was loosening her grasp at last and even the sound of china slipping from Sophy's hands to the kitchen floor would hardly have roused her. Celia, though her time was no longer claimed, spent as much of it as she could in the bedroom where white crochet mats covered everything coverable and faded photographs of women with lockets and men with side whiskers looked smugly on this scene of dissolution. She wondered how many of these pictured people were themselves still living, how many would arrive with head-shakings and black-edged handkerchiefs for the funeral. They were the kind of people to spend much more than they could afford on a railway journey for such a ceremony. In the meantime the question of expense weighed rather heavily on Celia herself. She did not know how Gerald was paying for the only extravagance of Mrs. Marston's life. He had refused the offer of Celia's money; she was not to be allowed to make amends, and if, in spite of this new care, he was younger and livelier, perhaps it was unnecessary to worry. All she could do was to sit in his mother's bedroom, so that she should not start on her mysterious journey without someone to see her go, and this slow dying seemed to Celia like the meagre preparations of a lonely old woman doomed to unwilling emigration. The ship was at the quayside and though the passenger might linger, she had to be on board before the time of sailing, going with hardly a farewell and with no knowledge of the kind of welcome waiting for her. Celia knew she was not much more than the emigration officer, she had very little personal interest in the matter, but she fulfilled her duties conscientiously, sitting on a hard chair beside the window, looking at the weather which was still warm and brilliant and watching some of the world go by. It was weather for sitting in a garden, for wearing pale, pretty frocks, but it was a long time since she had had a garden at her command and her dresses were of serviceable colours and materials. It was weather for young men and maidens, playing one kind of game while the light lasted and another when it became too dark to see a ball. It was weather for charming grandmothers becomingly arranged on a veranda while the grandchildren sported on a lawn, not the weather in which a grandmother who was not charming should be dying on a brass bedstead, while a daughter-in-law who was neither young nor old, who could play neither game and was not a grandmother yet, looked from the window at the errand boys, at Mrs. Sanders going out with a basket to buy the provisions Catherine had found inadequate, at a pair of gipsies, going from house to house, with their hair arranged in plaited loops, babies supported in the shawls slung over their shoulders and much heavier baskets of pedlars' stuff than Mrs. Sanders could have managed. They were muscular, swarthy, no doubt un-savoury on a near approach, yet even without the babies they would have remained, in their own world, intensely feminine; in Celia's world they were somewhat rankly of the female sex, but, from her seat among the crochet covers, the side whiskers and the lockets, she felt a kind of scorn for the unadventurous respectability of her own existence, and because they had seen sights hidden from her, endured hardships, fed coarsely and experienced rough love, she thought they must know more of life than she did. She felt a little ashamed and apologetic when she shook her head at their proffered wares. She could talk to most people but she would not know how to talk to them. They would think her a poor weak thing, unfit to face the world, and, indeed, as she had once said, she had lived chiefly in the passive mood, the passive mood and the past tense, in a past episode so tenuous that it had taken all her time to preserve its being. She ought to have had half a dozen children; she ought to have been handled as these women were and to have learnt to use her nails on anyone who destroyed her peace instead of submitting to mental gnawings, but she could hardly persuade Gerald to take to drink in the hope of a salutary beating; she was the product of her environment and upbringing and scratching was not part of her equipment. She had to get her peace in a harder fashion, by learning a sort of indifference to self which was not lack of interest in it. That would be death and she did not want to die. On the contrary, not yet having learnt her lesson, having, as it were, merely supplied herself with the necessary books and fluttered the pages which must be closely studied, she opened her doors to a strong resurgence of her youth, the last chance it was likely to have. She wanted something to happen, and that was the cry of youth, something intense but simple in its emotions of happiness or grief. It was the simplicity of some emotion for which she craved and in which only youth believes and, as it would not come to her in this little house, she must go abroad to look for it..

Mrs. Marston, only half-conscious, was lying very still, and, in answer to Celia's raised eyebrows, the nurse shook her head reassuringly.

'You go out and enjoy yourself,' she said. 'What weather! I'd like to have a bit of fun myself. And it's not as if there's anything you can do.'

'I wanted, I rather wanted to take some clean clothes for Catherine, to my sister's house,' Celia said, and there was a little hesitation in her tone, as though she wondered whether this excuse would do. 'And if you want a bit of fun, Nurse, and can get it, why don't you take half a day to-morrow? There's not much you can do either.'

She made a neat parcel of the things she had washed and ironed for Catherine, then she went home to change her frock. She took the french hat from its box and put it back, and then she took it out again. It suited her. Richard and Susan had made no mistake about it. It suited her and it was suitable, whether for joy or woe, a wreath of laurel or a crown of thorns, and she made a bitter face at herself in the glass, knowing that the laurel of victory would mean defeat and a crown of thorns was not for her small sorrows. Nevertheless, she would wear the hat and when she had put it on at a becoming angle, powdered her nose and found a clean pair of gloves, she made a rapid inspection of the flat.

Everything was in order. Miss Riggs had seen to that. Her sitting-room, though it was spotless, felt neglected and forlorn. The dining-room, on the other hand, had come into its own. The baronial furniture seemed to assure her proudly that this was the favoured apartment. A thick roll of architect's plans leaned against the sideboard, there was a pot of wallflowers on the table and Celia wondered whether they had come from Jo's back garden. Miss Riggs, less happily, had spread a dustsheet over Catherine's bed, as though she were never coming back; her little treasures had been put away and Celia quickly shut the door on that sad emptiness. But Jimmy's room was as it had always been. He had innumerable small possessions, pencils and keys, knives, little boxes, notebooks and pipes, kept in a sort of orderly confusion, like that on a mechanic's bench. And his pyjamas, folded neatly, as she had taught him years ago, were under his pillow, promising that he, at least, intended to return. She gave the pillow a pat and, on an impulse, returned to her own room. There was only one pillow on the bed. Unlike his mother who preserved the one Mr. Marston's head should have pressed, Gerald had removed her own. But that might be Miss Riggs's doing. She had a mania for putting things away, it would go to her heart to use two pillow cases when one would do and, giving Gerald the benefit of the doubt, Celia ran down the stairs before she could vex herself with the unreasonableness of troubling to doubt at all.

She went up Barton Street and across The Green and then took the pleasantest, leafiest of the roads leading to May's house, but they were all pleasant, all leafy, all drowsing in the summer afternoon and informed with the serenity bestowed upon a place when most of its male inhabitants are safely collected in another part of a city and, as she approached the house, she was glad May was still away. She would not have learnt what she wanted to know from her. The holiday was being prolonged by the weather or its own success, but what on earth, Celia wondered, could they find to talk about? And she cast a thought towards Hester, taking other people's dogs for walks in the parks and doing errands for women who thought they were too busy to do them for themselves, while Stephen was doing the right thing according to the bond he had made when he was too young to know better, the thing that probably caused the least unhappiness and what Celia had never succeeded in doing properly herself, and when she saw the house in its clean cream coat, the windows wide open and the garden gay, she thought he had done well. This was a home and one could not destroy a home.

The front door was wide open, too, the gate into the garden was ajar and Celia did not scruple to walk upstairs and put Catherine's stockings, her handkerchiefs and white school blouse in their appropriate drawers. She had left traces of herself between morning and afternoon school. Her shoes, hurriedly kicked off her feet, were lying on their sides, like derelicts at low tide: the wardrobe door swung on its hinges; there were, most regrettably, a few hairs adhering to her comb; there were books on the bed and, on the table beside it, Celia was surprised and touched to see an old photograph of herself, a snapshot taken she could not remember when, but evidently on a windy day when a thin dress was driven against her figure.

'Dear me,' she murmured thoughtfully. 'What a pity!' And she forgot to straighten the shoes, shut the wardrobe and purify the comb. There was no sound to be heard from the landing but, thinking the girls might be in the garden, she went into the nursery whence she could look out at the lawn and as she entered the room she decided that Catherine's description of looseness in the house might certainly be applied to many of the doors, for here, an unprecedented opportunity, the front of Susan's doll's house had been swung back and left in that position, and the beautifully appointed little rooms were at anybody's mercy.

Celia would not take advantage of what might be an accident. She went to the window, stepped back hastily, then advanced again, like someone who shrinks from the first flash of an ugly sight but gathers courage in taking it piecemeal. And, visually, this was not an ugly sight. It was only that of a middle-aged gentleman smoking a pipe in a basket chair on the lawn and a girl sitting near him in the pretty attitude of sewing, the head bent, the hand poised. They looked like a father and daughter enjoying a calm companionship on this summer afternoon, but Celia, supporting herself against the nursery table, was trembling as she always did when she first saw Richard after a separation. His stick was beside his chair; there was a certain stiffness about the stretch of his left leg; he supported his pipe in the way that had always charmed her because it was his way, yet she knew she was seeing him with fresh eyes, as though his neglect of her and the judgments of Hester and

Susan and Catherine were lenses clarifying or distorting her earlier view, but chiefly it was her certainty, long kept at bay, that after the first difficult years, there had been no reciprocity of feeling between them. It would have lasted if they had been together but, separated, his share of it had fallen away from him while hers had lasted because she had cherished it with infinite care. Yet he had sent his love when he was ill, she told herself again, and he had never married. The impression must have sunk deep, though, long ago, the die had lost its value, but last year and the year before, for many years, they had met in the sure, natural friendliness which must always exist between them. 'Then, why not this year?' she asked, and looking at Susan, she found the answer, and that snake in her breast moved sluggishly, then seemed to settle again to sleep, for Susan, raising her needlework, had unmistakably concealed a yawn and her eyes raked the back of the house in the manner of one who looks anxiously for relief. Celia, seeing this and remembering how she had treasured all her own moments with Richard in a garden, felt a momentary anger, but no more jealousy, against the girl who was so little appreciative of her privileges. Then, behind her, she heard quick footsteps and a voice raised at the top of a scale and running down it with joyful, effortless precision, and Prudence appeared in the doorway and stood for a moment in astonishment.

'I walked in,' Celia said. 'The door was open. All the burglars in the world could have done the same.'

'Yes, but Susan and I are in and out all the time.' She joined her aunt by the table and, laughing a little, she said, 'We're taking turns! He's a nice little man and very amusing when he likes, but after all, he's old enough to be our father and we have a perfectly good one already. And he knits, Aunt Celia! He makes his own socks! Don't you think that's rather an effeminate thing to do?'

Celia, listening, her eyes downcast, possessed by the inward trembling of her indignation, suddenly raised her head and looked at Prudence fairly. She did not notice the girl's little start of surprise at the sight of the widely opened eyes, a dusky blue, normally a cool and tender colour and now like smoke from a banked fire, presaging an uprush of hot words, but Celia looked down again and said coldly, 'Your generation seems to have no imagination. It doesn't seem to be conscious of its debts.' Then she paused to ask herself whether she were widely enough conscious of her own. 'I don't think you need despise Mr. Milligan because he knits his socks.'

'I'm sorry, Aunt Celia,' Prudence said meekly enough. 'I suppose it's because I'm rather bored with him to-day. He's been here since eleven o'clock. Yes, Mrs. Carey asked us if we could have him to spend the day. Rather absurd, wasn't it? He might have been seven years old, but that's the way she treats him. And he's very easy going. He does what he's told. And he's just as happy in our garden as he would be anywhere else.'

'Happier, perhaps.'

'Yes, he's rather taken with Susan and a little bit with me. He likes girls and Mrs. Carey finds us useful to amuse him and he's going away to-morrow.'

'Already!' Celia exclaimed.

'Why, he's been with Mrs. Carey for three weeks or more.'

'I didn't know. I think I've lost count of time.'

'Is it so dreadful, over there?' Prudence asked gently.

'No, not really dreadful.'

'But it would do you good, wouldn't it, to stay to tea? We'll have it in the garden.'

'No, I won't stay. Has Susan been showing Mr. Milligan the doll's house?'

'No, he's not so young as that! Besides, she wouldn't. Not to him. Jimmy ought to have locked it up. He has the key. He's fitting it with electric light and he wants to put in a cistern, but it's sure to leak and spoil the furniture.'

'Not if Jimmy does it,' Celia said with great simplicity, and carefully she returned the front of the house to its place. It was her way of renouncing all judgment in his affairs and Susan's.

CHAPTER LI

'I'LL come down the road with you,' Prudence said. 'It's really my turn for Mr. Milligan, but I do love strolling about these roads in the summer. There's always a sort of holiday feeling. Such ugly houses, too, most of them, in this part of Upper Radstowe, and rather dreary in the winter, but now they have a charm. All the windows open and people playing the piano abominably. If they played better, it wouldn't sound so gay. But I don't suppose you feel very gay just now, do you?'

'No, not very,' Celia said.

'But it's nice for us to have Catherine and she's very good for Priscilla. She keeps her in much better order than we can. Priscilla thinks our standards are old-fashioned but she accepts Catherine's. And she can't play at the pretty spoilt child with her. She won't even dare to do it with Mr. Milligan if Catherine has her eyes on her, but she'll have her chance to-day because Catherine's staying late at school and we haven't to take Mr. Milligan back till six o'clock.'

'Haven't to?' Celia said.

'Those were our orders,' Prudence said demurely. 'I don't see why I shouldn't tell you, though we're not supposed to know, but Mr. Milligan must have thought it looked odd for him to spend his last day with us. Too attentive. Or perhaps he can't keep things to himself. Mrs. Carey wanted him out of the way and he didn't want to be in it, because she's bringing that poor boy home. He's coming to-day and he'll be tucked up in bed before Mr. Milligan gets back. I don't know why she couldn't have waited another day until Mr. Milligan had gone, but I think she's like that. Rather sudden. Or perhaps he hadn't the sense to go. And she won't bother about us any more. We shan't exist. But I can understand that she wouldn't want anyone else to see the boy, can't you? Just his father and mother,' Prudence said with comprehension.

Yes, Celia thought, with a different kind of comprehension, not another woman, intruding where she had no right, and as she remembered Pauline's cold voice over the telephone, she understood the ensuing silence. She knew her instinct about Pauline's ruthlessness was right. She had offended the passion of possession brought to its maddest point and her charitable mission would never be forgiven. It explained Pauline's share in Richard's absence and why she had taken care he should not stray to-day. His own share had to be explained in another way and already she was adapting herself to what was no more than tenderness for an old memory when it was brought accidentally to his mind. Yes, Pauline must have inspired him to send his love. She would not do that now if the opportunity occurred, and Celia, who had come out to find a great emotion, a fierce jealousy, a bitter renunciation, had for her only feeling one of emptiness, her friend and her lover gone; his admirable self-control changed to a pleasant amenability. She felt empty: worse than that, she knew she had been a fool.

'His father and mother,' she murmured.

'Yes, they've both gone to fetch him and I feel half-ashamed of knowing. It's too — too private, isn't it? We ought not to have been told,' she said, and Celia silently agreed with this condemnation of Pauline's brother. Twenty years ago, would he have been so confidential with strangers, outraging Pauline's hard reserve? Did people grow less sensitive as they grew older?

'But we can forget,' she heard Prudence saying quietly.

Yes, they could be trusted to do that, and, without knowing she was breaking a settled habit, she kissed Prudence at parting, instead of offering a cheek.

'You look so sweet in that hat,' Prudence said. 'From a long way off it looks quite ordinary and then, when you get closer, you see how clever it really is. And that's what happens with you yourself.'

'But I'm not clever,' Celia said. 'At school I couldn't even do long division. I never knew what to put inside those ears, those brackets, at the sides. The whole thing always looked to me like the back view of a cat. No, I'm not clever.'

She was an ordinary woman in an ordinary hat that was neither a wreath nor a crown, but she was clever enough to make a good guess at Pauline's mental processes and it was these that chiefly occupied her as she walked back. She could understand them well enough to forgive the injustice of resentment turned against herself and she was generous enough to be glad if her intrusion, her sight of Meredith, her companionship of Reginald on his sad errand, had united him and Pauline in a single purpose. Perhaps she had been trying to spare him all the time and he, almost hating her for it, had imagined she only spared herself. Strange how people could live together for years and never touch at the important point! And these two had been ardent lovers. She liked to think they might be lovers again, at an age when such as Susan and Prudence would think all passion must be dead, and she paused, as usual, on The Terrace, to look at her favourite view, feeling curiously free of any desires for herself. She stood there, considering the incalculableness in their results of human words and actions. Good, sometimes, for someone, produced what, according to man's judgment, seemed to be immediate evil, and evil produced good, but the final reckoning could not be made until the end of time and no human being could do the sum. And she wondered what harm, what benefits had been set going when, as naturally as drawing a breath, she fell in love with Richard Milligan, what would have happened if she had acted differently then or if she had refused to feed herself on an illusion. But that food had suited her. It had kept her sweet-tempered, and tolerant of much that might have fretted her and Gerald had lost nothing he might have had. As far as she knew, she had cheated no one but herself and even that not all the time, but then, she reminded herself, she could see for such a very little way. Within those limits, she had no regrets and as she looked at Easterly church tower, very certain to-day of its knowledge of right and wrong, she refused to repudiate the past for some of it had been good; she could not do the proper thing and look towards the future with tragic or dull eyes. In the course of an interesting journey, she had lost some of her luggage and she must learn to do without it. She had lost the luxuries, the perfumes, the little decorations which had made her feel romantic, which no one else had noticed. She could do without them; nevertheless, she knew, as she walked on, that she would always want them. However, she still had a home but, when she entered it to restore her hat to its pretty box, she was distressed to find that the one room she had really made her own seemed to agree with her that its former occupant had gone for ever. It was like a room sentimentally preserved in memory of the departed, the rocking-chair in its place, the lid of the bureau shut, all the books neatly ranged on their shelves. There was nothing on the table except a jar which ought to have held flowers, nothing in the bureau she would rather an unfriendly eye did not see. 'Nothing!' she said aloud, opening her empty hands. No longer could she pretend that instead of letters and sentimental little mementoes, she had a better treasure in Richard Milligan's silent love and considerate restraint. How easily she had befooled herself, she thought, but though she might be empty, she was far from dead and she gave the rocking-chair a vicious push and took a few books from the shelves. She could beguile herself with these while she sat in Mrs.

Marston's bedroom, and she hoped someone would notice the gap in the shelves, notice it to-night, before Miss Riggs could do something about it in the morning. She left the hat-box on the floor instead of hiding it in the monumental wardrobe, she dropped her gloves on the sideboard, but she knew Miss Riggs, coming in to get the supper and turn down the beds, would whisk these things out of sight before Jimmy or Gerald could set eyes on them.

She set her own eyes on the roll of Gerald's plans. Was it these that kept him up so late at night while she walked alone on The Terrace? She felt some curiosity about them and believing, illogically, that she now had the right to look at them without his leave, she spread them on the table, but she did not look very far. The topmost plan was quite enough for her and she rolled them up again rather quickly. It seemed, then, that there was still something to be taken from her; she was deprived of her comforting ability to relate some of her dissatisfaction with Gerald to the meretricious mediocrity of his work, for what she had seen, if it was not original, was sober and solid. It owed a good deal to the kind of house she liked best, the kind he had told her he liked best himself, though she had not believed him, and she was disappointed and most unreasonably angry with the woman whose name was neatly lettered on the front elevation of the house. Could this be Maudie? No, Maudie would surely prefer one of the little villas with senseless decorations, or one of those like a child's arrangement of square bricks. Well, she thought, picking up her gloves, he had been able to do something good after all, without her help. He had found his inspiration elsewhere. It was not impossible that, in some indirect way, he had found it in Maudie and it seemed to her that Catherine was the only person who had the slightest need of her. Why then, had she not gone away with Richard while there was no Catherine, while they were in love, while they were young, before he had become a nice, funny little man, a middle-aged bachelor with a taste for the company of charming girls, or she could look at him from the nursery window and go away without a word? It would have made no difference to anybody in the end, except to him and her. If Jimmy had been left in the gutter, he would have picked himself out of it and found, with cheerful determination, a better place in the world. He had always been a self-reliant child and he would have managed very well without a mother, while Gerald, after a short time of wounded vanity and grief, would have found another wife and one more to his taste. He would have felt just as she did now, she thought, sinking into a chair beside the imitation antique table, laying her arms on the oak and then her head on them. She was no longer like a cistern emptied for cleaning; she might have known that strange vacuity would not last. She was like a cistern slowly filling up, with humiliation, with loneliness, with humiliation again, because most of the qualities on which she prided herself, and especially that rhythm to which she had always tried to live, had been dependent on a conductor who had stopped beating the time, controlling the music, long ago. He had probably never realized that she was more faithful, or more foolish, than he was. He had been happy in his not too arduous work, with a settled income and such social pleasures as he chose to take. He had no responsibilities and no cares but, having avoided some of her own, she need not blame him for his immunity, and she thought she saw that not loving was no reason for not caring; it was, indeed, an added responsibility and the loss of the one which had always lain close at hand in the shape of Gerald was made apparent to her in the ironic moment, now, when she needed all the justification she could get for her existence. And it seemed to her that it was expediency as well as kindness to serve whenever the opportunity arose.

This kind of knowledge, the painful getting of wisdom,

seemed to come too late, she thought, yet there was no sense in life unless such learning had a value of its own, unless, without evident practical results, it existed in unseen fruitfulness. And she had no doubt about the value of courage as a quality, she blessed a middle-age in which she could see herself for what she was, with humour, without despair and, in that spirit, she returned to the little house at the end of The Terrace to learn that Mrs. Marston was very restless, and the nurse, who could not make out what she wanted, hoped Celia might be able to calm her.

Celia bent over the bed, feeling, for the first time, a sort of tenderness for Mrs. Marston in whom some old distress had risen from the past and become a present and an urgent one and, straining her ears and her wits to understand, she heard in Mrs. Marston's voice not the assurance Gerald had given Maudie, but a prayer that Gerald would look after her.

'Yes, yes, he'll look after her,' Celia promised in a confusion of pity and astonishment, amusement and unworthy rage, for here was another loss. She was robbed of the idea of a Maudie who, on an infinitely lower level, was for Gerald what Richard had been for her. This ought to have been a gain, but all her efforts to find a serious fault in Gerald had the humbling effect of revealing some weakness in herself and, in this case, she was afraid it was perilously near a hateful vulgarity of the mind, something worse than the vulgarities she had suspected in him. Here was more knowledge, she thought grimly. It was a day full of lessons and that night, she disciplined herself to ask him who this Maudie was.

'Does it matter?' he said coolly.

'I should like to know how to comfort her.'

'I don't think she's really suffering much. Couldn't it happen that something you'd thought about a great deal might pop out just because your defences were all down?'

'Yes, I suppose that could happen.'

'As in sleep,' he said.

The tone, more than the words, startled her. Its tolerance seemed to put aside some knowledge to which he was indifferent; it also put her very far from him and, raising the eyelids which, after all, had not been quite the screen she had believed, she saw him at a great distance across the narrow space of Mrs. Marston's dining-room and there was all the difference in the world between the distance she had created and the one he was keeping now. Hers could be contracted or expanded at her will, but she could do nothing about his and her womanhood resented what her mind accepted as her due. But was she to blame? Could she control love?

Aloud, she persisted in a low voice, 'But who is she?'

A shade of embarrassment crossed his face. 'A sister.'

'A sister? I never knew you had one.'

'No.'

'But how extraordinary not to tell me!'

'Was it? You see I was very fond of her,' he explained, and she thought this was the unkindest thing anyone had ever said to her.

'I don't deserve that,' she said in a quick, stifled voice.

He got up and stood gazing over the flower-pots into the street. He blocked what view there was and any sight of the passers-by whose footsteps went clipping or shuffling on the pavement. He made the room dark, too, and the cold of the slippery leather chair went up and down Celia's body. Her small world had grown smaller, darker and colder. She felt hemmed in by the bulky man at the window, but her thoughts leapt over him to Catherine in May's house, to Jimmy, there too, putting electric light into the doll's house, to Meredith Carey, indifferent to his surroundings and to Richard Milligan, packing his bags for his departure to-morrow. She imagined him bending over them stiffly, arranging his belongings neatly and looking, with mild anticipation towards the work or pleasure awaiting him elsewhere, while the sweet smells from the garden came through the window.

'You know yourself,' she heard Gerald saying, 'there are certain people, or ideas of people, that get spoilt when someone else looks at them. Well, I had my ideas. But that wasn't the reason at first, not at first.' He paused and then, still addressing the street, he said painfully, 'She wasn't quite like other people. She would always have had to be looked after. And I was in love with you. I knew you weren't in love with me. I had a feeling that Maudie might tip the scales against me. A rather feeble-minded person in the family.'

'You ought to have told me,' Celia said.

'But it wasn't madness. I wouldn't have risked that.'

'You ought to have told me. I should only have been sorry for you.'

'I think you were sorry already,' Gerald said dryly. 'Yes, I think that was what you felt. Going to the war, poor boy, might never come back, so you gave him what happiness you could.'

To that true statement she made no reply and when he had waited for affirmation or denial, he said, 'I knew you'd find my mother quite enough to swallow. I couldn't give you Maudie too, and then she died, while I was out in France. It wasn't likely I'd tell you then.'

'Why not?' she breathed.

'Dirty, disloyal trick,' he muttered, 'telling you about her when she was safely dead. I was fond of her,' he repeated, 'and, you'll be surprised, but I meant a lot to her. You see,' he added, 'she wasn't quite like other people.'

'But,' Celia said, 'you are not fair to me. I should have been kind about that, kinder to your mother, too,' and she thought true kindness involved a willingness to let other people show it.

'Would you?' he said. 'You must remember she was a Marston, not a Carey.'

There was a bitter truth in this suggestion, too. The undeveloped brain of Meredith Carey, the son of brilliant parents, seemed like a tragic accident, while a feeble-minded Maudie Marston was a not unfitting complement to her mother, the odour of camphor, the crochet mats, the side whiskers and the lockets. It seemed to matter less and she knew that this sort of prejudice, a form of snobbishness from which she had believed she was free, had always subtly tinged her view of Gerald. In the son of a belted earl some of his gestures and habits and tricks of manner would have missed the criticism to which they were subjected in the son of the lawyer's clerk, the grandson of the dealer in small quantities of coal.

'I believe you hate me,' she said, not angrily, but thinking he had good cause.

He did not speak. Still looking out of the window, he shook his head very slowly.

CHAPTER LII

THE best Celia could say for Mrs. Marston's funeral was that it might have been worse if Mrs. Marston had herself arranged it, but not very much worse, for there was something inherently ugly in the processes necessary for the disposal of the dead. The hoarse, respectful whispers of the undertaker's men in consultation with the relatives and heaven knew what ribaldry and roughness when they were left to their business upstairs; the coffin, approximating so callously to the shape of the body; the flowers nodding jauntily to the movements of the hearse; the rain tapping on the umbrellas of the little gathering round the grave; the earth glistening with moisture — it was all ugly except the words pronounced hurriedly and mechanically by a clergyman none of the family had ever seen before. Mrs. Marston, on her arrival in Radstowe, had not attached herself to any place of worship, and this man, indigenous to the cemetery, conducted the rites at a rattling pace. It was not the weather for dawdling, he knew nothing of the person in the oak box and no doubt he was thinking of his own affairs. Which of the company was not? If Gerald had invited friends or relatives from the Midlands, none had appeared. Here, besides Sophy who sniffed occasionally and had been busy during the last few days in finding virtues for Mrs. Marston, and the night nurse who liked to see the last of her patients, besides Stephen and, rather surprisingly, Julia and John, was only Gerald's own family, Jimmy, looking solemn and uncomfortable, and Catherine, holding her mother's arm in horror at death itself and in shrinking from the thought of that particular body in the coffin and the coffin in the oozing earth. Of these, only Gerald could be much concerned with the woman who had gone, and Celia did not know how much he had really cared for her or what kind of mother she had been to him when he was young. She realized how little he had told her or his children of his own childhood and his past seemed to be barren of those family anecdotes, jokes and sayings which are handed down from one generation to another. Perhaps there was none to tell. Mrs. Marston could not have been productive of much merriment in the home or have said anything pleasantly memorable, and, in Gerald's memories, there was always the restraint of Maudie who must not be mentioned. Celia pictured her as amiable, quickly responsive to smiles and frowns, walking with the gay, hopping movement peculiar to her kind, not in the least like the Maudie of her own invention, with the bright hair, the high bosom. But such women existed no longer, she thought impatiently; she had never honestly believed in anyone so crude, and glancing at Julia whose face was composed in an expression of complete oblivion to the heavy rainfall, she decided that there was not much to choose between her silly sister-in-law and herself. They could both take a fraction of a fact and build an improbable story on it. Nevertheless, it was odd that Gerald should have addressed Maudie in his sleep immediately after that glimpse of him like a man about to run a race, and it might be the fault of her own limited outlook that she could not believe in any inspiration coming to Gerald from any but a feminine source.

The last words had been said. A handful of earth, finer and drier than that from which the grave had been dug, had fallen on the coffin and the parson, mistaking John and Julia for the chief mourners, was offering a damp hand and insisting on telling them where to look for comfort, in spite of their modest attempts to disclaim the post of honour. He had made his choice and he abode by it for already, far off, a procession like a black insect with white spots was crawling through the cemetery gate.

'Isn't he hateful?' Catherine muttered and turned away.

Yes, he was hateful, Celia thought, like a ghoul, seeking the next corpse, and the planks round the grave, the newly-turned earth, the wreaths dashed by the rain, were hateful too. This seemed so poor a way to deal with anything as magnificent as death, yet she could not connect magnificence with Mrs. Marston; this setting for her final scene did very well and, as she stood there in her old mackintosh, duly returned by Julia, and looked round to see Gerald speaking to a woman she did not know, and then, when he left her, receiving a brotherly and somewhat diaconal handshake from John, who came of a line of deacons, as she noticed John's protective and propelling arm round Julia's shoulders, she felt a sudden uprising of energy in her mind and body, for in the midst of death she was alive and these ordinary people, this somewhat sordid scene, were of absorbing interest. In this advance of John and Julia, for instance, she saw a slightly defiant demonstration. Here they were, they seemed to say, so firmly united that one could not attend a funeral in the rain without the other.

'You mustn't grieve. She is much happier where she is,' Julia said gently.

Celia gave her an unsuitably gay smile and, for John's sake, because she could not help being fond of him, she refrained from thanking Julia for this assurance and asking for more detailed information. She would much rather have been told how these two had come to terms and what they were. Terms had to be made between two people who had started on a journey and were bound by their own natures to continue it together. It was useless to reproach and wrangle because one of them had forgotten to pack something the other wanted, muddled the arrangements, mislaid the tickets or taken the best seat. People who rather recklessly accepted each other as companions had to be very careful with their memories; they had to forget the

403

unpleasantness of the day before and start the next one in a spirit of amiability and trust; they had to cultivate the trick of seeing and hearing the things they liked and becoming blind and deaf to the others. Yes, Celia thought, she knew all the theory by heart; she could have written an excellent manual on marriage. The practical difficulty was to subdue a consciousness of self in a situation which forced it into prominence, to forgive the faults which were a reflection on her own judgment, the errors in taste which were a condemnation of her, too. It was necessary to realize without indignation that the other partner also had dissatisfactions, but dwelt on them less because he was more generous and not nearly so exacting.

'And so,' said Julia, flapping her eyelashes, 'you must be happy too.'

'Yes,' Celia said obediently, but she wished she could be sad, or happy only in the belief that Mrs. Marston and Maudie were together in a heaven where the feeble-minded had their wits restored to them and the grim were transformed into all that was lovely. And perhaps Mrs. Marston would not have been grim if she had not shut her mouth on all reference to Maudie and her heart against those who did not disgrace her with their afflictions. She and Pauline Carey, living worlds apart, speaking different languages, had their point of resemblance in a primitive maternal instinct of jealousy and defence, and Celia, more fortunate than either of them, cast a possessive look at Jimmy who stood with his hands in his pockets and his hat pulled over his eyes, waiting with decent patience for the moment of departure, and she looked at Catherine, whose patience, on the other hand, was intended to attract attention and whose wounded glance, avoiding the cemetery and the monuments, was fixed on the highest chimney within her view and, like nearly everyone who stands beside a grave, Celia wished she had been kinder to the dead.

This regret came too late to be anything but an admonition for the future, yet, as Stephen approached and even though he, like all mortals, might die to-morrow, his air of health, his bronzed cheeks, assured her she might risk a touch of malice in her tender inquiries about his holiday and, with a momentary accentuation of his occasional squint, he acknowledged her intention before he assumed as bland an expression as his thin face could manage. He must be sorry he had confided in her, she thought, and she was glad she had confided in no one, but she had no right to feel superior for she had merely relinquished an illusion and his task had been harder, yet she knew she would never forgive him for not having held his tongue.

'Do you realize', Catherine inquired with polite exasperation, 'that it's pouring with rain and my feet are absolutely soaked? This seems to me a very strange place for having a sort of family party.'

John and Julia had already made for their car, Stephen hurried off to his; the hired ones had discreetly crept as near as possible to the group and Sophy, who would gladly have wandered among the tombstones and unostentatiously joined another funeral, was bundled into one cab by the nurse while the family took its places in the other. Their wet mackintoshes glistened, the rain streamed down outside and glistened on the marble crosses; it must have been thudding like drum taps on the tarpaulin drawn over Mrs. Marston's grave until the thick, wet earth could be shovelled into it. This was a brutal sort of leave-taking and there was no help for it, but Celia shuddered as she half-dared to fancy what she would have felt if it had been Jimmy or Catherine who was left alone in the rain.

Gerald turned from his contemplation of the streets and no one could know what memories of his mother, to look at Celia and hope she had not taken cold. It had been a small shudder, but he had noticed it, and a slight sensation of warmth stole over her, a slight consciousness of power.

'Oh no,' she said, 'I shan't get cold but, if we weren't all so wet, I should like us all to huddle up together.'

At that he smiled uncertainly, lifting his eyebrows and she added sadly, 'But it wouldn't do. We should all hate it. We must have hot baths when we get home, instead.'

She was trying to hold her umbrella clear of herself and of Catherine on the opposite seat and, looking at it, she said, 'Did I ever tell you about the woman who was sick in the tramcar when I was a child?'

'Oh don't, pet. Yes, dozens of times!'

Celia would not be stayed. 'Into her umbrella,' she said impressively, but Catherine had her hands to her ears and Gerald and Jimmy, leaning towards each other, were discussing strains and stresses.

'I don't think it's funny,' Catherine said, when she thought she might safely remove her hands.

'It isn't meant to be. I tell the story as a tribute to great presence of mind and, but for me, that woman would be unhonoured and unsung.'

'She ought to have stayed at home,' Catherine said positively, 'and you know, you do tell your stories rather often.'

'How else do you think the folk stories were handed down to us? And I expect the young people got very restive when the old bard insisted on singing them all over again, but it would have been a pity if he hadn't, and some day, when there are no umbrellas left, your great, great, great-grandchildren will like my little story and be proud of it. We're making footnotes to history all the time.'

'I don't think we're as important as all that,' Catherine said.

The car was labouring up The Slope and, from her corner, Celia could see the University tower. That, she hoped, would still be standing when umbrellas, clumsy contrivances, had long been obsolete. There were plenty of them to be seen to-day and if anyone had moved his own aside and could have seen through the windows of the car, he would have agreed with Catherine that the four people within seemed of very little importance, of about as much importance to the world as the man who looked at them, but Celia was realizing that the centre of her own world lay within the confines of the cab, one of the millions of little worlds that made up the whole. For practical purposes, so it had always been, but the best part of her imaginative life had been lived elsewhere. Had that all been wasted? she wondered. She could not believe it. Loving her children, she modestly believed, at least as much as most women loved theirs, she had been, in a sense, detached from them, their confidence and affection was not her first need and it was comfortable to think this might have been well for them. She took no credit for it. What might have been the result of wisdom in someone else was that of folly in her case.

'So you see,' she said aloud, 'you never know.'

Gerald and Jimmy turned their heads towards her without lifting them; Catherine said calmly, 'She's only thinking out loud. She often does it. Who was that woman you were talking to, Father? The one in the red mackintosh. A nice colour, but still, rather gaudy.'

'Friend of mine,' Gerald said cheerfully.

'Well, of course. Friend of' — she could not be flippant to-day and she chose the respectful title — 'Friend of Grandmother's?'

'No,' he said shortly, and added quickly, 'I'm building a house for her.'

'Then', said Catherine, 'she must be awfully pleased with it, or she wouldn't have come out on a day like this.'

'And so she ought to be,' Celia said slowly. She kept her eyes shut, she seemed to be lazily relaxed, but she had never felt more possessive, less generous or more determined, for the conviction had come to her in a flash, while Catherine spoke, that the safety of her world depended on the betrayal of her past and her pride, and she would allow no private world to Gerald now that she had lost her own.

'So she ought to be,' she said again. 'A nice, warm brick, the same red as the mackintosh. It must be a favourite colour. And a good house. I'd like to live in it myself.'

CHAPTER LIII

'WHAT do you know about that house of mine?' Gerald asked.

Celia was in her rocking-chair beside the fire lighted by the wise Miss Riggs to cheer the funeral party. The tea she had prepared for them was a model of good taste, the well-buttered toasted bun appearing in the form of comfort without any suggestion of festivity, but that meal was over long ago. This was the hour when Celia was usually left alone in the sitting-room and Gerald should have been out or working in the dining-room. Jimmy had disappeared very quietly, doubtful of the propriety of seeking pleasure elsewhere, but sure he would not get it in his home, and Catherine had gone to bed with a night-light, like a baby, because the rain still fell heavily and she would rather have looked forward to a perpetuity of paper bags and gingerbread than remember the drenched earth in which her grand-mother was lying.

As Gerald asked his question, he stooped to put more coal on the fire, and Celia said, 'Oh don't! This will last as long as we want it.'

'I'm not so sure,' he said, and chose another lump. 'What do you know about it?' he repeated. 'Or were you just pretending, for Catherine's benefit?'

She shook her head. 'I'm a much better pretender than that. I shouldn't have risked talking about red brick if there'd been any chance the house was made of stone. No. I looked at the plan. I thought you wouldn't mind.'

'Not in the least.'

'It's a good house.'

'Ah, thank you,' he said dryly. 'It must have surprised you.'

409

'No, I wasn't surprised.'

'But not exactly pleased,' he said, smiling a little. 'In fact, rather disappointed.'

It was true. He had disappointed her judgment of him in connection with her money, with his house, with Maudie, and she decided sadly that she was not clever where her men were concerned. She was much too ready to fit their characters to her needs and they would not be fitted. Gerald's last words and his next ones assured her of that.

'But anyhow,' he said cheerfully, 'you have the consolation of knowing you didn't bring the disappointment on yourself. You had nothing to do with that house — nothing. Much more with the little ones you despise. They seemed to flourish in the domestic atmosphere but when it came to something better, I had to get out of it. You've never done work of that kind, even as ordinary as I know mine is. You don't know how distrust and scorn at one end of the passage can deaden the mind at the other. But, while you were away, I could work here. My mind, what there is of it, was free.'

He drew a breath, as though to remind himself of that past freedom and she thought he had been right to build up the fire though, even now, it was not big enough to warm her. She felt frozen, rigid, more with anger than with grief, because he could say these cruel things so gently and disregard all her years of service, of living poorly without complaint. And her chief pride, in having made a home where people lived in liberty and without wrangling, would have been in the dust if she had not been sustained by another pride, in herself, in her qualities, and by a deep-rooted disdain, which did not eliminate suffering, for the adverse criticism of any-body in the world. This was not as simple as conceit which is the offspring of a shallow mind. It was composed of inde-pendence, humour and a value for everything that was individual, even though it might not be good. But this dis-dain could not refuse to see the truth as he saw it, or relieve her anger and pain. There was no relief for these. She neither knew nor loved him well enough to pour out her thoughts tumultuously, knowing that understanding or passion would deal fairly with them all, assimilating some, refusing others, forgetting those which should not be remembered.

What she remembered herself most clearly now was the night when she had made for home along The Terrace and seen the light in the window where he was working happily because she was not there. It was lucky the door had been shut, she thought, lucky for her pride. She had always reckoned on its being opened if she cared to give it a little push; yes, coming home in the cab, she had meant to push it. Now, the only thing to do was to turn away again. But she knew, too, that the door would not have been so securely shut if there had not been a new self-confidence behind it.

'Then,' she said, 'I'd better go away.'

'Where would you like to go?' he asked kindly.

Controlling her indignation at this compliance, she thought of the sedate Georgian house in the picture she had destroyed and how she had imagined herself living there, her days spent in the walled garden, the long, still nights in a room unencumbered by baronial furniture. But something had happened to the house. The dreams had gone out of it; the uneven footfall could not be heard. It was raining in that garden as she thought of it, just as it was raining here and she stood at the window and looked at the dripping trees and felt behind her the emptiness of the rooms. She was alone there, useless and idle, deprived of irritations and anxieties and, turning from the imagined trees, she looked round this room where her body was. An open book lay, face downwards beside her chair, there were flowers on the table, the lid of the bureau was down, showing the homely muddle of bills and letters.

'I don't know. I don't think it matters much,' she said.

411

'But, wherever it is, I won't go without Catherine and how can we afford two homes?'

He got up and moved about the room, then stood with his back to her in front of the bookshelves as he had stood, not long ago, at his mother's window. Though he was tall, he had a bulkiness on which the best of clothes would not have set very well and instead of a knife-edge to the back of his trousers, there was a series of horizontal creases. He was not a romantic figure, but he could have applied the same words to her. Her maturing shape needed a garment better cut than the cheap black dress she had bought lest he should think her wanting in respect, and suddenly her anger died. There was no place here for great emotions; she always missed them. Here were merely two human beings in middle life who still pathetically sought happiness and that hope had to be resigned if the spirit were to be freed. But this thought came easily to her from whom the hope was already taken and perhaps Gerald saw happiness within his reach, just beyond the unhappiness she made for him.

Suddenly he turned, a look of rough determination on his face. 'Why don't you go and live where you love?' he asked.

There was a bitter humour in the question, but she hardly had time to savour it before he said, 'The mistake you've made with me, one of the mistakes, has been thinking I'm much stupider than I am. I may be rather stupid, but not where you are concerned, because I have loved you very much and so, you see, I know a lot about you. All the tones of your voice, the one for Catherine, the one for Jimmy, the one for me. You shouldn't have expected me to miss the other, a little higher, a little harder and quicker.'

'Then,' she said, and she spoke in that harder, quicker voice and her cheeks were flushed, 'Why do you say this now? Why now? Why only now? Because you can do without me?'

'Because I want you to be happy. And the children are

older. And we shall have more money. My mother lived on a small annuity and I thought it was all she had. People seem to suspect me, as you know, where money is concerned. But you shall have your share.'

'Are those the only reasons?'

'What others could there be?'

'You might love someone else.'

'I've often wished I could.'

'That woman you built the house for . . .'

'You wouldn't like her.'

'What has that to do with it?'

He smiled at her simplicity. 'I suppose you've set a standard,' he said with a simplicity of his own. 'You'd think her vulgar, but she's a good friend and I'm afraid I rather like vulgar people. They so often have kind hearts. Kind hearts and rough tongues. She gave me the rough of her tongue and then a chance and some faith in myself. Now, you've always been so damned polite. You've spared my feelings. You always think before you speak. You must be as tired of that as I am. Can't we have done with these evasions? We've been living on them for years, for all the years that you've been in love with another man. Don't you see that I'm trying to make it easy for you to go to him?'

She suffered then the last pang Richard Milligan could give her. There was a kind of pleasure in it because she knew it was the last, and she said, 'But I don't want to go'. And seeing Gerald's face grow taut with hope, she was inspired to say, and salvage what she could, 'I haven't been a success. He doesn't want me either.'

There was something ridiculous in Gerald's aspect, his face red and frowning, his eyes bulging a little as he shouted the one word, 'Fool!' and under her startled laughter, she exclaimed, 'Well, isn't he just like you?'

'No,' Gerald replied, still shouting, 'he is not!' and he went out and banged the door.

So, she thought, like the others they would just go on and, as Stephen had said, it was not a bad thing to do. It was a pity she had not miraculously fallen in love with Gerald, but she had her first real satisfaction in knowing he was in love with her. She had no illusions about a future in which they would be much the same man and woman as they were before; she was humbled by the necessity of building on another woman's foundations, but she knew there was hardly an ancient fabric in the world that had not an older one below it, and experience was not something peculiar to each separate person but a possession held in common, a mass of good and evil, failures and triumphs to which she had given her share and in which she need not scruple to rummage for what served her best.